Overlay
A Bed of Money
Underlay

The Horseplayer Trilogy
by Barry N. Malzberg

Stark House Press • Eureka California

OVERLAY / A BED OF MONEY / UNDERLAY

Published by Stark House Press
1315 H Street
Eureka, CA 95501, USA
griffinskye3@sbcglobal.net
www.starkhousepress.com

OVERLAY
Copyright © 1972 by Barry N. Malzberg and published by Lancer
Books, New York. [Grateful acknowledgement to Howard Rowe of
the *American Turf Monthly* for permission to paraphrase an
excerpt from *Aqueduct & Santa Anita on $105 a Day* (Copyright
© 1970 by Howard L. Rowe) in the prologue of this novel.]

A BED OF MONEY
Copyright © 1970 by Gerrold Watkins and published by The
Olympia Press, Inc., New York. Reprinted here under the author's
real name.

UNDERLAY
Copyright © 1974 by Barry N. Malzberg, and published by Avon
Books, New York; reprinted by International Polygonics, Ltd.,
1986.

All editions reprinted by arrangement with the author.
All rights reserved.

"My Mission in South Ozone Park" copyright © 2015
by Barry N. Malzberg.

"Preface," "Szygy In The Home Stretch," "Afterword:
A Bed of Miscalculation" and "Afterword To An Afterword"
copyright © 2020 by Barry N. Malzberg.

ISBN-13: 978-1-951473-12-9

Book design by Mark Shepard, shepgraphics.com
Proofreading by Bill Kelly

PUBLISHER'S NOTE:
Without limiting the rights under copyright reserved above, no
part of this publication may be reproduced, stored, or introduced
into a retrieval system or transmitted in any form or by any
means (electronic, mechanical, photocopying, recording or
otherwise) without the prior written permission of both the
copyright owner and the above publisher of the book.

First Stark House Press Edition: November 2020

Author's Preface

A Letter to the Publisher: Some Late Thoughts On The Sport of Gniks

This traffic of the trilogy is another version of our world; our world as seen in a crazed Coney Island mirror which both refracts and reshapes our self-image and our world in ways indescribable other than in its own desperate terms. It is not clear to me at this perilous juncture or junction, the era in which human civilization will either turn or disappear, transmogrify or die that the racetrack, its ambiance, the totality of the sport of gniks (as was so deemed by Howard Rowe) has any future, that it may as all of the myriad fortunes and disasters of the world we knew be swept furiously and finally past the horizon by fervid waves of circumstance and that as close in time as say the roller derby or dance marathons are chronologically to our present, so horse racing will be understood only as a part of an ahistoric past. Those who follow, if they follow, may well see the subject as distant as Roller Derby and to read the novels will be to embark upon a vision quest. Who now can imagine the lives of the marathon dancers, the slyness and emotional bankruptcy of the jockeys room or the grooms' secret? Can the racetrack seem to make sense to those who follow after? It made a terrible kind of sense to me and I tried to import that into the works at hand: it was more than a metaphor, it was too harsh to be a metaphor. No, if anything our world was a metaphor for the races as we struggled up and down in class, scratching out of claimers for allowances, shifting from sprints to routes or back again to make the odds shake; it may be a practice as arcane as that depicted in Gissing's GRUB STREET which dealt with British publishing in the 1890s and just happened to be about the world in which we still live, an outcome which would have jolted Gissing who probably thought he was a satirist, not a prophet.

I paid for that sentimental education in hot blood and cold treasure and that knowledge inflames these novels; seeks in this era of doomed postulate to burn down the house. All of the scenes are apocalyptic, all of the characters at the precipice. All are apocalyptic, all foreshadow the present terrible moment as the splinters of what we took to be G-d's grandstand shiver and with stately elegance fall. I learned, I tried to learn, I can learn and I will again by going not only where I but the victimized planet itself will have to go, into the barn, into rehab, maybe back into training or—equally likely—maybe behind that portable screen of concealment placed at the stretch turn far from the landscape, that screened turn for home shielding the crowd from the Grassy

Knoll, the waves of pain, the shouts of deliverance. Ruffian's bones, dry bones in the name of the Lord lying full fathom five under the infield, the filly's scream as her leg snapped echoing through the crowd who came to see her beat Foolish Pleasure, the Derby winner. She was the favorite, the filly, but she did not, dying instead on the backstretch in that collapse. Falling, falling, in the sullen early twilight toward that big hole in the ground, under the huge canvas of sky.

—Teaneck, NJ
April 2020

Overlay

Barry N. Malzberg

TWO EPIGRAPHS FOR HORSEPLAYERS

… He had had an unusually bad day at the flats and now, as he left the track disconsolately, a small voice seemed to whisper to the horse-player: *go to the trots, go to the trots*. He was most astounded because nothing like this had ever happened to him before but he resolved to follow the advice and see what would happen. Arriving at Yonkers, he purchased a program and took a position by the rail, waiting confidently for the voice to address him again. Three minutes before first-race post it did. *Bet number five*, the voice counselled and without hesitation, the punter bought five ten dollar win tickets on that horse. He then watched with delight as number five paced home an easy winner, paying $52.80.

… It continued that way all evening, the voice waiting until near post to whisper its selections, the horse-player following them in parley until, just before the ninth, he had over seventy-five thousand dollars which, in response to instructions, he sent in on number three. Driven down to 1–2 by this enormous bet, three broke at the start and trailed the field throughout, losing by ten or fifteen lengths.

Stunned, shattered, the horseplayer collapsed over the rail, waiting for the voice to explain itself. At long last it did. *Son of a bitch*, the voice said in wee small tones, *son of a bitch*.

—by permission of Howard Rowe

"*Clocker Lawton* we have sinned. *Clocker Powell* we have failed utterly, we are washed in the colors of our inequity. Oh *New York Turf Letter*, *Top Turf*, we have gone astray; plunged into a sea of darkness; we have lost our way. We have forgotten the lessons of the Fathers: no fillies against colts; no maidens in straight claimers; no workout line, no bet. We have been greedy. We have chased longshots. We have failed to learn the awful lessons of the tote. Verily we say unto you that we have lost our way, we are utterly cast aside, our bones are made to run out like sealing wax. Faith of our Fathers, Word of the Prophets, we are lost and cannot be found. In the dread machinery of the tote we faint from sickness, pray for your blessings. Oh may your mercy find us again and may we never stray from thy teachings, thy sacred Word until restored again to the freshness of our youth, we play and gambol like lambs on the fields of desire."

—*The Loser's Litany*

FIRST PROLOGUE

In the year 1978 (433 Galactic) the attention of the Bureau fell to the planet Earth which, Headquarters decided, had reached a point where it furnished a clear and present danger to the cause of Galactic Unity. With some regret, tempered by a long and hard-bought sense of bureaucratic anomie, a plan was put into operation to rid the sector of the menace by sowing the seeds of disunity within.

SECOND PROLOGUE

Calamity. Or cataclysm. The implications of entropy seem to dominate the universe, all drive and desire to the contrary. Vanity, vanity, and so forth. Of course it is hard to be precise about this; not as precise, in any event, as one would like to be. Perhaps the basic problem is that I am simpleminded; I give myself credit for potential which never existed. I cannot be blamed for this; it is a natural error. My position in the Bureau, after all this time, would certainly hint toward that explanation.

On the other hand, I would still like to believe that I have been the victim of inequities, terrible inequities—politics and maneuvering, cunning and deceit, manipulation and torment—and that in the long run, all this will come clear. I am still young, relatively speaking. My career in its richness lies ahead of me. There will be other opportunities, assignments more worth taking seriously than this, demanding my best.

Assignments. Beyond calamity, assignments. A one to one ratio of devastation and manipulation which would be depressing if I did not feel that fighting the battle against entropy was the Good Fight. We must conquer malevolence, mindless breakdown, social fragmentation. By using them on the point of origin. Blight. The obliteration of destiny. Every living being, every social unit has a moral right to. Its own extension and so on. Granted this and granted that. Taking into account. As you can see, I am quoting verbatim but with certain gaps and inaccuracies. Fortunately, rote memory is not necessary in this job. We may refer to procedure when it is needed.

"The next one is a tough one," Hemmings said. (His name is not Hemmings and he did not really say this, but I am looking for equivalents in pursuit of communication. I do not want to make jargon of these notes. What good would it do to describe what Hemmings looks like or the method by which he communicates? The important thing is to achieve a dry universality, a point of common approach. Perhaps I should point out as well that I have no idea as to why I have decided to embark upon this diary. Agents are supposed to leave no written testaments to their mission, even when it is highly unlikely—as in this case—that our symbols will ever be discovered and interpreted. I could get into serious trouble at Headquarters were they to ever discover that I have decided to record. On the other hand, who cares about Headquarters at this time? The situation has become progressively mindless and deteriorative. Those bastards couldn't possibly understand what is going on here. One must learn to Follow the Right.)

"These people are dangerous and insane," Hemmings said. "The polarities, the constants, the projections, and so on, all of this would indicate that within a very short amount of time, even by our standards, they will pose a real menace. We have to stop this, of course. Onward! We must protect our interests and so on. Unity!"

"Of course," I said deferentially. (Deference is one of my assets: I owe much of my reputation in the Bureau to my ability to be deferential without obsequity. Obsequious without deference. It is all a question of semantics.) "I've already done some reading in the case folder. Dangerous people. They appear to have a real streak of malevolence accompanying their dangerous technology. That makes them doubly fearful."

"Well, not the malevolence itself," Hemmings said. "Malevolence isn't quite a constant, you know. You'd have to virtually admit a construct of diabolism to make that work and, as far as we understand, they fail now to accept diabolism. Instead, they've settled for a weak causality. Explication of all acts through consequence and so on. Actually, and this is rather frightening, they tend to consider themselves basically good. Perhaps it's the pantheistic instinct once again; you tend to find it in these limited cultures."

(We tend to talk in sophistries at the Bureau perhaps more than is truly good for us. Perhaps this has to do with the rather simple and dreadful nature of our work as well as its mechanical overtone. More will be said of this later, I think, if I get around to it.)

"You want me to break down the institutions, of course," I said. "Get into the core and concentrate on the devastating urges which lie at the center of their behavior." (We also try to get into the center of issues without dissembling. There are so many cases, so many caseworkers, so few supervisors that we must cultivate efficiency. In a way, I am very proud of the Bureau. It struggles against difficult odds and does a fine job.)

"More or less," Hemmings said. "There's a rather special overcast to this assignment, however. As far as I can see, we'll have to get into this rather unconventionally. Attempting to buckle them through the rational devices won't work; they're too technocratic, and their mores— or those which they think are the mores—are totally insane. So we have to approach them from the edges, concentrate on mysticism, spirituality, the occult, the irrational. That's the only way to topple them. You go in through the approved institutions and they'll eat you up alive. They're more insane now than we could possibly make them."

"That means a subpopulation."

"Exactly. As it so happens, they have a very convenient subpopulation which is exactly suited for this kind of work. That makes things much easier for us. Through this subpopulation, their energizing I should say and its manipulation, you can work in toward the center and bring the whole thing down very quickly. They'd be most vulnerable to this type of approach."

"A subpopulation involved with mysticism, the occult, and the irrational," I said. "I suppose that you want me to become immersed in their reform politics."

"Well, not exactly," Hemmings said. "The fact is that, as I told you, their most insane devices are considered to be supremely rational—by them. That wouldn't work at all; you'd only make the structure appear more solid. No, we've carved out the proper element with which you're to deal. We have it all written down on these charts and so on, a selected bias, research, collation, etc. All that you have to do is to go to work on them within the limited scope. Plan D, I suppose. Or perhaps Plan E. It's all relative. You'll have to use some judgment."

"Good enough," I said. "What is this subpopulation?"

"Well, I don't exactly know what their name is," Hemmings said, tilting back and casting a wistful arc of smoke toward the ceiling. (No arc, no smoke, no ceiling but I am still hustling equivalents: familiarity must be preserved in these wretched circumstances, goddamn it.) "But I can tell you what they call themselves and then go on from there."

"What is that?"

"Horseplayers," Hemmings said. "The subpopulation calls itself horseplayers."

"Horseplayers?"

"That's the appellation used."

"Horseplayers. That means they—"

"Play horses," Hemmings finished. "Of course, they don't consider it exactly play."

This is the origin of the peculiar circumstance in which I now find myself. I have the feeling that my time here is distinctly limited; likewise these circumstances which are wretched, foul, dealing for the most part with a series of furnished rooms outfitted with stacks and stacks of desiccate racing newspapers or "tipsheets" from which all power comes but which smell (I have the sense) terrible and cast an added gloom over the entire operation. For these reasons, I will try to cultivate a seemly brusqueness, an artistic conciseness, as I move toward the heart of the matter.

Which yet, I do not understand.

What is this doing to me?

CHAPTER I

Simmons. Simmons the horseplayer. Let us consider him for the moment if we might. He is leaning against the rail at Aqueduct, surrounded (he feels) by wheeling birds and doom, clutching a handful of losing parimutuel tickets in his left hand. His right hand is occupied with his hair; he is trying ceaselessly to comb it into place, a nervous gesture which caused one of his drinking companions (he has no friends) to call him years ago, Simmons the Dresser, a nickname which, unfortunately, never stuck since his other drinking companions knew his habits too well.

It is 1:43 now, some twelve minutes before scheduled post time for the second race and Simmons is desperately seeking information from the tote board. He has already lost the first race. The results posted indicate that the horse on which he bet finished third. Simmons did not have the horse to show or across the board. He is a win bettor only, some years ago having read in a handicapping book that only the win bettor has a chance to retain an edge and that place and show were for amateurs and old ladies. He does not know who wrote this book or where it is today but ever since he read this information, he has never bet other than to win. He is not sure whether or not this has made much difference but intends to draw up some statistics sooner or later. He keeps a careful record of his struggles; the fact is though that he never totals. (For those who are interested I say that Simmons has lost slightly less than he might have otherwise lost had he bet place and show, but the difference in percentage terms is infinitesimal and the psychological benefits of having had more tickets to cash would have well outweighed the insignificant additional losses.)

Simmons has, then, blown the first race. He has, for that matter, lost seven races in a row, going back to the third yesterday, a dash for two-year maiden fillies that produced a seven-length victory for an odds-on favorite. Simmons collected $7.50 for his $5.00 ticket on that one. Before then there is also a succession of losing races, although here, perhaps, Simmons loses his sense of precision. He is not exactly sure how many races he has recently lost or how long the losing streak has gone on. All that he can suggest at this moment is that he is deeply into what he has popularly termed a Blue Period and that his situation will have to markedly change for the better shortly or he will be forced to the most serious and investigatory questions about his life and career. Such as, what is he doing here? And what did he hope to gain? And why did he make that famous decision some months ago to have it over and done with the horses once and for all and to make them pay for his psychological investments? And so on. Simmons will phrase these questions to himself in a low, frenetic mumble, somewhere midway between *sotto voce* and a sustained shriek and those people in his presence at the time the inquiries begin, will look at him peculiarly or not at all, depending upon custom or interest. If he chooses to ask them of himself at the track, he will incite no response at all. There are, after all, so many questioners at the track. The churches—and I intuit a little of this subject—have nothing to compare with the track in the metaphysical area.

"Sons of bitches," Simmons says, but he says this without conviction or hope; it is merely a transitional statement in the category of throat-clearing or manipulation of the genitals and means, hence, absolutely nothing. The fact is that Simmons is not clear as to the identity of the sons of bitches, and if he were confronted by them now or several races in the future, he would not quite know what to say. Manners would overcome reason. "You could have helped me a little with that four horse in the first," he would probably point out mildly, or, "Gee, I wish that that kid on my eight horse in yesterday's starter-handicap had tried to stay out of the switches." Overall, an apologetic tone would certainly extrude. The fact is—and it is important that we understand our focus at the outset—that Simmons is both mild and polite; also, that he expects little beyond what he has already received and that when he is talking about the sons of bitches—well, it would be naïve and simplistic to say that he refers mainly to himself, but as one who is extremely close to that situation, I can suggest that part of this is valid. (Part of it is not. Everything is irretrievably complex. This must be kept carefully in mind here. The distance between a winning and tail-end horse in the average field is, at the most, five seconds—five seconds upon which rests the ascription of all hope and, in certain cases, the actual lives of these creatures. One must be respectful of any institution which can so carefully narrow the gap between intimation and disaster.)

"Sons of bitches," Simmons says again and opens the copy of the morning *Telegraph* which he is holding to full arm's length and begins to look, with neither anticipation nor intensity, at the expert's selection for the second race. Because this is both a Thursday and cloudy, Simmons is able to perform this gesture, articulate his feelings, in isolation and quiet; there is no one within several yards of him in any direction. The fact is, although he would find it painful to admit this, that Simmons despises company for private reasons and is able to find his fullest sense of identity only at the racetrack precisely because it both heightens and renders somehow sinister his sense of isolation. He knows that he would never be able to get away with his rhetoric in a social or subway situation, and he would not dare to do it in his room because he has long been conditioned to the belief (alas!) that any man who talks to himself in his own quarters is probably insane.

"Ah, there's no goddamn percentage," Simmons now mutters, as he looks at the *Telegraph*. As always, this ominous newspaper renders him little comfort since its selectors, like all selectors everywhere, are oriented toward favorites or logical choices and tell him only what a sane, conservative advisor (Simmons envisions him as a portly man who inhabits the clubhouse, has a mild cardiac condition, and calls all trainers Willie) would offer if this advisor were, for some reason to take an interest in Simmons and his plight and attempt to turn the situation around. Simmons, who once wanted exactly such a friend, now hates the spectre of the Advisor, feels that the Advisor—like *Clocker Lawton, Clocker Rowe* and *Clocker Powell*—simultaneously embodies and parodies everything about successful followers of racing that he has come to hate and feels that he might as well kill him on sight as not. He has, therefore, transferred his revulsion to the selector pages, which he now turns away from with a moan. He goes instead to the past performances which he regards with a glazed and horrified expression as he comes slowly to understand that he has seen them all before, most of the night in fact, and that he knows less about these horses than he did at the beginning.

For the first time (this afternoon) it occurs to Simmons that he might be losing his mind. Meanwhile, the bugler walks to the front of the paddock and blows that call to indicate that the jockeys are to mount their horses. It is almost time for the field in the second race to come out.

Simmons has lost twenty dollars on the first race. He has lost two hundred and sixty dollars during his most recent losing streak. He has lost $1,680 (plus expenses) since he made his Career Decision some three months and sixteen days ago. I offer these statistics without prejudice and only because, unlike Simmons, I am in a position to amass them, reconcile them with a larger scheme of possibilities and, see them in what might be tastefully called an overall perspective. Therefore, they cause me neither pain nor pleasure to recite. Simmons, on the other hand, confronted by these figures would be unable to speak them distinctly. I am not saying that my position (I have discovered this with some surprise) is necessarily superior to that of Simmons. Unlike him, I take almost no emotions from event, this being, I am led to understand by the Headquarters briefs, a defect in their terms. I hold my own judgment in abeyance. Certainly Simmons, in the short time that I have dwelt with him, has taught me a great deal.

Now he sighs, mutters, stretches, curses. He wishes, of course, to make a bet on the second race (he always bets on every race, being unable to cope with the fear that he would otherwise know of missing out on the Ultimate Coup) but has no firm choice; he cannot, pity him, arrive at that careful, judicious balance of speed, windage, condition, manipulation, desire, weight, and intrinsic class which is the key to approaching the variables of even the cheapest claiming sprint. Or, as he would put it, he cannot seem to get an edge. It is at this moment, therefore, that I decide to make my entrance; seeing little enough profit in delay and realizing that the Simmons who needs my help at 1:46 may have a definite superiority over the Simmons who would reject it at 3:10. For the fact is that I see already the pattern of Simmons's last thrashings and it is not pleasant. (Which is not to say that I cannot stage-manage it. Only a Simmons could think that the unpleasant is necessarily disastrous.)

"Look," I say without introduction, "do you want a play in this race? I think I can give you something interesting."

"Oh boy," Simmons says, looking up and then rapidly down toward his newspaper. (I should point out that this is not the first time I have approached him so abruptly, but he is still finding it difficult to adjust to my presence.) "Oh God, it isn't you again, is it?" Simmons's initial resistance toward my appearance has been somewhat blunted, but the fact remains that he finds me almost unbearable. While his hold on sanity (I can attest) has never been in the least precarious, Simmons thinks that it is and that I am a manifestation of his breakdown. I have made progress in this area but not quite enough. "I just don't want to listen," he says and covers his ears. Perhaps he is thinking of blinkers. "I don't want to hear any more of it. Losing is one thing but this …"

"Nonsense," I say and then address him with enormous tact and personal force. The covering of the ears means nothing. "We don't have time for overlong discussions, and besides, I must warn you that unless you take some good advice quickly, you will be verging on a truly massive disaster, one with overtones of violence and a sense of intrinsic loss more acute than any you have ever known. I am afraid that I must get to the simple gist of this: bet the three horse, win and place."

"Oh no," Simmons says again but obediently. (There is an enormous and satisfying submission to all horseplayers because the fact is that they need to be told exactly what to do.) He opens the newspaper to the past performances and looks at the horse in question. "Make Peace?" he says. "The number three horse, Make Peace?"

"That's the one I say," and partake of the sensations of his finger against the newsprint. The faint impression of type slides across his skin with an almost erotic smoothness. I can understand what is erroneously called the power of the printed word. "Win and place. Place and win." I articulate distinctly. "My time, after all, is not unlimited."

"But that's ridiculous," Simmons says. "This horse is already thirty-five to one on the board. He's the only maiden in the race. He hasn't shown a thing since February at Bowie and that was in a claimer two thousand dollars less than this one. The French bastard who's riding him stinks, the trainer is in a bad losing streak, and if that ain't bad enough, the weight is the heaviest in the race. I don't see it. I just don't see it." (It is well known that with such rationalizations about his marriage, Simmons walked out of his home several years ago and never returned. For this reason, and others, I do not take his rationalizations seriously.)

"Reason enough," I say. "He doesn't figure. That's the point I was trying to develop. It wouldn't be a good tip if it were logical, would it?"

At this moment, the bugler blows the second call and our conversation is halted. We stand in almost companionable quiet while the announcement is made and the horses come onto the track, some of them with a curious, skipping gait which indicates incipient lameness, others with a somnolent prance which might indicate either good spirits or the presence of undetectable drugs. The seven horse, a brown six-year-old gelding, moves somewhat ahead of the field and comes toward us, turns at a point in front of our section of the rail and then, with some encouragement from outrider and jockey, both of whom are singing, breaks into a sidewise gallop which quickly carries him past the finish line and out of sight along the backstretch. The other horses follow less eagerly and at a cautious distance.

"Front bandages," Simmons says, "Front *and* rear. And he seemed a little rank, too. I don't know. I just don't know. Look, look: he's fifty to one." In his rising excitement—this is, to be sure, the very first tip I have given him, although on previous occasions I have gone so far as to offer advanced handicapping advice—his hostility has vanished and his very disbelief seems to wave like a sheet between us, punched with enough holes for random communication. "Ah, it's crazy, it's crazy," he says. "I mean, I'm willing to listen to anyone but I just don't see it. Fifty to one." The tote winks. "*Sixty* to one. Do you think—"

"I do not think," I say. "By the way, I can't talk any longer," and add something about probability currents and cross-angles of time which Simmons is expected to find obscure and to ignore. I leave him rapidly and in such a state of elemental self-absorption that I know he will hardly detect my absence and then only with an abstracted glare. For the fact is that I have put Simmons on to something.

As the horses gather in the upper stretch to talk things over a bit before getting into the dreaded starting gate (I am also privy to the emotions of horses, limited creatures but none the less poignant, at least to themselves), Simmons turns and begins to move at his own sidewise canter toward the parimutuel windows. Together we join a short line of ragged men, most of them pallid, who shuffle their feet and clutch their wallets while their duplicates ahead pass the windows and scurry by, looking at the tickets they have bought with wonder. It is the ten-dollar window, an excellent sign in itself, because Simmons does almost all of his business at the two- and five-dollar slots. He does this, as he once explained to me, not because he wagers little but because he simply feels more comfortable at these more modest windows. Perhaps it is a question of his heritage or only the class system at work. In any event, it is a fact—and I have witnessed this—that once Simmons bet fifty dollars on a filly to win and did so at the two-dollar window in the form of twenty-five tickets. He simply feels more in place there, the clerk's glare to the contrary. In that case, incidentally, the horse won, profiting Simmons fifty-five dollars, something which he considered an excellent omen as well as a sign that his humility had been observed and respected in Higher Quarters. Nevertheless, he is now on the ten-dollar line.

"Got anything?" the man behind him asks in response to a certain stimulus which I have implanted midway between the medulla oblongata and the *vas deferens*. I am curious about the degree of confidentiality which Simmons feels invested in our relationship. But I have not been cautious, technically, and there is a terrifying moment during which I fear the questioner might faint. Fortunately, he does not, but the reasons he has worked out for betting the eight horse are now and will remain irrevocably wiped from his mind.

"Nothing," Simmons mutters, "oh all right, the six, the six. Just got a tip out of the infield but I don't know if it's worth a damn. I'll stab, though." For an instant I feel a jolt of disorientation: has Simmons misunderstood me or already forgotten the advice? But then as he comes to the window, I understand that he is only being what he takes to be very cunning, and as he leans over he makes the clerk lip-read the word *three*. He has decided then to posture as a deaf-mute in order to protect his information, and this is safe since no ten-dollar clerk at this track has ever before seen him. As he now mouths, "Three ten times," the clerk returns that timeless embracing nod of one who has seen everything (this look is also available in whorehouses but then only on reservation and for special customers) and punches out ten tickets. Simmons, the recent deaf-mute, puts down a hundred dollar bill, leaving him with only a couple of dollars and change, and takes the tickets, cupping them so that the man behind cannot see, and then moves to the rear of the line. Pausing there he verifies the number as he always does (although his losing streak has now reached such proportions that when races are over he finds himself reaching for his tickets and praying that the clerk has made a mistake or that he, Simmons, has begun to lose his vision and did not verify properly). Then he returns slowly toward his place on the rail, pausing for a brief cup of coffee which he does not taste, although he can distinctly hear the clerk cursing him for not leaving the change from a quarter. I understand with disgust that Simmons will not visit the place windows, preferring to back up his bet with insistence rather than circumspection. It is an old failing.

The rail is slightly more crowded now with only two minutes to post, but sufficiently uninhabited at the edges that he is able to leave out the yardage which he feels he needs as he prepares himself for the running. As he curls his hair, wipes his forehead (although it is a cool day), runs a left hand absently over his genitals, his inner wrist catching the comforting bulge of the tickets in his trouser pocket, he begins a thin, shrieking monologue which he believes to be private although, of course, I am privy to every word. I listen to it with relish, delighted as always to see that my effects upon Simmons have not been imperceptible and that now as in the past (and in the imponderable future as well) I have the capacity to move him. Of course I have had to change many of my devices and manipulations in order to do so but the synapses are well covered, and it is this, along with a few other things, that gives me hope. If I have possessed Simmons to this degree, then there is absolutely no saying how effective the mission might be, and, in the bargain, I have been able to keep abreast of his development. This is no mean accomplishment since Simmons has been even more variable within the last couple of weeks than in the past, (I refuse to believe that my presence has had anything at all to do with this.)

"Oh you bastards," Simmons is saying, "oh you bastards, *please*, please give me this one; it's so little to ask. A hundred dollars, seventy to one now, that's seven thousand, just seven thousand dollars. What's the difference? Who cares? What difference would it make to the bastards if I won? Favorites can lose, longshots win. Longshots win big. Everyone gets out sooner or later, later or sooner. Oh God, give me just this once and never again. The three, the three, just once the three. What difference does it make to you, you dirty sons of bitches? But think of the difference it makes to *me:* a new chance, a new life, well, maybe the old life but certainly better, a *lot* better. I deserve it. Oh give this one to me now. Forty to one. Big drop. Here comes the money. Oh God, four thousand dollars, maybe more, never less. Oh please, please; it won't cost you a thing but think of what it means to me!"

There are two aspects to this monologue which I find objectionable. The first is that the main thrust of Summons's appeal is to the sons of bitches rather than to the one who gave him the tip—that is to say me. The second is that Simmons knows as well as I that were he to win four thousand dollars he would have no more idea of what to do with it than as to what to do with the hundred he has just bet. It is various and peculiar, but it is the very perversity of Simmons, and by inference of all these creatures, which has so involved me and made them—*pace*, Headquarters!—sympathetic in my eyes. Who other than themselves would have ever conceived them?

In any event, Simmons is now barely coherent. "Oh, I picked him for God's sake, let me know that I still have my wits about me!" He moans and this, as everything else, I try to find amusing. It is not the fact that my tip has been so rapidly transmuted into judgment that titillates. No, it is something else; it has to do with the certainty of Simmons's conviction that massive things now work in the balance. This is an emotion only fully apprehensible at the racetrack, although other situations occasionally come close. None of those situations I have noticed, however, are at all accessible to what Simmons or I would think of as the "working class."

It is now post time. No, it is some seconds after post time, one of the horses in the gate having clearly, to Simmons's anguished but far-sighted gaze, unseated his jockey. "Oh God, not the three, not number three!" Simmons pleads and the announcer says, "That's number one, Cinnamon Roll, unseating the rider." And Simmons gives a gasp of relief as the announcer adds, "That's Cinnamon Roll now running off from the gate." "Oh boy," Simmons says as several patrons to his right and left begin to spew curses at the same time extracting tickets from shirt pockets which they regard with loathing. Cinnamon Roll is the 7–5 favorite, as one glance at the tote quickly affirms. "I really can't stand this," Simmons says to no one in particular and bangs an elbow into the mesh, giving him enough distracting pain to keep him functioning while the outriders meanwhile recover number one, gently urge her toward the gate, stand guard while the jockey remounts, and then tenderly pat the horse into position. The grandstand mutters angrily; they feel that the horse should have been scratched for medical reasons. But Simmons himself is beyond judgments; he has moved into an abyss of feeling so profound that only the announcer's statement that the horses are out of the gate is able to move him to passion.

The effect of this is, however, galvanic and would surprise anyone in the vicinity of the ten-dollar window who had decided to take a tip from the mute. "Oh, you bastards, here you come!" he says with conviction, a sidewise glance at the board now informing him that the horse is at least ninety to one. "Oh boy," he says, "come on, come on, get me out of this, *Come on!*" his voice winding its way up the scale during the final words and impressing me, as it always has, with Simmons's utter lack of obscenity under stress situations. It all falls away in the same fashion, I understand, that soldiers in mortal danger of their lives or with broken morale, are apt to curse somewhat less than a cross section of the Mothers Superior. Obscenity, according to those studies with which I am familiar, occurs only during the relative contentment of hope and tends to vanish when the stresses become evident. "Oh please," says Simmons, and clasps his hands prettily.

(Once, Simmons had made a resolve to not address horses or jockeys during the running of races. He came to this decision on the basis that he was trying to be businesslike and participating in an investment program not dissimilar to stocks and bonds. Did brokers or customers, he wondered, scream curses at the ticker and shake their fists wildly when old IBM went up at dawn? Of course they did not, so neither would he. This resolve has lasted four races, until Lopez had done something really disastrous with a longshot who was caused to bear in on the rail, and from that time on Simmons has comforted himself with the new certainty that without air conditioning, all brokers would work in their undershirts.)

The horses come toward the stretch turn. It is difficult to pick up the call in the midst of the shouting and difficult as well to see the numbers of the leading horses as flashed on the tote board because of the angle. It is for this very reason—a sense of rising mystery during a race, all possibilities enacted until the deadly, final knowledge—that Simmons has elected this for his vantage point. But now, past all shrieking, his voice is only a terrified whisper as he says, "What's going on?" Hurling himself half over the rail, he is able to see the race for the first time—and he cannot spot the three horse. Four is on the lead and seven outside of it coming on. The three must be behind another horse on the rail; either that or it has adjourned from the gate because, as the horses pass, he is quite unable to see it. "Please," Simmons begs as he watches the field scuttle from him. There are diminishing cries in the distance and then a silence so deep and white that it could turn flowering acres into glowing bone.

Numbers come on the tote which Simmons is unable to see. After a time—and it is a considerable time, for the horses must return to the paddock to be unsaddled and the jockeys must weigh in, but for Simmons there is no sense of chronology whatsoever—the announcer says that the race is official and reads off the money horses. The three finishes third which is a remarkable showing for a ninety-to-one shot. Only one ninety-to-one shot out of ten beats even a third of its field; this one

has beaten fully three-quarters.

I point this out to Simmons in a mild, apologetic tone. "It was rather remarkable, you've got to admit that," I say, "and you could have had the show bet which incidentally paid only eighty sixty due to the two favorites running in."

Simmons says nothing. He is beyond modest mathematical calculation. Instead, he is shaking his head, up and down, his neck constricting, his brow bulging, his eyes fluttering. He appears to be entering a period of sea change, or at any rate it seems to be Simmons Transmuted which I see before me: an older, wiser, infinitely altered Simmons who looks at me with compassion and loathing intermingled. As palms spread before me (figuratively) I back away, apologizing for my faulty information, my impulsiveness, my overextended and already-familiar desire to please my landlords. My suspicion is that I too have become a compulsive gambler—even though I had reasons for this.

But after a long time, Simmons says something in a low voice, and it is difficult for me to distinguish it for a moment. Then the words seem to explode through me with the force of a grenade, or perhaps I am thinking of a waterfall (my taste for metaphor being as faulty as my way with horses). Nevertheless, I find that I am drenched in knowledge, swaying, gasping, so moved that I am virtually inarticulate—and then the silence further deepens as we plunge toward Saturday's True and Final Disaster and the wondrously grim events of the deservedly famous Last Descent which will then begin.

"You can't win them all," Simmons says.

CHAPTER II

First Recitatif: Seen from the outside, all of these minds are the same, leading to the unfortunate stereotype, the steady delimitation of outlook so common to the sport, etc., and all of this composing another in that series of humiliations which must be suffered by the "horseplayers" of this good brown Earth. Inside, however, it is something else entirely as only I would know. The variation of these minds is splendid: no two of them alike, no three of them in concordance, a range of opinion, response, personality, superstition, which is truly astonishing, the more so because it does congeal around a point of shared rage. Rage and instinct. That is where it all begins.

Consider, gentlemen: at the moment I occupy four minds. All of them employ the same rhetoric, all have similar "goals," none of them differ in degree of ambition ultimate from the others—but, nonetheless, the range is extraordinary. The one revolves around small angles, small plans, the other around devastation and its personal impact, the other yet around prophecies and admixtures (she sees omens in the weather, to say nothing of the amalgam of glances she imagines herself to gain from post-bound jockeys), another around a certain eclecticism combining scatology, theology, sexual perversion, and certain sociological constructs which make no sense to the outsider and yet seem to form a compelling statement for the one so afflicted. And so on. And so forth. The sprawl! The conflicts! The holy, holy difference! And I selected them all at random in the bargain! That such diversity could breed unity; that such a unity could come from coincidence. Any four would have been the same. This is the terror of it.

Terror! Terror! A reflective individual (and I must use that term advisedly) could do worse than to spend the rest of his years with the seeking of correlative coefficient and conflicts among this breed. Unfortunately, I do not have the time.

No, I do not have the time. My mission is specific rather than general, goal-linked, highly motivated, and will work toward a visible conclusion.

(It is hard to control their language. It is so clumsy and imprecise, further, that subvariation, English, with which I struggle is particularly wretched since a given word or phrase may have ten meanings or more depending upon context. "He rode the mare," for instance, does not mean the same as "he rode the mayor." "He got trapped on the rail" is opposed to "he railed at the entrapment." There are individuals here, believe it or not, who devote a substantial proportion of their time to language, either its expression or analysis, and it is understandable, granted their poor equipment, why language alone should underlie so many of their problems. They simply do not know what they are talking about.)

Bear with me. I cannot justify these digressions but find them uncontrollable: there is so very much to record—now that I have decided to break the policy—and so little time to do it; one must so to speak, seize the moment. The hour? The time? It does not matter. Were I more organized, I would not be in this post in the first place, would doubtless be comfortably ensconced in the Bureau passing on the work of wretched hacks like this undersigned who, because they lack discipline and seniority, are forced to perform the, uh, field work.

No time, no time. It is the feeling of *disaster* which so overwhelms at this time, so inexplicable and yet in its oppressive weight and dimension hinting at a veracity that cannot be avoided. A feeling of enclosure, of the most inexpressible *limitation*, the lurkings of a devastation so complete as to sink without trace not only those well-meaning individuals whom I tenant but the *occupant* himself and at the end of it—

Enough of this. To facts and the clear basic extrinsics of event from which all real conclusion will come. (Do it, I said to Tony this morning, do it, do it, you know you want to so much so go ahead because you have the right.) Everything is under control and will remain so. (He looked at me, his face pale as a shadow roll and said, I'm afraid. I want to but I can't. No fear, I said, the fear all comes from inside, they can't do a thing to you. And I know he will do it.) Lacking physiognomy, I have no emotional liability. Lacking presence I am not culpable. Lacking form, I am free. Remember this, remember this....

All of them are waking now, turning toward the dawn which comes in lurking slowly from the direction of Ozone Park. It will soon be Saturday, June 4, 1987. Belmont Day. The third jewel of the triple crown at a mile and a half for three year olds.

CHAPTER III

Mary. Consider now Mary. (She will insert the fuses.) The room is full of bags and bags; bags and tipsheets that is to say. On the near wall are lined the bags which she uses both for shopping and accumulation, some of them still filled with the evening's pickings, others clean and reconstituted for later adventures. The bags are stencilled with messages like FREE THE THREE or GIVE THE RIGHT A CHANCE or DON'T BUY FOREIGN, some of them evincing not only rhetoric but a certain fusion of poetry and appeal. PRAY FOR THE TIMES. But Mary, it must be clearly understood, reads none of this; is as impermeable to rhetoric as only a woman of her age and means can be. She is no longer interested in Messages. She has not believed for a long time that the Answers lies anywhere outside of her skull. She still, however, does believe in the Answer. We shall see evidence of this now and again.

The near corner is, of course, that against which her bed is placed and it is for this reason that the bags are there; it enables her to collapse for a rest immediately upon dropping the bags in her wake and, conversely, she is then able to go through their considerable contents later and at some leisure without ever leaving her bed. Despite the fact that she is in relatively good physical condition, this is an advantage not to be disregarded, although the contents of the bags themselves are often disappointing, Mary is seventy-eight years old.

She has been a collector of used merchandise now for some ten years or shortly after she hit the six-four double for three thousand five hundred eighty-nine dollars and forty cents at Belmont on a cheerless fall afternoon. Feeling that the end of her horseplaying career was now imminent, she looked for another activity which would divert her in her old age. Unfortunately, she lost almost all of the proceeds within six months, largely on hot tips and new tipsheets, and thus the bags, instead of being her main occupation became only a sideline, a satellite as it were to the business at hand. But the mechanics of collecting kind of interest her, even now. She knows that some day she will hit a large double again and this second time around she will not be so foolish; she will invest half the winnings in reliable stocks. Once she found a current *Telegraph* folded neatly in a collection of orange peels, smelling vaguely of lint. In terms of collections, this has been her Main Hit, although there have been a couple of lunches.

On the other, more important side of the room, lie the tipsheets. Mary has the most impressive collection of used tipsheets in the city of New York. It is possible that it is the only such collection (I have not re-searched this) since, unlike the *Morning Telegraphy*, tipsheets are not meant to remain on file. Bought for the instant at the track and used only for an afternoon, they tend to be an ugly reminder of losses or de-pendence, and horseplayers discard them somewhere underfoot or in the lavatories shortly before the last race. All of them, that is, except Mary who has been saving tipsheets since she first went to the track, some fifty years ago. They lie in even, multi-colored stacks on the far wall: the *Lawtons* in an orange pile, the *Rowes* in a yellow, the *Powells* in a green, the *New York Turf Letters* in a blue and white, and so on. In composite, and there are several hundred thousand of them there, they compose a living anthology of defeat—or perhaps it is victory depending upon the luck of the tipsheets and the faith of those interpreting them. One of the piles contains what Mary feels to be the prize of her collection: the only twenty issues ever published of the *International Astrological Predic-tor* which, attuned to the various zodiacal signs, attempted to give each horseplayer an individual reading. The trouble with the *Predictor*, as Mary understands it, is that it often gave twelve horses in a race.

(It is understood that the use these people make of "astrology" is mega-lomaniacal and insane. They feel, some of them, that the "heavens" somehow gave them a "sign" for their "destiny" if not convenience, and this is worth an ironic essay of some length and judicious weight. Un-fortunately I do not have the time now, but it should have been pointed out to them a long time ago that inasmuch as some "planets" are "in-habited" and the zodiacal signs for the tenants of these planets would be in contradiction to their own, what can be made of all this? Multiple destiny? Law of entropy? Gains and losses? This is only part of the am-bivalence of the construct. It is a pity that I will not be able to go into this in sufficient detail.)

Mary did not buy all of these tipsheets, of course. Their gross value, purchased, would be upwards of $75,000. (It is important to be precise; it sculptures out a kind of balance in the madness.) Mary has never had this kind of money, even during winning streaks. She buys only *Law-*

ton, following the Orange Madman's prophecy with a kind of dazzled compulsiveness which would be founded upon design if there were any kind of consistency to it. The others she has collected on her own, either from the pavements of the track, or by begging them from horseplayers as, tipsheets under arm, they prepare to leave the scenes of their demolition. "Pardon me sir but may I please have that *New York Turf Letter* you're holding? I want to compare selections and surely you'd bless an old lady, won't you?" This is Mary's standard line and has met with unified success.

But occasionally a stubborn or lunatic horseplayer has actually withheld the goods, depositing on Mary a slow burning glare of knowledge and saying something like, "Huh, you old bitch, you just want to pick up the systems without laying out the cash, right?" It is at times like these that Mary's truest and most subtle diplomacy has come to the fore. "Oh no sir," she says, "I just want to mail it to my son who is overseas now in the army and used to love to play the horses; it gives him a feeling that he's got a part of home with him if he only has his *New York Turf Letter* that he loved so, or do you think that he loves fighting the war for you?" And this has never failed to work, not even once, since the only thing more characteristic of horseplayers than desperation is their guilt. (If they lose, they are being punished, if they win the money is not really theirs.) Every one of them—I have done a little survey detail— believes that he would be best and truest to himself in a state of terminal diagnosis or mortal combat. "Oh sure, lady, for your son in the war," even the most maddened of those petitioned will say, and Mary has another *Turf Letter* to add to her collection. Or *Top Turf*. Of those two she finds the *Turf Letter* more sensible although *Top Turf* is not afraid, every other race or so, to give a real longshot just to show that it has courage and imagination. Perhaps the proprietor of *Top Turf* has a somewhat larger mind than the rest of them.

(One begins to wonder: exactly who *are* the people behind the tipsheets? Are they businessmen cynically manipulating the drives of horseplayers to their own mild profit or, as it increasingly seems more likely to me, are they horseplayers themselves—horseplayers into losing streaks so long and cruel that they have been forced to sell their intimations rather than follow them? For the same reason that most bartenders in working-class bars appear to be alcoholics or barely reformed alcoholics, I think that the latter suggestion is probably the more viable.)

It is hard to say exactly what Mary has in mind for the tipsheets, once she has acquired them. She collects them for a certainty and enjoys looking at them in the aggregate as her first act on awakening. On sunny mornings in the summer there is a virtual blaze of color and cheer vaulting from the side of the room toward her bed, catching the beam of daylight through the window and sending it to Mary in clouds of orange and green which makes her feel as if she were celebrating the force of nature itself. But witness is not the sun of her activity; she spends long mumbling hours, two or three evenings a week, during which she crouches by the sheets and runs her hands through their weary selections cackling to herself. Now and then she is apt to pull a tipsheet at random from the stack and point a finger at something she sees.

"You look here!" she will say to the ceiling, "on November 5, 1958, Lawton picked Egg Nog to place in the third race at Jamaica, and I remember that race as distinctly as the day I was born. That horse finished *fifth*. Went lame, the son of a bitch. This *proves* that they don't know what they're talking about! Not one of those sons of bitches has any sense at all!" she will say and put the tipsheet back into its proper place with a flourish, thereby ending the discussion.

"Ah, the stupid bastards," she will say, "they don't know what in hell they are doing, not a single one of them and that's the whole trouble. The thing is in the hands of idiots, just like this jerk Powell here who always goes to maidens in mixed claimers because they get light weight and he feels they can't lose—but what Rowe does to a maiden claimer, shouldn't be done to a dog."

God, the actual degree of heat in Mary's apartment: it is late spring and what with the steady deterioration of the climate through the last half-century on the planet due mostly to radio-actives and the effects of the post-industrial period, it is almost unbearable here, even for Mary, let alone the man who is at present occupying the space with her and, so to speak, making things even hotter. This man is short and fat, and can be most conveniently located somewhere in his late forties. He is Mary's only son, a stockbroker named Julian, and he is at the moment attempting to complete a dialogue with Mary which has gone on for several hours now, has become increasingly painful, and has, several times forced my own intervention into Mary's brain in order to protect her against the chance of cerebral seizure.

"I won't go," she is saying, "and that's final. I won't have any part of it. I'm an independent woman and I live my own life and can live it until I die which will not be soon, thank you. You'd take me away from all this?" and motions toward the stacks of tipsheets on the left, the bags on the right, consecutive gestures which seem to make Julian (he prefers, in his trade, to be called Jules but reverts to a kind of stammering Julianship with his mother; somehow things never work out with her as they should) stagger in the foul, shifting breezes of the room and then clutch something in the vicinity of his chest. He feels that his physical self is deteriorating but his mother has always done this to him.

"Never," she says. "Oh no. Never, never, never, never!"

"You have to, Mother," Julian says with what he takes to be filial discipline. "You can't live here anymore. The whole section is coming down for urban renewal, anyway."

"Ha!" Mary said. "They'll have to carry us out dead. We're suing. There's a tenant committee and everything. I'm a woman who knows her rights and they aren't going to renew me."

"And besides that," Julian says, "and let's be realistic about this now, I can't stand your losses anymore. I cannot finance this. I can help you with the rent and so on, but I can't back the horseracing. I mean, I've put up with it for a long, long time and I've been understanding and I know what it means to you and so on, but—"

"It's just a losing streak," Mary says. "Anyway, didn't I always steer you right? Just a little losing streak, nothing serious. Didn't I get you through college on my information? Wasn't it because of me that you had the clothes and car to get that bitch of a wife of yours? So I've had a tough time adjusting to the new surface, doesn't mean a thing." (The answer to all of Mary's questions is no. She is falsifying her past, but since she has been likewise falsifying the future for so long now, the discrimination is merely a nicety. She dismisses it. It is beneath her.)

"I don't care, Mother," Julian says, resisting at cost (I am omnipotent in these circumstances, as you know, and can deduce not only motive but ambivalence) an impulse to sob. "I don't care whether it's a little losing streak or a long one. I can't argue anymore. I just can't *afford* it. We have to get you into—uh—well, we have to get you into a more controlled environment. Somewhere where you'll be protected and taken care of and—"

"No," Mary says with a pleasing finality. In profile, her face seems to Julian to be that of a woman years younger, perhaps a woman transmuted by rage and suffering into some earlier and better vestige of herself. "I won't have anything to do with it, Julian. I'll never go to a nursing home and I'll never stop playing the horses. I'm in a little trouble right now but nothing serious and I'll get right out of it. It's my entitlement. I devoted my whole life to working out the system and just when I'm finally on the point of seeing a little return from all my interest, just when I'm about able to enjoy my old age, you come—*you* who I put through college and got that bitch of a wife for—and tell me that you're going to take it all away from the old woman. I won't have it. I worked too hard. I deserve my pleasure, it's the only thing we got."

As she says the last of this, with a pleasing dramatic flourish and an absence of self-pity which even I can find commendable, Mary stumbles back from Julian, over-balances, and without dignity or ceremony, topples heavily to the floor, her passage somewhat deflected by the bags which give her a nasty thump in the back and then deposit her, on her knees from which she regard Julian with a faint and uncustomary glare of appeal. Trembling, he reaches forward to bring her to her feet. (This is not the first time that Mary has fallen in this way, although she rather too often has a habit of doing it before relatives and acquaintances during a period of intense argument. As he does so, as he feels the pressure of his fluttering old Mom moving within his cupped palms, what is left of Julian's reserve, not to say his exterior, crumbles. He feels totally out of control and does not know if it is rage or fear which drives him to say what he then says, holding onto her tightly.)

"I won't have it!" he shouts, giving Mary's lines back to her with a considerably different reading. "I tell you, I won't have this anymore, I can't stand it. I won't be associated with you! I'll pay for the room and I'll pay for the food, all right and I'll give you an allowance even—but I won't, I absolutely won't, I absolutely refuse to give you any money for the horses now. It's not fair! It's not right! I have no interest in horses! They don't mean a thing to me! All my life I somehow managed to avoid them, it isn't reasonable that *I* should be a loser." He backs away from her, and when his pelvis bumps against the wall, he feels a certain grinding presence and manages, not unhappily, to bring himself back to a true confrontation of the circumstances: his mother's age, the condition of the room, the flies which whirr absently, suspended in the gelatinous air, the snap of horns outside, the cries of children pelting the window. It is really insane. Even in a calamitous market he still holds down a desk at Hochstein & Super, and lunch hour, even the lunch hour of a broker, is now ending.

"No more time," he says. "Now you make the decision: either you go to a nursing home or you stop playing the horses but you can't do this to me!" Julian moans and with this arietta seems to spin slowly through time itself, moving flylike toward the door. When he gets there, he looks at his mother for a moment until her gaze rises to his and then he leaves the room, slamming the door firmly. It seems that he had said all that he is going to say.

This has been Julian's fifth visit to his mother during the past six months, all of these visits having had the same subjectual basis but never before has he spoken with such commendable passion, forthrightness, lack of ambiguity. It is something which I, steeped as I am in the deadly circumlocutions of language not to say implication, can appreciate, and I savor it sidewise while with a thin harumph I clear my throat to reconstitute my dialogue with Mary.

Mary and I are on excellent speaking terms. Of all of them, she has been the quickest to accept me; the friendliest, the least reserved, the most reasonable. She has managed to accept both my existence and her sanity, a speculative vault which would be surprising under the circumstances if it were not so very moving. She trusts me. Mary, for all the bad press which she has received, has an open mind and a communicative intelligence, and one would wish that these qualities were not trapped into a corpus as luckless, superstitious, and panicky as hers often tends to be. On the other hand, she was picked at random, so I have no complaints.

"The son of a bitch." Mary says, sitting on the floor again but with a certain poised dignity and grace which would surprise the puffing Julian who I happen to know is now hurtling through the stones and garbage of the Upper West Side, looking frantically for a taxicab, blinking his eyes against tears and smog. Never, he had resolved, will he have dealings with his mother again. He will not sustain her horseplaying anymore. What terrorizes Julian and adds no small impetus to his flight is this: he realizes that he still believes that his mother is somehow the precursor of Information and that lurking behind her whines, sobs, accusations, and wrath is always the possibility of the Ultimate Tip of such dimension as to whirl him free past stockbrokership (to say nothing of his wife) and to some unchartered vintage of possibility where he will be able, in peace, to wangle alternatives forever. Julian hails a cab. He stumbles into it gasping and leaves the Upper West Side forever. Two days later he will have a coronary which will hospitalize him for six months and leave him thereafter a bloated, pallid, wreck, only barely cognizant through shifting eyes, of what has been done to him. Three years from today he will die gracelessly at noon. I am sorry. I am sorry about this, Julian. Nevertheless, there is really nothing I can do about it; I am not your tenant and you are not a horseplayer. Enough. Enough of trajectories.

"The son of a bitch ain't got no perspective," Mary says, "no damned perspective." She gasps a little, prowls through the tipsheets, removes a 1957 *Powell*. "The bastard went off Gallant Man in the Belmont," she says. "Look, it's right here. It was there staring him in the face how that horse couldn't lose and he went to Bold Ruler. What the hell are you going to do when idiots like this are on top?" Her eyes dazzle; this has been a comfort line and yet, somehow, she is not yet eased. "Ah the bastard, the dirty bastard," she mumbles and crawls over to the nearest of the bags, extracts half a salami sandwich carefully stowed a few days earlier against this kind of crisis and begins to eat sullenly. "He doesn't care what comes of me and after I got him that wife, too." A certain plaintive note extrudes which I cannot miss and which gives me, to the extent that I can feel emotion at all, a start of genuine satisfaction.

"It isn't fair," she yells. Mary does not subvocalize like some of the others; if worth saying, she feels, it is worth screaming. "It just isn't right. And after I spent all those years working on the system and just beginning to get it nice and tight, just began to work in the factor for maidens and the odds angle, after all of this the son of a bitch does this to me. Well, I shouldn't call him a son of a bitch. Well, yes, I *can* call him a son of a bitch. I guess it doesn't matter one way or the other." She chokes down the remainder of the sandwich with difficulty. "Ah, Christ, they're all out to get you anyway."

"Listen Mary," I intervene. It is important that I seize this moment to make my points as efficaciously as possible and yet, confronted by this opportunity I have a feeling of what could be termed inadequacy which makes me stumble just a trifle for words. Perhaps it is the very imminence of a qualified success which blocks me, or perhaps it is merely that congenital streak of incompetence which was responsible for my decision to join the Bureau in the beginning (civil service, even at the highest levels, is security rather than achievement oriented). "Listen, Mary, you can see the whole thing happening, you know what I mean? I mean if the kid pulls out the support then you won't be able to stand the losses anymore and the whole thing is going to go down the drain, of course it wouldn't go that way if you started to win, but the system doesn't look very good. Let's face it Mary old girl" (a certain leisurely informality can be assumed to work itself into many of my dialogues; one cannot stand on ceremony with these creatures because the only rituals which are meaningful to them are self-imposed), "it's right down the drain now and downhill all the way. No way out, just the nursing home and rockers at three instead of the fourth race; a little bowl of soup at five instead of the ninth, lights out at nine instead of studying the *Telegraph*. See it straight, Mary, there's only one way to go and it's the big bad way—but there is an escape, one escape that will solve everything if you do it now. But you can't wait, Mary, you can't fake it. You've got to seize the moment or should I say the time and follow through."

"What?" she says, ingesting the sandwich and taking another half from the bag. She is completely fixated on me, thrilled, as it were, into a kind of heightened consciousness, perhaps by the intensity of my appeal (I have heretofore been reasonable with her and attempted to do by rational means what is seemingly impossible through the melodramatic), perhaps by the intensity of her plight. She has always accepted me but it is now as if I, along with the sandwich, am suffering the excursion of ingestion. There is some greed to her intensity as she says again, "What do I do? What's the answer? Tell me? Because I don't think that anybody knows, that's what I'm beginning to learn. Not a one of them."

"It's obvious, Mary," I say with a pedantic gentleness and render upon her trembling, grey little psyche a pat almost affectionate in its tingling connection, it not only quiets her but brings certain centers of the brain into a howling awareness. "You've still got a little bit left. Not enough to carry you at all but something you managed to squeeze away out of the budget and even away from the horses. You still have it, don't you, Mary? Five hundred dollars, right between pages 102 and 104 of the *Monthly Chart Book* for December of 1972 which is under your bed."

"How'd you know that?" she says. "I mean how could you tell? There's no one—"

"Isn't it obvious, Mary?" I say. "Isn't it obvious to you how I knew? Come on, be realistic now. There's very little time left. You can see it all before you, can't you?"

She thinks about this for a while, the planes of her simple, weary, honest old face seeming to muddle together in some anguish of heat and light, and then she says, "Of course. Of course I had to understand. It had to be that way, didn't it?"

"The answer, Mary. There's only one answer, you know. Unless you want all of it to go away and then all you will know will be light: light coming in through the windows of the nursing home, light from the examining tools of dishonest young physicians who, for a small retainer will pronounce you dead or alive depending upon the vigorish in the book; light from the trays of food winking in the corridors, light from the stethoscopes gleaming like an inquiry sign as the solemn, serious, blunt young face of an orderly turns downward toward you and—"

"The answer," she says. "Just give me the answer." It would seem that I have had some effect upon her. Painful this but necessary. I do not like to hit them so hard—they are, for all their degeneracy, so infuriatingly vulnerable—but this is the only way that they can be encouraged to listen. "Just tell me the answer. Come on."

"Don't you know it, Mary? Haven't you followed it in the alleys of your mind night after night dwindling into sleep, the slow extinguishment, of consciousness leading you toward that epiphany, that sense of connection which came out of necessity and told you that this was what you had to do? Haven't you dreamed it Mary; touched the torch a thousand times?"

"Ah, don't give me none of that bullshit. I can't pay no attention. Just tell me what I should do, will you?"

"You tell me, Mary."

We confront one another then in an endless, unchanging silence for a period of time which could be seconds or several years (depending upon one's planet of origin, its cycle of revolution, the nature of its ecology) and then she says, "What you mean then is that I got to take the whole five hundred—"

"The whole five hundred, Mary. Every cent of it is right."

"And I've got to take it to the track."

"That's right, Mary. You've got to take it to the track."

"The whole five hundred. You want me to take every cent of it?"

"That's right, Mary. You can't leave any of it out, now. It has to be everything because that's the only fairness."

"And I have to put that whole five hundred—"

"You can't hold back. It has to be one shot and out because that's the way that you always wanted it, isn't it?"

"The five hundred?"

"Come on, Mary. You're almost there now. Just a little bit more, now. You have to take the five hundred and lay it—"

"Lay it on a selection and hope that it comes in," she says and leans against the wall gasping hoarsely, wiping an arm against her forehead, overcome, one might think, from the speculative vault except that I know Mary too well and that it is only a certain pathos which is inspiring her. She sees herself at this moment as a small woman against Doom and if there is little ennoblement in it, then the background must be seen. "Lay it all on a selection and hope it comes in." She croaks, and her eyes flutter. She feels overcome by fatigue. She shifts on the floor, adjusting her limbs. "Hope it comes in," she says, "and all comes in for the selection that's out, and then everything is in and out, out to the inness, shade to the darkness, dark to the light." Her breathing becomes slightly more regular and she seems to subside against the wall in a long, rolling slant which carries her, in stages, to the floor.

A cheek nestles against one of her bags, an orange peel coming to fall atop her forehead and giving her the aspect of a still life: Woman with Fruit at Night. It is a touching and affecting scene rendering her a grandeur and grace which even the doomed Julian might appreciate. Prayers come by bets; they come in oranges as well. "Hope it comes in," Mary murmurs to the orange and falls into a deep sleep so deep and true that I can barely encompass it (being sentenced merely to sentience and disaster a thousand light-years from her); a spiralling circular sleep for Mary at the end of which it can be assumed that Judgment resides.

Or is it a horse? Yes, it is a horse, the three horse. The three horse is coming on the outside, now, moving fastest of all at the finish, hooking the field, the jockey rolling on the flanks like a puppet, and as the field comes by Mary's point of view, the three has hooked it. It has come head to head with the leader and now it is passing; the three is winning. The three is winning, the three is winning, the dim shriek of the crowd rises toward lustful knowledge as the field stumbles and staggers, flutters and leaps toward the wire. And at the wire there is a sound: shatter of cannon bone, twist of foreleg, cry of horse and bleat of jockey and somewhere between Mary's point of view and the clubhouse a horse has gone down. It is impossible to see from this angle the number on the saddlecloth but the horse is thrashing in agony and as the field comes by

slowly and grandly, rearing to reverse, jockeys swaying to an upright position to bring them into assembly on the backstretch, as the rites of the
race move toward conclusion, Mary waits in a poised and terrible uncertainty, looking at the board, waiting for the number of the winner to
go up. The judges, it seems, have called for a photograph to determine
the order of finish. All tickets are to be held until the result of the race
is official. In the next race there are no changes. In the seventh race
there is a change of jockeys. In the eighth race the five horse is wearing mud caulks. All tickets to be held please. Do not discard your
parimutuel tickets until the result of the race is official. Mary rams herself against the rail like an insect, she is trying to tear the information
from the board but the board is blank. Everything is blank.

Mary slowly falls open-mouthed away from the bags and into a protective ball against the floor. She snores. Mary is now sleeping. Witness
her sleep. True and central, deep and final, she plunges toward that fire
as her son eats a sandwich at Hochstein and all of Manhattan curls into
the sea.

CHAPTER IV

Second Recitatif: Most of the racetracks are built between ten and
twenty miles from the center of large urban areas. In the less populated
areas of the country, of course, they tend to be somewhat closer than that
to the main belt, but as a general indice, it is safe to say that the racetracks are conterminous to but wholly without the central cities of their
country. There are two reasons for this.

One is the question of real estate values. The average racetrack covers several hundred acres and property and land values in the city are
such that the racing associations simply could not afford to have their
enterprise directly in the metropolitan areas. (It is remarkable how easily I have assimilated their filthy jargon, with what swooning facility I
can regurgitate this rhetoric. It hypnotizes to think of what they have
done with language for now, it virtually obliterates all meaning. Nevertheless, one must go on. There is so little time. The circumstances are
so foul. The aura of these people is so disgusting. But a certain tacitness
extrudes, a limited sense of delicacy. They sweat. They confuse mortification with corruption.)

The other reason is co-equal and possibly the more significant in the
long run. It is the question of displacement. The race tracks must be
away from the center of the metropolitan areas because they represent—at least, to those who patronize them—the excision of all those
values on which the metropolitan areas are themselves based: ration-

ality, causality, consequence, effort, consumption, production, accretion, etc. The racetracks are founded upon something different; they are selling (and selling well) the conception that there is no simple way out, that causality is meaningless, that accretion has to do only with psychic conditions and not with possessions (which must be metaphors for true gain) and if they are too close to the metropolitan areas, the message might move uncomfortably near to a larger heterogeneity of the population. They represent an alternative. And the alternative is one of annihilation, devastation, and waste.

Annihilation! Devastation! Waste! Or: waste! annihilation! devastation! However you want it, you can score this gloomy triad for chamber orchestra. (I think of a flute concerto backed by double bass and a simple string continuo). It could be the basis for a massive contrapuntal chant: one could, with the more likelihood, install these words on placards in every place of public assembly within these aforementioned metropolitan areas, undoubtedly to stunning effect. Seeing for the first time the true sum of their lives humbly inscribed in florid script before them, would the mortgagees and tenants be driven toward a kind of insight? Who knows? Is it not worth a try?

Perhaps I ramble. Looking back on these notes to date—hasty, wandering, faulty in their apprehension of the truly fascinating individuals with whom I have come to deal—I see that to a certain extent I have already defied my purposes which were not so much circumlocution as the act of explication. I wanted to make it clear what is going on here. I wanted it to be understood, and understood well, that what is going to happen would happen anyway; all that I am providing is a shade of haste and manipulation. I wanted to make it clear how they deserved what they were going to get. Yet I have not quite succeeded.

To the contrary, skimming rapidly, I see dialogues, retrospection, institutions bargained with and unyielding, complaints and so on. A certain characterological sense seems to be lacking. My own motives, shining and bureaucratically pure as they may be, seem shrouded in mystery, my eventual purposes highly qualified. I did not want this. I wanted to, as they say, "go with the chalk." Yet this is so intolerably difficult.

A lesson can be drawn from Simmons. Simmons has (who would have guessed it?) something to teach me. His exercises in self-justification are purely external and for himself. Having settled his scores he finds no need to break into new ground; he can settle them over and again, each thread a shining element in the tangle. What he lacks in gesture he provides in flourish. Nevertheless, I cannot take the course of a Simmons. I come from different stock. Other formative experiences and so on. Also my range is somewhat wider.

One senses the slow convulsion, the slow turning here toward absolute disengagement and confrontation. One can feel the disaster palpable in the very air: the salt marshes surrounding the racetrack stink with an awful poignance which on certain cloudy Tuesdays and Thursdays penetrates the infield itself, wraps all of its occupants into a spirit of mortality, and whisks them with dispatch to grandstand and mutuel machine where, in some slender compensation, they proceed to place the remaining parts of themselves on the line. The smell, composed of urban decay, ozone, and something even more profound which might be the signal of ecological rebellion, fills even the insensitive horseplayers with grief and nostalgia. They seem to smell their history. Speechless, it can address them only through the nostrils.

Meanwhile, the swans who paddle the infield lake here tell no secrets whatsoever, preferring to concentrate upon a small enclosure within the reeds. Perhaps they are copulating, working on the next generation of swans to inhabit the lake in, say, 1988. What mindless certainty! But they are only swans; they do not understand that the racing association in its wisdom and efficiency imports a new crop every so often, returning the corpses of previous tenants (too much pollution) to some version of the Swan's Motel. One wants to think of a bevy of late Aqueduct swans, laid neatly in the reception room of some hideous rest stop, sheltered in glass coffins over which are neatly arrayed wreaths made out of mutuel tickets. But somehow the metaphor involves too much struggle.

I do not sentimentalize the swans! One must learn to over-sentimentalize nothing. Time and again I have had to counteract this tendency, remind myself (as Simmons does often enough but he in the matter of prostitutes) that it is needless, destructive, and deadly, to sentimentalize that which has no feeling for you. I am not to be blamed for the individual fates of swans, let alone horseplayers and horsemen who are, as they should know, acting as mere correlatives for the overall condition. Certain folklore in their history and ours holds that a given number of individuals are the repositories and focus of all guilt and suffering for the unburdened millions who live in their times, and if that group happens here to be horseplayers, how can I be blamed? I did not crawl into their beds years ago and whisper talk of hits. I did not create the circumstances that sent them here. I came onto the scene long after they had completed their undeviating journey: rip of ticket, flicker of tote, scream of dismay, bellow of rage, whisk of horses, tap of jockey, speckles of mud on their feet as they patter to the windows. This was the situation I was given, not created.

Nevertheless. Nevertheless: why do I feel *culpable?*

CHAPTER V

Simmons is now tapped out. He sits on his sofa and for the first time regards his notebook. The statistics are so clear that he can barely come to terms with them. But the truth can no longer be escaped: he has no money left. Or, he has fifteen dollars left. In either event, he has no means to pay the rent which is already due. He is unable to repair his shoes. The cry of an illegitimate baby down the hall reminds him that he has no means of a sustenance. A scatter of roaches across the floor reminds him that he has few visible means of sanitation and that his wardrobe has expired. The hoots of children on the street below remind him that he has cast his seed upon the ground. The baby sputters. The roaches dart. The children throw or seem to throw a ball which clatters ominously against his windowpane and then, dislodging one of the land-lady's flowerpots, falls to the street with an augmented crash. Toilets flush down the hall. The sound of a broom in the corridors. Simmons sighs and opens the new morning *Telegraph* which, with a doughnut, he has just picked up for dinner. He opens to the entries for the first race, shakes his head, mutters something, shakes it again, and warily puts his index finger on the page, runs it down loosely. Figures seem to daz-zle his eyes, past performance workouts flow dimly against the seat of his consciousness. He pauses to look at the form for Never Far Back, an aged gelding who has been running in bad form recently but who, Sim-mons noted the last time (he bet him and the horse finished seventh) has now had his appearance improved through the colorful addition of pastel foreleg bandages which quite glisten and catch the sun as the horse stumbles lamely through the stretch. Appearances are vital.

"There's got to be a spot," Simmons says and shakes his head. "There's just got to be a *spot*."

"Simmons," I say, "Simmons, if you'll just listen to me a—"

"Shut up you evil, foul-minded son of a bitch," Simmons says.

CHAPTER VI

Despite my good efforts, Mary awakens blinking to a stab of urgency and phones the turf information service for the *Clocker-Eye Racing Note-book*. The service offers the results of each and every race at the New York tracks about forty-five minutes after last post, thereby enabling its readers and followers to avoid the agony of waiting for the morning papers somewhat later on with a handful of bookie slips or advance tickets clumped against the change in their pockets, slowly turning to glue under the pressure of anxiety. The service of the *Racing Notebook* (one deftly drops jargon in referring to it from now on; it is my analysis that the more mystical the pursuit the more heavy-handed the titles, we can safely ignore this) is the uniquely valuable dedication to improving not only the breed of horses but horseplayers. The only problem is that in order to circumvent federal and state laws the *Eye Mouth* would be more appropriate) cannot give out the results by names of horses. Instead, they are forced to do so by number; the numbers being the order of selection made by the *Eye* itself in its issue for the day. That is to say that if the *Eye's* third choice in a given race won, its seventh choice finished second and its eleventh finished third, the efficient but nervous secretary who takes these calls will announce the results as three-seven-eleven, necessitating that users of the service must have a copy of the *Eye* before them in order to make sense of the results.

(Nonusers are, however, entitled to take their chances. The *Eye* has been deep in a losing streak for many years now and a disproportionate number of winners turn out to have numbers like twelve and eight and six; that the *Eye* should so publicly reveal its incompetence is something that Mary would find difficult and puzzling if she had not come to understand herself a while back that the seventy-five cents invested in each issue of the *Eye* can be said to cover not so much information as the result service. In fact, the man who makes the selections for the *Eye* is the publisher himself, an eighty-three-year-old man with a lisp and stammer who, some years ago, lost his entire sex book factory during a disastrous week in Saratoga and was forced to find some useful way to get back at the system. He has, in certain senses then, been getting even ever since, but he has picked the wrong set of victims. His predilection for selecting horses moving up sharply in class after a disastrous race is well known and celebrated in the trade, and the fact that this did produce a $116.20 winner some seven years ago is still accounting for a full ten percent of the tiny circulation of the *Eye*. (Mary calls it the *Evil Eye* but for all her shrewdness she is rather simpleminded and certainly gullible.)

It is that tipsheet which Mary now holds before her as she dials the requisite number and asks for the winner of the ninth race at Aqueduct held some ninety minutes ago. Through a friend who goes to the track every day (Mary only goes four or five times a week) she has placed a two dollar bet on a longshot, Mr. Mal, who, she figured could not possibly be lower than 40–1 and was a sure thing to finish at the very least sixth in its large field.

"Ninth race," a querulous male voice says over the phone (perhaps the publisher himself, in order to save on overhead, is now taking the calls), "ninth race at Aqueduct, June 6, 1978. Winner is number ten. Second number three. Third horse number five. Buy the *Clocker-Eye Racing Notebook* at selected newsstands or at the grandstand entrance to the racetrack. Thank you for your interest," and hangs up with a clatter. Mary opens the *Eye* to the inmost page and finds that the tenth selection was a colt named Northway, listed in the morning line as 6–5. Her own selection, she finds grimly, was that of the *Eye* itself and can be presumed then to have been out of the money. She throws the *Eye* away in a kind of fury, removes a large notebook from one of the bags and makes an entry. According to her calculations, she is already seventy-three dollars behind for the week.

"It's only a little losing streak, the system is sound," she mumbles. Finding no comfort in this she adds, "Lawton picked the bastard as a longshot special only four races ago, damn it. Sons of bitches, it's all rigged. *All rigged.*" And then she does something very unMarylike, something so much out of the pattern of her previous behavior as to disconcert even me: she folds her arms tightly across her cheekbones and begins to cry. It is a high, falsetto wail, not totally unpleasing in the aesthetic sense and even rather soothing and I listen to it for a few moments, amazed as always by the capacity of these people to move me.

Finally I intervene. It is not, after all, my intention to prolong their suffering; as a matter of clear evidence I am doing everything within my power to end it. "You see, Mary," I say gently, "it can't possibly work. It just won't work that way at all. Even if the horse had won, you only would have made eighty dollars. You're in too deep. You've got to bail yourself out of this the only way you can."

"I know, I know," she says and her voice comes out clear and strident against the sobs, a kind of double-stopping of vocal effects showing real virtuosity, "I know that, but who would have ever known, when I got started, that there would be so much pain in it? You know? You know what I'm saying? Who would have thought that it would come to—"

"It would have to, Mary. The whole game sits on disaster. The disaster inflames it, informs it, gives it color and credence. You knew. You knew that from the first day."

"I want to go back to sleep," she says. "I didn't want I should have gotten up in the first place to find out how the race went. I wish I was still sleeping. I'm going back to sleep."

She folds herself on the floor, sighs, scrapples her feet into the wood, and using a bag as a pillow, begins to snore again.

It is a most convincing picture of human degradation. Except—and how can I sufficiently emphasize this point—except that Mary is not genuinely degraded, not in any sense that I have come to understand this word. Rather, she is apotheosized. Looking at her from this angle, my own sensibilities somewhat blurred by the grit in this room, it is as if I see not the common Mary to whom I have adjusted over this period, not the common Mary at all but instead a Mary Transfigured, one elevated by her passion to an assumption so vast and impermeable that nothing can really touch her.

If it is the horses which have brought her such comfort, say I, then may they run faster and forever. And if, like all qualities, they seek not only Transfiguration but Declension; if it is true that the obverse of every quality is that which would destroy it … Then seeing all of this (and how peculiarly they live what with dreadful counteracting tones of guilt, as if they do not desire their own mortality) one still wants the horses to run; moving with grace through the banked surfaces of the track, skittering down the backstretch like birds caught in the Hunter's Eye, vaulting into the homestretch with the heaving ecstasy and sense of connection which these humans themselves can only know in that most banal and struggling act which they think of as love. For love, for Love!

Mary dreams. In her dreams now she is winning forever. I gather myself into her and we make the passage together, toward that track without a tote, where all bets are prayers and the distant backstretch becomes another alleyway of the unspeakable human heart.

CHAPTER VII

Consider now, Tony. (He will procure the materials.) Tony is the problem. My communications with Tony, minimal from the first, have become bankrupt. It is as if there is a wall firmly lodged between his reason and myself; behind that wall Reason vainly kicks and scuttles, looking for a chink that would mean an arc of connection. But Tony's wall is firm, composed of forty years of rage, humiliation, defeat, disgust, etc., and it is not about to be kicked over by such feeble dwarves as compose his imperfectly contained sense of reason. Over this wall Reason and I are able to exchange confidences, pejoratives, and prayers, all held against that time (we do believe it) when the wall will collapse and we will conjoin, but for the time being it holds and there is little we can do other than to cheer one another. His reason, which I have said to be composed of dwarves is not to be underestimated: misshapen they may be but a certain piercing quality to their little eyes and lower features indicates that underneath it all the dwarves would be estimable people if only given the opportunity.

"Don't take this guy as permanent; he's a rest stop," Reason had consoled me, and I have, after a fashion, agreed, although it is perfectly clear to me that Tony and his reason are linked together as only suffering bedmates might be. Left to its own devices, Tony's reason would be in severe trouble: where would it find the ironies to feed it? The conjunctions? The endless gap between ambition and fulfillment which is the very stuff of which the dwarves' suppers are made? (Of such questions we need make no more, although it is no small insight into my own nature to point out that it is questions like these which tantalize me the most and which seem central to my own existence. What means Reason? What value irony? What price conjoinment? How long a longshot? The conditions from which I come put high premium on this kind of metaphysic. Nevertheless, it is extraneous.)

It is Tony himself with whom we must deal: the stolid, obdurate, externalized Tony who, listed in the programs and entry sections of the *Telegraph* as Trainer: A. Miller operates a public stable in and out of the New York tracks.

The public trainer, of course, is one who accepts horses to train from owners of any stripe or persuasion, this being in contrast to the private trainer who works only with the horses of the one large operation which employs him. Practically speaking—and this is the only means for Trainer: A. Miller—this means that private trainers are able to cultivate, at least externally, a certain air of gentility, weary bohemianism, usually minor statesmanship, whereas public trainers, who come into a somewhat larger view of the world's maddening heterogeneity, get all the nuts. To A. Miller come people like the doughnut manufacturer in Queens who owns three or four dismal thirty-five hundred dollar claimers and does not understand why his colors of cinnamon and sugar consistently fail to come in front of the fields. To A. Miller come failed mobsters with a vague desire to claim or run a couple of horses but lack connections. To A. Miller come old ladies from Mamaroneck who would emulate the popular admired Patrice Jacobs but instead come off as more reminiscent of Cowbell Hilda. The ladies are not the least of Tony's problems—he has a certain freedom of language which is not to be indulged in front of them, but there is simply no way in which he can otherwise express satisfactorily what he thinks of them and their miserable horses. However, it is not the ladies who at this time are imposing upon his time and talent.

Rather, all of Tony's energies, such are they, are presently fixated upon a small horse which is standing nakedly in the paddock area at Aqueduct, a number three thrown over its back. Blinkers are now being adjusted by one of Tony's grooms, a thin, whining boy with pimples who came to work for Tony some months ago because he believed that "tips" would augment his salary and expenses but who has only succeeded in losing all of his salary plus a bit of his resources. (This makes the groom somewhat bitter but we can happily pass him by. His possibilities are not linked in any significant way to horses, and in any event I find his mind dull and imperceptive. In a pinch he might show some ability with dynamite, but who needs him?) Tony is shaking his head with growing ferocity that is meant to signify despair, and as he backs off from the horse, hands on hips to regard it better, a certain shadow of genuine sorrow glazes over the face of A. Miller, giving it a rare (but moving) tragic overcast. He does not know what to make of this horse.

The horse, a four-year-old gelding named Make Peace, is one of Tony's own. The fact that the public trainer works with the horses of outsiders does not block him from trying to run a string of his own (this being the only sensible way out) and Make Peace is one of the three horses of twenty in Tony's care for which he possesses a trace of feeling. Most of the feeling is, naturally, not for the horse itself so much as for this extension of Tony, but this is not to be derided. In or out of the racetrack, one takes his feelings where he can, and Make Peace is one of the few elements in his life which can drive Tony into a genuine and urgent sense of connection with extra-Millerian matters. "Goddamn it," he says with growing wonder as he watches the horse now being led slowly into the walking ring by the disconsolate and cursing groom, "the son of a bitch is lame. He's lame, I can tell it from here. Who did this to me?"

Make Peace is not precisely lame; Tony knows this as well as I, and the horse would have been scratched by the stewards if its incapacity were as great as Tony would have it, but it is fair to say that for the last six months or so, he has performed as if he were. Tony who is, perhaps, somewhat more emotionally involved with his horses than the run of the mill public trainer has taken the horse's dismal performances to heart, as something of a personal comment (as it were) upon his training abilities and has been forced to rationalize the performances as being the willful efforts of a horse desirous of humiliating him. (This is a common frailty among these people; the buck is always passed. This is interesting and useful in the particular but tends to become something of a stricture when it invades their "international politics" or "urban renewal.") The horse, when he first came into Tony's care, was a $12,500 claiming animal capable of winning occasionally in races above that level and frequently in races below, thereby establishing his limits far better than Tony's ever could be (until recently). It was out of a $12,500 race that Tony claimed him at the behest of the prospective owner, an underwear manufacturer who had a couple of other, cheaper horses in Tony's care and wanted to go to the class. For the underwear manufacturer, the decision to claim an animal worth some eight thousand dollars more than any he had ever before owned might have been an existential leap of no small proportion, meaning that like many Americans he was trying to move up and on through the categories. But although the manufacturer attempted to move up in class through this purchase, the horse had other ideas. Perhaps the horse, in painful, instinctive sympathy with the truest and darkest urges of his new owner, felt that a declension in class was immediately necessary so that he could meet his new owner, so to speak, halfway. It is this animaline perversity that killed the underwear manufacturer recently and allowed Tony to purchase the horse, cheap and less training expenses already incurred, from the estate. He had sentiment.

Make Peace has however gone above and beyond the call of overcompensation. He is now about to compete in a $3,500 claiming race, the lowest offered at Aqueduct, and, as Tony's one sullen glance at the tote board confirms for him, the horse is hardly the favorite even in these wretched circumstances. In fact, Make Peace is 40–1. This, in the sense that all tote board statements can be assumed to represent the ultimate truth less seventeen percent is a fair summation of the animal's standing and chances at the present time.

The career of Make Peace over these months has been true and unique, a subsumption of disaster so concrete and exquisitely enclosed as to move me into a kind of metaphysical ecstasy. In so many ways, the history of this horse seems to have paralleled my own progress: it is as if some mutual doppelganger inhabits Make Peace and myself, or perhaps we are only influencing one another without the necessity of common denominator. In either case, those facts about the horse's history which I have been able to infer from my acquaintance with Tony's unconscious mind, are fascinating and utterly moving. He has raced seven times in the color of the underwear manufacturer (green with white stripes, stars on the cap, bottles of liniment with crossed T's) and five in Tony's (black and white, red circles, bow and arrow in the center, yellow checks) and has beaten a total of twelve horses in these twelve races which is to say that the average number of horses he has beaten at any given time is one point zero—in fields averaging ten or more. His most significant accomplishment during this period was a fourth (in a five horse field) on April 16th, when competing at six furlongs against $7,500 horses. Tony had advised the underwear manufacturer before the race that this looked like the proper spot, and the u.m., with several hundred relatives in tow, had appeared at the track precisely seven minutes before post to lay virtually all of the recent proceeds of activity on the horse. Leading to the eighth pole, Make Peace ceased entirely to lead thereafter, and Tony waited out the night in a grim soaking sweat of anticipation: he wondered if the u.m. had contacts. The only contacts the u.m. had, however, were with the emergency room of a famous private hospital in which he died of cerebral exhaustion toward dawn.

(Another parenthetical notation is in order: Tony had known, toward the heart of it, that the $7,500 race was not the spot for the horse and that the animal, no less than his owner, was doomed. He had tipped the u.m. on the horse as a kind of subtle and refined aggression, this being the only way that Tony feels he can get back at the forces and maddened animals which contain his life and have done so very much to destroy it. Of course he conceals this knowledge from himself and attributes his false notification to irreducible optimism and pressures from owners, but he really knows what he is doing. There is so little time, so much mortality so much of horses, so little of identity, poor Tony can only seem to break the cycle through misleading owners and it is a habit he will not break. It is to give no unusual knowledge to reveal that Tony no less than the late u.m. despises horses and wishes for their misfortune in a way that could be entertained only a man by totally dependent upon them.)

Tony got the horse from the estate cheap and heard nothing further from the relatives. Perhaps they were glad to have the u.m. out of the way. He suspected that the u.m. had lost rather a lot (but does not know the half of it: the u.m. lost fifteen thousand now uncollectible dollars).

Since his latest dreadful performance Make Peace seems to have found his destiny. He will now follow horses in a straight line as quickly as possible, being careful not to break the intent of the formation but not following too far behind, either. Somewhere within the simple but crystalline depths of its mind, Make Peace has now reached an accommodation with racing: the idea is to be symmetrical and not to give the other horses offense. There is no seeming way that Tony can break him of these habits nor is Tony anymore convinced that he should try. There is something graceful, even touching, about Make Peace's latest habits and in the bargain the horse has no trace of viciousness: like many horses descended to the cheap races a certain humility seems to have overtaken him by the withers and moved gently to his neck and pointed ears. Make Peace seems to have become smaller, lighter, less present. He does not, in any event, want to make his presence very well known.

Tony examines the animal in the walking ring, his hands on his hips, puffing on a large cigar which he has somehow forgotten to ignite. Led more quickly now by the groom the horse seems to work out of some of its first stiffness and even whinnies a bit, a sign of factitiousness or perhaps mere anxiety to get to the starting gate and be done with it. The dull bay seems to compliment its background; it is a cloudy day with a dense, swaddling humidity and Make Peace fits into it well. Tony curses and decides, not for the first time, that he made the wrong career choice and should have given himself a chance to finish high school before committing himself to a profession. Maybe he could have become a pharmacist and drugged horses on the sly.

The jockey, a small bitter man with compressed features, comes over to Tony, aimlessly swinging his whip and looking at the sky. Of French extraction, this jockey has been riding at the New York tracks for a couple of years now; he is not much of a jockey but then again there are very few trainers and agents who are unimpressed by a French accent and who, in the presence of this jockey, do not feel themselves to be of a somewhat higher, finer, more refined stock by virtue of giving information to a figure which interprets it with Gallic nods and shrugs and will even mutter curses on request. Most of the participants in the mechanics of horseracing consider European racing and things European to be generally superior and it is largely for this reason that the jockey has had a kind of success. He cannot really ride very well, being cowardly and arrogant by turns, although some of the more ignorant horseplayers have come to think of him as a "longshot specialist" because inevitably, one in fifty of the miserable horses which he rides will be able, through the incorporation of unknown medicants, to stagger home in front of a field of horses as bad or slightly worse.

(In such cases, this jockey demands of the trainer before even dismounting that the proceeds of a hundred dollar bet be turned over to him instantly and refuses to believe that the trainer has not bet for him in at least this denomination. This has led to several very ugly and public scenes and once he was suspended ten days for attempting to bite the knee of a steward. His most notable achievement, in his chosen sport to date, has been his identification in one gossip column many years ago as a playboy because he was seen "on the town" with a minor and fading starlet. The starlet was associating with him because he was her one and only reliable drug connection, but this falls totally outside the compass of narrative.)

At this time, the jockey's mood, in its bitterness and dismay, approaches Tony's. He has had a very bad series of unsuccessful sexual maneuverings having led him to question his height for the first time in several years, and in addition he has been in the siege of a long losing streak, forty-two or something like that. He knows that there will always be enough bad animals around these New York tracks to provide him with a minimal career but still he is being led into self-doubt, an emotion which he cannot really handle since there is so little of him. What he fears is that depression will lead him to a massive swelling of the sphincter which will in turn block evacuation and cause his weight to rise hopelessly despite all his efforts. He will go to one hundred and twenty-five pounds and will be reduced to exercising horses in the morning, jogging them hard in order to bounce his goddamned ass against the saddle in the hope that it will open and disgorge him by proxy onto the racetrack again. He is very prone to fantasies of this sort and allows them to create more internal disorder than, possibly, they are worth. Most of this jockey's problems come from the fact that like so many others in the profession he has an imagination and compulsion far beyond the reach of his sensibility. This drives him into compulsions far beyond the reach of imagination, the most extraordinary reactions merely to shield knowledge from himself.

"He win today?" the jockey asks, looking at Tony with dull eyes, cracking the whip over his head. "He lose? Or what? Give me instructions, I do exactly what I am supposed to do." All of this is said in light of the fact that this jockey has already ridden Make Peace three times, in his three most recent races in fact, and probably knows somewhat more about the refinement of the horse's peculiar habits than the trainer. Nevertheless, this is the only way in which the jockey can express his own aggression, much as Tony works through false tips. The trouble with trainers and jockeys is that for all their seeming control and autocracy, they have very few options. Professional actors could talk to this point with vigor.

"What do you think you're supposed to do?" Tony says harshly. "You know the damned horse better than I do. How the hell can I tell you how to make him run?" He does not like this jockey very much, to tell the truth of it, and the only reason he continues to use him is the insistence of the jockey himself who swears that he and the late owner had a close relationship and the jockey's continued relationship with the horse was in the nature of a dying request. Tony does not believe this but has no better ideas. "You think I've got the goddamned race set up for you and all you got to do is to take it home? What the hell kind of goddamned thinking is that supposed to be? I thought people from Europe were supposed to be smarter than us, goddamn it." In sadness, it must be admitted that Tony's rhetoric is quite limited.

"Don't know, boss," the jockey says, cheerfully enough. "I just try to follow the instructions, check what you want. First time you say, let him out on the front end; I let him out on the front end and he finish last. Next time you say rate him and I rate him right into the grandstand. The third time you say use your head, I use the head and the sonabitch almost throw me off. So this time I think maybe you try different advice. Maybe worse, I don't know. I stand here to listen, chief."

"You dirty frog bastard," Tony says, "you dirty arrogant son of a bitch, you should get packed into the rail on a blind switch and go into the infield," but of course Tony does not say this at all; things would perhaps be much better for him (and for me) if he did, but at his present state of evolutionary development, so to speak, Tony has only reached the point where he can entertain this kind of discourse at the level of internal monologue. At some time in the future this may change, conditions permitting, but if it does it will probably happen only at a private time and in a context having nothing whatsoever to do with the racetrack. "Oh, I don't know," Tony says mildly enough. "maybe you can just, well, kind of rate him close to the pace into the homestretch, leaving enough ground to get wide and then set him down. Maybe he'll finish third that way, you never know. I'm not putting anything down on him though. No side bets. Not for you, not for me, not for no one. I got to let him run loose. You understand the record."

"Oh sure," the jockey says. "I understand everything; you say no bet it's no bet. Just give him some good exercise and maybe we all have something to sing about in ten minutes, yes? Maybe a bet is down if he wins, you know?"

Someone in the paddock says, "Riders up." (It might even be me; I tend to get very involved in the affairs of this subpopulation and sometimes have the feeling that my subvocalizations are being broadcast at an ever-enlarging audience. This does not really discomfit me since I am sure that I would make a superb track announcer in other circumstances.) Then the groom leads Make Peace to where the jockey is standing. The jockey winks at Tony and in a little springing leap hurls himself into the saddle from which he regards Tony now with a strange revulsion which always comes from a sense of elevation. Make Peace twitches and his coat seems to break into a premonitory sweat as the jockey whispers something in his ear. What he whispers is an ancient and terrible Gallic curse which he has employed with his mounts for some time now; it may not make them run any better but it most certainly does not, make them run any worse.

They parade uneasily in concert around the walking ring as certain horseplayers lean uncomfortably over the rail to direct comments to the jockeys. It seems that they believe Make Peace's rider has not ridden as well in the last race as he might have were he truly motivated.

Tony, mumbling a bit himself, walks from the groom toward the horsemen's exit. He could, if he wanted, remain in the ring and accompany jockey and horse to the track entrance but at this moment he finds himself overcome by a kind of revulsion. Not for one more instant, he feels, can he bear to stand by and watch the activities before him; this horse has hurt him very personally and profoundly. It is as if the horse, in its incompetence, has rejected all of Tony's history, and the trainer, although he does not quite understand this yet, takes his work far more seriously than he would like to admit. It is a fact that he wants to win desperately with this horse; if not today then at some time in the near future, but every sight of the animal only goads him into furious and renewed realization of the pointlessness of his life. He cannot make a bad horse good. Make Peace has turned worse under his ownership, now his hocks have turned outward and the horse's eyes are dull with a complex intimation of defeat which even the most optimistic of horseplayers would have to note. Make Peace looks as if he is in the throes of a terminal illness.

"You gonna win today with this horse, Miller?" someone says over the fence and Tony shakes his head, looking at the ground, trying to act as if he were the assistant trainers or groom, but this doomed horseplayer knows faces as well as names and says, "Miller, you son of a bitch, go back to Dover Downs and stiff them there," referring to the little known fact that Tony, years ago, was involved in a nasty drugging incident at that little track.

"Drop dead, you bastard," Tony says, containing the words behind his lips but does not know if he is talking to the horseplayer or only to himself. Before the incident he had been leading trainer at Dover. He finds himself thinking of that now—his lost promise, his broken possibilities—and increases his pace. The trouble is that there is no part of your history which is not, somewhere, labeled, filed, and part of the public domain.

It is at this instant, when Tony removes a new cigar from his pocket and chews it, licks his lip, imagines that the horseplayer talking to him is dead, that I make my entrance. It is about time; I have, after all put up with so much on this day: Simmons's apostasy, Mary's stupidity, my own growing dismay, a nest of other aspects which I will not go into here, but there are limits to this as to all other things and perhaps I have now passed them. "Hey you," I say, settling upon a fashionable bluntness as, perhaps, the easiest way to set the tone. "Hey, Tony. The horse is going to win today. Sure as hell he's going to win. Stick a hundred on him, just for yourself. No one will ever know. Go on, do it: what the hell. You don't want that frog bastard to put him over behind your back, do you? I know how his mind works."

This is not the first of my interventions. Tony thinks that he now knows how to deal with them. "Cut it out," he mumbles. "Cut it out. If I go crazy, let me do it in my own bed with the sheets pulled up over my head. Please. I'll find a fast track. Let it not be right in the clubhouse walking ring. Give a man a break. Oh Jesus, I'm hearing voices again."

"You're not crazy, Tony. This is reality. Don't you think our—our relationship is getting a bit ridiculous? I mean, sooner or later, we've got to talk; there's no way you can keep on avoiding the issue. I'm only trying to help you out, Tony."

"It ain't here. There's nothing here. It's just my nerves and losing all the time and tension. I know what it's like. Okay, okay, I'll take a week off starting soon and rest up. Then my nerves will be back in shape and no more voices."

It is at this point that all of our discussions to date have terminated. So Tony has a predictable ease of ritual accomplished as he moves swiftly through the conversation, but there is no time for me to dissemble now. I have realized, with a thrill of yearning, that matters have reached quite a critical pass. Conditions are clipping right along. "Throw a c-note on him, Tony," I say. "You listen to me, you spot a hundred on that horse right now or I'll make you scream fuck you! right at the stewards and that will be the end of the trainer's license—to say nothing of all those nifty little arrangements with the other public trainers. I'm onto you. Tony. I've been following you for weeks. A c-note Tony and toss a fin on it for the groom or your first fuck you comes out in thirty seconds."

Oh yes, Oh yes indeed, my speech has an effect upon Tony—although it is not exactly what I have calculated. I have misjudged his stubbornness, his desperate sense of connection to what he likes to think of as the normative life. "Oh, you son of a bitch," he says. "Real or not I don't care. Who has to take this kind of crap? Get the hell out of here *right now,*" Tony says and, squeezing his fists, closes his eyes tightly and tries through extraordinary force of will to remove me. If my origin were sheerly metaphysical (it is not although my tenants often think so) or psychic (it has nothing to do with that at all) the gesture would probably succeed, Tony having an extraordinary if limited sense of presence, but under the given circumstances, it is, of course, futile. But it is enough of this. It is a call for action as clear and beautiful as the sound of the bugle to the post. It demands that I take measures of my own. Time is limited and factors, otherwise very much in hand, would go out of control entirely were I to allow Tony's gesture to succeed.

And so it is then, in the passageway between the walking ring and the clubhouse, that I am forced to commit an act which I know will be regretted forever after. I am sorry about this. Our orders are peculiarly explicit after all: we are to accomplish our mission at a maximum of general devastation but we are not, under most circumstances, to bring undue pain to any individual. It is as if the bureaucracy enables us to perform the most shocking acts upon abstractions while deferring to our basic instincts for the concrete which are always kind, gentle, and somehow benign. The fact is that I find it almost unbearably repellent to do any of these people injury, although I know that they deserve only a maximum of dislocation. This sense of ambivalence, this peculiar feeling of balancing delicately between two alternatives equally poisonous adds in no little degree to the pain of this assignment and is something which I will want investigated carefully at some quiet, enclosed time.

Perhaps during a sabbatical. Meanwhile, and with all this regret to the contrary, I perform certain adjustments upon Tony's nervous system, cause two synapses to lapse in their conjunction most alarmingly, create an electrical framework in a lower synapse which filters through sensations subtly altered and, then, with a scuttling gesture, I take the whole bloody network in psychic arm and I—

But why go into it? It is, after all, primordially disgusting. There is something about the very nature of biology which repels me: one understands that situations and their fulfillment can come only from organism; that it is the pulsing of fluids through stems which generates all of those actions and reactions which make the reversal of entropy possible. Still, the sheer corporeality—they are so *disgustingly* corporeal—of these people is nothing on which I intend to dwell.

I do the necessary. I do what has to be done. Throughout the procedure, I don blinkers and a shadow roll to shield me from too close an apprehension of the mount's reaction to track conditions. A noseband would have been helpful to accompany the shadow roll but I have no nose, not even its equivalent. The entire action takes less than three-tenths of a second, objective time, although for its subject it seems to go on and on. To Tony it seems he is moving endlessly on a frozen, unrolling strip of track, working out furlongs and furlongs on a cold plain without furlong poles, looking agonizingly for a finish line that cannot exist. Excruciating! enough even to cause me to lose momentary control of myself and to whinny in response, a failure rare in one as disciplined as the undersigned. But Tony is restored, although his condition is understood to be irrevocably changed. He looks at me, driven, desperate, and then the wall begins to crumble for the first time, the wall begins to crumble for real. It is now as if the massive iron of the tote itself has become disassembled and from the secret heart of the machinery pours forth numerology: odds spill out and calculations and possibilities, illuminating our stricken features in the sudden fluorescence, the central mystery finally exposed for all that it is worth, and it flickers before us as Reason shyly pops its head over the wall and nods at me. I return Reason's nod and in that doomful silence we exchange a look of perfect understanding and then join, never to be separated again.

In the distance the crowd mutters A horse has tossed its jockey and it's running free on the track. (Fortunately the horse is the favorite, not Make Peace.) The tote flickers to a new set of odds reflecting this disaster. Birds flicker and wheel in the sky. The bugler blows a mournful recitatif and departs.

"All right," Tony says, "all right. *All right!* What do you want me to do? Just tell me what you want me to do and I'll do it. But you listen to me you son of a bitch: I'll do it and the hell with the whole thing—but I don't believe a word of it. Not a word of it, do you understand me? And I never will. What should I do? Tell me."

And talking gently, insistently, calm Reason helping to buttress my tones, I guide Tony toward the one hundred dollar window (a flock of horseplayers following us like dogs tracing out a bitch) and tell him exactly what to do. And then, to be on the safe side, I make him do it.

CHAPTER VIII

Simmons removes his resources and considers them at some length in the vanquished silence of his furnished room. He has three hundred dollars in an unadmitted cash hoard, fifty-seven dollars and twenty-five cents in silver quarters, and a bank passbook indicating that a minimum deposit of one dollar is being retained until the end of the interest period. He has been holding the three hundred out on me, the son of a bitch; there is no end to their duplicity. There is no value to his possessions, although he does feel a certain sentimental attraction to his back issues of *Turf & Sport Digest*, some of which go back consecutively to October of 1953. He shakes his head at the small secret pile and then, muttering, goes to the window and considers the outside for a long time. It is really strange that he would have been able to have held back the three hundred on me; it means that my methods are not conclusive—this must not happen again. It is a five-door vault to the street and he thinks of this possibility without enthusiasm or hope. His consciousness remains at rest, its pendulum suspended dead center, waiting for further urgings. The small, shrieking, internalized voice which has brought us this far is now gone. At my instructions, he sits on the bed, puts his palms flatly on the blankets and then heaves himself into a crouching position, cupping his hands to his ears. He seems to be in the starting gate.

The marshal talks to him patiently, lovingly, insistently, confidentially, at great length. He takes his time. There is no reason to rush. The gates are locked. Certain basics have been accomplished and it can be assumed that in certain senses, Simmons and the marshal now have all the time in the world.

He nods understandingly. His eyes flicker. One can sense a simulacrum of the old Simmons in the glare that slowly, wistfully, fades back to blank. A hint of his old horseplaying energy returns as his larynx barks harsh symbols of agreement. "Yep! Yep! Yep!" The marshal soothes him, comforts him, leads him down the alternative byways of fulfillment and he must spend, Simmons and the marshal, several hours talking on this bed and—oh yes indeed!—what an intense and meaningful rapport we have when it is all concluded.

It is all quite wonderful and means that I was right about everything after all. Dismayed in certain subtle ways by the collapse of Tony's resistance I can nevertheless understand this: I have pushed him very hard. It was to be expected. Everything is to be expected. Everything fits together. Nothing is changed. All moves in a slow and sweltering constancy, embracing the future like fish in a pond might absorb the slow sift of food poured by the keeper into those cool and greenful depths. Light on the water, flicker of silver, birds dancing in the air.

CHAPTER IX

A race:

The horses, panting, terrified, are forced into position. They never outgrow their fear of the starting gate; they only learn to fear punishment the more. The gates are locked. Starters and assistants shout at one another. In the enclosure of the stalls, the horses whinny and stamp, shaking their heads, trying to dislodge the bits. Jockeys hang on and whisper curses or comforts to them. The 35–1 shot and the 6–5 favorite alike twitch their ears and caress the iron with their tails. A bell sounds, locking parimutuel machines against further wagering and the gates open.

The horses stumble to the track, some of them moving quickly, others caught in a slow frieze of dismay, finding their pace only irregularly. Jockey and horse fight for position, some of them diving into the rail which will give them the least amount of ground to cover, others moving to the outside where they will be free at last of the other horses. Moving down the backstretch they see the grandstand as a dim, thick, gray piling in the distance, catching the afternoon sun, pouring it back across the infield but the horses can see nothing, hear nothing, work the more intensely into the far turn as they come into the stretch. The early leaders, packed into the rail, are beginning to lose stride now, fighting for wind, and the jockeys flail them harder. Some of the come-from-behind horses are looking for position, moving up on the outside, diving for holes in the clutter. The field staggers into the homestretch like bees scattering before a hand and the positions begin to change. Some horses fall back but on the other hand, other horses are coming forward. There is always a balancing action at work; nothing is constant.

Forty-seven and three-fifths for the half-mile. One minute and two for five furlongs. The jockeys begin to work on the horses with renewed energy, the sounds of the grandstand pouring over them in thick, uneven waves, speech vaguely discernible at the center. Curses, prayers, mutterings, threats. Giggles. Appeals. The last eighth of a mile takes only thirteen seconds or a little less, depending upon the class of the horses. Those massed at the front make one last vault as they approach the wire, seeming to disconnect slightly from the mud of the track as they hurl themselves toward the finish. Behind them, beaten horses are no longer punished. Jockeys on these beaten horses wave their whips for the sake of the customers but do little more than show them to the horses. (The horses understand. The horses understand everything.) The field goes under the finish line. The last horse, beaten fifteen lengths or so, may be two and a half seconds slower than the winner. Two and a half seconds! It is a small enough investment to make for such possibilities. Possibilities!

The result of the race is not yet official. Please hold all tickets. Tickets are held tightly. Men hawk and spit on the gray of the lawn. In the grandstand, customers press against one another to get a closer look. Numbers come onto the board. The crowd roars (in certain countrified tracks, it gasps). The result of the race is not official. The result of the race is now official and the winner is. Jockeys leap from their horses in the walking ring, nod to the stewards, and, hands on hips, stand on scales until the clerk says they may leave. They learn to submit to this kind of thing early. Moving from the paddock in small clumps, some of them talk earnestly, shaking their heads. A few stragglers, eyes wide and misunderstanding, are already fixated on the question of the next race.

Post time for the next race is. A man leaps from the grandstand and falls three stories, his body pulped like a flower at the instant of demolition. Another man says words to his fiancée (who he has brought there for what was to be a casual date) which he knows must destroy everything they have and which can never, under any circumstances, be taken back. A welfare client looks at the tickets on which he has invested a month's rent and wonders what will be the best line to take with his investigator. Three horseplayers at the top of the grandstand take rifles and begin to shoot at the tote, neatly puncturing the greenery and causing lights to wink. An old woman who has played Heart's Device as a hunch play dies of a cardiac seizure in the alleyway toward the gardens.

Seventeen children between the ages of five and eight run madly along the lawn, throwing empty beer cups at one another, screaming in a language which no one can understand. The infield quakes and seems to settle deeper. The swans in the lake see something and scatter in alarm. The sun becomes larger in the sky and begins to spit rays of poisonous illumination. The top eave of the grandstand breaks and five hundred people perish on the lawn still holding their programs, many of them with pencils in their hands. The track announcer misses a cue and is three minutes late getting back for the next race. The horses for the next race wait patiently in the paddock while the announcer is found. The announcer, it seems, has been copulating with a swan. The swan is copulating with a horse. The horse is copulating with his trainer. The trainer is copulating with a groom. The groom is copulating with a mutuel clerk. The mutuel clerk is copulating with a swan. Post time for the next race approaches. The race has taken one minute, thirteen and two-fifths seconds.

But ah! what speculation, what ecstasy, what degradation it has generated! the proportion of speculation-and-reaction to incident must be in the hundreds of billions to one. What to make of this?

What will one make of it? What does it mean? What can one say? Where is the beauty in it? Why does it all seem so beautiful? Why does it all seem so beautiful? Who would have thought—ah, who ever would have thought—that there would be so much pain in it?

CHAPTER X

Tony turns from the hundred dollar window with a dull glaze of sweat ringing that area from which he has just issued orders. He has bet his horse to win five times ("Is that ok, chief? five times on the nose? You want maybe to bet him place a couple of times? Up the bet? Anything you say, chief, I understand that the thing ain't personal at all and I just want to do the right thing here. Five hundred ok? Thanks.") and now wanders out toward the track to see what has happened to his money. He does not go into the walking ring or clubhouse pavilion as would be the trainer's right but instead walks abstractedly through the infield lawn and to the rail, a spot where he has not been for some twenty-five years when he was sixteen and used to stay out of school to watch some races. On the way he bumps into a tall, uncoordinated a man who curses him and then goes back into private fugue. Simmons is on the line as well. I consider having them talk and then decide against it; there is plenty of time. To Tony the rail feels comfortable in his grasp, shiny and comforting and he holds onto it, his hands trembling only slightly from the exertion of squeezing. (Gently I lay a further pall on his mind to ease the panic; I owe him all the peace now that he can be given.)

When the horses spring from the gate, it seems to Tony that it is not so much as they are running before him or that the events are consequential; instead, all of this seems to be taking place on a distant planet, the language and customs of which Tony does not understand, and which he can greet only as a kind of exotica. "Well come on you old son of a bitch," Tony says, realizing that he hardly cares what happens to his horse. In fact, if pressed, Tony would not be able to tell you exactly on what he has bet; he knows that it is a horse with whom he is associated, somehow, but whether the association is professional or only in terms of the losing tickets is an issue beneath discussion.

"All right, number three," Tony cries and claps his hands ponderously like a seal. "Let's see some action now, number three. Whoa, number three! Hit it, baby!" There is an air of jollity to these encouragements. Tony has become jolly. He has become a jolly fat man. He has become a mindless jolly fat man. In fact, Tony is happier than he has been for two decades (not counting the first time he got laid) not that the source of the happiness can be traced back to anything which is happening to him because Make Peace is running one of his classic races, out of the post at 15–1. (For some reason the horse seems to be picking up a little action not even to be explained by Tony's five hundred. Who in hell could want to play him Tony's Reason wonders numbly.) The horse has raced wide throughout, has placed his muzzle clearly on the fleeing rump of the horse before him, and now, coming through the stretch, is running third like a projectile, a bullet-shaped form of power and substance neatly cleaving his way through the tracks of his predecessor as the jockey, whip in front of his nose, attempts to show the grandstand that classic European form which has made him so popular at Aqueduct for this and many seasons. The jockey beats on Make Peace's withers, he digs his little knees into the horse's spine in a fashion designed to madden and excite, and Make Peace hangs like a checkroom. His form uncoiling loosely and with terrible grace he follows his predecessor across the wire and down the backstretch turn into eternity. Third.

The crowd applauds politely, saluting the victory of the 7–5 favorite who, unfortunately (I am a perverse creature but you must understand the stresses I have been under so recently and so long) drops dead exactly as he crosses the finish line and lies kicking in a kind of ecstasy as his jockey rolls off and eyes him with astonishment. The bettors murmur, mumble, consult rapidly among themselves: will the horse be disqualified by reason of having dropped dead at the finish? After some period of time, the judges conclude that this is not an indictable offense since the cause of death cannot be presumed, *ipso facto*, to have been the cause of victory and the number of the late winner goes on the board.

Tony stands over the rail, both wrists hanging loosely over sewage and says, "How about that? How about that? five hundred dollars right into the gut, and the winner drops dead. What a race! What a race! Never saw anything quite like it." Tony's tones are mild, remonstrative; he is not so much a participant as a commentator, and between these short bursts of phrase, or perhaps the word should be song, his eyes seem to go blank. The five hundred in losing tickets hang unbidden in his shirt pocket until he reaches inside and, whistling, destroys them. He seems to feel that he has business back in the paddock but cannot imagine what it might be; as far as he knows he is perfectly content, leaning here over the rail at Aqueduct, five hundred dollars to the contrary and hope you are the same. "How about that?" Tony says again, "How about that? How about that?" and demurely enough I tell him about that, whisper to him in confidential tones, gently and lovingly guide him through the spaces of the infield and toward the clubhouse. And I talk all the time, talking, talking, inexhaustibly talking, my teeny-tiny voice filling the wilderness of his mind so to speak, and by the time I have escorted Tony to his car in the trainer's area and have made clear to him exactly what must be done now we are in perfect accord.

Perfect accord. Reason and I join *a capella* in song over the embers of Tony's psyche. It has all been very simple. It is merely a question of being realistic about many things. "How about that, dig that cat?" Tony sings as he drives us sweetly all the way into Manhattan and the secret Army surplus store that only he and the favored few know. The surplus store that sells grenades, rifles and incendiary bombs at cost, simple cost, right from the battlefields to you and not a cent of vigorish in it.

Building up the margin.

CHAPTER XI

Third Recitatif (Retrospective): In the beginning, there were recriminations. There would have to be. All agents have them. Altering the state of a sentient race, soul of creation in all living people, mechanical pantheism and so on. Obliteration of possibility, the implosion of outcome. The usual. This is all part of the context in which we work. We are warned against it in training. Clearly warned. That it is not of any. Significance. Of no significance and cannot be. Unduly involved, or concerned by. Something happens to the smooth, insistent flow of my rhetoric when I tap areas of policy; it is as if chunks of glass were being rammed through Mary's throat during a process of expectoration. I think that Mary would know what I am talking about, likewise Simmons. Tony as well. Gardner? The question is: how about the Bureau themselves? Can this be understood at the remove of many parsecs and granted the glowing alienation which assaults me at this time? It is very hard to say. One finds it difficult to make orderly reason of this. There is no set pattern to any of it.

It remains to the nature of their drives, that is the fascination. No less motivated than any of us, no less driven than the least of us—but how narrow, how narrow! Simmons dreams of a Daily Double (or I should say dreamed; Simmons is beyond all of that nonsense right now) and this double of which he dreams will be for four thousand, eight hundred and seventy-six dollars even. It will manage to disengage him not only from his difficulties but his history. Blown free, into some new angle of perception, he will be Simmons Ennobled or at least Simmons de-Crucified. He knows exactly how it will happen. He will wheel two outside shots in the first two races with everything in the second and when one of his selections wins the first, paying $341.80, Simmons will have all the possibilities in the double covered, the least of them on the wheel paying some two thousand dollars. Just before the second race begins he will lean easily over the rail and the jockey on the nearest horse will say, "Jack, you got a big one," just as if he (the jockey) is acting only for Simmons. And then the race will begin and the third choice will pull away from the field by yards and yards, winning by daylight and causing Simmons to giggle because he will be unable to understand how they can do something like this for him. But in any event he will be a winner and put all of the metaphysics to the side, scampering to the two dollar show window to collect his double gently, modestly. Bowing to the throngs assembled behind him, he will tip the clerk five dollars. The clerk will beam and shrug modestly and Simmons will leave Aqueduct rapidly by a side (to avoid highwaymen) entrance and hire a limousine to return him to his rooms for the last time. He will mumble to the driver all the way back about his terrible losses so that the driver will not be moved to assault him and take everything away. At destination, he will pay the driver twenty dollars and hop off into his rooms, he thinks. And then—

And then—

Well, it is difficult to speculate exactly what Simmons's thoughts comprise past this point; he has not thought it out clearly. Dim images of horses, women, newspapers, steak dinners, rising elevators, breasts assault him but in truth none of these hold for him half the viability and interest of what he will do immediately upon collecting his winnings. This is one of those ironies to which I have referred throughout. Of course, Simmons has no plans. The track has defined his time for so long now that without it to structure his day it is quite hopeless. Perhaps he will go back on the following day and lose everything. It is worth considering, it lessens the guilt feelings.

Mary, on the other hand, dreams of a forest of bills, thick and the consistency of dough in her hand. They will come not from a double (Mary is afraid of the lines on the double) but from a 300–1 shot that shakes loose from the pack and in response to Mary's glare, Mary's bleat, Mary's necessity, will scamper home lengths and lengths to the good.

And she will take the money (about seven thousand dollars in return for her twenty-five dollar bet) and take the bus instantly to the residence of her son where, in the presence of his wife and four intent little daughters, she will throw the bills one by one in his face, every cent of it, telling him as she does so exactly what she thinks of him (nothing), exactly what she thinks of his life (nothing), exactly what he means to her (nothing), exactly what she will have to do with him (nothing), and then she will parade in military scavenger's triumph back to her apartment, snatching tasteful objects from surrounding garbage cans to add to her collection. And then the losing streak will be broken.

The winning streak will continue, she will win and win and win with a ferocity she has never found for losing, and although most of the money will come on chalk there will be a fine lavender of longshots. She will build up an enormous estate, five thousand dollars at least, and she will leave every cent of it—every penny that is—to the invisible track announcer who has so kindly called all of her horses home. This will take care of Julian and perhaps herself. The track announcer has been there for over forty years and is certainly due for retirement if not thinking of it.

Tony's fantasies are more practical, having largely to do with triumphant rides in stages, the conversion of lame and staggering animals into bright-eyed and fleet handicap horses so gifted as to do even a Frenchman's bidding. Tony's mind is not as explicit of these matters as the other two. (Tony after all is actually in the game and can be presumed to know a thing or three.) For that reason, I have never found his fantasies as interesting. This may be why he was the first to Alter although I wish it could have been committed in a less abrupt fashion.

And Gardner—I see that I have not yet introduced Gardner; we will have much to say of him presently. His fantasies are the most complex of all, having largely to do with fugal forms of devastation of which he already understands his bets, in part, to be metaphors. Gardner is extremely intelligent.

What do they want? It is questions like these which now rankle as almost none of the others do; this is not metaphysical torment or sociological upheaval but simply basics of the most mundane kind. What are they after? What might they have in mind? What did they intend to do about all of this? Left on their own, what were their plans? Where do they get the gall? Do these fantasies, in any way complement that is to say interest with the wonder, mystery and overwhelming terror of the track?

For that matter, what *are* they doing at the grandstand entrance? Where is the gain in it? What do they imagine? What is the point? Surely they realize that they are throwing themselves again and again into the jaws of machines so implacable and mysterious that they can be sure of nothing except that those machines will extract—*will remove from them*—seventeen percent of their common reality every time they come out of it? How do they not understand this? And what would the consequences be of an ineluctable reduction of seventeen percent from reality nine times a day? Fifty-four times a week. Fifteen hundred times a year.

And what is the difference?

One must cultivate, as Headquarters would say, a certain mythical sense of distance, a truly grandiose detachment which would enable one to function in this void purposefully and move toward that destiny which awaits all of us. But it is not easy.

Perhaps it concerns the landscape of the minds in which I am trapped. They are all urban blights: depressions and garbage surrounding a small evil glint of jewelry which may shine in the night but in the day only acts, through its own devices, to destroy the very air which surrounds them. The horseplayer being an urban phenomenon.

One must, however, be ordered. I have gone this far. I can finish the job. The major work has been done. Plans have been laid, groundwork blasted. All that is left are the few necessary turnings and gropings to blast the thing free past history. Hold on for two days more, three at the most, and the job will be done. I will hold on. I am invulnerable. There is nothing to touch me. I am unique, omnipotent, and totally in control. I know it.

Yet I cannot escape this recent and insane urge of mine: the urge to bet a 4–1 shot. Just for the hell of it. To see what happens. But where, oh where in hell would I get the goods to lay on the crippled animal? And in what coin would they pay me?

CHAPTER XII

Gardner: Gardner is the key to all of them. (He will set off the chain reaction.) We must, with as much delicacy as possible, subsume Gardner and try to understand him. But of them all, Gardner is the hardest to contain.

See him. See him now! He is copulating with a girl. Underneath him she lies, stretched and open to the skin, mouth against his, her breasts thrown into his chest, impaled on the point of his erect organ which I should say is already penetrating her with enthusiasm and efficacy, blasting Gardner toward an orgasm which he can already see as clearly as the hot hand of the tote dropping a horse to post time tells him that once again he has been shut out of an angle. She is moaning, speaking to him in the most ancient and constant of their tongues and after a fashion he is talking back, if unh! uh! and ah! can be considered within the terms of dialogue. Gardner communes with the girl on the aural as well as a sexual level; it is an old ability; he is having a rowdy fuck. I regard them with some interest.

I do not find their act of generation to be as self-contained as other things; it has always had some power to move me. Universals exist, some comity is known. Pity and terror tug at one another within this shell. How they heave! How they puff! How they groan and suffer! One understands that only such creatures as they could emerge from this pain. How stifled from grace. How distant from comfort. And yet they enact those qualities to excess and call them love. Love! *Love!* Who is to understand? Who would want to understand? What is there to know? What fury in an angle! Blind conjunction, coincidence, and connection! See them copulate! Watch them! Watch them …

Gardner works upon the girl with devouring intensity, managing to force, in these final moments, all thoughts of horses and horsemen from his mind. He has had a very, very bad day at the racetrack: a forty-dollar day, in fact, and since this represents almost half of his weekly take-home salary, it can only be interpreted as a disaster. (But Gardner enjoys disasters and the feeling of consequentiality they bring. Where? he asks himself, where would he be if the racetrack did not endlessly provide a sense of proportion, put him in continual touch with his destiny?) Still, he is free of it for the time, tumbling into a well of feeling which buckles and opens before him.

Ah! the girl groans. (She is yielding and permissive and naïve enough to still enjoy sex.) Oh! Gardner shrieks and performing small rites upon her distended breasts, Gardner distributes into her the full load of his love, laying it down in a screaming procession that seems to wind away from him timelessly and he can follow it only a little while before he descends into fog. He lies atop her dreaming.

The girl still in the throes of her own orgasm forces him up and down atop her, congealing her limbs for reciprocity but Gardner does not care. He wants only to rest. It is not precisely that he is selfish—Gardner has a true and meaningful sense of proportion—but only that at the completion of the act of generation he likes to obtain a feeling of power by transcending it, denying his own needs. Sometimes this has worked out well. At other times it has not. Gardner, who is only twenty-eight, feels that he has some time left to investigate the various alternatives offered.

After a time, the girl stops, her head lolling away in disinterest, her mouth opening to pour syllables upon Gardner to which he listens with little interest as for some moments she tells him exactly what she thinks of him, thinks of the act of sex, thinks of his approach to the act of sex, thinks of sex from the psychological standpoint. The majority of these comments are complimentary and would have pleased Gardner greatly five or ten minutes ago, but now they fall upon him only peripherally, like absent pellets of horse droppings falling from the tails of longshots before a big race.

He mumbles and shakes his head, moving down lower upon her. He wants to sleep, to dream. He looks for her breasts. She removes herself from under him however and continues talking. This time her conversation is somewhat less generalized. Gardner tries to shut off this discourse as he has turned off the rest but it is not so easy; the girl's rhetoric seems to have moved from a casually obbligato second violin to a more determined, carefree first, and he can no longer impose theme and mood atop her easy fifths and thirds. There are no more fifths and thirds. Instead, she is trying to force thematic material through, and at last Gardner turns his head and shakes himself into sweating alertness, disentangles his limbs from there and says, "Listen, I told you we couldn't. We can't until things look up for me, I'm just not making that kind of money now, Virginia."

Virginia—for that is her name, although she has always resented its somewhat stodgy overtones and has done her modest best, in person, to act against it—says, "But I'm working too, Gardner. My income and your income together are plenty. I mean I'm getting tired of living this way. A girl's entitled to some security."

"What living?" Gardner says and rises to a seated position. "What security?" Now, in the half-gloom of his bedroom, he can be seen to be a man of normal height, features, coloring, etc., the usual design of hair; in fact, his prior resemblance to a large hen poised hawking over a crate of hard-laid eggs has now disappeared, although Gardner would appreciate the compliment as little as the description. (I love invective, when it is correct it is so final.) "There's no security. When I get married I want to feel that I can support you. Otherwise, what's the point? Can't we leave it like that for a while?"

He leans upon her and begins to move his hands on the girl's stomach, his intent being only vaguely sexual, but she pushes him away with determination and fury saying, "Now Gardner, come on. Be serious. I think it's time that we got serious, Gardner, because we really can't go on this way you know."

Serious! The girl wants him to be serious! Considering that it is at such-named moments that these people approach the depths of their folly, the request cannot be strictly well-meant as the saying goes and yet it appears to have the proper effect upon Gardner. Heaving, neighing, he disengages himself fully from the girl and stumbles away, turns on various lights, flicks on a large fluorescent contraption above the couch, takes a sheet and idly tosses it to the girl so that she can cover herself but not, it must be noted, because he has taken a last look at her and has constructed in his mind a series of lascivious pictures and speculations which he knows will serve him well later in the event that the conversation does not work out well. He mumbles, shakes his head, takes a bathrobe from the closet and dons it grumbling, then removes a pack of cigarettes from his bedroom and lights one. Lights two. Hands one to the girl. Takes the other for himself.

(I realize that this issue of cigarette lighting and smoking has become the sandwich layer filling scores and scores of inferior novels by hacks who know no other proper way to get their characters through transitions from one room or emotional state to the next but what am I to say? I did not invent Gardner; I am stuck with him and Gardner is a chain-smoker.)

Gardner Quant and Virginia are both intensely heavy smokers. They feel that no proper discussion or drama is functional unless it is supported or enveloped by clouds of fumes, wisps of grayness already circling their heads like halos. And although Gardner is convinced that the habit will ultimately sever him from life short of his normal span, he cannot stop. Neither can Virginia, although her speculations are similar. What a pleasant, pleasant surprise it will be for both of them when they find out (thanks to my ministrations) that their unhappy addiction has cost them not one second of time, not one errant heartbeat! It will utterly delight them or would, were they not to be occupied otherwise.

"Listen, Virginia," Gardner says. (I am now going to compress a great deal of dialogue into quite a short space. This is in order not only to reduce the acreage of this journal but to establish that my sense of order and transmutation have not degenerated in these miserable surroundings, these people will not get to me.) "It's impossible for us to get married. I'm only at the GS-7 level as you know with the cutbacks and so on and with the problems with funding from the administration, I don't think I'll be GS-11 for at least three more years. GS-11 is the minimum salary for what we'll need to live. Also, as you must understand, Virginia, I am devoted to the horses—far more so than is normal for a man of my age. I know we've disagreed about this many many times and there hasn't been a word you've ever said that hasn't stung me and made me feel deeply regretful and moved ... but the thing is I have this problem with the horses. I know I can't beat them but there's something in me that won't let me give them up. I feel I've got to have a clear shot at it and find out once and for all if it's *really* true that I can't beat them or if it's only an emotional block that's kept me from following my intellect, and now with this new field position I'm able to get out in the afternoons and make the track *every single day* except for Mondays of course when I have to cover the phones in the unit on my emergency day but every single *day* except that I can get out there for at least a couple of years until they catch up with what I'm doing and fire me. I love you Virginia, I really do love you, you know, no question about it, it isn't just the propinquity that made me get involved with you and I think that you're the most important person in the world to me right now … but I just don't know if it's *people* that I need or something *else*. Anyway, Virginia, and I have to be terribly honest about this with you because we decided at the very beginning that honesty was going to be the most important part of our relationship or we wouldn't have it all, anyway, the thing is that I'm still so goddamned involved with the horses that I get sick at night watching them run when I can't sleep. I'm so involved with them even after all the talking we've done and so on that sometimes when I'm making love to you I'm not even thinking about you but about the tote board or the odds or some angle on an entry tomorrow or a jockey switch. I have to confess that to you and I do it straight out because that's how I feel. Now, you wouldn't want to marry a man like that, would you? Or would you? I'd think the less of you if I thought that you could."

The effect of all this compression, of course, is to give not only Gardner but the scene a kind of frozen-time aspect. Gardner, stumbling through torrents of rhetoric and revelation in a highspeed frame which is entirely out of synchronization with the background, the background remaining mottled and slightly blue, showing its age. Gardner in his hundred-year-old apartment (all apartments in that city are a hundred years old, either that or brand new), Gardner taking his ease by being uneasy. Gardner! Whatever alteration has been performed upon him, however, is as nothing to what happens to his girlfriend.

Unlike him, fashionable bluntness is her method of speaking, and now, as I recapitulate her end of the discussion, things seem to go quite out of control. I have the feeling, transcribing these notes hurriedly, that I am chasing a single line of rhetoric unsuccessfully through alleys and byways. The rhetoric is getting away from me however and the situation in full is analogous to Gardner's own sensations as he watches the fleeing rump of a favorite bidding a permanent farewell to one of his long-shot specials. I do not know if I am putting this together in the most efficacious format but one thing must shine through: the ultimate perversity of it.

Even when stripped to the essentials of their appeal, they must dissemble. Why? This is not a question which I would expect to have answered within my brief span here, brief by their standards that is to say, by mine it is becoming horribly extended and it is taking on that timeless sense of mortification so clearly associated with gangrene or other allied and hopeless diseases.

"That's nonsense, Gardner," Virginia is saying meanwhile. (I am already hopelessly far behind and lost in transcription; I know now that like almost all the rest of it, three-fifths is beyond me forever.) "I don't believe that you're really that interested in the horses; it's just an *excuse* you've held on to in an effort to avoid your responsibilities. No one as serious about horses as you pretend to be could *possibly* be losing as much money as often as you are over such a period of time, Gardner, it's over fifty dollars a week! You're losing half your salary! If I wasn't around to get you through the last couple of days before payday, I can't imagine what would happen to you! The thing is that you think if you can keep on losing money at the horses the responsibility for getting married is off your shoulders and you don't really have to make mature choices but that's very unhealthy, Gardner. I took this course at the New School and I understand all the psychology in it.

"But look, I just don't have the patience anymore. I'm not getting any younger, Gardner, and I can't afford not to get married because there's really nothing else I particularly want to do. I mean, I want to marry you. You're all right and everything like that but if I can't I'll marry someone else. You're not the only man who likes my body you know and there are a whole lot of other things about me that I don't think you've really noticed.

"Anyway, Gardiner, you're going to have to come to a decision. I'm giving you two days. Today is Wednesday, June 8th and I'm going to leave now. I'm not going to spend the night here again and I'm not going to come into the office tomorrow either. I'll take sick leave so that means you won't be seeing me for at least two days.

"I'm giving you until Saturday June 11th, three days from now at the same time for you to make your decision about this one way or the other. Either you come to me and tell me that you understand my position and you'll stop all this nonsense to meet your responsibilities, get married to me that is, or we're finished Gardner. If you don't come to me saying that on Saturday night then I'll understand. I'll know you really don't want to get married and you want to bring the thing to an end.

"And that way I'll call in Monday morning and quit. I hate the job anyway and the only reason you should know that I've kept there is to be near you, but I have no other reason to stay. You'll have two days on your own to think this whole thing over and decide what you're going to do. That should be time enough and I think that three days is perfectly fair considering that this thing has been going on for more than three years.

"No, Gardner, don't say a thing to me, don't tell me this or that because

I won't listen. There's nothing you can say to me now that will change this. I've spent a long time getting to this decision and now it's definite. It's a definite thing for me. No, don't try any sex either, Gardner, that won't work. I've had enough sex for the evening, once is really enough for me if it's done right, and you do it right. That's something you'll have to learn to live with when we get married. I'm not crying, Gardner, that won't work either. I'm not crying."

Under certain circumstances, they can talk at an extended length and in their own eyes persuasively. This is something that must be kept in mind for the permanent records. Conviction such as they have is rare in this sector and might even explain many of their difficulties.

"I didn't ask you if you were crying," Gardner is saying. "For God's sake Virginia, that wasn't it, now *listen* to me. Saturday is Belmont day. They're running the Belmont at Aqueduct on Saturday, and it isn't fair. It isn't right."

"What isn't fair or right?"

"Well, Virginia, I mean the Belmont is a very important race. It's probably the single most important race in the country and every year you pin the whole season to it. The President comes. Half the cabinet is there. It's kind of the climax to a whole New York season, even though the season has six months to run after it. People think about the Belmont, Virginia; I mean they really can get involved. It isn't fair to force a decision like that on me just before an important race like that, I mean, Virginia, there's an angle to the Belmont. *Several* angles in fact. I've got to be free to consider—"

"Well I'm sorry, Gardner, that's exactly the kind of thing you're going to have to outgrow," she says and very competently she dresses, tucking all of her neatly inside a series of clothes which do not so much shield as insulate, and goes to the door of the apartment. From there she bestows upon him a final look of appeal and desire, although it may only be pity and terror (or perhaps love and trust: any combination of emotional states will do) and then, taking her overnight bag from the corridor (She had originally been supposed to stay all night. What the hell is *with* these women? Gardner thinks.) she goes through the door and bids him goodnight. Gardner hears her pattering on the stairs; presently he hears nothing at all, and in the empty spaces of his living room he now sits, lighting a new cigarette with the end of the old one, to consider all of this further.

He twitches. At the moment he seems bereft of answers. Peripety has never been Gardner's strongpoint. His specialty is composed of a smooth, even set of transitions rising inevitably to the next race, the next bet, the slick engine of a parley. As well as he thinks he knows Virginia, the fact of the matter is that she has upset his life style and functioning to the point where he feels the best thing to do would not to think at all for some time. Unhappily, this is not possible. As always my time is limited and now with the armaments to be procured, I have numerous small crusades to perform before the evening is over. I must find some reliable dealers and a good pamphlet or two on assembly.

She had no right, Gardner thinks. I mean, she had no right. It all could have worked out some way but she couldn't push it. It had to come right. Who's going to win the Belmont anyway? Why are they all out to get me? Is it possible that geldings can beat fillies $3,000 higher on the claiming level? What does it all mean? What does it come to? What would the effect be of weight at a route? Is it really five lengths for five pounds or are they exaggerating? What determines the class of the horse? How important is condition to class? What's the purpose? What are we living for?

(This is the way he thinks. Although splendidly organized in discourse, his mind and rhetoric prove to be disheveled and virtually uncontrollable in the interior monologue, amorphous thoughts whirl about some center dimly pieced out of drift and wreckage. In the midst of this sea, small obsessions dart like fish into the stream. Being in his mind is somewhat like inhabiting a stagnant pool that yet, miraculously, contains one of the few remaining schools of a prized species of fish. There is a nugget of insanity in Gardner's mind, a pellet of madness so pure and undefiled that it absolutely defies description and makes him by far the most profound of all those with whom I have dealt. Of course the competition is limited.)

He shakes his head and mumbles inarticulately, apparently giving himself the answers to these questions. Neither of us, however, can interpret them. The gist of the answers seems to be negative, although Gardner believes in the inhibiting effects of poor condition upon class.

"Listen," I say, "she's really quite right, you know. You can't go on like this. Sooner or later, the thing has to stop. You're twenty-eight years old and your earlier promise can long since be seen to have disappeared under a flash-flood of tipsheets, programs, horoscopes and bureaucratic petitions. You aren't nearly where you intended yourself to be when this whole thing began, and furthermore you're getting further away from it all the time. She is, by all your standards you know, an extraordinarily pretty girl and it's a lucky thing that she's even having anything to do with you. There are plenty of men in far better shape who couldn't get near a girl like this. Sooner or later, Gardner, you have to accept the realities."

"Listen old chap," he says. (Of all of them he is the most ingratiating and informal; it is true that we have a splendid relationship and have hit it off from the first. Finding no need to defend his sanity before me—

Gardner believing himself to be totally insane—he has been letting me neatly through his defenses so that I can see him, so to speak, bare; also he has a cheerful, almost demure manner in our private dialogues which shows a rare part of him, the Private Gardner that is, which is far different from the public, investigatory Gardner who is the bane of almost all the social security clients within a certain housing project on the north shore.) "Listen, that's perfectly all right for you to say but you don't have responsibilities yourself, you understand. You look at this differently. Also, your information is all wrong. If you want to know how I really feel, I have every intention of beating the horses someday. I happen to be not in the least self-destructive. She simply doesn't understand that it would be impossible for me to marry her until something decent happens. You wouldn't have any information, would you? Some angle tomorrow. No, I guess not; we've gone through that kind of thing before."

"As a matter of fact I do have some information," I say, leaning back casually, very much at ease, inhabiting the spaces of his mind with a grace and felicity which is rare and yet somehow familiar. Gardner's mind accommodates me comfortably indeed, swaddling me in layers of protective warmth which soothe and incite. They come so close to the spirit of Headquarters, as a matter of fact, that I am often driven quite beside myself by nostalgia. "I did not want to do this until we had come to the proper moment which would in the normal course of events have been some time from now but the fact is that I do have some information old friend, and I think that it would be worth your while to follow it up."

"I'll say," Gardner says and puts out his cigarette, lights up another with an immediate flourish and regards me expansively. "You'd better believe I'd take a tip. Even from you. Mostly from you. I mean it's not my fault you understand, if I can't beat the races. I really want to, you know, so that I can get out of this entirely. Then I can marry Virginia and live in a middle-income housing project and make GS-11 and, who knows? maybe go to graduate school for my master's degree at night. Funnier things have happened. Accomplishment! A little accomplishment would be a great thing."

"Yes it would."

"Tell me the tip."

"Accomplishment would, however, have two aspects, Gardner. It might well raise you to a level of feeling you could not stand."

"Tell me the tip."

"Ah," I say. "There's a condition which I must make explicit. I'm not in the information business for my health, you know. For every action a reaction. You have to promise me most explicitly to follow up this tip. In fact, to bet it heavily. Your trouble is that you don't bet heavily, Gardner. You say you do but ten dollars a race is your limit. I'm afraid that you're a little bit of a dilettante, not that I hold that entirely against you, but you've allowed attitude to overrun condition by quite a bit."

"Of course, chief. Anything you say. I figure information from you would have to be legitimate. Why shouldn't I listen?"

"And don't call me chief," I say, "I don't really like it. Grant me my few peculiarities. I understand that you have to cultivate a kind of borrowed flippancy to conceal the inner terror and I know full well that this rhetoric you use during stressful moments bears no relation to your vulnerable and rather gullible interior. You don't have to call me anything. You can just let our relationship define itself on its own terms."

"All right," he says, inhaling into the ashtray and then dropping the cigarette with a gasp. "All right, all right. I know nothing's your fault and nothing's my fault but this kind of thing isn't really necessary. I'll listen to what you have to say and that's it. I said, that's it. One shot and out. You sold me. Up to a point of course. Be reasonable. It isn't only the girl, it's other things. She's not the main course."

"You'll follow through?"

"Follow what through? I can't follow it through until I make some money."

"I'm talking about the tip, Gardner."

"Oh, the tip. Of course. Of course I'll follow through."

"I'm only checking, you understand. It's a question of evaluating intent. This is serious business, you understand. My motives here are very complex and not sheerly conversational."

"Just tell me," Gardner says, "just give me that damned tip. Lay it on me." He is attuned now, every fiber of his being tense and toward me, small thrills of blood coursing through his system, a sense of heightening and broadening at the hairline giving him the slightly wide-eyed aspect of a man who is nearing electrocution. His loins loosen slightly, his legs in the presence of the Ultimate Tip spread. Just as Virginia has opened before him so he is opening now, the eyelids fluttering. "Of course," he mutters. "Of *course*, I want to get out of this. Who would want to stay in it? What kind of a lunatic would get involved with it in the first place if he had any kind of choice?"

"All right," I say. "All right. I trust you. But you better follow through."

"I'm listening. *I'm listening.*"

"Make Peace in the second tomorrow," I say.

Then, there is silence.

CHAPTER XIII

The Belmont. The Belmont is one of America's oldest horse races and certainly her most respected. Three year olds (fillies are rarely entered, however, it is too testing for their delicate limbs, their oft menstruating pudenda) are asked to run a mile and a half under scale weight of one hundred and twenty six pounds, the longest distance that any of them have ever raced and a good piece longer than all but the best of them will ever be asked to race again. The only American race run at the classic European distance of a mile and a half, it is important not only to trainers and horsemen, but to breeders who feel that the combination of speed and stamina which appears in the ultimate winner makes him far more desirable than any of the winners of other major stakes races at stud. If he has won any of the other races as well, of course, so much the better. A winner of the Belmont, in any event, can have his stud fees nearly doubled from whatever they would have otherwise been. With the tendency of good horses to break down earlier and earlier in these times (because of the financial pressures to race them too early too often) and the virtual failure of any good horse to run past the age of five or six, the winner of the Belmont is usually considered to be the most valuable stud prospect in his given age group and usually goes on toward a long and successful career of copulation and its consequences. Modern famous sires such as Prince Graustark or Son Excellence can make as much as twenty thousand dollars for a single service to a mare in heat.

Run continuously at Belmont until the early 1960s, the race was switched to Aqueduct in 1962 because the imminent collapse of Belmont's grandstand forced authorities to condemn the track. Belmont was subsequently rebuilt at a cost to state and horseplayer of several million dollars and the race was switched back to its natural terrain in 1968. There, restored to the felicity of its origin, it appeared to be set through at least the end of the century.

However, in 1972, there occurred at Belmont the famous riots following the Third Religious Revival held at that track during the winter. The first two revivals had been enormously successful and had succeeded in turning over to the New York Racing Association, as fifteen percent of all collections, several hundred thousand dollars. Who was to suspect that fanatics or their satellites went crazy in the cold? But by then it was too late. The race was thus again shifted to Aqueduct where it has been run ever since, to the dissatisfaction of many sentimentalists who only grudgingly have accepted reality. Two renovations within less than two decades were beyond the means of the state during the Welfare Decade.

The arson of 1973 completely destroyed the clubhouse and paddock areas of the abandoned track and the Racing Association, in that era of increasing social dislocation and taxation, announced formerly that Belmont could not be rebuilt within the foreseeable future. Slated to be a commemorative historical site, Belmont was sold to the State University of New York which has instead decided to use the facilities to house faculty within the near future, as soon as plans can come out of the architectural unit, that is.

The race has done little to enhance the fading prestige of Aqueduct in the bargain, but this is something which must be accepted as the price paid for maintaining tradition. Under its original conditions, and since Belmont was the only mile and a half circumferential track in the country, the race was run comfortably with both start and finish directly before the clubhouse under the wire. At Aqueduct, which is three-eighths of a mile shorter, it must start far back, near the stretch turn and the horses are compelled to make a long straightaway run into the clubhouse turn which negates much of the strategy of the race as originally planned. This has bothered no one in the grandstand, however, and weaker jockeys are happier with the additional distance in which to maneuver their horses and arrange their chances.

Many amusing and interesting incidents have characterized the entertaining history of the Belmont. In 1961, for instance, Sherluck, an also-ran in the preceding three-year-old classics, won and paid $123.00, still the longest price ever recorded for the event. Shortly thereafter the horse broke down and was retired. In 1959, Black Hills, a longshot ridden by a celebrated jockey, fell heavily on the home turn while looking for position, and sent the jockey to the hospital for several weeks. The horse was destroyed. In 1973, Bold Master, a gelded son of Bold Ruler, appeared to have the race won in midstretch when, for reasons which have never been satisfactorily explained, he attempted to leap the inner rail (perhaps a swan's behind caught his mindless eye) and eviscerated himself neatly against a coincidentally placed furlong pole, thus ending not only his career but any chance at the romanticized Triple Crown. In 1976, Big Dipper and Candy Chief finished in the first and only dead heat in the history of the Triple Crown races, an incident which gave rise to the famous photograph which the President himself, the first fan of horse-racing, displayed during his inaugural address to the television cameras as an example of the unity which could come through shared effort. Still a further oddity, remarked upon by the President, is that both horses were sons of Candy Spots and that they were ridden by brothers, Robert and Richard Marshall, apprentice jockeys.

This is only a fragment or two of the fascinating lore and history of this tradition-laden race.

Some of the horses who have won the Belmont are: Sword Dancer, Jaipur, Damascus, Marking Time, Citation, Quadrangle, Swimming Hole, Ponder, Needles, Native Dancer, and the famous Military Hit. Some of the highly publicized horses who have lost this race are: Northern Dancer, Fabius, Bold Master, Ridan, Crimson Satan, Admiral's Voyage, Smash the Sea, Determine, Dedicate, My Dad George, Run to Mama, and Majestic Prince.

Many other oddities and tales about the Belmont are on file in the nest of clippings which I am bringing home and they may be studied at leisure. I have prepared a tasteful collection which combines scholarship and genial cheer in a fashion which will amuse and titillate even the uninitiate.

I trust that the aforegoing will prove: (a) that I am not in the least unbalanced, (b) not disconcerted, (c) not alienated from the situation, and (d) can write a level, undisturbed, Headquarterese prose with the best of the other operatives. The style adopted through the run of this report was exhibited only in order to put a little bit of—ah—color into the narration which would otherwise fail of the true import of what is going on here.

Plenty is going on here.

What in hell is going on here?

CHAPTER XIV

Fourth Recitatif (Confessional): Gentlemen! I have sinned. That is to say that the scar of my sin must be glowing darkly before you at this moment, hanging bloody and wet as a dashed pennant before your eyes; should you ever find, of course, and ponder these notes. Otherwise, my sin glows not at all and who would have it any other way? Who cares? What is the difference? My sin, in any event, is that as you now see I have failed to work in strictly chronological order and thus the narrative sense of some of this may have been a bit confusing from time to time to time. To time.

Order, gentlemen! Order! I can understand this. In my day I have grown to cherish order, praise it, enact it myself at all the myriad levels of possibility, to realize that it is order and order alone which so to speak stands between us and the impenetrable nightmare outside, order between us and the Engulfing Pit and yet, knowing all of this, I flout it with a certain élan, one could even say a certain kind of arrogance. After all, who can best decide what is to be done in a given situation than the operative on the planet, on the very planet! And if my tone takes on somewhat of a giddy air, if my characters seem to have perhaps decompensated themselves a little more dramatically than strictly necessary under the circumstances, still, who is best qualified to say what is and is not necessary: the bureaucracy or the operative? Come, gentlemen, think! I hear the rustlings in the abscess, I hear the sounds which can only be cheers. The operative! The operative! The humble, struggling, incorruptible operative!

After all, gentlemen, what did you expect? We have not taken on the upper classes of the society; we are not dealing with those cool, contained, ratiocinative types who have done so much to bring this state of affairs to its ghastly fruition. Rather, we are dealing with a simpler and altogether grimmer type, and if they tend to sweat, palpate and curse somewhat more than the average, then we must understand that they have their reasons! Reasons! Or, as the saying goes in this unique and pastoral land, as the saying goes indeed: horses for courses.

We are dealing with the events as best suited. You can see that I have kept the Objective firmly in mind from the beginning and all will capsulize appropriately on Belmont Day. During the Belmont itself, as a matter of fact. But we get there by most circuitous roots: Mary through Julian and Simmons via Make Peace and Tony through crude manipulation and Gardner—well, Gardner via Thursday by means of other antecedents. But it does not matter for they all will come together at that vital and terrible moment when the fires begin to lace the air like maddened insects and the hiss of flame, intolerable in its beauty, becomes a gigantic drone like the expulsion from a hive, and from this hive will burst forth then the flowers of destruction, wild and terrible in their multicolored beauty, fires which catch the grandstand and then the clubhouse and then the tote board and finally the track itself, until all is seen to be shadowed in flame: the forms of the horses and riders struggling through the brilliance of orange, the flicker of tentlike brown which can only be the collapsing grandstand, and through the eye of the fire one will see forms, forms shadowed and lithe, brilliant and round, forms of all shapes and sizes, needs and fulfillment, history and connection tumbling through the fire's veil … and somewhere at the dead-center of all this beauty will come a solution so terrible—

Will come a solution so terrible as to make you proud of me gentlemen! Be proud! Take counsel! Be patient! The fires are coming!

It is impossible not to become really involved in the affair. One understands that operatives are to cultivate a certain clear detachment, a dignified removal from the source of their efforts which will enable them to regard the consequences with quizzicality to say nothing of some amusement. No less than any of my associates, not a whit less than any of my superiors, I approached the mission in that spirit. Remember, remember if you will what I did on Capella L, with what poise and facility I did the necessary there. Remember the torture bins on the Centaurs? They were conceived and structured from this very mind's eye, jewels of pain as it were, and I was there, I was there! and never a twitch to betray my excitement and my passion.

But this is different.

I have never dealt with anything quite like this. What I cannot understand, and it may be this factor above all others which explains my peculiar rhetoric, what I cannot understand is that these people are serious. They are *serious*. They believe that if they can, through dealings with horses, irrevocably alter their lives, then they have solved something basic, and if that alteration is not accomplished it cannot be, no matter what, their fault. Parts and parts of them, whole grotesqueries of limbs and psyches they feel into these deadly machines day after day, putting in and taking out (always less seventeen percent) and at the end of all this suffering and penitence, involution and pain, will come, they believe, an apotheosis so profound as to yank them free from the trap of their passions and into a high, bright stratosphere of possibility.

It is this need for alteration which so seizes and maddens them, and if they cannot have it one way, well, then, they conclude that they will have it another. If they do not triumph over circumstance, then circumstance can only be their destruction. One has never seen anything quite like it.

They understand nothing. They care little of entropy. Questions of mortality and central fix in the universe do not disturb them. They are unaware of the greater principle of Cahn which states that it is the question of culpability which controls the destiny of races and that culpability is apportioned to the exact degree that they have aided the forces of entropy. (I quote from memory; Cahn's Law was always one of my interests but it has been many years since I wrote my paper on it.) They know nothing of the Lesser Laws of Straits which point out that for every act of grace there must be one of contrition in equal force, and therefore the duality of motives is intertwined. They giggle at the Five Principles of the Tork (which have a different name and numerology here but should be as devastating). All that they know is machinery. Machinery: putting it in, taking it out, exploding themselves again and again against that terrible wall and at the end … at the end, a missed angle, a lost step, a cowardly jockey, an unfortunate tip … at the end it is to those features where blame is ascribed, never to themselves. Ah, no, never!

And oh, the heat of the track: you cannot understand how it becomes in the late spring, gentlemen. It is somewhat nearer the shore than the central city but there is absolutely no breeze; it is airless, stagnant, a small flutter of frightened birds providing the only palpation, the smooth, rich, even stagnancy of the flats coming over the track on hot days, the sense of enclosure, the stillness, press of bodies, heat of damp, clutter of collusion as ten by ten they stumble to the windows to make their next bet, heedless of their sweat. Disgusting! Distasteful! Cry calumny in the temple! Sing to me of evil and loss, the beauty of the ruptured heart!

But the horses are beautiful; they are the last innocents and perform their dumb chores with that kind of grace known only to the unconscious. The horses rise slowly to meet their destiny in the scarred center of the track, poised like dancers as they lunge toward the wire; this is all they know and they do it so well, so superbly well! Hardly can they be blamed for what is construed around them.

Chronology fails. Only the metaphysic holds. But it holds. There is little time left: one or two days left to this wretched assignment and back to the shores. They cannot touch me as long as I concentrate and maintain professional discipline. They cannot discipline me as long as I concentrate. They cannot know me as long as I choose to be unknown.

It is not post time. The horses are on the track. In the first race, there are no changes. In the second race, number four, Hot Sun, is a bay gelding, and number seven, Green Power, is three pounds over. In the fifth race, a change of jockey. In the ninth race, number two, Run the Gauntlet, has been scratched. Scratch number two, Run the Gauntlet. Daily double windows close promptly at 1:20, and in the first race …

CHAPTER XV

Mary enters the track through the grandstand gate and stands numbed for a moment, before the tipsheet stand. On the train to the track it has been hot, has given all indications of being a stifling and bright day, but now, at the track itself, some errant cloudbank has covered the sun to retract visibility. Standing there, Mary has the feeling that she has been struck blind (probably in retribution) and she gropes for her eyeglasses, doing a good imitation of a woman bravely overcoming her handicap. As she settles the eyeglasses on her nose, the cloud goes away as rapidly as it has come and Mary feels herself literally pinned by the sun, all areas of her body seeming to heat and brighten to the ground as waves of radiation pass through her. "Son of a bitch," she says, and puts the glasses away again. "Son of a bitch, you just can't make a buck." It is as if the cloud, a 7–5 shot, has passed on in the stretch just in time to be beaten by the sun, a popular because sentimental favorite.

"Bastards," she murmurs and goes over to the tipsheet hawker. He is a small man, perhaps five feet three inches in height, who stands on a crate behind the stand in order to give the illusion of normal stature, but Mary knows his secret as well as he knows Mary, and they look at one another for a few instants while the man performs certain adjustments upon the hat he is wearing, pulling it down somewhat over his eyes. Mary's appearance seems to have sparked some core of the coy within him; he becomes winsome.

"Good afternoon, lady," he says. "What can I do for you today? A *Lawton*? A *Powell*? Schoolmaster hit the double yesterday, maybe you'd like to try that one. He's kind of a new item, just a kid, but he shows a lot of promise."

Mary shakes her head, puts her hands on hips, looks the hawker straight on until his gaze wavers and fails. "You have a lot of nerve," she says. "Do you know that?"

The man casts a frantic glance to his left and right (it is distressing to see how quickly they become discombobulated and for how little reason, the load of guilt they carry is that enormous) and sees that his partner is busily occupied in selling the *New York Turf Letter* to a businessman who cannot disengage his hands from a large blonde woman sufficiently to pay for it. The partner reaches over and gently extracts a dollar from the businessman's pocket, sees Mary then and says, "What did you say? What is it lady?"

"I said you have a lot of nerve," Mary says. "I been meaning to tell you that for a long, long time and you'd better hear me. Playing on the hopes of people like this. Telling them lies. You know that if any of these guys had decent information, they wouldn't be selling it for a buck. They'd be in there laying the bets on. Disgusting! Preying on a poor, helpless, lonely old woman who only wants a little bit of help. All of them liars and thieves. There is no information. *There is no information!*"

"But you're wrong, lady," the hawker says. He takes a *Lawton* and shows it to her, stabs something with a thumb. "You can see right here that this clocker hit the third and fourth races right on the nose yesterday with his Preferred and Most Preferred, and then here he comes back in the ninth with a $24.80 winner. Lawton's been at this for nearly thirty years, lady; he has bad days like any of us but they all even up and he's ahead. He's a real pro, Lawton. You got to have faith."

The hawker is appalled. He is having, although he tries to conceal this, a very bad time. Firstly he has never before spoken with Mary. (Their surprising sense of intimacy comes from sight and not from dialogue, this is the kind of thing which makes certain horseplayers feel that they have an understanding with a given horse or jockey.) Secondly their dialogue is beginning to attract a small but interested clump of spectators, all of whom look at Mary with something approaching fondness. It is as if she is speaking now for a large sector of the horse-playing population and Mary, sensing this, feeling a rising sense of power and accomplishment, says, "Don't give me none of that filth and lies. I know everything that's going on here. I been playing the horses myself for thirty years, girl and woman, and the whole thing is crooked. If any of you bums had the answers, you'd be inside making them and not trying to hustle six bits from a poor old woman who is down to her last couple of dollars. If you were men with any sense of respect and real cleanliness, you wouldn't be in this in the first place. You'd be doing something honest with your time. I bet you write all those sheets yourself, right, you bum, and sell them under different names, giving seven or eight horses in each and every race?"

"Lady," the hawker says, "lady please. I get five cents a sheet. I'm just trying to make a living, I never even *seen* the guys who do this stuff. I just get deliveries from some kids and try to do the best I can; what I can't sell I turn back and what I do sell I get a nickel. What are you laying into *me* for? I don't know who Clocker Lawton is, I never even saw the guy let alone know him, so if you got any problems—"

"Hah!" Mary says, pointing vigorously, "you admit it then. Clocker Lawton don't even exist. Listen, he admitted it!"

"I didn't say that. Of course he exists. I mean, he's writing the sheets, ain't he? Someone is writing the sheets and it ain't me. Hell, I don't know nothing about horses, I won't even play them. In my whole life I played a horse once and lost five dollars and that's it lady."

"Bum," Mary says. "Bum!"

"Please. Lady, please, lady, show some mercy, we got customers—"

"Oh no," a tall man says from the edges of the crowd. "That's perfectly all right. We'll wait. We want to listen to this lady."

"I'll tell you a thing or two," Mary says, raising her handbag and removing some coins from her interior purse. "I'll tell you more than a thing or two, you just wait and see. You're all filth and merchandising, that's what you are. You ain't got no proper sense of compassion."

She places seventy-five cents on the counter, picks up a *Lawton*. "But just to show you the kind of woman I am, the kind of spirit and pride I got, the way I always pay my dues, I'm going to buy your disgusting filth. Just to show you that I don't waste people's time or mislead them the way the rest of you do. To show that I got some respect. I care. I have compassion. *I follow through on what I say.*" This is not quite the reason of course. The fact is that Lawton's having named a $24.80 winner has excited Mary. Otherwise, she would certainly have tried *Rowe* today.

Vaguely conscious of dim approbation, perhaps a handclap behind her, Mary wanders through the alley under the grandstand, takes the old steps leading to the lawn. Then she moves abstractedly into the grandstand enclosure, reading *Lawton*. She thinks for a while of taking the escalator to her usual place in the grandstand but decides not to. A woman of her age should keep in condition; no reason at all to restrict the physical activity since it brought on heart disease. This is an unusual day, definitely a critical day, in fact it is a pivotal day, and the thing to do is to get a proper start and break bad habits. She goes to the bar in the rear of the enclosure and orders a beer, pays for it with a dollar, carefully puts away all the change and drinks the beer in slow, even gulps while she ponders *Lawton* further.

As always he is sticking to the chalk. There are a couple of interesting possibilities in the turf race but for the most part and predictably Lawton is once again picking horses which would have been favorites anyway, horses whose odds will be 3–1 at the most, 7–5 in the probable, and it is hardly worth seventy-five cents to Mary to see what is happening again to the timeless Clocker Lawton. Some time long ago, in his youth, Clocker must have had a disturbing series of incidents which had forever afterward made him doubtful of adventure and eager to clamber onto the familiar. Yellow should have been his color except that Powell picked it up.

Nevertheless, she thinks, one can never quite tell. Occasionally some of Lawton's choices do float up to higher odds and then, too, the real purpose of buying *Lawton* (she remembers) is to continue her file, her perfect file of *Lawtons*. It will be interesting in a few hours or more to look back upon this sheet and to understand that the mysterious, legendary, shrewd old clocker, no less than she, does not know what in hell he is doing and is vulnerable to whimsy, devastation, and the perverse. She places *Lawton* in her pocket-book with a sigh and resigns herself to the fact that there can be no answers from there.

She asks the bartender, then, if he has any information. Mary, like many regular horseplayers, believes that track employees (even the very humblest) are privy somehow to mysterious information, are hooked into some central sense of connection, have tapped sources so private and powerful that their jobs are meaningless to them only insofar as they keep them busy during the days and near the action. The bartender, for reasons of his own, has never tried to discourage this kind of misapprehension. (It leads to larger tips, although occasionally, very occasionally, horseplayers will come back to him later and complain. In that case he will say that Johnny or Joe had changed instructions at the last moment and decided not to go for it but next time for sure.... This enables him to string out his relations with customers indefinitely, although there is an aspect of intricacy, to all of this which makes his intellectual life, perhaps, somewhat livelier than he really wants it to be.) He says that he is not sure, not completely sure, but Floral Park in the fourth looks pretty good and that he, the bartender, is taking a flyer on the 5–3 double. He assures Mary that this is not to say that 5–3 will win, but on the other hand he isn't covering it because he expects it to lose either.

(Indirect dialogue is such a refreshing change of pace, gentlemen, I should have thought of it thousands of words ago. It enables distancing and in their case it is a pleasure.)

Mary explains that she is a very old woman who has been betrayed by her son. She has brought him up to a successful marriage and a prosperous career and now, when he has no more use for her, he has turned away. It is disgraceful. The bartender says that this is probably so, children being what they are these days, but the 5–3 double looks as if it might stand up; the figures on the five horse are particularly promising. He has just come from a track at Dover at which track he breezed an easy five furlongs in :58 3/5 unblinkered. As far as the three horse in the second race, the trainer, Miller, is thought to be one of the shrewdest and most corrupt men working out of Aqueduct and the horse is bound to win someday, why not today? Miller himself thought so highly of the horse that he bought it for himself from the previous owners, this being the kind of inside information you could pick up if you kept your eyes open at the track. Mary says that she noticed the very same thing in the *Telegraph* last night. (She is a liar however; she never reads the *Telegraph*, the figures frighten her and the excess of information strides her as the sheerest numerology: mystical and insane.) But you could never tell about shippers and trainers; they were too inconsistent. She orders another beer and tips the bartender fifty cents, explaining that thanks to her son's real ingratitude, she is in severe financial straits and must win herself out today or be gone from the racetrack forever. Forever and begone, she will fly away like a filly dispatched to the farm in heat. Perhaps she is getting a little drunk. The bartender says that this is altogether a shame but simply part of the whole generational breakdown which has led to the mysterious youth vigilantes and the dangerous hostile closed worlds of the commune. This bartender seems to have a shred of social consciousness or maybe it is only that he cannot pick winners and has been forced to educate himself instead.

Bedazzled in any event by this sociology (Mary knows that there is something which might be called an "outside world" but it has, at best, always seemed a bit of a nuisance), she downs her beer quickly and asks if Make Peace does not have a tendency to quit in the stretch anyway. The bartender says that he does; he has shown this tendency many times before but Miller has been tightening him up for months and is probably ready for the crackdown today. They nod at each other with sensations of power drifting between them, a true sense of collaboration. Two customers come over, holding *Telegraphs* and mumbling to one another and the bartender serves them at the far end. He comes back to Mary to say that he has now considered her problem and all things kept in the balance, he could now advise her to bet the three horse in the second race particularly heavily, lay off the double because of the uncertainties of Dover but go heavy into the three. Mary thanks him and tells him that he is a lovely man who understands old women and their terrors. She tips him another thirty cents, getting a house beer in return. (The house beer is absolutely remarkable, a once-a-year-occurrence, but the particular problem of this bartender is that he has always wanted to be loved and has found so little of it; perhaps this is why he gives so many tips. It is not a question of venality but abandonment.) The bartender says that the beer is his pleasure and he wishes her luck.

Mary is quite definitely drunk at this point. She has absolutely no capacity for liquor, the poor lady, and she has not eaten at all today; also I am making myself lively in the cerebral hemispheres. She staggers from the stool beaming and wanders off toward the infield. Halfway there she realizes that she had left the *Lawton* on the counter and returns to retrieve it. The bartender is reading it assiduously and hands it to her with a shamed grin. "He seems to spot the same horses in the eighth as I do," he says.

Mary returns to the infield and notes that it is 1:15, five minutes until closing of the Daily Double windows. She decides to heed the bartender and lay off the double. Instead, she will bet the number three horse in the second race heavily and bail out in that fashion. The trainer is shrewd and in any event she deserves to win: God would not let her lose after all that she has gone through. She will take half her winnings to Julian and throw them in his face. She checks her handbag to make sure that the five hundred dollars is still there. "Son of a bitch tipsheet bastard could have stole it," she mumbles but without conviction. She knows as well as I do that the hawkers are too shy to make dramatic gestures such as theft. Under pressure, they flutter like birds.

Horses come onto the track for the first race, examine Mary with mute disinterest, and wander up the track. She follows them, bumping hard into a thin, gangling madman hanging over the rail by his elbows, frantically trying to control his trembling forefinger as he points it at the tote. "Watch it goddamn it lady," Simmons says. "Don't you know where the hell you are?" Mary says that she is sorry but certain people should learn that they don't own the entire area of the rail, even on Thursdays. They part from one another with some loathing, not understanding the great compact in which they are soon to be united (just as well). Simmons, shaking his head, decides to go off the chalk this time.

Mary looks over the rail for a while, then goes to the windows and makes a two dollar show bet on the number five. She finds it impossible to watch a race without having a bet of some sort down. She feels that this would mean that she was somehow losing control of her situation. (Overall her "interest" bets have done somewhat better than the "serious" ones but this is something which I would never point out to her, being of a rather sensitive nature overall.) She pushes back through the crowds, mumbling and cursing, the *Lawton* flapping in her hand and stands near the glass doors to watch the first race, putting her hands on various ribs in order to separate bodies.

The Lawton horse wins it. Lawton's second choice finishes second. The five horse, closing rapidly but caught between horses is third after all. There is an objection but it is disallowed and numbers go up on the board. Through all of this Mary waits patiently, singing beer songs. The five horse pays $7.80 to show, very mediocre for a 42–1 shot but it is, after all, $5.80 more which she will be able to put on the fervent nose of the number three. She walks with some grace to the payoff window, feeling that she is bestowing favor upon multitudes of losers she passes and waits for her payoff. The $7.80, clinked deeply into her palm from the hand of the mutuel clerk, has an aspect of blame to it and Mary rubs it almost lasciviously as she drops the seven dollars into her purse. The eighty cents she takes to her bartender and exchanges for another beer plus tip.

He nods and says that Willie dropped in the news from the backstretch exactly one minute before post that he did not like the conditions at all and would not be going with number five today. Perhaps next time or the time thereafter. The third-place finish is to be considered a kind of gift from Willie to the across-the-board bettors, a small reward for their willingness to limit their greed. The bartender says that this kind of thing can happen anytime at all but the number three still looks very solid to him and he has not had any advice yet to the contrary. Perhaps if he does he can catch her. He goes to the other end to pass some rye and whiskey over to two tough-looking women with sagging breasts who are examining the program and giggling about the peculiar names of some horses.

Mary sighs. She now finishes her fourth beer. She is staggeringly drunk, well beyond her means but I will maintain some reserve about this matter and not be unduly clinical. She goes to the hundred dollar window which is unoccupied except for a thin man in front of her and a Pinkerton glaring from the left, his eyes turned inward toward some awful knowledge, his badge glittering in the flicker of the inner tote. The man in front of her is talking earnestly to the clerk. "Come on, come on," he is saying and with some reluctance tickets appear, ten of them in fact (Mary, in drunken compulsiveness, counts the whirs) which the customer seizes.

"Where's the money?" the clerk says. "You haven't given me the money yet." The Pinkerton stirs, examines the situation and grumbles.

"Don't you trust me," her predecessor says and places ten one hundred dollar bills on the counter. "There," he says, "there." The Pinkerton's eyelids flutter and he mumbles. The clerk disgustedly counts the money, raps it on the counter, and puts it in the till saying something about insane horseplayers who not only make asses of themselves but feel that mutuel clerks should have to *trust* them and put up the tickets before they put up the money. This appears to sadden the clerk (who has always had a higher vision of humanity then his position can perhaps sustain) but not the Pinkerton who now whips a program out of his shirt pocket and begins to study it assiduously.

"Yes lady," the clerk says, looking at her through a suddenly acquired eyeshade. "You'll put down the money before you order the tickets, OK? It's not that I don't trust you or anything like that but I can only take one scene like that a day, lady. It's in the contract. There's a condition in my heart about tension and also, lady, what we don't get paid for we have to take ourselves. That means a very steady man has to be at this window or else you could wind up betting hundreds and hundreds of dollars on every horse in each race and that isn't good."

Despite the fact that hundred dollar clerks are known to be relatively proprietary about their business and their customers, this intimacy is a new experience for Mary and she takes it as a good omen. (She has no choice; she has never been at the hundred dollar window before, even to run bets.) "The number three," she says. "The three horse in the second race—five times."

"The money, lady," the clerk says, "the *money*," and Mary extracts it from her handbag. Five hundred dollar bills, her sinking fund, all the money she has, and she lays it carefully in front of the clerk like an offering. Involuntarily her hands clasp, she bites her tongue, nibbles her upper lip. At this doomed moment she tastes a wafer.

"Three?" the clerk says and she nods. He pushes the key five times, very carefully, and tickets emerge slickly, coming from the machine in the way the pellets of feces (Mary yet has a scatological mind) slide cleanly out of the rumps of nervous horses when they approach the starting gate. "Three," the clerk says and hands the tickets to her. "Five times. One. Two. Three. Four. Five. Five times on the number three. Five hundred dollars. One. Two. Three. Three again. Four. Five. Five hundred dollars. Correct, lady, and good luck. I happen to know that the three in this race has a good chance," and the clerk bestows upon her a perfectly wonderful and merry wink.

Mary takes the tickets and clutches them to her, then deposits them in her handbag and wanders off toward the infield. Halfway there she thinks about yet another beer but a deep, glowing belch, grinding out of the very center of her and seeming to send out slivers of fire reminds her that she is dealing with certain issues of mortality about which, perhaps, it is wisest to maintain a sort of deference. The hell with the beer, it only exhausts the heart anyway. She looks at the tickets, verifies the number by the winking lights of the tote, and goes out again to the track. The horses have been warming up for some moments and are already circling into the starting gate for the mile and an eighth race, staring at one another sullenly. "Come on, three," says Mary hoarsely. She had meant to shout this but is surprised at the noncooperation of her vocal cords. It seems as if she has lost momentarily the power of declamative speech. "Oh come on, three," Mary says, "come on!"

I speak to her then, I say, "All right, Mary, here we go. You're hooked in deep now, eh?"

She looks at me with revulsion. Then the knowledge hits her like a blow and she gasps but it is too late, the bets are placed and there is nothing she can do. "You," she says, "*you—*"

"Too late, Mary," I say cheerfully. "Consider the odds, however. Just think of them."

The gates spring open and the horses lumber out. "You bastard," she says and the race is run, truly contested all the way for all its cheapness and the three shows a certain rigorous grace, a good deal of courage for once and certain moves as well but for all his efforts he cannot improve in the stretch drive, and hanging on for all he is worth finishes third, beaten five or six lengths.

"Son of a bitch," Mary says, stunned, as the official light goes up. "Son of a bitch."

"Sorry, Mary," I say. "It was after all not very nice of me but it had to be done. Besides, the horse was an overlay at good odds and you had a run for your money, what the hell?"

"Oh God," she says. "Oh God," and a rotting belch springs from her stomach, her hands spring to her heart; her head sinks to her chest, her body folds around her chest, her knees fly toward her face and rolling and rolling on the infield lawn, Mary thinks that it may be a heart attack after all (she has waited for it so long) but at the center knows that there is no such luck. It is only an attack of hysteria or guilt or something because, otherwise, why would she be laughing so? Laughing, laughing, laughing to split the sun, and in the third race there are no changes.

It is harsh doings and fills me with a twinge of pity but there is no other way in which it could have been done. Now Mary knows too. The third race is to be won by a 10–1 shot whose form Mary has been watching for some weeks and whose name she had escaped in the program. She would have bet him heavily win and place. She would have won over three thousand dollars.

CHAPTER XVI

The roots of Gardner's condition are not quite as easy to assess. The interesting thing is that he comes from generations of horse-players; his mother and father were brought to divorce through the ministrations of the track and his paternal grandfather (although he has never heard this) was a bookmaker in the Old Country many years before Gardner's time. By being mistaken for an important secret service operative by the wrong people, the grandfather, it can be said, joined a long succession of people who have given their life for art.

His mother and father on the other hand were relatively less rigorous cases. His father was a longshot stabber and his mother an adherent to the chalk, and it was this more than any other factor which wrecked their marriage and sent them springing apart some months before poor Gardner was even born; his father committed suicide by leaping from the roof of the old Jamaica grandstand one afternoon when a long shot which he had taken himself off came in.

In recrimination, his mother swore off the horses forever and Gardner had to find the pursuit on his own as it were, recapitulating all of this ontogeny with a mad phylogeny of his own which would see him, some seventeen years after his birth, greeting his home from work with the word that he had gone to the track for the very first time and had liked it very much, so much in fact that the seventeen dollars he had lost were not even a concern to him. His mother's reaction was so painful that, more than a decade later, Gardner cannot still bear to think of it; since that one painful scene he has never again discussed horses with his mother. For that matter, he has not seen her for some years. Her obligations, she told him, ended when Gardner went to the track for the first time and so it is a testimony to his motivation that he was able to get himself through the city university of his choice. Exhausted, he had joined the civil service after his seven-year career in this university and for the first time found that he had betting money. The rest is understood to be inevitable. Since he has not seen his mother for years, Gardner is always promising himself that he will call and perhaps some day he will but it would, I have assured him when we discussed the subject one time, make no difference either way. His mother has a frenetic terror of horses to this day; Gardner would have nothing else to give her.

The pure fine blood of generations of horseplayers can thus be said to course restlessly in Gardner's veins. It is not only his psyche which he brings to the rail when he cheers one of his horses on but his very heritage, a mélange of history going back hundreds of years (his paternal grandfather learned everything he knew from his uncle) and which in terms of cultural tradition and lore should be almost overwhelming. But the sad fact of the matter is that Gardner has inherited not only his doomed family's interest but its ill luck, and he is (I say this in all sadness) one of the worst serious horseplayers in New York City, having been embarked long since upon a losing streak so grim and vicious that it can be assumed to be a direct reflection upon his intelligence and not his desires. Gardner wants to win, but, he is gullible, superstitious, panicky, ignorant, and impatient and time and again he forgets the lessons which he feels that he has so painfully learned and has paid for so expensively. He becomes unduly excited by tote board changes, he allows women at the track to excite him, he looks for information in the bottom of urinals, and he feels that the Stevens counter clerks know him and are out to get him personally. Gardner has long since made the track a mad extension of his own interior which is not so damned placid to begin with. Gardner. Pity Gardner! Consider him if you will and try to understand the perspective.

It is the series of lessons he has learned, as a matter of fact, which Gardner now recites to himself as he drives his ancient car to Aqueduct on this fine Thursday afternoon. Free from compulsory duty in the office by virtue of a new procedure, freed by virtue of the car from the various unpleasantness of the subway, Gardner feels as always that he is entering through damnation into apotheosis. The car was purchased as an investment in concentration and he is now trying to instill within himself that cold and bright band of logic which he knows must light his path home. Don't bet longshots to win only, Gardner thinks, always always back them up for place twice as much as win. Bet odds-on favorites to place only. Never bet fillies against males under any conditions. Never bet a horse moving up in class after a good race. Never bet a horse moving down in class after a bad race. Watch out for jockey switches. Never bet a horse carrying more than three pounds over the weight he carried in his last victory. Watch out for four year olds and up that have engaged in driving finishes in their last two races.

Watch for last minute flashes down on the board, he reminds himself. Look for a well-spotted horse from another track moving down at least a thousand dollars in class and with a leading jockey on him. Never bet horses that have been claimed for the first race in new colors. Insist that a horse has had a workout at least twice during the past seventeen days; on the other hand, pay particular attention to horses that have no workouts whatsoever listed in the past performance line because the trainer may be trying to cover up something. Forget any horse overweight more than two pounds. Do not bet unknown jockeys on horses in the 5–1 range. Gardner continues this litany, achieving in some parts of it a genuine fire, others a rather mechanical sense of iteration. All of it is quite interesting, adding as it does to my own observations, opinions, and insights about the track and there is very little of it which should be disregarded—even though Gardner, under normal circumstances, will certainly forget every word of it the instant he comes to the track and sees that A Certain Horse which he has been following is listed in odds of upwards of 10–1. Of things such as this is Gardner's destiny woven, all of it richly tapestried from his history.

One can conceive of generation after generation of disasters which have somehow conspired to bring about this modern Gardner who sits singing in his old Torquefast, spacing out his encouragement with high-pitched bleats which are understood to be limitations of bugle calls. Gardner is an optimist. He knows that somehow he will, on this very bright afternoon, win all the money for Virginia today and then he will be finished with the horses forever and the two of them will be married, *Married!* From their loins will spring a succession of dour and uncomplicated children all inheriting Virginia's stamina and Gardner's intelligence, none of whom will know or care that workouts in even furlongs of twelve seconds each usually are the key to a hard race on the succeeding day.

Gardner. Gardner! All kinds of impulses spring to mind and memory. One would (if only one could) reach over the seat and give him an encouraging pat on the back to put him in the proper cheer for this afternoon's battle. Or perhaps one would remonstrate with him, try to lead Gardner to understand that the kind of answers which he seeks at the track are generally for people far older and more self-enclosed than he. Or perhaps one would merely want to join him in his bugle calls which have a certain rustic charm and in their imitative aspects come close to giving a good representation of the track. But one does none of those things, one does instead what one is best suited to do by nature and custom. One must understand limitations. So one talks.

"Gardner," I say, "you have to be reasonable. You cannot win all the money in an afternoon. You would need thousands and thousands of dollars in order to recoup your losses, give you some savings and provide you with the kind of margin you would need for Virginia to quit her job. It's far better to be realistic about this. Try to be realistic. You have to do this thing in small quantities. You wouldn't expect, after all, to make a year's salary in a day, would you? It takes time."

"Of course not," he says, "but this is different." He shuts off the radio which has been giving the news in a low rumble behind the bugle calls. (If there is one thing Gardner possesses it is unfailing politeness.) "Nothing's impossible. Listen: if I can run a ten dollar *show* parley through nine races, I'd have a thousand dollars. And any idiot can pick a show parley. That's no real challenge at all and it doesn't mean a thing. I could do it anytime I wanted if that was my kind of thing. A ten dollar place parley on the other hand would be five thousand dollars at least and any idiot can pick a horse which will finish second. But I'm not going to do that either."

"What are you going to do, Gardner?"

"I'm going to bet every cent I have on Make Peace in the second," he says. "I've been watching that horse for months. He ran a good third in Florida not even six months ago and since then he hasn't done nothing but the trainer's been bringing him along slow and liked the horse so much he bought him from the previous owner which trainers rarely do. Miller is smart. Now he's running the horse back against thirty-five hundred dollar pigs for the first time and that's the angle I wanted. I mean, it's *proven* that the horse can win in this class because he already proved he can beat better; it's a matter of timing, of knowing when they're going to go for it seriously, the dirty bastards. I figure that today's the day. They can't ride him forever, they claimed him after that business in Florida and they've carried the damned horse along ever since. Today's the day. Today's the day! I feel it. I *know* it. It's got to be!" He slams his fist to the steering wheel and simultaneously navigates the car cunningly into the right-hand lane to be prepared for the exit which is less than a mile away. "He ought to be thirty to one at the least. But I figure much higher than that."

"Cinnamon Roll's got a chance," I point out.

"Sure he's got a chance, sure he does; he's the favorite for one thing and favorite's always have a chance. But it's too good on paper, too good to be true. The horse finishes second beaten a neck four days ago with seven thousand dollar horses and yesterday he works out in .46 so you know he's sound and the dropdown in class is because they want the purse badly. It's *too* good," Gardner says and slams his fist on the wheel again somewhat less indolently. "It's just too good to be true. The horse figures to win so there's no way he can, that's the way they rig these cheap claiming races."

"But listen Gardner," I say with enormous calm and a kind of ease. "I point this out with sorrow but Make Peace was entered in the second yesterday. He was running against four thousand dollar horses then and what he did was to run off from the starting gate and must have rapped himself somewhat seriously because the stewards scratched him out."

"Aha!" Gardner says, "that's precisely the point. And now they bring him right back so he can't be at all hurt. They pulled that whole little scene yesterday to build up the odds for today. What the idea was was to make him look as bad as possible, but they're bringing him right back, aren't they? They aren't even laying him off over the weekend! The next day. The next day! The horse has got to be ripe if they're pulling off something like that. And he takes another drop in class. Aha! That ought to build up the odds to a pretty penny. It all fits in with my theory, that's what it does."

It is really quite hopeless. Nevertheless I say, "But you see, Gardner, the stewards will never scratch a horse for running off from the gate unless they have reason to believe that the horse is unsound and that he hurt himself in the excitement. They may be bringing him back today only to find out how badly he is hurt and entering him in a race he can't win because they know that they won't lose him. Or more likely, come to think of it, they *want* to lose him and figure that an angle like this will surely draw a claim. It isn't safe, Gardner. I can't call it gilt-edged. It's all really suspicious. I feel it's my obligation to warn you off the horse, you can't predict this kind of thing."

Slamming the car out of gear and coasting through an underpass, he says, "So, what's safe? You know it's all a swindle anyway. So what the hell, you have to stab on something long and hope for the best. It's the only way."

It is this aspect of dualism in their function which I find the most thoroughly infuriating. They will enunciate logic, defend it, struggle to acquire it, seek, enfold, and manipulate; they will justify all of their acts, when they choose, under the tenets of logic and then at the least likely time and for the most perverse of reasons they will deny it and lurch instead toward mysticism, the occult, the laws of chance, the question of fraud, etc. It is as if this constant swing between empirical order (or the faith in it) and subjective chaos is their own carefully prepared metaphor for existence, developed with some cunning over the course of years and years, evolved painfully and with intricacy as the sum of many experiences and the result is chaos—absolute chaos. This is the most depressing aspect of the situation: one can simply not *reason* with them. They are not rational. They will do the strangest things and call them logic, do the most justified in the name of impulse.

"All right, Gardner," I say, "have it your way then. I'm just trying to be helpful and enable you to see angles that you may have overlooked. I consider it my duty." Gardner, at least, accepts me. Our relationship from the first has been distinguished by its cordiality. This is more than can be said of any of the others and it enables me to forgive him many things—although, you can be sure, not quite enough to do him any good.

"Yeah, I understand that," Gardner says, "but after all, you're just along for the ride, you explained that part already, and if you're just along for the ride, then you've got to give me room and let me do what's best. I know what I'm doing and it's necessary. You've got to have respect for the fact that I know what I'm doing and that I came to it the hard way. After all, I've been chasing them man and boy for ten years and I should know a couple things. Stick with me, and you'll see some angles. Of course, there's nothing personal in this; if you got some other business you want to catch up on—"

"No," I say, "I'll stick around. That's perfectly all right." I have brought him to believe that I am a special projects director for a psychological research firm conducting extraordinary research under government grant and that I have been able, in my technical pursuit, to succeed in the routine transference of my consciousness to other minds. Precisely why such insanity should seem credible to him and why the matter has been so informally granted from the beginning is anyone's guess, surely not mine. It may have to do in part with the fact that Gardner himself works for the government and in that context one can accept the possibility of this agency doing almost anything.

There is another reason of course. Gardner has cheerfully courted insanity for many years and welcomes concrete manifestation of the fact. There is no point in being insane (Gardner cheerfully believes) unless you have something to really show for it and now he most certainly does. Auditory hallucinations. (The racetrack does not count; he sees nothing insane about it.)

"Stick with me, chief, stick with me," Gardner hums, pulling onto an access road and passing several competing cars in a dangerously low arc while he up and down shifts in a rich full clang of gears. "Stick with me, chief, you won't be sorry. No sorrow on the morrow, for Gardner's going to town." He is always this way before he witnesses the first race. Sunken into a gleaming optimism, all possibilities fraught with meaning and spread before him, Gardner succumbs to his more realistic state of mind only when he has actually passed through a series of occurrences which manage to wipe out of mind any recollection of the previous idiocy. This means that there is no possibility, anywhere along the way, of Gardner uniting these separate selves and managing to apologize—to me, to his history, to his girl. I understand that in certain cultures this constitutes a perfect definition of the schizoid condition but I do not have enough to say on this to make myself of much interest.

Gardner, singing, hauls the car past trees and dogs, housewives and children, greenery and bonfires, past an intersection and then into the main parking lot of the racetrack. He pays the attendant three dollars for parking and then, instead of swinging left toward the grandstand lot, turns briskly right, heading toward the preferred. A surge of liberation accompanies this simple act for Gardner has decided to treat himself. He will be a huge winner this afternoon and the extra money will mean nothing. He pays the sullen attendant and puts the car in back of the clubhouse, wedging it in with an evil glint of satisfaction, between two large aircars, leaving small scratches on the left rear door of one. The attendants will be blamed for things like this. He gets out and in a curious, skipping gait (his anticipatory amble) pays his way into the clubhouse and taking the escalator finds himself an excellent seat on the first level, overlooking the finish line. It is the first time he has ever been to the clubhouse.

Gardner is humming. It is a very old popular song about shrimp boats: "Shrimp boats are a-coming, their sails are in sight. Shrimp boats are a-coming, there's dancing tonight." Gardner is hurrying home. He is hurrying, hurrying, hurrying home. Apotheosis approaches. Gardner can see his destiny hovering, singing, in the air.

CHAPTER XVII

Tony looks at the weaponry without opinion or interest. His eyes glaze, his limbs are waxen, his movements stiff. What I have done is effective but I have the feeling that perhaps I have pushed past some unnecessary limits. It is all to be regretted but on the other hand, Tony has served his function and now must do some work.

"The assembling, Tony," I remind him gently. "The fuses. Put those fuses inside."

He rubs his hands, sighs, looks toward a corner of the room from which a roach scuttles in astonishment, stamps out the life of the roach with deliberate flinging ease and then turns back to the grenades. "Fuses," he says. "Where are the fuses?" His hands dangle over them without impulse.

"Get them Tony," And so I assist him. It is not difficult, in this state, to guide his old hands into the appropriate gestures. The weaponry itself is childishly easy; there is nothing to it at all. Hands which have broken a yearling into the gate and which have worked many a frightened gelding in the slop are capable of doing it easily. Slowly, lovingly, with many caresses and blandishments, I guide Tony through the act of assembly, my words of praise like the gentlest of woman's gifts, small kisses on the wounded core of his psyche, my murmurs of encouragement as distant and beautiful to him as the colors of the horses now streaming before him on the backstretch of their delight, moving toward their last home, the glow of the finish wire suspended like a necklace in the dusk.

CHAPTER XVIII

"I can't stand it," Mary says. She is not sure of her whereabouts but she believes that it might be a bar. The bar seems to be empty and this means that she can talk to herself without embarrassment, but on the other hand the hell with it. Who listens? Who cares? Where are the feelings anymore? She is very drunk. "I can't stand it anymore," she says again. "I really can't take this. Who can take it? All of them bastards driving you crazy. I won't live with it. No one should."

The bartender, wiping his hands slowly on a towel, turns toward her menacingly and seems to be on the point of having a dialogue. Hastily I make several clumsy adjustments and he returns to his glasses. On an impulse I force him then to remove an unopened bottle of rye from the cabinet, twist the cap free, and down several ounces in two gulping swallows. He chokes, but then accommodates himself. This along with the adjustments will settle him for the time being.

"No way," she says. "Just no way at all."

This is where I come in. "You don't have to take it, Mary. There is a way out of all this you know."

"Don't have to take it? Way out?" She is really stupefyingly drunk. It has been a slow process of accretion, moving from the second race to here, a process involving easy transitions from beer to rye to mixed drinks. She shakes her head uneasily, feeling that it is somehow disengaged from and yet menacingly near her body. Small implosions rock her joints; she shifts on the stool. At the fringes of her consciousness death peeps out to cast a hopefully quizzical look but then retreats discouraged. "What's that? Way out? Speak sense to me now, will you? Can barely hear a thing with all that buzzing. Come on lad, speak up, speak up. You have something to say? Then just say it!"

"You can be free, Mary," I point out. "You don't have to put up with this again. No more longshots, no more blind switches, no more bastard jockeys, no more crooked trainers. No more hot horses, no more tiring in the stretch, no more bearing out. Think of it! None of this, none of any of it, just a straight ride into peace and release."

"Well then, what is it? Come on; I'm listening. Don't tell me about that bastard, Julian. I won't even hear that bastard's name mentioned to me again. Not ever. He doesn't matter."

"It has nothing to do with Julian. Listen, Mary; it's a way out of Julian too. It's a way out of everything and it's so easy. All you have to do is to see it."

"All right, then," she says, gesturing with her left hand. She knocks over the glass of liquor which runs unheeded down the bar. The bartender regards this with some interest but then decides to make nothing of it. "The hell with it. I'm listening. What do I have to lose? What do I care anymore? I know that I lost my mind with all my luck."

"You can break free, Mary. You can have your life the way you always wanted it to be and the answer was in front of you all the time. All you had to do was to look."

(It is truly shameful that I must lead the poor, drunken subject on in this fashion. One would hope for somewhat less dissimulation by this time. But it is necessary. Only by building the requisite sense of attention can I be sure that she will pay heed when the time for revelation comes. The details are quite simple but they must be explicit—and then too she is, as I have already said, quite drunk and I am not really responsible for that part of it. By proxy as well—all right, I shall admit it—I am rather drunk myself; it is difficult to maintain contact with a mind in this condition without feeling the dismal undertow.)

"I'm looking," she says. "I'm looking now, damn you."

"It's just a question of bringing it down," I say. "Making sure that if you can't beat it then no one can. And there's nothing to that because it's been sitting on disaster for two hundred years."

Then I talk to her explicitly, persuasively, subvocally, patiently, documenting all of my observations. She listens with swollen eyelids, an open-mouth. Once or twice she moves to protest weakly but I quickly dispose of that by pointing out that anyone in her position would be glad to do what she is in a position to do and would consider it an honor. Besides, she has no choice. Mary nods and agrees. She removes, at length, the used *Lawton* from her handbag, and ponders it for a while, the names of the horses weaving mysteriously in and out of her consciousness, names of Preferred and Most Preferred seeming to obliterate the necessity for further thought. "And they both run out," she says. "Both of the sons of bitches run out. That goes to show you about Lawton, doesn't it? He doesn't know what the hell he's doing."

"No," I say, "he does not."

"I don't even think he exists. I figured that out today. It's a hoax, the whole thing. There's no Clocker Lawton. It's all made up."

"He exists," I say. "I can assure you of that."

"I ain't never seen him and he ain't never done me no good so there can't be none. He's just a bunch of guys in a back room somewhere knocking out hot tips. He don't exist."

"But he does. He does."

"Well he doesn't know what the hell he's doing even if he does exist."

"That's right," I say with some passion. "Yes, yes, that part of it is a fact. None of them know what they're doing. They stumble through their lives with the schizoid glare of maniacs. They enact their lives in the way that inferior jockeys try to survive in tight quarters, holding on, just holding on and creating for themselves the illusion of alternative, dreaming as all the holes close in front of them, seeing their history collide and recede in the background, staggering through an endless stretch with dirt and film kicked back at them, the wretched fog of the flats filling their nostrils with a scent that they must call ambrosia. That's how they live their lives, do you know that, Mary?"

"I don't know what you're talking about. You talk too much for me."

"Then concentrate."

"What does that mean?"

"The stupidity, the calumny, the sheer waste of it," I point out, somehow caught by my rhetoric and unable to stop, but for all the good that it is doing I might as well be the liquor glass itself. This would have more effect. Still, I am entitled to some expression of my views; I have taken far too much of this and for what end? How much can I take? I have feelings too, gentlemen. I suffer, I react. I am not your run of the mill agent. For all of this time I have kept my views tightly wrapped within, scuttling in the bottle of self, observing everything, questioning nothing, performing the slow, slick moves of manipulation, retracting that cold and bold edge of myself from event because only in that way were it possible to achieve any kind of reason. But I am entitled to better than this. How far are *my* limits, goddamn it?

"If they could only understand the waste, Mary," I says, "it might be better because then they could face the sheer bankruptcy of their lives and do away with themselves but they cannot. Oh no, that is not for them! Instead, they interpret the waste as accomplishment, the loss as annealment, the denial as grace, the suffering as passage, the corruption as change, the wickedness as transition, and immersed in this sea of rationalization they traverse slowly and awkwardly to a kind of doom which would absorb them totally were it not that they can supersede even doom having found so well other ways of doing past themselves. Nothing extrinsic to these people. They make their own hell."

"You talk like some kind of a conservative."

"I don't think labels are the point, Mary, that's too easy."

"Well, you got to have sympathy. Whatever it is you're saying, anyway, you got to try to have some feeling. Horseplaying is a very tough racket, you know. It's all rigged against you from the beginning and you get nervous."

"It's more than the horseplaying," I say, "it's everything," but then I feel a kind of twinge, it is infuriation passing by because the fact is that she is right in more ways than she can possibly guess and I add, "Well, you can beat it if you only showed any patience but they don't have it," and try to drop the issue. I have gone too far, for once. Even I can see that.

Mary, however, is on top of me and asks, "How can you beat it? You have a system? Tell me how do you get around it?" It is the first time she has talked to me with any interest, let alone passion and although most of this can be ascribed to liquor and despair. I find myself pleased enough to say, "There's a very simple, basic method Mary but it's too late for it to do you any good now. The money's all gone."

"Yes," she says, "yes, yes, but just tell me, just so that I know I knew it. I have to know."

What the hell. I give the bartender a cautionary look and then a precautionary jab in the medulla oblongata just to make very sure that he is out of commission. "Well, if you must know, you have to play favorites to *place only;* you consider only favorites and eliminate those that failed to finish first or second in their last races and that system will show you a twelve percent profit over the long haul with no other adjustments necessary. If you tinker around and put in a distance condition it goes up to fifty percent but you get less action of course."

"Favorites," she says with some contempt. "Favorites? Oh hell."

"It isn't spectacular, Mary. The prices are terrible as a matter of fact, averaging only slightly over $2.80 but it's the only foolproof system there is and it's tight."

"Favorites," she says, shaking her head and nearly falling off the stool, "Why I wouldna bet that way even if I had knew it. What kind of a cheap hustle is that? That's no way to beat the track. It's no fun! It's just like investment or something."

(I sigh. They are really all the same at bedrock, Simmons has the same difficulty, so does Gardner, they have contempt for small winning prices because they believe them to constitute some kind of a judgment of cowardice.) "Well, it's too late anyway," I say, "so forget it. Anyway, if you had used the system and become a very rich old lady you wouldn't be having nearly half so much fun."

I proceed to remind her of what she must do. She is extremely drunk and beginning to belch back liquor now, wavering on the very edge of sickness, and I must talk very slowly, calmly, expansively indeed, but after a fashion my words permeate and I know that she will be all right. Her role, in any event, is a relatively minor one, peripheral to the basic adjustments to be made by the others, and I know that in the crux she can be counted upon. When, I am quite sure that everything is in order, I allow her to pass out over the bar, cradling her old head in her thin hands, sighing, sobbing, and smiling wearily as slumber licks at her.

The bartender grunts and collapses, afflicted with another kind of somnolence. I leave this *ménage à deux* with some regret but move to scenes less pastoral instead as things begin to move, lurching toward a definite conclusion. Only a little bit more now. Certainly, I can hold on.

CHAPTER XIX

Gardner stands by the clubhouse rail with two hundred dollars' worth of win tickets on Make Peace in his shirt pocket. His good intentions to the contrary, he has found it impossible to remain in the clubhouse to watch the race. Too much is invested, his confidence to the contrary. He stands by the rail now instead, beating his thin fists on steel and reciting small cheerful rhymes to himself composed of popular song and scatology: moon and June, spit and bit, whip and shit. Gardner mumbles and then checks the odds on the board again: Make Peace is holding steady at a little over 40–1. Eight thousand dollars for Gardner if he wins. Capital enough to marry Virginia and abandon the races, he decides. He begins to sing again, more sentimentally this time, trying to dredge up dim memoirs of old handicapping hints or special angles to compliment the songs but finds that his mind has somehow been drained of pedantry at this moment. It is inhabited only by winding snatches of lyric and a kind of empty anticipation.

The horses move by in a stiff gallop, one by one, and Gardner and the jockey on Make Peace exchange what Gardner hopes is a look of true understanding and level communion. "C'mon, Jean," Gardner says in what he had intended to be a brightly encouraging tone but the words come out in a dull, stentorian rasp, which frightens him, and he hawks out phlegm in a series of choking sounds, wondering whether he may have a fatal chest disease. "Boot 'em in, Jean," he says with somewhat more volume, and the Frenchman casts back one quick glance over his shoulder and then whips the horse out of sight. Cries from the clubhouse, as Jean knows, are always to be more heeded than the grandstand grunting and Jean seems to respond, his buttocks move far up on the horse and he briskly bounces a couple of times, making Gardner think of intercourse and entrance. (This is his terrible problem: while engaging in sex he thinks of horses and while playing horses he is apt, at the oddest moments, to be seized by lust.)

Gardner searches for more rhymes, finds that he has nothing left to sing and quiets. He fumbles the tickets and feels them seem to somehow bulge and enlarge as the winking tote now cheerfully whispers to him of eight thousand dollars. Eight thousand dollars. *"Eight thousand dollars!*" Gardner says. "It's an angle!" and reminds himself to definitely give the payoff clerk a hundred or so when he collects. It is the least gesture a gracious winner could make for an employee.

It is a splendid, chastening scene, this, and one which I could observe without boredom for hours and hours but there is no time to enjoy it. Of them all Gardner is the only one who truly interests me, who I inhabit comfortably, and whose every action I find meaningful. As always, one remembers that business is, after all, business, and the controlling sense of mission must decide. "Gardner," I say easily from the background, then strolling into the forefront of his consciousness as I continue, "Gardner, you do understand that you don't want to win this bet, don't you? That has got to be made perfectly clear."

He jumps. He has not been expecting me. Usually we do not converse at the races themselves, settling instead for prognostications and postmortems. "Huh?" he says. "What's that? I thought you had gone. What do you want now? I can't talk; I'm really kind of involved now. Why, don't you come back after the race and we'll talk then? That would be the right instance; really, I'm just kind of tied up now and I think—"

"No time," I say, and then add rather unkindly, "bullshit. Gardner, I must make it perfectly apparent to you that winning this race could only constitute an absolute disaster. Fortunately you have no chance and we can expect that in terms of that loss, things will take a somewhat inevitable course. But before all of this is done you must understand that you truly can't afford to win. You don't really want to win in the first place you see, and in the second place, winning would destroy you—absolutely destroy you! Luckily for you, you subconsciously apprehend most of this already and that is why you're such a successfully inept horseplayer. But we can't leave all of this to the subconscious, Gardner, we have to get at least into the preconscious levels of inference, motivations, the blending of will and activity, this is the least that can be asked of you."

"Come on," he says. "Get out. Out! Not now. Sooner. We'll talk about it later. Later, I told you." He waves a hand in front of his eyes, having localized me apparently toward the prefrontal lobes of his brain. His tone has become harsh and strident and that casual amiability which has distinguished almost all of our dialogues until now has departed.

"Soon enough," I say. "First, however, a couple of things must be made understood, Gardner. You see, if you won this race and collected eight thousand dollars you would no longer have any excuses against abandoning the track and marrying Virginia. And the painful fact is that you don't really want to do either, Gardner. Let's have it out: you're a suppressed homosexual, your relationship with this girl comes only out of a sense of justification and you wouldn't know what to do in a productive situation if you fell into one. Winning eight thousand dollars just to face this kind of stuff isn't worth it, Gardner. Cheaper to drop the whole matter, not that we can anymore now."

"Listen to me you evil son of a bitch, I don't know what—"

"Oh come on, Gardner," I say wearily, "I've really been very patient and kind throughout this affair and my patience has had severe strains recently. It's just about gone, as a matter of fact. I want to break this to you gently and help you prepare yourself for certain eventualities but if you want to get nasty I have that capacity too. You've misread me and my motives from the start Gardner. You thought I was a whimsy or projection. I'm not you know. I'm quite something else."

I show him what else I am. For the first time with any of them, I remove all barriers, all controls, and let myself be looked upon. This would destroy Mary or Simmons or Tony, but Gardner is of stronger stock and has a trace of intelligence and can handle this although barely. I let him look at me in full for some five or ten seconds, turning in profile so that he can see a suggestion of the edges, then wheel back to full confrontation. I show him other things. I show him what Virginia is and what she means to him. I show him what he has really been doing when he thinks he has been copulating with her, I show him the basic significance of the horses. The horses are demonstrated to him in terms of their essential needs and purposes instead of those kindly rationalizations with which Gardner has spaced out his afternoons at the track. I show him their pain, their anger, their fury and that for which they are only a metaphor.

It is this, not surprisingly, which proves to be the most shattering part of it. Gardner covers his face with his hands. "Please," he says, "please don't do it. Please stop. Please!" The covering action means nothing of course (the pictures being internal) but I take pity on him, not for the first time, and clamp down the shield.

Gardner stands by the rail gasping, retching, inhaling choking mouthfuls of air which seem to pollute his lungs and cause his consciousness to balk. "Oh God," he says. "Oh God."

"I'm really quite sorry, Gardner," I say, "but I can't be taken for granted. There are certain things going on here which are too important to be mishandled. The stakes, as you might say, are a bit too large. I wish we had the time to let you win or lose the race and work through to your own conclusions, but this might take forty or fifty years and that kind of time simply isn't available. I've got too much invested in you now though to abandon this so we'll just have to do the best we can with what we've got. The best we can with what we've got," I repeat, and cast an eye down the backstretch. "Well, Gardner," I say, "it is now post time. You might as well watch the race. Go *on*, Gardner, watch the race. I don't intend to do anything more just now so enjoy yourself."

He looks toward the backstretch numbly. In this instant of extremity he seems not to care or perhaps I am missing certain points. I do not know. Clearly, he does not eye the tote board, if he did he might note with interest that the unfortunate Make Peace holds steady at 40–1, making the eight thousand dollars still visible but Gardner seems to have lost at least temporary interest in the race. His mouth sags, he tries to form words but cannot. His eyes blink and water and he rubs them. (I did not mean to have quite this kind of effect upon him but, gentlemen, what else could I do? Time is running short. Short!)

The horses come out of the starting gate in a kind of suspension, hung in the air in slow frieze and Make Peace dodges into the middle of the pack. (How bored one could become with writing the same race several times! but it is a fascinating race and, like the Scriptures, the riches are endless.) "He's rating him," Gardner might comment in other instances but at the moment Gardner is saying nothing. I say nothing as well; races are interesting and always pleasant to watch. Along the backstretch, Make Peace can be seen to slowly poke his way to fifth or sixth coming slowly clear toward the middle and Jean rises in the stirrups with Gallic abandon, whip and flails at him. The horse seems to lose its action for a moment and then recovers, swings wide, comes behind a horse making a charge and in tandem they close on the leaders. Coming into the stretch he is third, beaten three or four lengths and moving with some vigor. "Come on, Make Peace!" I shout (the first time I have ever cheered a horse but then I have found it unnecessary until now, my patrons having taken care of all that for me), "whip and drive, whip and drive!" genuinely caught up in this Make Peace is not to fulfill his potential today; something seems to happen to his rear action (perhaps an errant dart of poison which I have thrown because, regardless of my emotions, he must lose this race) and the horse slips back on the track, throws it in without ceremony and staggers home third. The jockey, shaking his head, eases him under the wire. A peculiar look of frenzy haunting his enlarged eyes as he ducks in toward the rail and then up the clubhouse turn, the horse looks entrapped but this is as nothing to the rider who lets out a stream of curses which Gardner imagines he can hear. Perhaps he has taken the race personally. Perhaps Jean even thought that he had a chance to win. Who knows? Who cares?

Gardner turns slowly from the rail. He is changed. Gardner transmogrified looks toward the upper grandstand with sinking eyes. He still bears enough resemblance to the Gardner I have known to be, however, rather recognizable. "Two hundred," he whispers.

I say, "Believe me, it was really for the best, Gardner, completely for the best … you don't even know how lucky you are."

"Two hundred dollars," he says.

"You couldn't win," I say cheerfully enough. "Face it Gardner, you never really wanted this girl anyway. It was always something else you saw when you entered her, something terrible and bright at the far rim. Why do you think you were thinking of horses and odds and tote boards and spots when you were screwing? Do you really think that it was simple obsession? Come on, Gardner, you're a college graduate. What else was it, what were you touching?"

He raises a waxen hand to pick hair away from his forehead and says, "I don't know. I just don't know. I can't understand. Why did you do this to me? Why did you have to hurt me so?"

"Oh come on, Gardner," I say, "you're taking the whole thing personally, as if all of these events trigger in on you when they actually only concern you peripherally. That's the end of the horses now and you're fine, just fine, never better and everything left to work. Come on; you've got five dollars left to go home with and plenty of gas in the car so let's just go out to the parking lot and have a long talk. We can sit in the car and do it right there. I have any number of interesting things to tell you and if we do it now we can have it all behind us."

"Two hundred dollars," he marvels. "Two hundred dollars."

"It's cheap at the price and besides, Gardner, if you had won it only would have made things more difficult."

"You don't understand. You just couldn't understand. The *pain* …"

"Think of the universals."

"You stiffed the horse," he says, "that's what you did. Now I understand everything. You must have stiffed my horse."

"Oh come on," I say, "don't be ridiculous; do you really think that if I were capable of stiffing horses, Gardner, I'd take the time and trouble to deal with *you?* I'd have the whole thing all wrapped up by now."

This out and out lie is really disgraceful but procedure allows ethics to be defined as the situation warrants and it apparently gives Gardner some comfort. In a childlike and touching gesture, he sticks his thumb into his mouth for an instant, biting on it, and then makes his exit from the clubhouse, clutching the escalator handle as if it were handlebars. We ride down and on the way I begin to talk; calmly and soothingly, patiently and caressingly, I acquaint Gardner with the facts of the issue and by the time we have reached his car he is already on the verge of an accommodation. It is a painful thing to see how easily I have destroyed him but Gardner was the most submissive of them all. There has been no question of resistance. He is too lost, and now even the horses have been taken from him.

CHAPTER XX

Simmons, seeking extinction, has gone to a bar. (It is one in the same neighborhood as that which Mary tenanted some hours earlier.) Because his funds are limited, however, because he cannot in any way understand the mechanics of serious drinking, he has been sipping only rye and ginger ale slowly for the last several hours and now finds himself with a third in front of him, three dollars and change in his wallet, and a timorous understanding of the fact that he has not quite obtained what he has sought. With a cry of sheer self-loathing he opens the *Telegraph* again to the entries for the Belmont and looks at them without understanding. There are eight horses entered for the classic and he knows as surely as he has ever known anything in his life that one of them must win and that he is looking at the name of the winner right now, but he cannot, for the life of him, allow this insight to lift him the necessary step further into selection. It is this peculiar frustration of horseracing more than any other single factor which has so inflamed Simmons: the fact that the goddamned winning horse is always *right there* as ubiquitous as the losers and yet time and again the names of the losers seem to overwhelm, tantalize Simmons irresistibly and he has only, in retrospect, been able to deduce the offering of possibility. There has, after all, been so little to separate him from a fortune: a flicker of eyeball, a trembling motion of the index finger, but it is enough to make a man cry. He could be Simmons in a penthouse now, or at least a townhouse, getting laid or otherwise disporting himself, and instead he is drinking rye and ginger ale in a goddamned stinking little bar in Flushing and has absolutely no idea of where he is going or, for that matter, of how he has reached here. Simmons would weep for himself if he were capable of self-dramatization. Unhappily, he even lacks that. He does not consider himself truly important anymore. Bitter, bitter: it is really all too much.

"Sons of bitches," he says. This attracts no notice. Right and left, places are being occupied by men very similar to Simmons who are also looking at their copies of the *Telegraph* in hopelessness and rage, shaking their heads. The bartender (a wonderfully jolly fellow with whom I dare not tamper; a mask so splendid should not be altered) looks at Simmons for a moment, winks at him, rubs a cloth over the counter and says something inaudible. "Sons of bitches," Simmons murmurs and returns to the form. (It is painful for me to note that once again he is becoming interested in the names of all the wrong horses. In extremity, he becomes even more fully himself. Clearly, I have done him a favor.

This man has no future.)

"Hey pal, you're crowding me," the man on his left says and pokes Simmons violently in the elbow before he returns to the newspaper. "No goddamned manners these bastards," the man adds and it is this, possibly, which sets off Simmons. Certainly, nothing else which has recently happened could account for the explosion which now ensues.

Simmons mutated! Simmons reborn! Simmons raised to new levels of rhetoric and action! Simmons raised from the cocoon and deposited breathing and wild upon the brow of the world! It is surely enough to move even a less reflective (or reflexive) creature than myself. It is astonishing. Simmons falls upon the man on his left like a horse devouring oats and before the astounded bartender or other customers can intervene, he has made several attempts to strangle him.

Action! Pounding! Force! The mortification of the flesh! (Surely and as you can see, it defies my simple narrative powers to recount what is going on at this moment; I have never been good at the rather distasteful physical scenes into which these people often move themselves. Enough, I will invoke transitions.) The victim, after a few, stunned instants, comes on strongly in the stretch, launching a rally of some force and dimension and begins to turn upon Simmons several skillful hooks and twists which come with stunning force into his pallid features and deposit him, in very little time, upon the floor of the bar, on which he begins to thrash and mutter. The victim, as if totally uninterested now that this minor source of friction has been removed (Even casual horseplayers have learned to function in this way; there are nine races a day, a thousand in a season. How much memory can one have?) shrugs and returns to his paper, mumbling about lunatics. Simmons is escorted to his feet by several men and hurled from the door with rapidity and some ease. He lands on the pavement on all fours, shaking his head. After a moment, his *Telegraph*, still folded precisely to the Belmont entries, joins him. He clutches the paper to his chest and staggers to his feet. His eyes glint madly. His mouth heaves. His hands tremble. Simmons has now hit what could be called the bottom of the ladder or possibly its apogee, the end of the rope or the top of the mountain.

Chest heaving, mouth salivating, limbs trembling, heart palpitating, Simmons rears back toward the bar, puts his head into the door and screams. "You sons of bitches I'll get you for this!" and then makes a hasty, scuttling exit. He has got the customers all mixed up with trainers. "I'll get you, I'll get you!" he shrieks and breaks into full storming trot, moving down pastoral Queens Boulevard in the borough of Queens, New York, eyes fixed and staring, feet pattering, wind gasping.

"I'll get them," he says, "I'll get all of them. All of those thieving bastards." He stops suddenly, poises the *Telegraph* in his hand and then throws it with enormous force toward a random window. It breaks through the plate glass of a florist shop in a shattering burst and Simmons finds himself surmounted by gasping cackles as he looks at the ruin: the *Telegraph* has landed in a flower pot and is now surrounded by sprigs and sprigs of gardenias which have fallen to circle and seem to enshrine the newspaper with the delicacy and finality of an artifact. This is how, Simmons thinks, the newspaper might look if centuries later, alien beings came to Earth and began to order the ruins: the *Telegraph* would be granted a spot of honor by these ignorant invaders who would probably devote whole volumes to speculation on its origin and purposes.

(Simmons is an idiot. Any self-respecting member of that which his xenophobia terms aliens would deduce instantly what the newspaper had in mind and would only feel pity for a race still dependent upon numerology of this sort. It should have been pointed out much earlier that long long ago, before Headquarters itself, to say nothing of the Fellowhood, evolved, we had had something roughly similar to horseracing—and took care of it in the Fires. It is a transitional point on the way to a greater maturity until it begins to occupy the place in racial history which it does here. Then, somewhat stronger action is demanded.)

"Look at that," Simmons says. "It serves them right." He is not exactly sure who the ones served right are but one can have some sympathy for the point of view. I understand this. Then sirens go off, whistles begin to sound, an alarm clangs with rage and fury and Simmons breaks his posture and begins to scuttle full tilt toward the subway. "The hell with them," he says, "I've had it. I've got a couple of dollars and I'll make a new start in life. I don't give a shit who wins the Belmont," by which he means only that he does not care about his inability to deduce the race but this is close enough. Simmons and I have voyaged far and wide together and finally we have come to a lovely intersection.

I say, "Do I hear you right, Simmons? Do I hear you correctly? Do you really want to bring the whole thing down?"

Hardly breaking stride he says puffing, "You again?"

"Who else? Of course it's me, Simmons, did you expect maybe Willie Carbellini?" (This is an old and cheap racetrack joke but even at this moment of tension I believe I am entitled. For one thing I am bouncing around in him like a madman and for another the trap of Simmons is at last closing.)

"Yeah," he says, running, "I'd like to get rid of the whole damned thing, no question about it. It's lousy and it stinks and it wrecks all the households and starves children and it drives guys crazy. It's poison, that's what it is, but they got a whole new generation coming in there every week or so and thus it won't ever end. Sure I'd like to reunite the families and save the little children, besides that, I think that *Clocker Lawton* is a phony. There's no Clocker Lawton, no such person."

"You can, Simmons," I say. "You can end it. The whole thing can end, and the means are within your hands." An edge of triumph blares into my voice.

Scuttling upstairs meanwhile into an elevated subway, flinging coins into the cupped hands of an attendant as he bypasses the gate, Simmons throws himself into an about-to-be-departed train just as the doors slam and with no loss of breath or continuity he says, "Tell me how, that's all. I'm listening. I don't care if I'm crazy or not, you just tell me some way that I can take care of this thing, get rid of it and I *will* because I can't stand it anymore! It's too evil and besides, you just can't work out a system that will stand up. It's too unpredictable."

"All right then," I say, somewhat moved by this new reformer's zeal which, as is always the case with people of Simmons's unsuccessful stripe, comes to the fore only when they feel in very bad need of reform themselves. "It's very simple, there really isn't anything to it at all. All you have to do is to go right to the center of it and undercut everything."

"You ain't telling me nothing," he says, rocking on the seat. "I mean, I don't get the words here."

"Don't worry about the words." I begin to subvocalize. I paint him pictures, provide him with a forest of images, a nest of metaphor from which easily spring thickets of speculation, the thickets in turn bear blossoms and I pick and cull these for him, talking merrily all the while. His mouth opens and he reacts with wonder. Two old women eye him strangely, a young girl out on her first date looks at him and begins to giggle. Simmons is oblivious. He is fascinated. He hears (or sees) me out, a process that takes only a couple of moments but which for him, subjectively goes on for quite a long time.

"Well I'll be damned," he finally says. "You mean, that's all there is to it?"

"That's all," I say. "Of course there's a question of ethos, and so on and so forth but that comes after the fact. The basic process is pretty much as easy as that."

"Why that's nothing! That's the simplest thing I've ever seen. You mean that that was all there was to it all the time? That all I had to do was that and it would have been over?"

"Exactly."

"That all of this is going on, all this suffering and crud and so forth and it really comes down to that? So simple a thing? Well I'll be damned," Simmons says, and crosses his hands, looks down meditatively at the floor. "It don't figure," he says after a pause. "It's *too* simple."

"What's that?"

"I said, it's too simple. If it was that simple, somebody would have done it a long time ago, you know? It wouldn't have waited for me. It all would have happened already."

"No it couldn't," I say. "Let's consider that." I draw him another portfolio. This is a handi-pack, so to speak, and takes much less time.

His eyes widen and then glaze and finally narrow. "How about that?" he says. "How about that? That explains what you're doing here. Ain't that something? And you picked me. It's kind of an honor, I'll say that. That I would be selected and everything."

"You and a couple of others," I say. I beam under his praise. It has been so long since I have heard a kind word. Of course I have taken him far more greatly into my confidence than any of the others and perhaps more than I should have but then, I am entitled to certain prerogatives, am I not, gentlemen? There are limits to the abuse and rigor of any job. Then too, I have a right to establish an identity. "I must admit that you're my favorite, however," I add. "Of all of them. You have the most sensitivity and your mind seems to be the most—uh—receptive to what I'm doing."

"You don't say. You don't say, really? And you mean that something as simple as that would have brought it down all the time? As simple as that? It's the damnedest thing. When do I get to meet those others?"

"I'm going to take you to Tony right now. He and you will be working together as partners. The others will be at the edges."

"Tony's the trainer, right?"

"Right. He trains horses at Aqueduct."

"That wouldn't be Tony Miller, would it?"

"That's who it is."

"Well, I'll be damned. That's something!"

"My pleasure," I say. "I told you, I work efficiently. I take only the best people."

"Be damned. Son of a bitch," Simmons says quite loudly. The girl summons her date to another seat while giving him a look of terror. The two old women, on the other hand, eye him with modest smiles and begin to pat one another consolingly. Perhaps they think that Simmons is announcing himself. I regard the mixed reactions with some interest; it is so strikingly close to what I have myself contemplated. The girl begins to whisper intensely to her date and he shrugs, looks toward the ceiling of the car. One of the old women makes a circling gesture around her head which might have driven Simmons, even an hour ago, into murderous rage but which now escapes him completely. "Son of a bitch," he says somewhat more quietly. "Anthony Miller, the trainer. You mean, I'm finally going to meet that character. Isn't that a killer? You know how much money I've lost on that bastard in the past couple months? I been following him all along like he was related."

"You've lost eighty-six dollars and twenty cents on him."

Simmons rolls his eyes inward in astonishment. "Yeah, something like that. I never added it all up. You mean you know all that kind of stuff too? Everything I lost and all that?"

"Of course I do," I say. "Among other things, I'm a documentarian. It's a requirement of the job."

"How much have I lost since I got started back in this game?"

"You don't really want to know."

"Sure I do. Sure I do."

"Sixteen hundred and eighty dollars plus expenses," I say.

He shakes his head and rubs his hands reflexively. "Oh boy," Simmons says. "I knew it was something like that but that? Wow! No, it's no good. I got to get out of this game somehow. You're right. It gotta go sooner or later and maybe sooner. Why did I ever get back into it in the first place? I thought I learned my lesson five years ago for good."

"Do you want the answer? Or are you just making conversation?"

"Do you have the answer?"

"Of course I have the answer. I have the answers to everything. Simmons. There isn't a thing your miserable little operation holds down here that I don't understand completely. You can't slip a thing past me." (I seem to be slightly inebriate again. Perhaps it is merely the effects of being so close to two stinking drunks within a couple of hours. Although I am not at all susceptible to liquor it is possible that its emanations have an effect not suggested in the manuals. For whatever reason, it occurs to me, that I am beginning to get fed up with Simmons. He is all right up to a point but I can see why he has been forced into largely solitary activities.)

"Oh, you don't have to call it miserable," he is saying, "I mean, it's the only planet we got. You can understand that. Yeah, tell me. Why did I get back in this game in the first place? Don't tell me about coming in to make a fast buck, I know that part already. What's the other part? Is there another part?"

The train yanks itself into a station and groans open, four forms tumbling out. They flee into the night or maybe it is only another car. The doors close again and we are alone except for the hiss and clutter of the fans which, of course, provide a ruminative background for our discussion. "Or is there another reason?" Simmons repeats, taking my silence for an unwillingness to speak when it is only gratitude because now the final hurdles have been leapt over with the casual grace of the good steeplechase horses. He has taken on the denouement himself.

"Surely there is," I say. "In fact it's the only reason; it's the basic form which all the other factors emerge. You came back to it, Simmons, to suffer, but your suffering had to be of a very particular nature. It had to be self-enclosed, you see. The ordinary kind of suffering you could find anywhere, it tenanted all the spaces of your life, but the thing was that it was diffused, it was uncontained, it spilled out everywhere, and that part was no good because the thing about most suffering that is unstructured, and, clearly to be ascribed, is that it is so pointless. The nature of you people is to put up with anything, the worst horrors, as long as you could be assured that there is a meaning to it. But you couldn't find the meaning to your suffering, so what you gravitated toward was horseracing which gave you, at the least, a kind of self-containment. It gave you perspective. The rationalizations you couldn't find outside you could find inside. It isn't very nice to hit you so hard with all of this but you did ask for the truth you know and you might as well be a man and take it. Grow up, Simmons. It was a bad move leaving your wife I should point out. That really made no sense at all. She was cut out of the same material that you were. You could have had many years of contentedly playing the horses and losing together if you had only been willing to share your insights. But you thought that cutting her out of that part of your life guaranteed you importance. Well, that's your asininity Simmons. One thing is clear and that is you cannot, as you have said, possibly win them all."

He shakes his head, poising on the seat and says, "It wasn't that way. I mean, it wasn't that way at all. I mean, I didn't come to suffer. The suffering came afterward because I was losing. I only wanted to win. I thought that you could win at the game and if you only could then—"

"Oh come on now," I say, my patience quite destroyed by this nonsense. "I have no respect at all for the way you're talking now. If you cannot assess the nature and value of your more unspeakable drives well then so be it, but at least be realistic. You're getting exactly what you came for Simmons. This is what you wanted all the time. You wouldn't know what to do otherwise."

Simmons sighs, purses his lips, shifts again on the seat and stares out the blank, dusty counterpane into the night. There seems to be an impression of lights in the distance or perhaps it is only another train passing and carefully he moistens an index finger, wipes it across the pane until a small spot clears and then looks intently through it. Forms seems to be struggling on the tracks, branches wave. The train hoots and plunges underground. "You don't understand," he says, "it wasn't like that at all. It was something else too, another part ... but essentially you're right."

"Of course I'm right. I'm always right."

"I mean, it's too rotten. The whole thing, the corruption. It's got to come down, somehow, you're right about that."

"Of course it's got to come down. That's why you're all in this in the first place, to make it come down. But try a little realism, Simmons, won't you? That's all I can ask. Some willingness to come to terms. That's the least that can be demanded of a man in your situation."

Simmons puts his hands on his knees heavily. He stands, wanders toward the door, leans against it. The next stop is the one that I have instructed for exit, as always he tries to be a little ahead of the game.

"You really know everything," he says. "I mean, I don't even dispute that. I see that you're right. I know that you see more than we ever can about every single thing and that you got to have the truth and we be wrong—but there is this one thing you don't understand, that's all. I swear it. I mean I know I went into it probably to suffer if that's what you say and I wanted to be unhappy and look for answers and all like that but there was something else too. Can't you try to see that?"

"All right," I say. "I'll try." I am ever willing to expand my notes, my research, my point of view. My omnipotence is only relative; there are some things which I can never know. "What was it then? Tell me if you want."

"Oh," Simmons says with a sigh as the train comes into the station, "it was just so beautiful. It was just such a beautiful thing, that's all. Can't you follow that?" He steps outside. "It was just the most beautiful thing," he says and then he goes into the night, shaking his head and clutching his eyes. Perhaps it is an emotional seizure of some kind although it might only be the dust. I follow at a respectful distance.

No less than he, I can understand the problems of emotional affectation and what it can do to all kinds of beings. Is not my own life and progress testament to the fact?

"It was just so *beautiful*," Simmons says.

CHAPTER XXI

In Tony's room, Mary and he assemble the weaponry. They work with much effort, little conversation. I direct them idly from time to time, making sure that they comply with the basic nature of the instructions. Mary sticks her tongue between her teeth, tears apart metal, inserts wiring, closes things and passes on the materials to Tony who carefully feeds them through a large hole. The assembled materials are then put to one side and more are taken. Thirty completed bombs lie in one corner of the room. Ten more need to be assembled.

Mary is confused. She is not quite sure where she is, or precisely how she has gotten here, or what the point of it all is. (It has been necessary for me to use forceful and abrupt action to guide her to these rooms, on her own she might have lain in the bar for hours and hours but time is now running short and I have thus been compelled to intervene dramatically. This will damage Mary as it has already damaged Tony but it hardly matters.) Nevertheless, she works with some efficiency. From time to time they mumble at one another, most of their comments having to do with horses. I allow this since it cheers them on in their work. At some ease I lean in a corner and watch them. The concentration! The scuttling! It all bears a strange and amusing resemblance to the gestures of horseplayers as they drink with one another before making their bets on the next race. The consequences are similar.

"Don't bet fillies," Mary says. "Never bet fillies against males and lay off the fillies in the girl races. They go into heat and like that and you can never know what's going to happen."

"An angle," Tony offers. "You got to find yourself an angle. Like every now and then the racing secretary will write a race that's just right for your horse and you know that he's had you in mind when he's done it but you can't ever let him know that you know because then it gets into collusion and everything. You got to watch out for those kind of races. The best way to get him to write one for you is to run and run and run your stock, even if it's all broken down, just so that the races can fill and the suckers feel that they got lots of bets, but how can you do that if some of your stock can't even take a crap in the mornings? All these horses are broken down. And then those big owners and trainers, they get all the breaks from the office whether they run their horses or not. Class. All they want to do is to go to the class. It's disgusting. If it weren't for guys like me there wouldn't be such a thing as racing but they'll spit on you each and every time."

"You got to watch routers," Mary warns, carefully inserting some dynamite into a tube (very carefully indeed), "when they get dropped down into the sprint races. The thing is that they almost never win, but the next time they go back to a route they lower the boom. Of course it isn't always that way. Sometimes it's even the reverse."

"You try to look for a spot," Tony says, "but you finally find a claiming race, say, your horse might take and there are three or four other bastards looking out at the same spot so nothing's sure. And then if the horse is worth anything at all, they're just as likely as not to claim it away from you. What you got to do is to run a horse over his head or at the wrong distance for so long that he looks terrible and then kind of *sneak* him in somewhere. Usually you got to ship them out. But how does that pay? Then they lose their form in the vans." He taps some armaments together, whispers about vans, adds armament to the pile.

"Now a real good overlay, the kind of thing I like," Mary says, "is a horse that's been shipped in from some other track where it's done good and they slot it in a claiming level a couple of thousand higher and give it the same jockey from the old track. That's an angle. It's almost a sure thing. Of course it never happens."

"Now all your goddamned truckers are thieves anyway. They don't take care of the horses. And I know what some of the grooms do in those vans on the trips. I won't even talk about that stuff. You see, the fucking grooms got angles too. All of them bastards drink with each other every night and practice ways to stiff their horses for the other guy. Maybe we should of got them some goddamned pension plan, then they would take a little interest."

"And when a jockey pulls a horse in the stretch so instead of finishing fifth he's last, that means they're setting him up for another day. They don't like to whip horses that got a chance next time out. What you do is this: you get yourself a little pair of binoculars and sit up high on the grandstand and you can watch all that kind of stuff. Dozens of possibilities if you don't get eyestrain."

"No possibilities," Tony says. "No luck. Nothing to be done. The whole game is rotten to the core and then they blame us just for trying to make a buck out of it."

"Gotta watch everything. Gotta watch the tote board like a hawk. Look for the smart money coming in there with about a minute to post." Mary passes over another assembly to Tony, he tamps it down, passes it to one side. And the arietta continues.

The arietta continues! I listen to it with warmth and affection. They have so much to say to one another and yet they can barely communicate. The interweaving of voices, the shards of speculation, the aphorisms and tips which would come from them compose a satisfactory primer for anyone interested in the sport of horseracing except that all of it is somehow contradictory and no one except the undersigned is listening. Their heads move in conferral over a particularly resistant piece of metal. They poke one another affectionately in encouragement. The scene is companionable in its warmth; it is truly unfortunate that neither is really aware of the presence of the other. Still, one must take what profit one can from the situation. Certainly, there is a good deal of information being bestowed in this room and if there is no one else to partake of it, then I most certainly will. I am of a saving nature. I do not like to waste knowledge, no matter what its source. Every loss a gain, every injury a thrust, every disaster an epiphany. Conservation of resources. The battle against entropy. Holding against the void.

In a few hours they are finished. The armaments go into two large valises which Tony has been holding in his closet for two decades against the necessity for a quick exit. The valises are locked and put into the living room near the door. Gasping, wheezing, Tony and Mary go to the refrigerator one by one, find themselves a can of beer apiece and drink it solemnly at separate corners of the living room. It is a situation ripe for lively social intercourse except that they are still very much unto themselves, even now.

"Lousy racing, secretaries," Tony says, still interested in the issue. "The goddamned blueblood owners who shit on all of us. The stinking jockeys, the fat exercise boys, the dirty grooms. The racing association. The government. The American Totalisator Company. The damned fire traps on the backstretch. Breeders with deformed merchandise. Yearling sales. Crooked auctioneers. Gotta go. The whole damned thing's gotta go."

"Hot horses," says Mary, "and crooked trainers. Horses that bleed or quit in the stretch. Favorites that don't run back to their form. Dropdowns that bear out. Early speed that don't carry further. Platers which lug into the rail. It's just gotta go. I tell you, I can't stand any of it no more."

"Ogden Philips," says Tony.

"Jean Cruguet," Mary says.

"Calvin Rainey."

"Larry Adams."

"Eddie Neloy and Horatio Luro. Pancho Martin and Sigmund Summer."

"Harry M. Stevens concession company. Olympia Parking service."

"John Cox Brady."

"Subway specials."

"Clocker Lawton."

"Clocker Powell."

"Assistant starters."

"Cruguet. Jean Cruguet."

"Julian," Mary says. "*Julian.*"

"Butazolidin."

"It's got to go," Mary says, "the whole thing, I can't take it anymore."

"Blow it up," Tony mumbles and inverts the beer can over his shoe, watches the liquid trickle darkly into the rug like the blood coming from the nostrils of an overworked horse. "Blow the whole thing up. It's no good anymore. It's just not working. It's not doing what it was supposed to do."

"They lied to us. Every single one of them lied to us. They said we could make it and we couldn't. It was all a lie. Every single one of them. Colonel Bradley. Charles Hatton. Tom Ainslie. They said that it was sensible, that it was somehow sane and decent, that you could make it that way if you tried. That it all came together. They knew the difference all along."

"They all lied," Tony says contrapunto, "every single one of them. They knew better. But they didn't care. They simply didn't care. The truth would have hurt them so they gave us the lie instead. They didn't care about us."

"The New York Turf Letter."

"The Totalisator Company."

"Got to go," Mary says. "The whole thing. It's got to go."

"It got to blow," says Tony. "The whole works."

Now, in the darkness of the room, they see one another for the first time. Rising to that conjoinment their eyes stare, hands flutter, noses twitch. They confront. They see the other. They merge. They sink into one another, coming together in some strange unity of the spirit, something which, at extreme moments only I can provide. They aggrandize in a way that has never been necessary before. I am moved, even though I created it. (I take pleasure in my work. I do good work. I do.)

Tony and Mary no longer exist.

Tony-Mary breathes heavily, harshly, raggedly in the dawn. It blinks, flutters, gasps, rolls into itself. After a time it sleeps. The sleep is long and full, possessed of images. Birds dreaming in the night. Horses running in the gray of the dawn, hurtling on the training track, moving, rising, successive levels of speed and anguish as they try to bank the clock before it runs down all the way. All the way. One eleven and two fifths. One minute flat. Forty-eight seconds. One minute and thirty-eight. Thirty-five seconds breezing. Two minutes handily from the gate. The sun comes over the track and dries the mud puddles, brings the hard brown dirt to the surface again where it will shine oh so brightly in the afternoon.

CHAPTER XXII

Fifth Recitatif (Apocalypse):

Now it is all seen before me: the devastation, the wreckage, the beauty and the death. Shattered bodies of horses, the corpses of horse-players rolling at attention in the mud, still alert and poised to that shank of fire as it races from one tier to the next and then in a low, crumbling snort the track itself is imploded. Now, there is only this low, flat plain on which flesh, paper, and machinery mix and meld, shattered in the stink of ozone. All done, finished, there is nothing more here, but I look upon it for a time, contemplate all of it: the meaning, the implications, the consequences, and I do not quite know what to think. Two or three of the forms are still alive. They flop in the ooze, perhaps seeking recapitulation of their history, a primordial kind of adjustment. Terrible, terrible! I kill them indolently and with a kind of caress. High squeals from the shattered hulk of the totalisator, the tumultuous whine of the Stevens coffee-maker as it continues to idiotically percolate.

All done, gentlemen. Finished. Are you proud of me? Mission completed. My obligations are terminated and shortly I will return. I look through the wreckage quizzically, trying to find that one necessary artifact which I can enshrine as emblem of the mission, but there is nothing. A torn program flaps in a hiss of expiration, I do not want it. I do not want to know the entries or the program of band tunes saluting the President. From the backstretch comes a high panicked whinny. A gelding struggles to its feet and looks dumbly about; sees what it has to see and screams in terror. He is not the only one. *I have forgotten the horses!* Behind the backstretch are stabled hundreds and hundreds of horses, horses stabled in the hulk of Belmont as well. They must be taken care of. They must not be left to panic and starvation, these innocents. Weeping, I perform the necessary. I have performed the necessary all along. Only the one basic act was outside my ken and now it is done. Simmons said that it was beautiful: he spoke of the beauty of it. They only love that which they can encompass with their hatred.

The horses are off the track, gentlemen. It is now post time.

CHAPTER XXIII

Gardner huddles in the upper grandstand, wrapped in his overcoat, shuddering against the wind and the rain. He has been here for several hours now in the same spot. Now it is almost time for the Belmont stakes itself and he consults his program, muttering and shaking his head. He has no selections. But then he has no money. He is merely waiting. Everything is going on schedule. Earlier this morning he had called Virginia to say that his final decision had been made. (He was almost inarticulate; much coaching and prodding was necessary from me to keep the conversation going.) "I lost everything," he said, "I lost everything and still I want to go back so that's your answer, isn't it?" The phone was silent for a while and then Virginia said she guessed that she had her answer and without saying anything else she hung up. (She was a limited girl, Virginia, but she had a certain facility for gestures which can never be slighted.) Gardner then went to his automobile and drove straight to Aqueduct, abandoning his usual prerace concert because there was nothing to sing and for that matter nothing to bet. His losses on Make Peace left him with little more than ten dollars, none of which is instantly available to him since it reposes in the savings account that he had opened for emergencies some years ago and toward which end had been depositing twenty-five cents a week. He could have had a last shot at a parley but he has been screwed: it is Saturday. At the track he had parked the car about a mile from the lot (not having the money) and then had hiked in through wind and rain muttering all the way to the grandstand entrance where he had used three dollars for entrance, fifty cents for a program, and fifty cents for a copy of the *Telegraph*. He has only thirty cents left none of which he intends to wager.

It has been an unusual experience for Gardner, attending the races wholly without money that is, something which he had thought could never happen to him, although he has been aware, as has any horse-player late in the days, that some of his companions' interest in the races is no longer empirical. Seeing the horses run in this way, taking part in them from the heightened and deepened alienation of powerlessness, Gardner has begun to understand for the first time what it might be like to be an imbecile wandering the streets of Manhattan on leave from the institution or a eunuch at an orgy. There is, as well, a feeling of culpability which he cannot escape (a responsibility for everything that is going on at the track since, having no involvement in the outcome, he can see the full picture) and also a sort of bizarre and tragic elevation. He had never realized until this afternoon what racing might really look like to the uninitiate. It is maddening and dull, insane to imagine that so much of his life has been wrecked by what was obviously an amorphous rite. In the bargain, none of the horses on which he would have bet has been anywhere in the money at all, increasing his feeling of disengagement. Gardner shudders and puts his hands deeper into his pockets. He is quite cold but he is not yet even into the Belmont and in any event, there is really nowhere for him to go. Nothing seems to interest him quite as much as it did yesterday. He thinks for a moment of Virginia but then puts her out of his mind. He comes to understand (through my slightly mechanical aid) that he was never very interested in her at all and that it is just as well that he will no longer be involved with her, although he still wishes that this could have been, somehow, accomplished less disgracefully. Gardner is wistful.

He checks out the entries for the big race as the horses come onto the track, shuddering a little in the cold. The band plays *Hail to the Chief* for the post parade (once it was *Sidewalks of New York* but with the transfer of the Racing Association's authority to the aegis of Federalism and with the President of the United States now at each and every Belmont as a gesture of his solidity with racing, a move which has assured him of a wide range of support in what is unfortunately not a voting population) and the horses struggle up the track, jockeys flailing them to keep them attentive. There would be nothing worse than a disinterested horse in the Belmont post parade, and the air of somnolence which creeps from one or two of the entries makes the jockeys savage. They begin to pummel their horses and the entire field begins to chase one another up the stretch and into the turn. Jean is riding an 80–1 shot whose female owner, having failed with it in sprints and claiming races, now feels that the horse must have classic potential. Gardner sighs. It is a colorful spectacle and has a great deal of sentimental appeal, but somehow he does not feel really moved. He looks at the entries for the last time. As usual, they disclose nothing except that Jean's chances are somewhat limited. Still, one never knows.

This is the first two hundred thousand dollar Belmont. That amount of money has been added to the entry and eligibility fees in order to keep the race, in the words of the track management, competitive with most of the major takes. In truth, the Racing Commission has been disastrously cheap about this race for many years. There are now a multitude of two- and three-year-old races that offer four to five times the Belmont prize but the question of tradition has long been the Commission's retaliation for expense. It was only a threatened (but little publicized) strike by several trainers of promising entries which caused the committee to up the purse some twenty-five thousand dollars. The favorite is an ex-two-year-old claimer named Knocker who, after winning the Derby on a disqualification, took the Preakness driving by three lengths in the slop, and although there are certain sectors of opinion which hold that the horse lacks essential courage and can handle nothing other than an off-track, the conditions and the hope of the Belmont crowd have knocked him down to 2–5 on the board with only some seven minutes of betting left. Gardner extracts the thirty cents from his pocket and eyes it longingly. The odds would make him twelve cents but that is not precisely the point; it is a strange thing not to have action on the oldest and most prestigious stake in the country. Or so thinks Gardner but then his state is perilous and has been carefully moved to such a point that he can now barely function at all.

"Come on, Gardner," I say as the horses turn up the back-stretch. "Enough of this. On your feet. Let's go." Unresistingly he stands and I urge him with several nudges and prods in the cerebellum towards an exit. "Time to get to work," I say, almost cheerfully. Gardner shambles along unprotestingly. His movements are somewhat uncoordinated, hardly reminiscent of the lively and spritely Gardner of so many race-track successes but I have had to make a whole series of radical adjustments which have disturbed the synapses, and under the circumstances (this is not my specialty) I am grateful that he is ambulatory at all. I guide him through the exit and onto a long, high ramp. Gardner walks up puffing, fumbling in his pocket for the thirty cents. The thirty cents has somehow become very important to him, comprising one of his few remaining connections. "All the way up, boy," I say cajoling him, and he groans on.

At length we reach the very top of the grandstand, the rear balcony before the seating area that is, and as I urge him on his westward way he bounces as far to the left as he can and then walks down the shallow incline and into the very last row of seats. Because of the rain and huge expanse of track, this row is almost empty. In the middle, Mary and Tony sit surrounded by valises which occupy a chair between them. They look at Gardner without interest, then resume their survey of the valises, taking only small, greedy looks at the track from time to time. Gardner moves to Mary's right, sits beside her. She takes little interest.

I have reduced their minds to a small, tiny point apiece. The point is fine and concentrate, takes in only the valises and what must be done with them and I am able to abandon them fully now (they are really quite out of commission) to devote my energies to Gardner.

"Open them," I say. "Come on. Open those valises."

His head jerks and he asks, "What for? Who are these people?"

"No questions Gardner. No time now. Open the valises. Open them now."

He shrugs and leans over Mary, touches the brass locks and forces the first, then the second open. They fall apart easily to the sides, disclosing armaments. Mary and Tony eye it fully, licking their lips and then Tony runs a hand affectionately over a grenade.

"What is this?" Gardner says. "What is going on here?"

"You know what it is. You know exactly what it is. Now do what you have to do."

Gardner's mind struggles. I can sense it like a bird fluttering under my grasp and in rage (never expecting so much trouble in the last moments from one so simple) squeeze perhaps a bit too hard. He succumbs with a gasp, still fighting. "No," he says. "*No!*" How does he manage it?

"Come on, Gardner. It's so easy. We went through all of this yesterday. There's nothing to it at all. Just come on."

"You're crazy," he mumbles. He is still staggering for the rhetoric of resistance even under this kind of pressure. It is remarkable but I have no time to be moved. "You're insane."

"No," I say. "I have a mission, that's all. I have a mission and I'm trying to be expeditious. Be reasonable about this. Gardner, really; there's no time to waste. Come on. Reach over. Take one."

In tandem, Mary and Tony humbly take their own grenades, look at them with intent and serious profiles, then wait obediently while I say again, "You too, Gardner. You're not cooperating. It's too late for that kind of stuff now. Just take one and be glad."

"But listen," he says, sweating, wriggling, gasping. "Listen to me, will you? You don't need me for this. You've got *them* to do it. They'll do it. What do you need *me* for? What have you done to them?"

"You don't understand, Gardner," I say, a little sadly, with circumspection and low force. "You still don't see it. I need a complete cross-section so that the fire can be total, I need every single representative of every sect and you're one of the four."

He moans and crumples. He reaches out a hand ever so delicately and tentatively for a grenade—and I help him, Tony helps him, Mary passes it across her lap and Gardner clutches it damply, groaning. The horses go into the gate up the turn for post time and the megaphones squeal. There is a clang.

The gate opens, the horses pour out and just as they do so I give the signal, give the signal, "now!" and the grenades arch. (Oh it is so beautiful to see them! I have waited so long!) From Mary's hand and then Tony's and after a short interval from Gardner's as well, they are tossed down toward the track and just as they reach the lip of the first grandstand they explode in lovely, curling threads of fire and they dip for more grenades and Tony says, "Whoopee! Whoopee! Go get them you bastards!" and throws one which explodes off a customer's head. Mary tries to spot hers on the ears of the favorite but misses and destroys instead a Harry M. Stevens concession carriage waiting in the rain. And Gardner, the youngest and most vigorous of them all, scores a dead hit on the pink cap (white stripes, yellow sleeves, stars on the hoops) of Jean who was trying to make a move on the clubhouse turn and now it is almost impossible to see the track for the fire.

See the fire, the smoke, the anguish. The race disappears and faces begin to turn, burn. Heads and bodies, mouths open, pouring anguish. The President dies in his blood. More grenades and more grenades and …

CHAPTER XXIV

Simmons is standing on the lawn by the finish wire as the first bomb hits. The role he has been assigned is very difficult and testing and I can only hope that he is ready to meet his obligations as he turns, drops his hands, faces the crowd and begins to roar with enormous intensity. (The exertions to which I put his vocal cords will render them surely useless thereafter but under the circumstances this is moot. I only hope they will hold up.)

"I want you to know why this is happening!" Simmons screams. (I have selected him for the role of Explicator; nothing so well suits the basic didacticism of his nature and no one is more entitled to try to sum up the sense of this.) "I want you to know that this is no prank you sons of bitches. It's real! It's something that was planned a long, long time ago! It's too rotten and too corrupt and it has got to go!" Simmons bellows and, amazingly, despite the turmoil, he is getting attention. Certain members of the crowd, partisans to the last, cheer thinly, trying to distinguish horses up the backstretch. Simmons continues, "From this spark will come a fire and the fire will wage the world; world enough and time and besides, how much of this can anyone take!? It's impossible! *Impossible!*"

Momentarily I leave him concentrating upon certain important alterations in the clubhouse that demand my immediate attention and as I do so, Simmons breaks into the lovely litany which I have so carefully prepared for him.

"*Clocker Lawton*, we have sinned. *Clocker Powell* we have failed utterly, we are washed in the colors of our inequity. Oh *New York Turf Letter, Top Turf*, we have gone astray; plunged into a sea of darkness, we have lost our way. We have forgotten the lessons of the Fathers: no fillies against colts; no maidens in straight claimers; no workout line, no bet. We have been greedy. We have chased longshots. We have failed to learn the awful lessons of the tote." Threads of fire frame him as if in a halo. "Verily we say unto you that we have lost our way, we are utterly cast aside, our bones are made to run out like sealing wax." Three owners are incinerated in the clubhouse bar, the charred fragments of the ex-favorite roll in the wind toward the swans. "Faith of our Fathers, Word of the Prophets, we are lost and cannot be found. In the dread machinery of the tote we faint from sickness, pray for your blessings. Oh may your mercy find us again!" Simmons shrieks, "and may we never stray from thy teachings, thy sacred Word, until restored again to the freshness of our youth, we play and gambol like lambs on the fields of all desire."

More bombs rain. Mary has fainted but Tony and Gardner are still going strong and Gardner in particular, with a series of two-handed efforts is showing real promise. "Pray! Pray!" Simmons says. One more hail of bombs … and now the lawn begins to heave, the very stretch to dissolve as the chain reaction begins, just as promised, right on schedule. The true and calamitous chain reaction, here it is! And now there are only forms, forms darting and screaming in the network of fire, and Simmons, his arms outstretched, seems to sink into the concrete and is utterly consumed. "We have sinned! We have sinned!" his last words as he falls beneath sight and is lost. Mary topples from the grandstand and is gone forever. Only Gardner is left, chuckling madly as he opens the second valise with the atomic assembly, a merry light in his destroyed eyes as he connects the wires leading to the power plant and then skillfully he flips the switch and it is at this moment …

EPILOGUE

… that my mission ends. Their world, their personal universe, is no more. I feel a yanking, rending pain like nothing I have ever known before. When I come to my senses I am standing in Headquarters, sweating against a wall and they are looking at me. Hemmings and people even higher than he are looking at me and Hemmings is saying: "You stupid son of a bitch, you weren't supposed to get *involved*, just set the machinery and get out. Now you've made reclamation utterly impossible. Why the hell did you take this *seriously?*" And, "You lunatic, what made you do it *that* way?" And things like this, oh just terrible things I can barely stand to hear and I smile weakly (oh so very weakly) showing them the scarred palms of my useless hands. And then they come toward me, all of them in a row, screaming and hissing at me and it is not difficult for me to understand; even a man of my limited mentality, that they are very mad. Oh boy, oh boy, are they ever mad! I know that my fuckup will be the talk of the Bureau for years and years … to say nothing of my imminent demotion.

Nevertheless, one tried.

THE END

Afterword: Syzygy In The Home Stretch

"*Underlay* is not a horse-racing novel" my friend, editor and occasional collaborator Mike Resnick (1942-2020) said to me long after the fact, "It is a horse *playing* novel" and on some reflection I had to agree with him; that novel like *Overlay* was set at the track, used the track, drew upon its language of enticement and disaster but focused upon the entrapped humans, not the exploited horses whose concerns were perhaps not metaphysical. Harry the Flat was neither Citation nor that wretched allowance four year-old Branch who cost me heavy money and hope in 1970, Simmons the Horseplayer in this novel could not be confused with Bold Ruler who in his last race broke down in front of the Belmont Grandstand and sent himself off to stud; Bold Ruler's breakdown occurred in the Brooklyn Handicap run on my first day at the racetrack and, consequential as it was, occurred at a distance from my position at the rail and had less of an impact than the third place finish of the gelding Find which paid four dollars on my two dollar show bet and helped propel me toward a wasted and eventual life of witness: breakdowns here, sudden swerving there, lost action on the far turn to take me out of the race. Bold Ruler recovered, had a long and presumably happy life at stud, sired Secretariat, perhaps the best and always the most adored horse of the second half of his century. This cascade of events and consequence bemused me on my first day at the track (escorted by my Aunt Teresa who felt that experience beat yearning even in the pastel 1950s) and they continued to amuse me, right through to these late races, these twilight events on a racing card which by this time is crumpled almost beyond recognition. Anticipation and loss, loss and hope, calculation toward derangement, these were some of the lessons of South Ozone Park and Elmont, Long Island and they were indelible. I still shudder within their consequence.

"Anticipation and loss", "calculation toward derangement": surely I could have given my departed friend Mike Resnick (an expert and dedicated handicapper but never a bettor; he just liked to see them run or so he maintained) an argument on the horse-racing/horseplaying novel argument; I could have pointed out that they could not be separated, that they were Sturgeon's syzygy, desperately and eternally combined, melded into one another. The horses, sometimes adjusted by careful or careless administration of drugs ran through all levels of possibility or loss; strained against themselves, born to run of course but also born to quit, born to flag, born to bear out, born to lose. Strained against themselves the horses knew pain if not regret; they knew fear if not surcease and so of course did the horseplayers leaning on the rail or soaking in whiskey or juleps at the upper levels. Extending those barriers of possibility, moving up or down the scale of qualification: allowance horses and claimers, gentleman owners and captains of industry, dead beat or broken grooms washing down the horses in echoing barns, horseplayers of all background and ambition joined in hopeful or hapless bellowing for the struggle in deep stretch. "For relief, go to the racetrack" A.J. Liebling suggested long ago, "It opens the lungs and empties the mind."

These are both factors in *Overlay* which was the second novel in the chronology of the trilogy, written in a tumultuous and angry rush in March of 1970 and given to my friend and editor Robert Hoskins almost on the morning of the Sixth Day so that I could rest, every page almost autobiographical in its conveyance of the experience I was having weekly in those months of my wife's mid-pregnancy, the perils and pressures of a market which was suddenly like Gorky's lower depths opening to me, with all the sudden and shuddering possibility which seemed to merge in the spectacle and events at South Ozone Park where every afternoon except Sunday my own destiny and possibility seemed to be refracted in the gyrations out of the starting gate, the frantic maneuverings of the undependable Angel Cordero on overplayed favorites, the scramble of Woodhouse or Ussery as high in the seat they would pound their fading horses in the stretch. Animal rights were no more favored on those afternoons than the concept of indigenous rebellion held much sway in the Pentagon and through all of it, equipped for the immersion with an eleven-year-old rusted Buick I solemnly attended services two or three times a week, services which unwillingly took on the aspect of the memorial, the Yahrzeit rather than of the Festival. It is not a time of life which I would want to relive, not even for the questionable pleasures of being 30 and a fool again and I look upon that time not so much as a sentimental education as a guided tour—Clocker Lawton's picks and suggestions in hand—of hell. Or, as Laurence Janifer would have typed: Hell.

Well, that was half a century ago. Off-Track Betting opened a few weeks before the Triple Crown won by Dust Commander, OTB grew, grew some more, became a derelict heaven, shriveled into a charnel house and in a clutter of dropped programs and crumpled *Morning Telegraphs* disappeared and I have lived on and on, into the era of the postponement of the Kentucky Derby from the first Saturday in May to at least September (I write this with the conviction that it will be cancelled). I am Lear without the poetry; I have seen such things as will never be seen again. This novel is of course a crude and somewhat cruel takeoff on Theodore Sturgeon's *More Than Human*, his exploration of syzygy; my four horseplayers of the Apocalypse are a version of the cast of that novel, randomly assembled and conjectured into an amalgam of Earthly destruction. To the Committee of the Whole which had sent my protagonist to this planet to gather the syzygy for the amalgam which would produce the Big Bomb, to that wretched group humanity, had been weighed in the balance by the Overlords and had been found wanting. *Mene mene tekel upsharshin.* The horses are on the track. In the distance, blazing South, that consuming fire. The horses are at the gate. It is now post-time.

The Sport of Gniks scratched.

May 2020: New Jersey

A Bed of Money

Barry N. Malzberg

writing as Gerrold Watkins

For Lenny Brown, Moe Wasserman and Joe Jedel
and some good afternoons.

ONE

Foster has always had this desire, this real strong desire, to immerse himself between two breasts so huge that he would feel himself literally choked, drowning in the surrounding flesh and now, at this late moment in the day, he sees no reason not to indulge himself. Grunting, poised over the girl on the bed, he cups the enormous weight of her breasts, two palms to one of them, and rubs the flesh back and forth, sobbing, choking back the whines and cries in his mouth, then opens his lips to their fullest extension and plunges the breast in, slobbering, moaning. At some distance of detachment it occurs to him that his cries might well be those of a man in agony rather than one who is, indeed, on the verge of his largest and most hopeless kind of ascendance, but he tries to push these thoughts back into the dim corner of his mind where all the difficult thoughts often come and concentrates only on the breasts: on sucking, tasting, exploring, nibbling. The nipple erects inside his mouth with a kind of uncoiling flourish, showing that the girl too has been aroused—women have their fantasies also; it is only the media that would seem to make sex a man's preoccupation, a woman's indulgence, he reminds himself—and curls his tongue around her nipple harder, imagining that somehow she is excreting milk toward him, the salt taste of his own saliva coming back faintly to him as beneath he feels her limbs shift then spread to accommodate him. He makes the oozing thrust of penetration slowly, slowly, feeling the exquisite slivers of pain that it sends through his prick, already so hard-used this evening that it seems to be somehow apart from him, a flower open to a kind of agony he has rarely suspected and he has to groan and let himself settle into her through the sucking, pulsing motions of her cunt, rather than the hard, easy way of slippery penetration. It hurts; the more sensitive the prick becomes the more agonizing its copulation he had read somewhere once and had hardly believed it. It was more medical book nonsense but now he knows it, knows it for a fact and yet cannot stop. Below the waist he is one enormous ache; his prick and balls thick with pain and necessity, yet three orgasms or four orgasms later he is still seeking, still looking for the Ultimate Fuck. It is about time, after all, he deserves no less and so he swings his concentration fully back to the girl, feeling her nod and jerk under him. "Oh God," she is saying, "Oh God, it hurts so much I can't stand it but don't stop, don't stop," and he wonders idly if she is just trying to please him or whether she is as deep into sex at the moment as he is; it hardly matters, none of that matters at all, he is going to get his ashes hauled as he never has before and so he moves in and out slowly, letting her make the motions, dodging his mouth from one breast to the other, feeling the hot swirling center of her open and close beneath him and then, so quickly, he is at orgasm again, pain and fire shifting through him and as he comes, feeling a surge of power which almost lifts him to the ceiling, he clasps her right breast in his hand and squeezes, squeezes to bring down upon her thirty years of renewal and betrayal, deprivation and loss and she squeals, "Oh God, it's so good!" And that is the way he comes into her, annealing and receding, moving and retracting and falls on top of her at last exhausted, his breath coming faintly against her, the oven-smell of her flesh full in his nostrils. He wonders idly if he should check his wallet.

"Oh, George," the girl is mumbling. "Oh George, that was fantastic, I've never had anything like it; where did you learn to fuck like that?" and he tries to prepare himself for sleep with that approbation drifting through him but she says, "It was terrific, I never knew anyone who could do it in just that way, you're really fantastic, George, just fantastic," and he feels a shudder of revulsion moving slowly like a fish cutting through the waters of his fatigue; there will indeed be no sleep for him at this instant. After fucking, they want conversation, at least those whom he has known. And beyond that, too much has happened today for sleep: it has been the longest and most apocalyptic day of his life and sleep, that anticlimax, cannot be imposed so early. He sighs, settles off her, reaches toward his cigarettes from the table, takes one, lights it, gives it to her and then lights another for himself. Then puts it out; he has resolved to quit smoking and even though he carries a pack for occasional lapses he has only had ten today. There is no point in carrying on such a dangerous habit, particularly now when his net worth has increased so remarkably and he is, for the first time, on the verge of becoming a valuable piece of goods.

The girl blows out some smoke wistfully, turns to him. "Talk to me," she says. "You're so quiet."

"No I'm not. I'm just thinking."

"Tell me how it was for you."

"It was all right. I mean, it was really good. I've never had it quite as good as we just did."

"And wasn't there a lot of it? But do you know something?" she says with a faint pout and runs a finger down his arm. "I bet that you don't even remember my name."

"Of course I do."

"So what is my name?"

"It's Dolores."

"Ah," she says with a satisfied groan and slides fully against him, running her hand up and down his body, touching his weakened genitals deftly, tweaking his flaccid prick. "I thought you wouldn't remember. I only told you once in the bar and I didn't think that it meant anything to you."

"I remember everything."

"George?" the girl says in a different tone, and runs her hand up and down his thighs briskly, "George, will you tell me again? Just like you did before?"

"About what?"

"You know. The money. What happened today to you at the track."

"Oh for God's sake," Foster says, but the trouble is that he does not say it seriously, hears this in fact with a twist of pleasure because on whatever level it is obvious that he has impressed this girl most profoundly and she is really a very pretty girl with the largest tits that he has ever seen, let alone handled. "You don't want to hear all that again. I went through it."

"Yes I do," she says huskily and begins to squeeze and manipulate his prick with real professionalism, real skill, her breasts juggling slightly with the energy that she is putting into that twinkling grasp. "It really thrilled me. I mean, the way you told it and everything."

"Is that the only reason you came here with me?"

"George," she says, and sits up with a quiver, dropping his prick, confronting him between her bobbling breasts with a look of high dismay settling into her brown eyes. "Do you really think I'm that kind of person? I don't even know how you can ask. I'm really insulted, I—"

"Okay," he says, more shaken by the loss of physical contact than he would have thought, needing her in that instant only to settle down and grapple with him once again. "Okay, okay, I'll tell you if you want to hear. But there really isn't too much to it at all."

"Oh yes there is," she says, winking at him almost in a kind of confidentiality and settling against him. "Oh yes there is, George; you really shouldn't underrate yourself like that. You tell things beautifully and besides, it's such a beautiful story. Beautiful, beautiful, beautiful," she murmurs and looks at him with eyes alight and merry with anticipation, her fingertips grazing his balls as he settles himself again, thinks *the hell with it*, and takes a cigarette. She lights it for him with her own, a gesture containing a kind of devotion as he sucks and grasps at the proffered flame, then takes in his first lungful of smoke in—well—two and a half to three hours. "Do you want to hear the whole thing or only about the big race?"

"Oh just the big race. I mean the whole thing is just great but it's the big race that turns me on so. I think it's fantastic, George, I really do. Tell me just like you told me at Mitchie's now, just the same words and everything."

"Well," he says, half-closing his eyes so that only a thin white patch of ceiling protrudes on his consciousness; he could be in the open air now, lying under a thick cloudy sky instead of the confined spaces of a motel, listening to the pleasant hum of air conditioners, the dry groaning of plumbing somewhere above him. "Well, at Aqueduct today I came into the sixth race already seventy-five dollars behind. It was disgusting, particularly since I had really had the daily double but didn't have the guts to bet the two horses together and then in the fourth I had forty dollars on the favorite to place and he loses out by a whisker. So I am in deep trouble you understand, feeling very gloomy because although there is no way that you can truly beat the races, there is also no way that you can convince a man that he should stop trying."

"And you've been trying all your life."

"And I've been trying all my life, that's right. Now, in the sixth race there is this horse called People Trap that I have been following for a long, long time. He is a three-year-old gelding with bad legs but a very stout heart and a good trainer who has been running him in and out of bad luck all year long. Six furlongs, a mile, a mile and an eighth, Monmouth, Rockingham, Pimlico, he has tried this horse at all distances on all tracks and still has yet to coax a win out of him although the horse is obviously sound and trying, simply very slow."

"But has a great heart."

"But has a very great heart, a remarkable thing for a three-year-old plater, the best he has done being a third in a bad allowance stake at Laurel too many months ago. I have been following this horse steady, finding something in him that I admire and I decide that once again on this day I will bet him. Even though he has disappointed me terribly many times."

"How has he disappointed you?" she asks, and once again begins to squeeze him limply; he feels the moisture trapped by her hand beginning to move in small curls and rivulets toward the bed and groans slightly, moves as if he would turn upon her but with a kind of grace which he has always found the most remarkable thing in women, she withdraws and begins to stroke his forehead rapidly, cooling him. He has been sweating, it seems. "How did he disappoint you, George?" she asks again, some urgency at the edges of her tone.

"In May I bet him five, five and five across the board in a situation which seemed ideal for his talents and trainer and he ran out, bearing in on the stretch turn. In June, I was sure that Rogaldo—he's the trainer—had found the spot in a mile and an eighth at Monmouth and I bet him fifty win, fifty place with a bookie of my acquaintance but although he finished second he was disqualified; he was bumping in the stretch, probably because of sore ankles. And in September in a six-fur-long race at Aqueduct I was sure that this was it and bet another fifty on him, but only to show. He finished fourth."

"That must have been terrible."

"Oh it was terrible; it happens all the time; you get hooked on one horse, like on a woman and you can't get out because you think that the very next time the horse will stop being a bitch and that's how you get sucked in deeper and deeper, like drugs or death."

"I hope you don't think that I'm a bitch, George," she says quietly, returning her hand now to his genitals, a mild warning tweak indicating that he is to mind his business this time.

"Oh no, I don't. Where did you get the idea?"

"Now tell me again about the sixth, George."

"Well, I was far behind on the day. And the damned horse was running again, under an apprentice jockey this time and the funny thing was that I didn't even notice until I opened the program to the sixth that he was running today. I thought he was some other horse or running to-morrow or something. But there he was. And I didn't even want to bet him; I was so disgusted with all the money I had lost on him and the lousy day I was having but I decided—"

"You decided that you better have a little action on him just in case."

"Exactly. I decided I ought to have a little action. The figures were wrong and the distance, seven furlongs, was wrong and the weather was lousy and I was feeling lousy and I was too far behind but I figure what the hell, be shorn for a sheep well as a lamb—right?—so just to have some interest in the race I bet him ten dollars to win."

"Right."

"And then I went out to the paddock and the horse looked really lousy, he had bandages on all four legs and red eyes and the kid on him looked like he didn't even weigh eighty pounds, let alone the hundred he was said to be carrying and the kid was so scared that it looked like his brain was showing behind his eyes. I found out later this was only the second time he had ever raced. And then the horse started to rear in the pad-dock which is always a real bad sign."

"Tell me about the tote, George."

"The tote? Oh the tote. Well the horse was 40-1 in the program on the morning line but he opened right off at 70-1 and then he started to go up and up. Right away, almost, he was at 99-1 which doesn't mean any-thing except that 99-1 is the largest boards the tote can show; anything above 99-1 is still 99-1 on the board but it could really be a thousand to one. And I followed my calculations and by five minutes to post, this horse was 343-1, approximately. Which was a legitimate enough thing considering his record and the field and the jockey and the way he looked."

"George, tell me about what happened then. The thing that happened to you."

"You really want to hear this?" he says and giggles nervously, caught up in the story now himself and vaguely embarrassed because even now it has the same effect: it is as if, from only eight hours removed, he can look back on the disaster of his earlier life and see it now for what it truly was: small farce executed with burlesque moves at the center of which moved the comic loser George Foster who never understood the simple way to get out of the scene: strike the set. "I mean—"

"I love to hear it, George. I really do. I think you're the most sincere man—"

"Well I got this feeling," Foster says. "Right before post, it was like a voice in the sky talking to me direct, it said, bet this horse. Don't let him get away from you; don't be a fool all your life, take chances. And I said back to the voice, it was a real dialogue, a two-way thing which was the unusual part, well look, I already got ten bucks on his nose. And the voice said, don't be an idiot all your life George Foster, reach out, take the chances, stop hedging or you'll be nothing but a loser all your life, your whole life. Bet the horse 50, 50 and 50. Just like that it said. Gave me instructions and everything."

"That's really something. So then you went to the window—"

"So then I went to the window, the fifty-dollar window and bought three tickets—win, place and show on People Trap. Number seven, I said, and the clerk looked at me like I was crazy."

"But you weren't crazy, were you, George? Not at all; you were never crazy."

"I hope not," Foster says, really caught up in it now; the girl seems to have disappeared, similarly the bed, even the various clever twitches and pressures on his body seem to have diminished to memory; he could, for all that it matters be back at Aqueduct now for the strangest, most thrilling afternoon of his life. "So they go into the gate. The horse goes off at 300-1, my bet driving the odds down a bit. They go from the gate, he takes the lead right away, another horse knocks him off stride in the backstretch—"

"But you weren't worried, were you, George?"

"Well I was and I wasn't; I didn't have time to think because the horse recovered so fast and got back to the lead and coming into the stretch he leads by three lengths. The horse is running like it's crazed and the jockey is holding on like he doesn't want to win but only stay aboard and the horse comes by me lengths clear and he goes on to the wire and he wins by eight lengths."

"Eight lengths," the girl says reverently. "Eight whole lengths. It must have been beautiful."

"And then when he gets right past the finish line he pulls up like he's been shot and then takes a tumble, the kid going right over his neck. Boy was he scared! I mean, I figured they had him full of speed but I didn't think it would hit him that fast."

"But it did. And there was no objection."

"No," Foster says, "there was no objection and there was no inquiry and they came out and pulled the horse away in a hack and he pays $604.10 for win, $142.10 for place and $70.20 for show, the longest price any horse has paid at the Big A in history."

"Beautiful," she says. "Beautiful. So how much did you win, George?"

"Well, I had the sixty for win and that was a little over eighteen thousand dollars. And I had the fifty for place so that was about thirty-five hundred dollars. And the fifty for show was about eighteen hundred dollars. So I won about twenty-three thousand dollars."

"Twenty-three thousand dollars," Dolores says. "Oh my, oh my. In one afternoon. On one race."

"It was beautiful," Foster says, sighing, "it was beautiful. And now I'm even and in fact I'm ahead and I'm never going to play again. It's like purged out of me, wiped. I pay off everybody tomorrow and start a new life."

"And you had the whole twenty-three thousand dollars on you when you met me. You went right from the track to the place, just like you knew I was going to be there or something. It was such a coincidence that we met."

"Yes," Foster says, "something like that," remembering even at this moment the knot of desire which had seized him on the way out of the track, the feeling of low uncoiling, some meshing of the network between his glands and the twenty-three thousand dollars in cold cash which lay in his right front pocket, held together and down by his fist. He had taken a hired car, of course, right out of the track—one of those dozens of limousines lying in wait for the big winners or worse losers who could not, in either event, bear the possibility of buses or the impact of the subway. The driver had looked at him a little peculiarly when he had asked for action in the neighborhood but when Foster said, "Action, I mean action. I mean I'm a big winner and now I want to find something. I'm entitled and besides that, what's wrong with asking? I'll give you fifty dollars if you take me to the right place." The driver had brightened up considerably and told Foster that he knew what he wanted, had just the place in mind, a fine café near Queens Boulevard and in the bargain all the women were beautiful. He had gone in there and all the rest had seemed a fine inevitability, now, half-turning, poising on an elbow to look at Dolores once again, the firmness of the breasts even without support goading him again toward necessity it seems to him that the day indeed is made out of one single ribbon of material stretching from the gloom and shadows of the morning to this rosy, well-lit fulfillment of the evening, all of it out of one piece, cleaved out of the simplest material like great musical compositions. "Oh boy," he moans, "oh boy," and leans forward to sink within her again.

But somehow it is not so good this time, not nearly quite so good although in her way she does all she can to help him, inhaling, thrusting out a nipple, bringing his mouth down to burning merger, accommodatingly flexing her thighs as he moves toward her center once again. Perhaps it is only depletion but Foster is not sure of this; he has come four or five times in a night before although never, he must admit, in the company of something nearly so persuasive and accommodating as what is in hand; more probably it is some thrust of intimidation, some feeling of responsibility which settles heavily over him as he begins to rock back and forth, talking about the twenty-three thousand dollars has reminded him of the heavy obligation it imposes; now he will really have to make something of his life. At the beginning horse racing had been an exercise and an amusement, later on when he got too deep into debt it had become an obsession but he had somehow never questioned the fact that it was a temporary part of his life, an indulgence which he would squander and move past even though he was thirty-three years old and obviously not in shape for any serious professional career plans. Indeed in recent months the thought had taken to attacking him during random evenings and during bouts of insomnia: *I'm sucked in so deep I'll never get out of this alive, I never really wanted anything else or I wouldn't have let myself get into this in the first place* and it had taken all of his bitterly retained faith in himself, all of his grim optimism to fight off these apprehensions as the twitches and obsessions that they had to be. He had managed to retain, at no small cost, his long belief that he was an exceptional person, meant for only the most exceptional of destinies: surely God would not have taken the trouble to put George Foster, this remarkable individual, full of such passions and torments, on the very stage of the earth if God had not intended to shelter him against an unbearably important destiny but it had been difficult, difficult: the losing was difficult and the shylocks were difficult and Tony the Fixer who backed up the shylocks with certain deft maneuvers and physical activities was difficult and the burning sense of loss, almost all of the time, was difficult, unbearable really; the color of losing tickets, the sense of disaster as beaten horses dropped back, winning horses failed to make their move, had been almost unbearable and now in one thunderous burst twenty-three thousand dollars had been handed him as tribute by this very same God to assure him what too many people along the way had almost forgotten: George Foster was exceptional. George Foster was meant for better things; everything in which he involved himself was only a preparation and a hedge against his outcome and now he had twenty-three thousand dollars to prove that he was not a loser but was, in fact, a winner, the biggest winner he had ever known in his lifetime personally. Perhaps it is only the thought of the twenty-three thousand in new hundreds that is tensing him so; it is over on the chair in his wallet in his pants, dangling somewhere in the vicinity of the floor and with the first flush of sex dissipated he finds himself thinking of it almost passionately. What he would like to do, if all things were equal, would be to disengage himself from the girl who is very pretty and a terrific fuck but something, in the last analysis, of a bore, and go over for a while to fondle the bills.

Perhaps then it is that which is disconcerting him and only those self-imposed flickers; perhaps though it is Dolores herself who is fucking him now with passionate energy, more energy than she has yet displayed, there is less flush in her breasts, less point in her nipples, less wetness in her cunt perhaps, but far, far more movement to her thighs, she is working on him now with the grim insistence and dedication of a horse clearing out on the stretch run for a final burst and whistling slowly through her fine nose, muttering to herself as she works on him. What she is muttering is *twenty-three thousand dollars, twenty-three thousand dollars*, faintly, almost lispingly—perhaps she had a speech defect when she was younger—and her face holds upon it a look of such enormous concentration that it goes far beyond anything in Foster's experience. *Twenty-three thousand*, she says a bit more loudly, a bit more disconcertingly and then reaches both hands down, takes hold of his balls and squeezes, palpates them until he feels the vanquished semen sigh within and begin to pour out heavily into her. It is an enormous, bursting, thrashing orgasm that he now endures and seems to take an eternity; when it is over he is very solemn indeed and falls away from her with a kind of heavy yielding which surprises him in the force of his exhaustion; he needs a long rest. He had tried too much today. Perhaps he should not have wanted to get laid on his first night out. In any event, he will get ready to go home now; it has been a long day and it is time to unwind. The girl has done very well for him but she is, when all is said and done, only a girl. Foster decides vaguely that he has drunk too much; there was no need to have what he did at the bar, even though it did not seem at the time to be catching up with him and in his days he had consumed far, far more than four Manhattans and a Gibson cocktail.

"Is it in hundreds?" the girl is saying. "That would make two hundred and thirty hundreds, wouldn't it?"

"I think so. That's how they pay out."

"Not thousands?"

"Not enough use for them at the rack."

"Could I look at them?"

"No," Foster says.

"You told me I could look at them," she says, moving warmly against him. "Oh boy, you've got a terrific body. Can't I please look at them?"

"No I didn't," Foster says, feeling finally and vastly irritated. "Anyway, there's nothing to look at. All hundreds seem the same, this is only that there's more of them."

"Oh, but I'd love to see them. I've never seen that kind of money. It would be a thrill—"

"No," Foster says, and rises. He has a panicky moment of disorientation during which he thinks he may faint but no, it is only fatigue, drink and too much sex, nothing fatal after all and he is able to stand quite securely on the floor, straddling his discarded shirt. "I think we'd better go now."

"But we booked the motel for the night."

"Yeah," Foster says. "But I'm tired. I'm sorry, but I don't think I want to make an all-nighter."

She looks at him, two spots of anger suddenly implanted on her cheeks and says, "Does that mean what I think it means?"

"No," he says, "there was nothing personal meant. Listen, Dolores, I'm just tired. It's been some day. It's been great and we'll have to get together again soon but right now I'm just so tired and I have to get home. My mother will be worried," he says which is half a lie because although he does have a mother and lives with her, she will not be worried; the old bitch having, if this is the usual weekday, been long stiff, since eight or nine or so, lying nodding beside the television set. "And I don't want to worry her."

"Well," Dolores says and stands herself, giving him a different aspect; her breasts if possible seem even larger when she is standing and the nipples have an interesting bluish tinge toward the edges that he had not noticed before, maybe it is merely his constant sucking. "Well, if you feel that way. It isn't very nice of you, George, after how nice I've been to you, but all right."

"We better get dressed," he says vaguely, feeling somewhat at odds and goes for his pants, for no reason fondles the wallet pocket, yes it is there. He finds himself seized suddenly by an urge to count the money again. "We'll be going."

"First I have to call my girl friend?"

"Huh?"

"My girl friend. I mean I have a roommate and she worries about me;

we have this agreement that if one of us is out for the evening and doesn't call in saying where she is, the one who is home notifies the cops right away. I mean it's a terrible city for a girl to be alone in, not that you would understand. I'll have to call her right now."

"All right," Foster says, wondering why the explanation has been necessary and then discarding it; all women are, after all, crazy in their individual ways, no less than men. "I have to go to the bathroom. So you can make your call and then get dressed and I'll get dressed and then we'll go, okay?"

"That's great," she says, "that's just great; you go to the bathroom right now, and I'll make my call." If he has in any way offended her that is all gone now; her eyes seem to dance and sparkle with light, with joy, with relief, with a mad, merry twinkle. "Just great."

"Fine," Foster says, feeling vaguely formal and nods at her, grabs his pants and goes into the bathroom, shuts the door and locks it. As soon as he is in those clean, white spaces he sighs, feeling tension move out of him and reaches into his pants, seizes the wallet and, extracting the huge lump of money, begins to count. He does it lovingly, passionately, his fingers caressing the surfaces of the bills, Benjamin Franklin seeming to wink at him in some ghostly communion of spirit as together they share the wonder of his ascension, this mood of his Night of Nights.

In the other room he hears the girl talking in a fast, low voice, doubtless assuring her roommate that Foster the winner, would not possibly make a false move at her.

TWO

But even in his losing periods, even at the sheer dumping point where disaster and inference have seemed to merge into a kind of ecstasy because there is, after all, nothing more fundamentally exhilarating to Foster than disaster, he has always had a kind of mediocre luck with women. This is the kind of thing that has never failed to surprise him: coming from a difficult, middle-class background he is still convinced to this day that women are somehow both moral and difficult and that they would mingle with the likes of him is something of an astonishment. Even more interesting to him—during the periods when he has thought much about this which are not very often—is the fact that he has retained, even to the near-middle of his thirties, a strong interest in women; most men who had led lives similar to his would no longer have the guts to try. Foster has a fair degree of insight, he is not entirely a fool and he is aware that most of the men he has known in circumstances similar to his have been far detached from women, stricken off in some spaces of their own where Chance takes up the terrain where Fucking has quit … and indeed Foster knows and not through folklore that the racetrack is one of the worst places in the world to try to get laid; the only worse place is the floor of the New York Stock Exchange but even the Stock Exchange has pretty little research assistants who have much thinking to do in between setting up the tapes and there are many red-faced men hanging around the area who believe that commerce can only be helped along by a little informed soliciting. The racetrack on the contrary seems to be populated, superficially, by only two kinds of people: young men and women on dates, dilettantes and the hell with them, interested only in using margins as an excuse for necking and older men and women who are seriously and exclusively interested in horses and who, locked into their particular computations, barely acknowledge their own physical presence, let alone anyone else's. It is true that there are, now and then, a few vagrant whores out there, working mostly in packs, trying to skim off some of the winnings of the winners and once, a long time ago, Foster met a very beautiful girl in the infield who said she was a secretary in the advertising industry but liked to come out to the track on her days off because it reminded her of the way that the people out there were really living. She liked to fuck too, this girl, and Foster had surprisingly little difficulty in smuggling her behind the interior tote, checking out the measurements of her tongue and breasts with scurrying hands and then arranging to take her back to New York on the subway special, at the end of which excursion he seems to dimly remember having screwed her in an apartment filled with mirrors and humming birds, the rising flip of her nipple sinuous and deadly in all that sound and glitter, but it has passed away, this particular memory; mostly he remembers that on this particular day he lost fifty-eight dollars and twenty cents, mostly as the result of an unfortunate bet on a favorite in the closing starter handicap and the trouble is that his longest memories, the ones that affect him the most and which seem to come closest to his sense of himself almost always have to do with losses and rarely with anything else. Foster had occasionally regretted this girl; regretted that he was too engrossed, even ennobled by the calamity to try to pursue her and since she had both an unlisted phone number and an imminent eviction he was never able to connect with her again. This struck Foster at the time as a loss—he had tried to find her on the evening of a day when he had hit the double and was forty dollars to the good—but looking back on it now, as he does occasionally, he has almost concluded that it was the best: the girl and he, in the last analysis, had very little to talk about and all the time that he was working over her long breasts and opening sprawl of thighs she had been querying him on the effects which windage in the backstretch could have on front-runners in the fall.

Still, and despite this pattern, Foster has never had any particular trouble in getting women: he has found them on the subways and in bars, he has picked them up on the streets and in restaurants, he has even found them in bookstores and liquor shops, standing with abstracted expressions, apparently waiting for him to come to the same conclusion on their bodies and condition that they have already accepted. While the major part of him has been involved in the large metaphor of the racetrack a small, shrewd, cunning gnome buried within has been looking out with a rather steely glint for his sexual health and he has therefore never fully closed his options that way although on occasion he has been tempted. Nevertheless, in the aftermath of the Big Hit this afternoon, it seemed both a natural and inevitable phenomenon that he would go in search of a woman to share it with, the more accessible and attractive the woman the better. Most of the men he knows would not have handled things in this manner of course: they would have scurried off to the trotters in search of a true parley or worse yet would have gone back to their furnished apartments to sit in wondering, numbing contemplation of the two hundred and thirty one-hundred-dollar bills, barely coming to the realization of the fact that finally having hit the score they hadn't the faintest idea of what to do with it but Foster is not in their category, never was as a matter of fact, Foster knows exactly what he is going to do with it. In a quiet way Foster has always considered himself a better, somehow finer type of horse player, a scholar, as it were, trapped with a class of people somewhat inferior to him; a man who got into a ragged game for purposes entirely apart from the normal motivation which purposes, when once satisfied, would send him swinging free, alert, glitter in his eyes, ready at last to capitalize. Foster knows that he will never play the horses again. There is no need to. They have served their purposes.

What these purposes were he is not quite sure yet but he will: he will as he stuffs the bills back into his wallet with fiendish speed, finding that he is suddenly chuckling madly and removing some complimentary toothpaste from the medicine cabinet he puts a huge gob of it into a drinking glass, fills it with water and begins to gargle merrily, singing almost, letting the clean, fresh ointment wash away the taste and smell of corruption in his mouth; bring him into a new state of consciousness and then he airily dumps the unused contents of the glass into the basin, runs a little hot water over it, listens to it simper down the drain and then steps into his clothing, admiring himself in the mirror while he does so and comes back into the room briskly, now confident of himself: everything must be taken step by step and he is already making the vital moves. Dolores is sitting on the bed, still naked, looking at the telephone with a vague smile, the kind of smile which comes over a woman when her breasts are being sucked rapidly, repeatedly and Foster observes that her clothes are still neatly piled in the corner, she has made no moves whatsoever. As she sees him, her expression drops to solemnity and then kindles ever so slowly toward reception and she beckons to him, putting a cool, fine hand on his arm, letting it move up gently toward his shoulder blade and then kisses him, tongue and teeth, grinding expertly and he feels himself within the shell of his underwear beginning to rise again. It is really quite impossible: the difficult thing about sex, for Foster, is that it opens up further and further, you are never more aware of its importance than when you are having it and this is why in the long run the celibates may have it right. It is far better never to get laid at all then to get laid occasionally because getting laid occasionally means that you begin to ask questions which in certain circumstances can be almost insupportable.

"Come on," he says, backing off the kiss, shaking his head, trying to feign briskness. "I thought we were getting out of here."

"Oh," she says moistly. "Oh Harry, I thought so too but I really can't keep my hands off you and when I saw you again after you being away from me and all I just lost control. Oh God," she says and drops his hands to his genitals, cups her own palms over them, begins to knead so that the masturbation-by-proxy sends shivers of warmth and intimation stirring through Foster. "Oh God, oh God," and comes over him with a moan, breasts flopping, squeezing against him and then encircles him with another kiss, one so prolonged, reddened and urgent that Foster feels himself gasping when they separate.

"C'mon," he says hopelessly, "we got to get out of here. My mother—"

"I spoke to my roommate. She's not worried anymore. She says I should stay out as long as I want. Grab the moment she said, grab the moment. You never know when it will come around again. Wasn't that sweet of her? I told her all about you, Harry. She says you sound terrific."

"Out," Foster mumbles thickly, choking, not even sure of direction now or why the question of exit has become so crucial. Is it so crucial? "Out."

"Oh let's stay," she says. "Let's just stay for a little while longer. We can go in ten minutes, twenty minutes, half an hour or so, but Harry let's take the moment. It's our moment; yours and mine. My roommate is named Sybelle, she's an actress too, she did some Shakespeare in stock two summers ago and she talks beautifully. Doesn't she talk beautifully, Harry? She's a beautiful girl too, not as beautiful as me of course but very nice for all of that and so sweet and sensitive and I want you to take my breasts in your mouth; do it to me like you did it before, bite them, bring the teeth together, make believe that the nipple is a piece of hard candy; oh don't you know, Harry, that every woman likes to be hurt there?" And quite lost now, quite entrapped, but liking it for all of that Foster collaborates: he can feel his body beginning on the slow drown of collaboration, first his fluttering prick, seized suddenly by her energetic hands seems to have assumed grotesque, swollen proportions, then his thighs, shivering and quivering, seem to have gone quite weak and flaccid; then too he feels as if he is falling into a cavern, a long, mindless, endless cavern at the end of which is some kind of Ultimate Bestowal, this being one of the familiar hallucinations of sex and finally his own fingers are collaborating, devils now, devils always, persistent toward their own knowledge they are moving down her stomach and up her thighs, around, in and down and he feels the juices of her cunt thick, welling, shoves three fingers into her snatch with such ease that he has the feeling she could, at this moment, take his entire hand, probes around there for a while feeling the beat of her swelling clitoris and then, groaning, helps her take off his few pieces of clothing, shifting, straddling on the bed, feeling the slow slide of pants below his knees and the enormous bursting power of his cock as she covers it now with both hands and then, with collaborative eagerness, moves briskly down the wedge of his body and proceeds to go down on him.

She goes down on him with unusual passion—that, as a matter of fact, is the culminating fact about this girl, this screw, what passion she is showing! What concentration! What single-minded devotion! Foster had never realized that he was capable of generating such response from a girl; it is probably the winner's aura that she has sensed and is trying to draw power from but that is perfectly all right with him; he has more than enough of this to go around to ten, a hundred, a thousand girls, the beneficence of Winning—and with a practiced ease which in other circumstances would lead him into some serious speculations about her background and gifts, certainly no girl that he has been with has ever taken the cock with the sheer professionalism that this one does; most of them, as a matter of tact, have been so tentative and uneasy with the thing as to fill him with pity for their submission and make him almost beg off. But not this one, what she is attempting to do, Foster gathers from his distance and in the numbing fire from his glans, is to ingest all of it into her mouth, take it beyond possibility, gather it unto her and he feels around him what might be the dainty tremors of her tiny esophagus, trying to judge through sensation whether this gift is edible goods or whether its possessor is once again Only Kidding, she moans and slobbers over him, whines and cries, squeals and jumps, rocking him back and forth with her fists as she does so, a hint of touch on his balls, touch of fire in his crotch, fire of tension in his asshole and more quickly than he would have dreamed possible he is once again surging toward her but what an orgasm it is this time! What an orgasm! It is to the other orgasms today as galloping 100-1 shot is to a 1-5 shot that you have bet to show coming staggering in wheezes into the money. He grunts, sobs, moans, twists, reaches her breasts with fingers that seem to have turned to ice and begins to squeeze her nipples then with the care and finesse which he put into the pile of $100.00 winning tickets after People Trap had won but before he had had a chance to collect. The nipples, seemingly huge as apples, seem to pulsate in his palms, his prick pulsates in her mouth, her mouth pulsates against his prick, the bed shifts, ceiling wheels, breath sighs and Foster comes in an explosion of such shattering power that he feels that his semen has turned to glass and must be shattering fragments within her mouth. She follows him all the way to the end of it and beyond, drawing out the last of him and swallowing with satisfaction, then, still cupping his prick with her hands—so that it doesn't get too cold too suddenly he supposes—disengages her mouth and kisses his hip, sighs, yawns on the bed. Idly he probes her open cunt from this easy access, then bends his head down the last necessary inches and begins to lap her, curling his tongue into the hairs, feeling the wedge of her clitoris—it must be her clitoris—open up. It really isn't too bad when you get down to doing it in the right context, he decides. Foster has actually never gone down on a woman. There has been no prejudice in any of this, simply a lack of what he would consider proper timing.

She moves with him but in no great hurry, her thighs flex indolently back and forth, her moistness increases a little but she is quiet, almost a dead weight on top of him and at a certain point he stops and asks her if what he is doing offends her for any reason or is not giving her any pleasure. "Don't be ridiculous, it's *very* nice," she says giggling. "Just take your time doing it; there's no rush at *all*," and so, dimly relieved, he goes back to it, exploring her cunt with real interest now, almost clinical, bringing his hands up and around to encircle the cheeks of her ass, faintly puffy but very firm, unblemished, smooth white, fully rising and to his astonishment finds that somewhere down below he is on the verge of yet another erection. It is ridiculous, absolutely ridiculous that something like this should be happening to him—sex for him has been a one-shot phenomenon, something very good like eating an excellent meal but who the hell ever sent the waiter back for seconds, even in the cheapest of restaurants?—but he tries not to speculate, his speculating days are over, the Foster who cancelled and balanced chances is far far beyond him: this is a new, a take-it-as-it-comes, a for lack of a better word existential Foster, a winning Foster and so he feels her mouth slide against him once again with an enormous detachment; if she can coax another orgasm out of him she is better than anyone he has ever dealt with and that is all there is to it. Her tongue protrudes, begins to work around him, he feels his concentration gather, he feels a surge of power, flicker of need and then a lunging toward and she encircles him; his tongue falls away from her cunt and he leans back sighing. This is the life. He concentrates, working on it by remote control from some vast distance as if he were operating a detonating device which, far down range, would heave clods of earth spectacularly but by no means effecting him in any meaningful way and it is interesting, that is the thing, it is really far more interesting than anything which has ever happened to him before with the possible exception of People Trap and he feels good, really good; this is the new Foster, all kindling connection, on the verge of ascension and there is absolutely no way knowing how far he would go, what outcome he would find, what meanings he would chase, what exaltation he would know turning from her as the All-New Foster—but at that moment there are shattering poundings and boots heard through the door; the girl sighs enormously and turns away from him, the room seems to turn away from him, shouts begin and moans and curses and the girl is saying, as if from a far, far distance. "Oh thank God, they're here. They came, they *came*." and he does not know, listening to her sob of release, if she is talking about some people who have come or is merely referring to him, Foster, the all-time winner who has not, after all yielded this second time and now, seemingly never will. Weakened he can only watch as the girl springs up, unlatches the door and lets the two men in. They regard him with vast interest. He supposes that he regards them in the same way.

THREE

"Well," the taller of the two men says; not that he is much taller and not that there is really any significant difference between the two except that this taller one seems to be amused while the shorter guy in the all-new, all-blue suit is searching the walls, licking his lips as if vaguely embarrassed. "Well, well, well. How are you, loser?" and looks down at him with a beckoning smile, almost as if he were on the verge of some meaningful embrace. "How are *you* Dolores?" He looks down at Foster with enormous contentment, not missing any angle of the bed or, Foster supposes, physique. "So you got the mouth treatment from Dolores," he says. "Well, you lucky, lucky man. There are very few of us."

"Stop it, Eddie," the girl says, now perched uneasily against the wall. "No cracks about me. I had to keep him in the room, we agreed that you wanted him in the room—"

"And here he is," Eddie agrees, nodding briskly and checking something in his pocket. "And couldn't look nicer. Foster is the name? Pleased to meet you. My name is Eddie as you have already found out." He shrugs, makes a tilting gesture at the ceiling, winks at Foster. "Sorry that we have to meet in such amazing circumstances—"

"All right," the shorter, all-blue man says abruptly. "Cut that out now, Ed. This isn't a party, it's business. Come on; get up and get dressed, fella. Go into the bathroom." Some delicate expression crosses All-Blue's lips, the sheer physicality of the situation seems to have upset him in some fashion. "There's nothing personal here."

"Listen, Al," Ed says. "I don't mean anything; I was just trying to introduce myself—"

"Cut it out. This is serious business. Go in there and get dressed, Foster. We're clearing out; this is no party, no social occasion. Dolores, show us the money. Let me see that money."

"I don't know where he's got it right now," Dolores says. "It was in his wallet in his pants but he might have put it somewhere else."

"Where's the money?" Al says to Foster. A kind of consternation seems to have come over him in the instant, it was as if he had taken the whole thing personally. "Where is it?"

"Listen," Foster says, very difficult circumstances these, but he is trying to deal with them, most likely by pretending that they cannot possibly be occurring. It is simply not likely that the girl could do something like this to him. "I don't think you understand. That's *my* money."

"Sure it is," Al says, "every cent of it yours. We're not talking about ownership right now, just location. Where the fuck is it?"

"Please, Harry," Delores says. "Tell him where the dough is."

"Now you're talking sensible, sweetheart. You not only got an excellent mouth, you can use it both ways. Tell me where the money is, champ."

"I don't like your cracks. Eddie."

"Fuck off," Al says with exasperation. "This ain't the time or the place and personally I think you two are crazy." He puts an arm on Foster's bare shoulder, kneels, regards him with a kind of complicity which suggests: *Stick with me, kid, you and I are the only sensible people in this room.* "The money," he says with sweet reasonableness. "You see, Dolores called us and said that you had twenty-three thousand dollars on you from this big score and we went to a lot of time and trouble to come down and see it. We're money-checkers, you understand; that's our function in life. Whenever we hear that someone's got a big wad of money on them we come down to check it out personal because we got their interests in heart and we wouldn't want to think that some guy was carrying around a whole lot of counterfeit, thinking that it was the real goods. It would let him down too hard, to find out that it was all phony. So let's see the money, sweetheart, just to check it out."

"Don't sweet-talk the fuck," Ed says loudly. "Just find out where the money is. Listen here—"

More to reconcile Eddie and Al than for any other reason; it is obvious that they do not like one another very much and Foster, even in his tension, has a flicker of pity for two men who must be so bound together by both work and hate—it must be a difficult thing—Foster says, "In my pants in the bathroom. The back pocket. In the wallet."

"Thank you, Harry," Dolores says. "Listen, fellows, I'm gonna get dressed."

"And deprive us?"

"Cut it out, Eddie," Al says with vast weariness and vanishes into the bathroom, comes back with Foster's pants, extracts the enormous wallet and looks at it with reverence for a moment. "My God," he says. "My God, it looks like the truth. Look at it."

"Open it up," Eddie says. "Maybe it's stuffed with toilet paper or something. She's not the first broad who could ever have fallen for a story."

"Ah, patience," Al says and with massive delicacy, a gesture of care, opens the wallet and takes out Foster's enormous wad of money, then looks at it with reverence. "My God," he says, "my God, it's really all there. Look at that. I never seen nothing like it."

"Beautiful," Eddie says and comes over, bends with Al to regard the contents, absently fondles the bills which are in Al's hand until a few on top flake off and begin to curl, waveringly, to the floor. With a sense of outraged propriety—this is his money after all that they are spoiling—Foster lunges forward, seizes the bills and makes to jam them in his pockets until he realizes that there are no pockets. It is a very difficult and embarrassing situation. Meanwhile, Al replaces the money in the wallet and then with a look of whistling care, restores it to Foster's pants. "For safekeeping," he says. "Just to show you that we ain't no robbers or nothing like that."

"I told you," Dolores is saying. "I told you sons-of-bitches he had the money."

"Yes," Al says, "I know you told us, sweetheart, but sometimes you aren't as dependable as you are at other times and sometimes you don't concentrate as hard as you do at other times and besides it is very difficult to accept the word that you are with a man with twenty-three thousand dollars, not because you ain't *worth* twenty-three thousand dollars, you understand, because you are, honey, every penny of it, but it is so easy for any of us to overestimate—"

"I can't stand it," Eddie says. "I can't stand this now. For Christ's sake, get the guy the fuck dressed and let's get out of here. They'll spot us any second."

"I'm sorry, Harry," Dolores says suddenly. She seems to be attempting some private mode of communication, above and beyond Eddie and Al all-blue and in different circumstances, Foster decides, it would be almost a touching gesture, operating as it does on the assumption that there is something very special between the two of them. "I really am. I didn't want to mislead you or anything like that. It's just that I have to do it because it has to be done if you follow what I mean and twenty-three grand is such an awful lot of money. But I really enjoyed it and I think you're a nice person."

"I want to get dressed," Foster says.

"Sure," Al says, "and just to help you out, I'll keep you company so you can figure out which is your pants and which is your shirt and so on. You and I will go in the bathroom to help you get dressed and Eddie can help Dolores get dressed and then we'll all go for a nice ride. Does that sound attractive?"

"Does she have to get dressed right away?" Eddie says and flicks out a tentative finger, touches one of Dolores's nipples. The thing is that she submits, a grotesque expression on her face, nostrils distended, eyes closed, apparently not liking it very much. Foster reflects absently that all things being equal he probably got a lot further with her than most men did.

"Cut it out, you goon," Al says with something approaching affection and escorts Foster into the bathroom, closes the door gently behind them, then perches with interest on the toilet seat while Foster gets dressed. He lights a cigarette, twirls the match, flips it against the mirror, winks his eyes again, both of them. "How'd you get hold of that kind of money?"

"I hit a horse at the track."

"Dolores told us that. I mean which horse at what track? That's a fantastic score."

"What are you going to do?" Foster says. "Beat me up or kill me and take the wad? I don't think you're here to admire it."

"Oh, I don't know," Al says, shrugging. "Let's not talk about that part of it yet. We'll do what we have to do. There's nothing personal you understand; the girl is just doing her job. She has instructions. Actually, she probably likes you, you shouldn't feel that you've been made a fool of or anything like that. It's just business. What horse did you say?"

"People Trap."

"People Trap!"

"In the fifth at Aqueduct."

"Why, that son-of-a-bitch," Al says, with real pain. "That son-of-a-bitch! I've been following him myself here and there. You mean to say he was in the entries today? I didn't even notice. Of course I skim too fast, that's my trouble. I don't have patience, that's why I never made a real horse-player. You got to have extraordinary patience."

"Listen," Foster says. "Can't we work this thing out like gentlemen?" He is still trying to function, past the shock now, like Foster the Winner: this reasonable man who could not possibly be in a hole without making reasonable, civilized, respectable efforts to get out without too much dirt on him. "I know I'm in a bad spot but I'm not without sympathy. I mean, I'm not entirely unsympathetic. Anyway, you know what I mean; I've had a little experience in my life with losing, once or twice: I know how it is. Couldn't I offer you a couple of thousand—"

"Oh, come on," Al says and looks at him unwinking this time, his face suddenly drawn back so that Foster can see all the bone in it, a suspicion of fragmentation, an indication that Al might have been, at one time, the victim perhaps of a really serious auto accident, something that would have left scars on a previously pleasant, bright, optimistic personality. "Come on, pigeon, get the score. Be reasonable. Any man who can pick 100-1 shots—"

"300-1."

"The sons-of-a-bitch, they really put that over, didn't they? Any man, anyway who can pick 300-1 shots knows better than that. Don't you, Foster? Don't you now?"

"Know what?" Foster says, drawing on his pants. The presence of the wallet there is slickly comforting for some reason; if nothing else, by restoring it to him they have obviously planned to make their move in some intricate fashion and this may be to his advantage. The thing about losers was that by thinking too much they blew it: winners, who could see straight down the pipe, were always ahead of them.

"Why should we take a payoff when we can get it all?" Al says with satisfaction and inhales deeply on the cigarette, dumps it off, begins to fiddle with the shower curtain. "Now that ain't, strictly speaking, reasonable, Foster; you ain't using your head."

"But why are you entitled—"

"Consider it stolen money," Al says with enormous satisfaction and, sighing, lofts another huge puff of smoke toward the blower unit. "The horse could've run out. You'd never know the difference. This way at least you have the satisfaction of knowing that you made the right choices. And had a pretty fuck in the bargain that didn't cost you a penny. Usually Dolores—"

"Cut it out," Foster says.

"Dolores? You don't like my bringing Dolores into this? Well, I can understand your emotions, Foster; it's not an easy thing to understand that a woman might have other motives. Anyway," Al says and rises, stamps on the cigarette, gives Foster an enormous confidential pat on the behind. "Anyway, you're all dressed now and looking very sharp considering the circumstances and we can go out and rejoin the people now and get ready to get out of here. The way we do it is simple and if you keep your head about you you may make it after all. We only carry guns for show. Oh, by the way," Al says with a tone of exasperation, "come to think of it, that's right; I never showed you the gun because I got all this cooperation from you and maybe you're getting to think that we're just a couple meatballs taking too many chances. I'm heeled though, very nice," and opening his inner coat pocket and stepping back a pace shows Foster a lovely small gun imbedded like a cherry in a Manhattan, faintly protruding from the all-new, all-blue inner pocket. "It's a nice little gun and it shoots perfectly splendid-looking little holes. I spent a lot of money for it, me and Eddie that is. It was either a gun or car so we use public transportation. But it was a wise investment, you know?" and swats Foster again, almost a trickle of hilarity this time and Foster leads him out of the bathroom and back into the main unit where Dolores, standing uncomfortably now in the tight sweater which he had been introduced to her in is looking with some distraction toward the window while Eddie strokes and feels her, bumps her breasts together, bends his mouth toward his shoulder. He is quite absorbed, quite abstracted, and Al has to boot him with painful force to break up the juxtaposition, this sending Eddie careening into the side chair, the window ledge narrowly missing his head. Eddie looks up with dismay while Dolores shakes her head and picks up her handbag to check it.

"Come on," Al says. "Just cut that out."

"But you don't understand," Eddie says. "She let me. She makes it perfectly all right. And besides, this is a party, a victory like—"

"You're an idiot," Al says. "You're a loser. You're an inept thief. You got no class and you got no conception of margins. Now let's get out of here—"

"But twenty-three thousand—"

"Twenty-three thousand nothings if you don't cut it out."

"I'm really very sorry, Harry." Dolores says again and coming over to Foster, takes him sorrowfully, gracefully by the arm and leans her head against his shoulder. "Like I say, it was business and I work with them. I could have taken the chance and never told them but then the rest of my life as long as I ever lived I'd be thinking about that money and passing it up and no matter how much I liked you I couldn't risk that. You follow? You follow me, Harry?" Foster nods to suggest that he follows her and Al opens the door with something of a flourish, beckoning. "Our guest first," he says as Foster comes toward him. "Then the rest. What we're going to do, I gotta explain, is to take your car, Foster. You sit up front with the girl and you don't say nothing, you just drive. Eddie and I in the back; we keep chaperoning you. Then when we get on the highway I tell you where to go and what's next. You still got your wallet, Foster?"

"Yes."

"That's good because I wouldn't want you leaving it in the room or something unfair like that," Al says, patting him. "That's good; you keep it right there for the time being and when we want it, we'll just give you a call. Ready?" he says with the forced benevolence of the social director. "Let's go then," and that is how they go out of the room, towards Foster's 1961 Plymouth with standard shift which regards them from a couple of feet away, a half-smile on its creased bumper, a pool of oil underneath the left rear tire. He will definitely now, Foster decides, have to get rid of this car. Sentiment is one thing and debt another but he really can hardly trust it any more. His speculations shift rapidly from the car however to Eddie and Al who are standing with grins, waiting almost deferentially for him to open the doors. He has never, Foster decided, seen anything like these two before.

But this is quite likely: he is Foster the Winner now, this new man only a couple of hours in being and Foster the Winner has so far had the opportunity to see very little: a pair of excellent tits, a steaming cunt, two hundred and thirty hundred-dollar bills, a couple of confused goons, the slick interior of a motel; it really has been a very short life so far and therefore to an ineluctable extent Foster the Winner must rely upon the counsel and advice of his old friend Foster the Loser with whom he remains on speaking terms even though the Loser has been exiled to some place deep in the skull and already sinking below memory. Foster the Loser knows these men very well, far better, perhaps, than they even know themselves: the fact is that the Loser has been toe-to-toe in subways with them, jammed up in grandstands, standing against their meat in crowded bars, listening to them mumble about odds, percentages, fatigue and probabilities; he has known them for a long time in one way or the other and now he is busy whispering certain information to the Winner who, like all Winners, is shutting it up and taking it in. *You got to understand that these guys would do exactly what I would do* the Loser says and the Winner asks reasonably, *What is that?* and the Loser says, *Well you got to understand, they got terrific energy and tremendous wants but no imagination; no goddamned imagination at all, that's what always fucks them up one way or the other: now they are going to let you and the girl get into that car first while they wait for you to open the doors for them like a proper chauffeur; because they've got the gun and they figure consequently you aren't going to make any wrong moves. They are incapable of perceiving beyond the limits of a given situation in its given context which is probably the reason why you are the man carrying twenty-three thousand dollars and they are the people with the guns. Isn't that interesting?* Foster the Winner notes. *Well, thank you very much for your time and trouble. No problems at all*, the Loser says, *There isn't too damned much to do down here, there never was, so anytime you feel like you need a little help, just give me a call.* Foster extracts his keys from the left pants pocket, opens the door for the girl while Eddie and Al all-blue stand uneasily watching them; she smiles at Foster— a strange smile, it is almost as if they are alone and he is packing her off deferentially now after services rendered—and gets in. "Watch yourself, now," Al comments, "just go around there nice and easy and open the door and get in and then let Eddie and me slide right behind you. There doesn't have to be no trouble; we can handle this like gentlemen." Foster reflects again that he has never seen people like this before; even if his Winner's career continues he doubts if it will be a common occurrence. He nods, winks back at Al, slams the door on the girl and walks almost jauntily over to his side of the car, uses the key to get in—she has not opened the door for him which is really not very nice of her but on the other hand she is under pressure too—and gets behind the wheel. He pulls the door closed; it thuds in with a solidity so convincing that on the instant he decides that the old Plymouth really isn't that bad a car after all, maybe he will hold onto it; if nothing else it has a satisfying door-slam, solid gold.

What goes on next is very dreamlike and very rapid and Foster feels more like a witness than a participant; he starts the engine and it turns over, thank God and for once, quite easily, races the motor gently, then suddenly slams the car into reverse, floors the gas pedal, comes wheeling out of the parking space at such speed that he almost hits a gentle tree planted for the guests' rural satisfaction in the rear of the driveway, misses it, brakes the car, races the motor again in neutral and then, slamming it into drive he gets out of there at an almost monumental speed, hurling the car down the pathway toward the highway with his eyes squeezed shut against the roar, the girl's shrieks, certain absent bee-taps that she seems to be inflicting on his wrists and shoulders. "Cut that crap out or I'll turn the car over and kill us both," he mumbles to her. Behind him, coming through the layers of glass, he can hear thin cries; rage, dismay and fury are probably what is being communicated but at this growing distance under such insulation they sound to be more like the whimpering of children or men in some post-orgasmic state and as he takes the car onto the Shore Parkway, moving into the center lane oblivious of what a large truck is doing or trying not to do behind him, he finds himself laughing, shaking, quivering, obsessed with the laughter, the tears blinding his eyes, shaking his belly, making him tremble and then it is all business, moving the car up to seventy, eighty miles an hour, swinging to the left lane to pass a limousine in which he catches a glimpse of some politician-like dwarf standing in the rear, shaking a tiny fist at him through the windows, then around and back into the center lane and he drives with exhilaration, a feeling of vaulting ascendancy, his mood broken for only an instant when he scrabbles around to his rear pocket to make sure that the wallet is still there … which it would have to be. For the first time in several minutes he becomes aware of the girl because she is crying and the sounds have finally come through to Foster the Winner. Her face is in her palms, her elbows are on her knees and she is shaking with sobs that would seem vaguely like laughter if he was not so aware of the circumstances. "Cut that out," he says. "Now just cut it out; you got me in this damned mess."

"The fools," she is muttering, "the fools—"

"Has nothing to do with them," Foster says. "It's just percentage. They've got none. None at all."

"Oh God," she says. "Oh, God," and then after a pause, "well, what are you going to do with me? I suppose you're going to beat the hell out of me or maybe just dump me from the car. I told you, I didn't mean to do it. But I had to; it was business. Didn't I tell you that in the room? I liked you a lot. It was only—"

"Sure, sure," Foster says, embracing other complications. "Sure you did. Shut up and let me think." Calculations seem to shift dimly through him, he almost collides with a maddened Corvette that bucks into his lane at an improper moment and at the last second out of it again. "Just let me think."

"They'll kill you," she says, "If they ever catch up with you they'll kill you. My God, what am I talking about *you* for?" she says and her voice breaks. "They don't know who *you* are. They'll kill *me!* Where are you taking me? What are you doing?"

"Oh, hell," Foster says, finally deciding that it's the only thing he can do; a bit stunned by the world of choices into which the Winning has placed him, a whole new arena this one is with certain problems which, even from this unfamiliarity, look to him like Moral Choices, something with which he has previously been unfamiliar. "I guess I'll take you home first."

"Take me home! They'll be lying in wait for me there. You can't do that to me! Besides, I lied to you about where I lived; it's really a residential hotel with a single room. I don't have a girl friend."

"Oh, not your home," Foster says. "Not yet. Not for a while. No, I'm taking you to *my* home. I'm not through discussing this with you, though," he reminds her and moving crisply into the right lane, missing a huge van behind him by less than he would like to think, begins to look for an exit sign, reflecting that for a man who has driven the Shore Parkway so many times in so many moods he is behaving strangely as if he had never been on it before. Which in several essential senses is, of course, true.

FOUR

The rest of the drive is a quiet one; whatever exhilaration has possessed him has been drained from Foster and he finds himself in the sudden aftermath of his mood to have been plunged into a state of high, tense apprehension which makes speech seem somehow frivolous and in any event leaves him very little to say. Perhaps it is only that he wishes he could show the girl something a little more imposing than Bay Ridge, not that he has at any time up until this moment been ashamed of his neighborhood or where he comes from. But this girl, miserable girl who has twice defeated him this afternoon, once dangerously, for all of this is still sitting beside him and the sheer fact that she is is some indication that Foster feels an obligation to show her a good time, even if that good time is only involved with him getting his head blown off in her presence or something exciting like that. The girl, meanwhile, has settled into a total quiet, broken now and then only by vagrant eddies of sobs and platitude during which she has said things like, "I don't know how I got into this," or "It wasn't anything personal, you got to understand that," or "Actually sex was never quite as good as it was this afternoon," or "Al and Eddie are insane; you couldn't understand how dangerous they were if you hadn't, uh, *lived* with them," or "But what's the use, you're only going to hate me and think I'm just like them," and when Foster, stifled deep in his mood and quivers had not answered her, the girl had given up all conversation and had settled only for that continued silence occasionally broken by heavy sighs and some pouting. She was a very good-looking girl although a bit treacherous but one thing was clear: she had too many moves on her and one way or the other they were going to have to be broken up. Foster wasn't ready to decide yet, however, if he wanted to do the breaking and in what way. He was just barely beginning, after all, to come to terms with himself, a difficult enough job. He brings the car into Bay 35th Street, checking right and left to see if there are any cars which look like those of bill collectors, parked near his two-family but there are not and he reminds himself that it is after working hours in the first place and in the second, Eddie and Al willing, he no longer has to be concerned with bill collectors. He puts the car into the driveway, steps down on the emergency brake and says to the girl, "All right. This is it. Everybody out."

"What are you going to do to me?"

"We're going to get out."

She shudders and puts a hand pleadingly on his arm. "Please, Harry—"

"Oh, for Christ's sake," he says, finally getting it. "Do you think this is the last mile or something like that? You got to stop watching all those goddamned movies; this is where I live and we're just going to get out and go upstairs and have a cup of coffee and talk a little. I don't know what I'm going to do to you; I can't decide if I'll just slap you and send you home or if I'll try to straighten you out but we'll work that out in good time and in the meanwhile we got enough worrying about the boys to do without worrying about me. Forget it," he says and opens the door, gets out abruptly and is surprised to see her slide across the seat and come crying into his arms as he helps her out. Once again she puts her face in his chest. "I'm just so sorry," she says. "You can't imagine how sorry—"

"Oh, come on," Foster the Winner says. "Stop that dissimulation crap," not really wanting to pull words on her but then he is a college graduate and every now and then, once in a great while, it comes in handy, usually with waiters who he is about to stiff. He encircles her wrist tightly, guides her into the side door of the house and, shushing her with a forefinger, takes her quietly up the stairs, pausing at the top to rap quietly at the darkened door. "Mom usually goes to bed early and I don't like to wake her if I can help it," he says but this does not seem to be one of those evenings for Mom herself, his mother that is, opens the door on him and stands there in the pale reflected light of the one-bulb lamp from the kitchen. So she has been up late again.

"Damn it," she says, her spectacles flashing faintly. "Damn it, don't you have a key?"

"I didn't want to wake you. Mom, this is a friend of mine, Dolores"

"Well, pleased I'm sure," his mother says and turns her back on them, goes back to the kitchen. Dolores looks at him with confusion and rage alternating on her face and he finds himself, saying, "Oh, you don't have to worry about a thing, she's just very caught up in herself." He guides her into the living room, flicks on lights, directs her to the sofa. She sits down slowly, looking at the pictures on the walls: his late father in a field, his late father riding a horse, his late father leaning easily over the rail at Aqueduct, oh, his mother is devoted to his late father, no doubt about it, for the first time it occurs to Foster that his mother might be a little bit too devoted. "She doesn't get involved with me at all," he says. "We go our separate ways." His mother returns, carrying her copy of the *Telegraph* this time, the pages flung open to tomorrow's entries, and also a plate of cookies. She puts the cookies in front of Dolores and shrugs, looks at Foster. "How'd you make out today?" she asks.

"It's a long story."

"I blew eighty-six bucks. I had it made until the sixth, then that goddamned Milk Wagon has to bear out in the stretch. You see that race?”

“I left early.”

“Oh. Thought you could tell me about it. I didn’t like the reports I heard. Seems to me the jockey was pulling him all the way through. I had a hundred bucks on that animal. Well, it just goes to show you.”

“Do you play the horses too, Mrs. Foster?” Dolores asks and this is perhaps not the proper question at the given moment because his mother breaks into a fit of hysterical whinnying laughter—in which she sounds surprisingly like a horse herself, a mare or perhaps a four-year-old filly trying to kick out her stall—and trembling with giggles, turns to shuffle back to the kitchen. “Now and then,” she says behind her. “Now and then.”

“Mom plays the horses too,” Foster says, feeling an explicatory fit coming over him: some latent pedanticism, some need to explain to this girl what is going on. He has never before felt the need, with any girl, to explain his household or to even consider it rather strange but now, looking at it from her vantage point, he sees where it possibly may be. “She usually plays them through the bookies but once or twice a week she feels well enough to go out to the track so she does. Up till five years ago, Mom was able to get out every day but then arthritis caught up with her and a big losing streak and she found she didn’t have the strength any more. But she still dopes ‘em out—”

“But that’s—”

“Oh, we don’t have anything to do with each other,” Foster says. “I mean, she’ll give me a horse now and then or I’ll give her one but I only live here because the rent is cheap and I have lots of space and she doesn’t bother me. She’ll hit me for a loan now or then when she gets behind but I’ll hit her for a loan too and anyway, the pension and social security and some money that she’s been into for years from somewhere keep her going pretty good. Actually, I think she’s ahead. She won’t say but I think she makes fifty, sixty a week out of the flats so that fills out things nicely. She’ll play the trots too.”

“I never heard of anything like it.”

“Oh, she’s all right,” Foster says vaguely. “She doesn’t understand pace factors and she gives too much emphasis to speed and she doesn’t understand the first thing about maiden claimer races but she knows a couple of angles to allowance races I’ve only learned to pick up over the years and she’s deadly in the straight claimers. She has an eye for trainers. Otherwise, she’s not too much of a problem. Don’t worry about her; sometimes she stays up all night and dopes them out when she’s feeling puzzled and sometimes she goes right to bed. It all depends.”

“My God,” Dolores says, “you know, I didn’t mean anything with Eddie and Al. A joke; it was all part of a joke, a put-on. Actually, when you think about them, they're really nice guys, it's only that they—"

Somewhere during this, perhaps, Mom has shuffled back. "Oh, come on," Foster says, with a little exasperation. "The young lady and I—"

"Ain't none of my business," the old lady says, tugging idly on her night-gown. "Don't care what you do. Wish you luck; she's very pretty. No, wanted to ask you about Belmonte. How he look out there today?"

"Pretty good. Two seconds in the first four races, didn't ride in the fifth. Then I went home."

"Did he seem to be riding easy?"

"Pretty fair."

"I'm afraid of him. This Pia Star looks very good tomorrow but I'm afraid of that boy. He's got a vicious streak and I think he's a little something of a crook too. They say he came out of Puerto Rico's biggest fix track, you know."

"Oh, come on, Mom, that's just your paranoia again. He's a decent jockey."

"Yeah," she says, "well, he *still* can't ride them in anything over 120. You make out all right today?"

Foster sighs and says, "Fair."

"Nothing special?"

"Average."

"That means you lost forty bucks."

"Give or take," Foster says, looking down at his hands. "Go get 'em to-morrow."

"Were you with him out there, Dolores?"

"Uh ... no. No, I wasn't. We had a date later and—"

"Well, that's just as well. Just as well. My son is a lousy horse player, young lady. He never picked up the fundamentals. Not that it makes any difference to me, you understand."

"All right, Mom," Foster says.

"All right. All right. I'm going to bed. You want me to run anything in for you in the morning or you going to go out there yourself?"

"I don't know yet. Probably go out. Anyway, there's nothing I like good enough to bet right now. Haven't even looked over the entries."

"I'll bet," Mom says and shuffles out of the living room, shutting off lights behind her until they are left sitting in a pool of darkness, only the one, thin overhanging bulb above the door enabling Foster to see Dolores. She looks even better in this light; it returns to her face the bare youthfulness and optimism he had seen. "For God's sake, keep quiet in the morning, I need some sleep," Mom calls back and then slams her door. Dolores sighs, twitches on the couch, looks at her hands, rubs them across her cheek. "Do you have a cigarette?" she says.

"I left them in the motel. I forgot to take them. I guess I was a little distracted."

"Oh," she says. "Oh, I guess you were."

"Don't worry about Mom. She's just a little bitter because she knows I'm a better horse player than she is. Even though she makes money and I've been a loser. I go into it more deeply, I see angles she misses. Of course I'm a little younger than she is. Actually she used to be pretty good; she still teaches me a lot."

"Why didn't you tell her about what you made at the track today?"

"Why should I? We have no relationship; we're just two friends who live together."

"But your mother—"

"Well, put it this way," Foster says and turns Al's wink on her, feeling his eye seem to pop and glow in the darkness. "Far as I know, I've only told one person so far and you see what I got for that. Now I figure if I tell Mom, she's a lot shrewder than even you are so I'll just triple my troubles. You understand? Not that I don't have a certain affection for the old lady; after all, she did marry my father who was the greatest horse player I ever knew."

Dolores shifts on the couch, looks at him, looks down at her feet. "All right, Harry," she says. "All right. What are you going to do with me now? This can't go on like this, can it?"

Foster the Loser would have had the answer for that. He would have said, "Well, we'll just have to talk this one through and see where we get because I'm still not quite sure." Foster the Loser would have tossed cigarettes all night and calculated percentages with and against the girl, proportions in and out of the light. But Foster the Winner seems to have lost the Loser's easy articulacy while retaining other, more vital things.

"You want to know?" he says and turns on her the first real smile of the evening, a loosening and lightening seeming to flood through him as he does this and even the girl twitches, sees it, acknowledges it, takes notice. "If you want to know the truth, I think I'm going to screw the hell out of you. Again. And for real."

FIVE

It is even easier than he has supposed. The girl says nothing, gives him no glance—meaningful or otherwise—does not recoil, does not shrug, does nothing at all, looks at him only with a bland level gaze which embraces both her own growing sense of salvation and his own enormous sense of power which, despite all the trials and tribulations, has been working within him all day. He reaches toward her, feeling the hard, yielding graze of her skin under his palms, feeling the slow kneading force of her body as she comes absently against him and saying nothing at all, he picks her up and carries her into his large bedroom, an enormous room papered with pictures of horses and strewn with back issues of the *Telegraph*, charts, chart books, racing manuals, reports, texts on gambling and the hell with all of them now. Fortunately he had remembered to make his bed that morning. He tosses her on it and lowers himself slowly against her, the very issue of clothes seeming to dissolve in the blackness. With a single preoccupied hand he reaches up and snaps home the lock of his door.

Because it is all very easy: he has suddenly come to understand that it has been a long time coming and may be a longer time gone but in that middle ground—that vast middle ground of purpose—there may yet be knowledge enough, the kind of knowledge on which he can structure the rest of his life. Because this girl is for fucking. That is her basic purpose in life: she may have others, there is no question but that she thinks she has others, considers herself a solemn, weighty person with a sense of mission, a purpose, a history (If she were not in earnest, did not see herself as a protagonist, how could she have called New-Blue and Eddie in the first place?), but in the last analysis the judgement must be made: she exists to be screwed. In the minds of all the men who have seen her, dealt with her, fucked her or not, she is seen only in that context; women hate her for it, older people misunderstand her for it, pre-pubescents miss the point, even her own flighty consciousness will miss it time and again but the point is that the woman is for fucking no less than a tote-board is for calculation and you only get into trouble with the tote when you ask it to supply more than it is able to do: like predict results or try to differentiate the smart money from the dumb. In the same way this kind of woman is relatively simple, even an easy process if she is seen in that simple context of need: to understand her function, Foster decides, groping, ah yes, to understand her function is not to say that you will be able to use it: to juggle odds on the tote is not to predict the winner but it at least establishes the fact that one is working on the right level, one is working with the instrument in terms of its capabilities, one is dealing with it on the level sought. The girl knows about fucking. About nothing else will she ever be as sure.

And that is a pity, perhaps, a pity: for all he knows this girl is possessed of enormous qualities both above and below her sexuality; underneath her gigantic, flopping tits beats a heart as huge as the Pope's, between her legs sighs not only her cunt but bowels constricted by woe, need, loss, sensitivity, pain, memory, her lips are not only rubbery impressions to be grasped and gobbled but capable of enunciating thoughts of beauty—but all of that will have to wait. After all, Foster reflects, it is not he but she who has defined this role for herself: as far as he was concerned, she could have been anything. She was not alone in the bar, drinking whisky and water, casting him sidelong glances and admiring his hundred-dollar bill on the boards because she was trying to reach him at some point of sensitivity. Was she?

So Foster fucks her then, oblivious for the moment to all but skin and scent, self and twisting, but it is in a way the most interesting fuck he has ever had because it is not the two of them in the bed but, interestingly, the three of them, his shadow-partner, Foster the Loser has returned and it is as if not only the Winner but the Loser himself is doing the fucking, enabling Foster to work at not one but two levels of connection and this profundity on top of his earlier depletion, the scent and feel of the girl and his commingled rage and need at what she has done for him manage to lend him a profound experience; it is as if, then, fucking on the two levels, he finds himself tossed to a level of perception so broad and so meaningful that he knows he will never, whatever he does, wherever he goes, quite be the same again and it is worth it, it is worth it, oh yes indeed, it is certainly worth it:

The Loser stretches himself on her abdomen then, knees poised between her, hands reaching to curl and grasp her tit and encircle the nipple and in an agony of dependency, pain and lifting in his cock, void and stumble of excitation in his stomach he bends down then to suck her, taking the curling nipple in deeply, moaning, whistling, trying to immerse himself in the smoothness and pallid warmth of her skin and she leans back sighing, sighing, as the Loser drinks deeply of her, grinding his teeth in, trying to imagine that there is not saliva but milk steaming back at him in the agony of his sucking and she says, "Ah, ah," in a distant way and cups him, drags him into her as if he were a nursling and then he

The Winner rises to enormous height against her, height and power, stretches down his hands and squeezes her breasts cruelly, bringing the swinging pain into them, scratching and beating at the nipples until they seem on the verge of opening and spouting blood, the fluids of her, then clenches his mouth, sucks at her carefully, listening as if from a great distance to the increase of her moans, pacing himself against her to make the bitch whine and sob and she opens her mouth gasping, gasping, tongue hanging loose and fluttering in her head as he brings her past pain to fulfillment, then shoots down a hand and seizes the folds of her cunt, now huge, wet and pouting beneath him and begins to work inside of her, feeling the rhythmic gush and swell of her body recan feel the tickle and pressure of her fingers against his cock, his cock groaning and unwinding beneath her, she takes it in her hands and cups it as gently as an infant and he says, "God, God, more, more," and she gives him an easy increasing pressure, giving him the sensation that his semen is literally rising and bubbling inside him, moaning, muttering, he feels the length of his cock extend and digs his fingers into her distant, diminished hole, feeling the tightness of the walls, the smoothness of the interior, imagining as he reaches forward to move into her that he can grasp the fullness of the womb itself, immerse his fingers in it as years and years ago the Loser had drifted inside the aqueous warmth of his mother, then a pregnant horse player, waiting for the Big Win to strike and the natal pressures to begin. He says, "Oh baby, oh baby," again, knowing his helplessness, his need, her dominance, his vulnerability, excited not only by what he is doing but the sheer knowledge of his need for her and how at any given moment she could turn away from him and leave him stricken, bubbling with his vulnerability, then sucks of her tits again and rises fully, flexes his knees, makes a slow, stiff entrance, feeling the tightness of her hole constricting around him, a sense of entrapment, a

sponding mindlessly to him, knowing that what he is doing is driving her past sensation, past response into some orbit of her own where she will be completely at his mercy, groaning and unwinding underneath him, he takes her thighs in his hands and begins to knead and squeeze, squeeze and knead and she says, "God, God, I can't stand it, more, more," and he squeezes harder and harder, knowing that what he is doing to her is driving her to a point now where she will be utterly out of control, able to gush and flood only in terms of what he will permit her to do, digs his fingers into her huge, overflowing cunt, then the fist, the whole hand, feeling the opening of the walls, the roughness of the interior, knowing as he moves his whole hand into her that he can do with her anything he likes, tear it off, rip, destroy, it would all be the same to her, the same agony, the same yielding vulnerability; the Winner did this to his mother, bursting the walls of her when he came into the world of possibilities and so now he does it to this woman, a Big Win but only in relative perspective. He says, "Come on and fuck, let's give it back, you bitch," knowing her helplessness, her submission, his utter control of her, her utter vulnerability and excited not only by what he is doing but the sheer knowledge of her need for him and how at any given moment he could turn away from this bitch and leave her sense of vanishing as his prick marches away from him and in some hidden corridor, extended to enormous length begins to pulsate, then drags himself in and out of her, out and in, biting her shoulders, biting her neck, squeezing her breasts, whispering to her his dreadful need, his hope, his desire, his intentions, biting desperately again into her breasts while she closed and opened beneath him and into the smoothness of skin, tautness of muscle, timeless and impermeable stretch of flesh he deposited into her all that he had to give moaning "Oh, baby, oh baby, oh baby, oh God, oh God," until he thought the very insides of him were spinning out in a vulnerability so great that there would never, never be an end to this lust, this flesh, this slap and scuffle of skin, this melding, beating connection on his Bed of Beds. What a favor she had done him!

stricken on the sheets, bubbling over with unwanted come, unneeded juices, her tits wet and aching for his sucks again and his prick rises fully, comes to enormous size, makes a lunging, viscous entrance deep into the opening of her, feeling the slippery looseness of her hole yielding to tautness as she closes her legs and squeezes, a sense of rising power as his prick leads him into her and in some hidden corridor, extended to enormous height begins to throb out its signal, its music; then he lunges in and out brutally, squeezing her tits, biting her shoulders, biting her neck, forcing himself on her breasts, cursing to her his dreadful control, the power he has over her, his intentions, her desire, biting viciously again into her breasts until she whinnies back in him and defeat, opening underneath him and into that rough channel, into her cunt, the slackness and unwinding force, the need and necessity, her open and defeated flesh he deposits into her all that he has to give her and then more, a little bit more just for the hell of it, saying, "Take that, you bitch, take that," until she seems to explode underneath him, the very insides of her spinning out in submission, her vulnerability so great that there would never, never be an end to her lust, his flesh, this slap and scuffle of skin, this melding, beating connection he was making on his Bed of Beds.

And then with concentration and cunning joined together, Winner and Loser both, went down to eat her, ate her with single-minded concentration and passion. He had never liked sucking women off before, that was the odd thing, not that he thought they were dirty or had any particular hang-up in those directions but only because the whole idea of going down on them was something like backing up a wheeled horse in the daily double with some new money; it was superfluous, added nothing to nothing, the breasts were to suck, the cunt was to fuck and that was the end of it but now, it has been such a perverse day, such a long and learning day and so complete his alteration that he has begun to understand what it is really all about, why some men in fact—quite normal men—might actually prefer sucking in certain circumstances to fucking. The thing about sucking was the sheer immersion of it, there were never any potency problems, no problems of obligation either or reciprocity, you could do as you liked without feeling that you were riding a force simultaneously tending toward doom and ascension, extinction and apocalypse, none of that now but only the simple, quiet, timeless seeking of the womb in the pouting curls and roses of her being and although he had done it a few times without any particular pleasure it was different now, it was not as if he were sucking off this one girl, eating this single cunt but was instead establishing some kind of connection with Woman herself, this girl only the surrogate, the representative if you would. Some men felt that way about the tits of course, each to his own. Foster had once seen a stakes horse, nervous before the race, urinate in front of the stands before the gallop to the post and the look on the face of the horse assuming that horses had any counterpart to human expression which was something that only mystics, Walt Disney and horse players could believe in the first place—had been more than anything else one of the most enormous relief, the injection of blessedness into his difficult tense situation had caught him more by surprise than anything else but the horse was pleased, pleased (the jockey too, the horse won it by seven lengths and paid $21.60) and Foster feels this way now working on the girl; it is a fascinating sensation, one so complex that he knows he will be working it out in and out of his head for a long time to come, knows that all the time that he is Eating he is Learning and this has indeed been a day of more Learning than any normal man could possible internalize.

She gathers him into her, clasping her hands at the back of his neck, drawing him up and in; perhaps she had fought him a little bit at the beginning, perhaps it wasn't resistance but fear guiding her movements, perhaps the yielding is only primarily out of fear but those are Loser's thoughts, have nothing to do with the two smug new Fosters tenanting the faithful body and he continues to eat her, her hips now moving in a seizure, her thighs fluttering like an enormous butterfly, her body trembling and unfolding underneath him and he feels the wetness increase, the petals of her spread, and drives her that way into an orgasm, his own shrivelled and exhausted prick under him on the bed flexing itself with a premonitory tremor or two, a sympathetic twitch as he feels her unload into him; women are not supposed to ejaculate or so he has read somewhere but if she is not ejaculating she is at least simulating it splendidly and Foster, more out of curiosity than lust (He has no lust; he is high, free, in a spirit of total ascendancy: how many times can a man come and still remain subjective?) drinks her come down, finding that it is oddly sweet and somehow tasty, perhaps he is thinking of the mustard on a Harry M. Stevens hot dog. She moans and sighs, groans and gasps, falls back and he lifts his head to find her eyes on him, open and luminescent. They flutter in the darkness much as her thighs had. "No one ever did that to me before like that," she says. "Oh, my God," and caresses his chin, ruffles his hair, then, perhaps is reminded of something, circumstances maybe, and retreats from him, going into herself, her body seeming to stiffen. "You wanted to do it, didn't you?" she says, "I mean, you didn't do it just because you felt it had to be done?" and Foster says," Of course not" and comes up to seek her on her level and then he does a surprising, perhaps it is a truly amazing thing, he will think this over later, at the end of this wonderful and terrible day, he drags her huge left nipple into his mouth and curls his lips around it and huddles against her and closes his eyes, pillowing on her breast, sensing as if from a great and increasing distance that she is shifting under him, dragging up bedclothes, but he is far gone, pitch black, deep descending and then Foster the Winner sleeps, at least for a while, sorting out all the colors and hues of his possibility, feeling that tickets are being strewn out to the wind, dreaming of the old pink, yellow and brown mutuel tickets that they used to sell at the racetracks until the son-of-a-bitching NYRA went in for the new computer system and made them all grey. The old tickets were lovely. They really gave you the feeling that you were exchanging a little bit of your life for a horse. They glowed at you. Foster does not yet know this but he is sleeping.

SIX

Once in a strange way he had connected with something at the racetrack: this was on a day four or five years ago when he had encountered one of the most monumental of all the middle-period disasters, the day that he had lost five-hundred dollars because he hadn't had the guts to bet his own selection but had allowed two fish in brown suits to take him off it, right at the window, standing on line to make his bet. "Nah, the eight horse won't make it; I got into on the number six," they had been saying to one another, over and over again, and Foster, from an old loser's dread which informed him that in a given situation his ideas were always inferior to his competitors, Foster had gone off the number eight whose figures he had so compellingly calculated the previous evening and gone on to the number six who got caught in several blind switches on the stretch turn and ended up a fast-closing third, the number eight winning it by a comfortable length and paying—what did it pay?—ah yes, it paid $18.10; you do not forget things like that. He had lost a hundred on the number six and four hundred on the other seven races he had stayed for and none of this was improved by the fact that he had to cash the winning ticket for his mother on the number eight horse; the old bitch had bet it ten and ten, precisely on his advice and this somehow seemed to be the final canker on his futility but when he stumbled into this girl in front of the advance-ticket window while try-ing to make a fast exit, and knocked her sprawling, the day seemed to have gone completely off its tracks, completely insane, absolutely un-controllable and it was this more than anything else, the feeling that he was no longer a rational person but a gnome living in a cave of winds that had made him stop and return to the girl and pick her up. In a nor-mal mood he never would have done it. Fuck them all. The girl was cry-ing and not because he had knocked her down. She had come out with her boy friend for her first day at the races but the boy friend had lost the first three and gotten drunk and had not been seen by her for two hours and she had started betting her own money, just for fun, because she thought her boy friend would be back any minute and bail her out of this but her boy friend was really gone and she had managed to lose twenty-five dollars on five races, right down the drain, not even getting a horse in the money anytime. Foster had pointed out that twenty-five dollars was not really so bad but had resisted the impulse to tell her of his own problems for reasons that evaded him then but which he came to understand only a couple of seconds later when it became apparent to him that he could pick the girl up if he wanted to and do anything with her he liked if he only gave her the proper rationalization for be-ing a girl that would screw a strange man to get $25.00 back. She was a college girl, a very nice girl really, but living in very tight quarters and forced to work part-time as a waitress to half-support herself and $25.00 was three days' wages for her or, looking at it another way, one whole credit hour of knowledge. Foster put her in his car gently—it had been a '53 Ford then, his own knowledge of auto models moved some eight to fifteen years behind the market, depending on his luck—and drove her to his place gently and talked to her gently and regaled her with a few of his own experiences gently—he impressed her as he wanted to as a Winner—and guided her upstairs gently and put her in his bedroom gently and paid his mother her money ungently and then locked the door against the old bitch and for the next hour and a half he gave the college girl the kind of screwing which she had perhaps read about but to which her own mind adventures with her boy friend—after a while she became quite explicit in describing his habits—bore as much relation as a gelded plater to a stakes winning stallion. He found her soft under him, yielding soft in a way which women very frequently were not, all of her skin loose and gathering around him and he did things with her which previously he had only considered abstractly, milking out her tits, using her tits to screw between, slipping it into her firm but surprisingly slack buttocks, testing her sphincter muscles with his nose and so on. It had been an education. He was not sure what drove him: whether it was need or sorrow for the girl or perversity or merely regret at his lost five hundred bucks. Perhaps it was all of them.

But the point of it was this and it was something he was not able to admit to himself until much later: he hadn't enjoyed it that much. All through, something had been lacking: the girl was cooperative, even enthusiastic, the decor of his room was okay, his own responses were excellent, her breasts were wondrously flexible, but deep in the dead-center of the last time he came he had found a kernel of woe so hard and bitter that it had almost destroyed him and he realized that what he was doing with her was something that he would only find exciting much later, to jerk off to maybe, but not at the source, not the real. It wasn't that he paid her because he had paid for it often before and that was okay; it was better not to pay for it of course but everything was part of context and if the whore was good enough or the need great, paid sex could be as good or better than the other kind: no, it was something else, something else that made him send her out of the room as soon as he possibly could when it was all over, something else that made him utterly unable to speak to her when they were dressing, something else that seized and clamped him in the car when he drove her back to the Fashion Institute where she went to school and left him even unable to mumble. He wasn't able to figure it out for quite a while but eventually he did and when he did he wasn't sure but that he was better not knowing. But knowledge being worthwhile for its own sake he tried to tell himself that he was better off knowing.

The fact was that Losers were unable to truly understand or enjoy sex because sex was Play and Losers saw life as an obstacle, as Work. And a Loser in the middle of a Losing streak couldn't enjoy sex doubly because ....

Well, he couldn't enjoy it because the Losing had already done for himself what the sex was supposed to do and it was like jerking off a corpse, was what it was like.

SEVEN

He wakes up trembling, not sure for a moment where or even who he is; feeling the hot breath of Al new-blue on him and feeling himself baking in the leer of Eddie, only when he sits up in astonishment, arms flailing, eyelids beating, does he become aware of who he is and what is going on now and then Foster settles back with a sigh, groaning as the bed infers certain adjustments in his back, springs squeaking, squealing. The girl is sleeping to the side of him, her back and buttocks juxtaposed into a V which in a way is both the most beautiful and graceful thing Foster has ever seen but it is as nothing to the aspect of her breasts which are moist and full and in this sliding, side position seem to be even larger than he had recollected them as being, the fine, flaring nipples tapering to a delicate point. He feels guilty, somehow loutish in noting the red streaks on those breasts, the hint of blue chewed around the nipples; he has brought to them nothing but marking but that is all in the past and in any event he restores to himself the insight that he has had last night about this girl and on the instant feels considerably better. He checks his watch. It is six o'clock in the morning; at most they have slept four hours.

Four hours at most and yet Foster feels himself full of energy, incapable of sleep, pistons moving stiffly within him, seeking some source of harnessing power and he knows that what is within him is merely habit: usually he oversleeps and has to hurry when he gets up in order to make sure that he is at the track in enough time to make the final *Telegraph* and program assessments. But he is not going to go to the track today, he did not even buy the *Telegraph* last night and at the realization that he has no idea of what is running today or what the hot horses are, Foster feels a flicker of dismay which he suppresses only with great firmness and then a sense of puzzlement. It is impossible to understand what is going on inside him anyway. He is not a horse player but an adventurer and has, in consummating his adventure, rid himself of the noxious need. He gets up again and checks his wallet carefully, counting the bills this time. There are 229 of the hundreds and a lot of loose-change which is perfectly all right since he had broke a hundred at the bar to impress the girl. Everything is fine. He counts again to make sure.

"It's all there," Dolores says. "I didn't take any of it." She is sitting up, her eyes wide and round, looking at him in a way midway between seductive interest and lustful memory or maybe that is only some aspect of his own response to her. Naked, her body falls in gentle folds and curves toward the bed, inciting a feeling which Foster takes to be protectiveness but may only be sensuality again. He tosses over an old bathrobe to her from the closet and stares at her until she puts it on.

"What time is it?" she says. "Do you have a cigarette here?"

"It's about six in the morning. No, I still don't have any cigarettes. I never have an extra pack because I'm always trying to quit and Mom did, three years ago, when she broke her ankle."

"It's early. Why'd you get up so early?"

"I couldn't sleep anymore."

"I'm afraid to go home." Dolores says. "They'll be waiting for me there. Outside. They'll wait around as long as they have to until I come back and then they'll beat me up. I know they will."

"They won't wait around forever."

"You don't understand," she says. "They have nothing to do, either of them. They've got all the time in the world. If it takes a week, fine. They'll blame the whole thing on me. Also, they'll figure that I'll lead them straight to you. They'll get it out of me too. I'll have to tell them."

"Not necessarily."

"You want me to go?" she says. "I'm really at your mercy. I mean there's not much I can do about it one way or the other. If you throw me out, I'll have to go. For that matter, you could beat me to a pulp—couldn't you?—and throw me out. Why haven't you done that?"

"Because it's more interesting this way," Foster finds himself saying with a kind of astonishment; he had not known that he had this precise and honest a mind. "The other way hardly isn't any challenge at all. Besides, I'm sick of losing all my life, I know what it feels like. There was nothing personal about the whole thing; you just wanted to get hold of the dough. So did I, only I went to the horses. You go to the guys. What's the difference?"

"I was rotten," she says, fluffing out the folds of the bathrobe, winking abstractedly, looking through the window. "I hope you don't think I'm just saying that to save my ass. I really was. But you got to understand my relationship with these guys. They been keeping me going. Also, they're very bad news. If I hadn't told them about this—"

"They'd never have known."

"But I owe them a couple of favors," she says vaguely. "Hey, is there any way to close those shades or something? I feel like everybody can look in on us and anyway it's too bright."

"It gets very sunny in the summer; it's a sun field. No, there aren't any ways to close those shades; they're busted and Mom doesn't have the dough to get any others. She's really no kind of housekeeper. I don't want to spend the money because I was always telling myself that I would get married or move out or something."

"Did you?"

"Not yet."

"Well," she says, crossing her arms. "What next? We can't do this all day."

"Do what all day?"

"Sit here and talk."

"No," Foster says, deep in his throat. "No, we can't; that's right." He moves toward her, takes a fold of the robe in his palm, squeezes it, runs a finger over it, then begins to ease the robe back over her shoulders. She shrugs violently and resists him.

"Oh no," she says. "No more of that. We've done all that."

"What does that mean?"

"It means that we've done it. This is the morning, I can't stand starting all over again in the morning what you did at night. Besides, the shades are up. Besides, do you really think you have the strength?"

Two years, a month, two days ago, Foster would have nodded meekly, given her a benevolent smile masquerading as a leer, patted her shoulder, said, *No, no, of course I don't have it* and capitulating to her good sense, her modesty, her sense of proportion, would have gone briskly, humming around dressing chores, trying to make a presentable front. Foster of two days ago would have shown up at the track too where he would have dumped another couple hundred. But Foster was not going to the track today; as far as he knew, Foster was never going to go there again and there had been other changes as well. Inside him, he feels a small unwinding of rage or maybe it is merely lust again, not that they both are not the same and he takes the robe with the other hand, curls his fists, yanks it back over her shoulder and exposes her nudity to the dappling sun, the fine lift of her breasts, the already familiar twist of her thighs; sighing he lies down against her feeling the seizure of an erection once again possessing him. He bends down and twirls her nipple with a thumb, squeezes her shoulder. "Listen, sweetheart," the new Foster says, "let me say it once and I'll never say it again. You are not exactly in a bargaining position."

"So does that mean you're going to blackmail me into screwing you?"

"Oh, but sweetheart," Foster says with real dismay, "it's not that way at all. You have it all wrong. You're not in a bargaining position because you really want to screw. It's your head that keeps on getting in front of your box, that's all. We got to work with your head," and moves toward her, groaning, spittle already rising to his dry mouth, an empty feeling in his gut, excitement curling in a hollow fashion through him and then, quite naked, he begins to knead and pummel her flesh, raising small pressure marks on it with his thumbs and fingers and with a dying sigh, a sigh of such sudden capitulation that Foster knows he has never heard its like before (although he suspects that he will hear many such in the future) she puts her arms around him, opens her thighs, thrusts up her hole and lets him work his indolent will upon her.

And this time he fucks her like a jockey would work on a dying horse in the stretch, kneeling over her, his mouth extended in perfect concentration, his muscles tight with tension, his belly hard, working on her belly to belly, measuring her paces, listening to her whining explosions underneath him he coaxes her into an orgasm carefully, carefully, feeling the pressure. Around him the field is gaining ground, charging on him: the field with entries like Memory and Manners and Suspension and Fear and Unhappy Circumstances; all of them dead-roan males from the stable of that famous owner and trainer Mr. Possibility but this entry, as powerful as it is (it is a 1-10 shot and off the board) has nothing on his dainty little filly who has something that none of these other steeds have ever understood: willingness. Oh, she is willing! Oh, she is eager! Oh, she will not give up! She flexes, screams, bicycles with her legs, pumps up her little cunt, doing everything within her power to extend herself and carefully Saving Ground along the inside of the track Foster uses all of that famous cunning and courage which have become a trademark for his skill among jockeys and manages to hold her together. He holds her all together, breasts like funnels, cunt lips pressed tight to knead, stomach to stomach so that there is no space between them and whispers encouragements into her ear to speed her home. "Twenty-three thousand dollars," he says and "Twenty-three thousand dollars," again and "Twenty-three thousand dollars," he reminds her and the filly plunges and bucks with enthusiasm, heaves herself into a wild, final lunge at the wire. "Twenty-three thousand dollars," he says, encouraging her. "Twenty-three thousand bucks," and all heart, all courage, showing her great strength she breaks loose, fluids surging from her, great clods of mud seeming to rise free from the track along with a generous supply of horse turds and it is all over then, done, the field vanquished and he rides her home in his victory lunge, throwing himself into her as they cross the finish line, trying to make his form as perfect as possible and the filly whinnies, canters, shows her spirit by frisking her tail high in the air and then, exhausted, collapses under him but what the hell, she won the race. For all he cares at this instant they could shoot her dead right on the track—after all she has served her purposes and he is the invaluable jockey without whom none of this would have been even accomplished—but a surge of remorse hits him at once and with a feeling of compassion for the poor filly he strokes her forehead which seems to be filled with moisture and then, still holding his arrow-sharp carriage, that which has made him famous and renowned as the King of Riders, vaults off her and lies beside. She mumbles something against his shoulder and then holds him and for a long absent time he lets her lie that way; feeling the slow cooling of her body, the settling consistency of her breasts which once gelatinous seem to be sliding back to rubber, her nipples spreading out and increasing their discoloration as they lose their point. She is really a very attractive girl, there is no doubt about it. Given the proper circumstances, the same circumstances which enabled him to vault free of his damaged and difficult history, he is sure that she would work out very well. And it is at that moment that Foster has his idea. It occurs to him all at once, the way he read once that certain kinds of novelists were supposed to be able to "see" a novel, the whole thing, beginning, middle and end in one flash, nothing to do but write it or do it and he says to her "Epiphany" and she looks up at him saying "What?" And he says "Epiphany," again. "That's what we need here, a little goddamned epiphany," and in the seeing, the totality of his realization he feels a relief so enormous that there is simply no way in which he can internalize it correctly. Perhaps it is only too much fucking. "Epiphany," he says, sitting up. "Exorcism of the devils. Coming to terms with all of it. Comprehension, understanding. The imminence of passage."

She is shaking her head. "I don't understand you," she says. "I think you're crazy."

"That's because you haven't had your epiphany yet. Every non-epiphanist would have to think that of a prophet. Don't worry about it. Get your clothes."

"What's that?"

"Get your clothes," he says, leaping from the bed. "Get your clothes and get dressed. Stick with me, kid, we'll see it all the way through. He that laughs last laughs best. A stitch in time. Don't bet fillies in boy races. Don't bet platers in allowances, ever. Don't play the hurdles races. Watch for hot horses. Look out for a distance horse that did bad in a sprint last time out. Don't follow jockeys, it's a losing system. Up and at them. *Up and at them*," he says with some passion and begins to pull on his clothes, making frantic gestures to her. "Come on now," and with the familiar sullen expression of confusion clamping down on her face she sits and then stands, looks for her clothes. She is really quite easy to manipulate, Foster decides, when you know what you are doing. Only a Loser could believe that a pretty woman is impossible to handle; actually they are far easier to handle than dogs because they exist only in terms of their prettiness and thus how they are dealt with. Dogs have elaborate and dangerous defense mechanisms which should be—but never are—equipped with Early Warning Systems. He finishes dressing somewhat before she does and then stands, beating his hands on his hips with frustration, urging her on to greater and greater speed as she puts on the rest of her clothing. Even the second day out in the same costume she looks very well; there is no doubt about that, in fact, a naive man would say that she is built to hell with breasts so firm that they stand up toward the ceiling rather than with the normal sag. Of course the naive man, having never seen her nude, would only be having his fantasies encouraged which is an old problem but wise trainers have succeeded on no more qualities than those possessed by the brassiere industry. This heavy and intricate chain of speculation makes him even more eager and he encourages her with swats on the behind, words of cheer and finally with his wallet which he opens, to show her the contents. "Twenty-three thousand bucks," he says. "You see?"

"I see," she says. "So what is it going to get me? *Or* you."

"An epiphany," says Foster. He takes her wrist, leads her from the room. Now, out of the relative soundproofing, he can hear noises in the hall, the dim sound of the radio, hush of electric clock, sound of the toaster working in the kitchen, the sound of cup and saucer meeting. Mom, as usual, is up, trying to get some early angles on things; trying to reach her own truest calculations in the clearest light of day. Dolores tenses for a moment, her hand trembles in his and he favors her with an enormous wink, mouths the word *epiphany* at her and leads her into the kitchen. "Hello, Mom," he says—she barely grunts, hunched over the table in a new nightgown, yellow this time, working with a pencil, her lips mumbling sounds which seem vaguely like curses—and takes two cups and saucers from the sink, runs a little water over them, then fills them with coffee from the percolator and hands one to Dolores, drinking the other rapidly himself. The coffee is barely lukewarm with foul grounds but that is fine; couldn't be better, it suits. As a special treat for Dolores he takes down from the hidden spot in the cabinet the emergency pack of mentholated cigarettes which he had saved for occasions like this—mentholated because he hated them and knew that if he was ever in so tight a spot that he would smoke them he *deserved* to have an emergency pack—and hands one over to Dolores with a slight bow, lights it with a flourish from the kitchen match, then lights his own, flicks the match carelessly across the table so that it bounces its way over the *Morning Telegraph* and on to the floor. His mother says *hunt!*, grumbles, glares at him, glasses shining. "Wanted to talk to you, Mom," Foster says. He makes a heads-up sign at Dolores who suddenly seems to have turned away from him, afflicted with disinterest; she is staring at some trees through the kitchen window. Oh, well. "You see, I hit a big horse at Aqueduct yesterday, People Trap, and I made twenty-three thousand dollars. Got it all from the window in hundred-dollar bills and got it with me. I just wanted to share my happiness with you and tell you that I'm clearing out personally. Immediately."

For a moment he believes that his mother may have fainted. On the other hand it is Dolores who evinces real panic, shrieking a high shriek, hand against mouth, as Mom falls head first past her coffee cup and diving into the *Telegraph* where the pages rustle, bend, form a cave for her head. She moans, twitches in her seat and Foster motions Dolores off, with massive good cheer sits his mother up again, slaps her briskly, competently, lovingly in the cheeks until he sees a little color and then backs away, approving what he has done. She will never look so well again.

"People Trap," she says, as if she had not fainted. "People Trap."

"Wasn't that nice?"

"Ussery, that son of a bitch," his mother says. "Ussery. Well, I'm sorry to see you leave but of course I know you'll be sharing your luck."

"Well, that's the point," Foster says. "You see, Mom, I'm not giving you a cent. Not for nothing."

"Ussery. He's only supposed to be good with speed horses in inside post positions. That's what all the sons-of-bitches tell you. So when he gets an outsider in the middle of the track, a one-run horse. But I wanted to bet him. I wanted to bet that bastard. There was something phony about it. I knew the odds was too long. I said, 'Murray,' I said to that little prick, 'Murray, I think I want to take a little action on People Trap,' and Murrays says to me, 'The horse is a stiff and I guarantee the winner of this race, look at the record,' and I say, 'Murray, I been laying 'em down with you woman and girl for fifteen years now, don't tout me off,' and he says, the little bastard he says, 'It's because you've been laying 'em down with me, Sonia, just because I consider you one of my oldest and closest friends that I tell you this, don't bet People Trap'. So I go off him to the three horse. And then the horse comes in. But that a stiff like you should have the dumb luck—"

"I been following him, Mom. Been following him for a long time."

"Ussery can't rate horses," Mom says. Her cheeks seem to be going a little bit pale again. "It's a well-known fact. He can ride them on the front end or he can take them outside from an inside post position into the wire. But he got no sense of pace!"

"Mom," Foster says, "I'm going to leave now. But I wanted to tell you that before I went. What I think I'll be doing is not coming back for my clothes and things but probably getting an apartment and then sending for them, you know, a messenger truck or something like that. So this is going to be goodbye, Mom."

"I said, 'Murray, as God is my judge, give me a piece of People Trap,'" his mother says. She is now absolutely white, sitting at a kind of loose attention. "And he says to me, 'Sonia, I cannot do this to you, as a person I know and respect I cannot allow you to throw your money away.' And I say, 'C'mon Murray,' and he gives me three. A *bookmaker* I'm letting tout me. A *bookmaker*. Oh, Sonia," his mother says in a high anguished voice, "Sonia Foster, you stupid bitch—"

"Mrs. Foster," Dolores says, taking his mother's hands and kneading them, a look of concentration and sorrow on her. "Mrs. Foster, please, it's only money. Besides, I know that Harry—"

"Leave her alone," Foster says. "Mom and I understand each other, don't we, Mom? You're just raving a bit, Mom, you can't stand it the way it is. You can't stand the fact that I hit the horse. Actually you never even looked twice at him. Your third point in the ten-point system you gave me in 1955 for my birthday is that you never play a horse out of form, no matter what the conditions and what the price. The horse got to show something and this horse ain't showed no one nothing. You didn't bet him, Mom. If you were going to bet him, Murray couldn't have touted you off with a gun."

"Oh," his mother says in short gasps. "Oh, you disgrace me! That you would come to this! A cheap, filthy horse player. A cheap, filthy little horse player who brings whores into the house under the eye of his only mother and then dares to insult his mother, tell his mother that her systems are no good—"

"Now, come here, Mrs. Foster," Dolores says.

"Don't you 'come here' me, you little bitch."

"Epiphany," Foster says with enormous satisfaction. He has never felt so fulfilled in his life. He goes to the stove and pours another cup of coffee, sips it meditatively.

"I begged him," his mother is saying, "I said, Harry, look at your father, the worst stiff that ever came out of Bensonhurst and all because he couldn't get away from the horses. I begged that boy. I did everything within my power to make a man of him. I did everything to show him the right way. That stiff, that George Foster, may he roast at least a little bit in hell, that George Foster ruined me but I had hopes for his son and now—"

"He was a lousy horse player," Foster agrees. "He really was. There wasn't a thing you could do for him but we tried, Mom."

"I begged him—"

"Didn't you, Mom? We begged him, both of us, to stop betting longshots to show. We tried to point out that if you won three bets out of four you were still an idiot. We showed him all the tables, didn't we, Mom? But if there were a horse of more than 40-1 in a large race he'd bet it to show. Or two horses or three horses. Oh, he was terrible," Foster says, remembering his father; for the first time in years feeling affection for the poor bastard who, after all, had worked so hard at being a lousy horse player. What no one understood until they fell into it themselves is that all horse players worked equally hard; the lousy ones simply turned out that way. It was not their fault. Perhaps it would have been better if the old man had not gotten too heavy to ride steeplechase although even then his mother was probably right; it was only a matter of time until the silly, clumsy bastard would have broken his neck. Or bet too much on the horse he was riding and gone broke. Or bet too much on the horse the race was being rigged for and been disbarred. Or something.

"I am not a whore, Mrs. Foster," Dolores is saying with fury. Despite all the passion Foster has coaxed from her, he has never seen it at this degree: she looks rosy and full enough for screwing right now, right over the table between the coffee cups, her little clitoris bobbing at the astonished eye level of his mother, not that this would particularly help Dolores's argument of course. "I'll have you know that your damned son—"

"Enough!" Foster screams dramatically and raises his hand. Dolores quiets, his mother turns penetrating, bleak eyes toward him, her face once again drifting toward dead white. The time has obviously passed for such maneuvers and Foster feels a twinge of guilt for an instant, then reminds himself that it is what he has been waiting for for years and in the bargain his mother would have done the same thing. And in her own ways has, many times. "That's enough. Dolores, are you ready?"

"Ussery," his mother mumbles.

"I'm ready."

"Lousy stinking platers."

"Goodbye, Mom. I'd like to give you some of my score but you see, I just can't. First off, I know it would hurt your pride too much to take it. And in the second place, I really need it for my start in life. And in the third place, you wouldn't feel right taking it because it would take away all the challenge. You've got to make your own pile, isn't that right, Mom?"

"Fuck you, son," his mother says but there is an overtone of real affection in this which Foster knows he will remember long past the words. "Go fuck yourself."

He bends down, inhales the dimness of her cheap perfume, kisses her old cheek. "Take care of yourself," he says and seizes Dolores by the hand, guides her through the living room and down the stairs. "Ussery," Mom is mumbling behind them and "Cordero," and "inside track" and "longshot" but all of this becomes very indistinct as they go further, of course, and by the time they are in the vestibule all that they can hear is something that sounds like "dunning witches muck." He helps her out, closes the door neatly behind him and locks it—this is, after all, his mother that he is leaving behind—and guides her into the car, politely opening the door for her, easing her in and then opening the driver's side himself. Once again she does not open it for him indicating that she is either not very thoughtful or at the time when she opens it for him they are Really in Love. This thought fills him with no emotion whatsoever and he starts the car, races the motor once to find that the miss in the goddamned carburetor has started again and then turns to her, touching her cheek gently with his right hand while with the left he rocks the steering wheel back and forth. "Half down," he says.

"What's that?"

"Halfway home. Now we have to do something to exorcise your devils. Epiphany, remember."

"I think you're crazy."

"Not a bit of it," says this new man, Foster the Winner. "Now you tell me where you live and I'm taking you right straight home."

"You're taking me home!"

"Oh, I'm going with you. I mean, don't you want to meet Eddie and Al? And after we take care of them, we can get to the real sense of the matter."

"Oh, my God."

"Well," Foster says cheerfully, "that comes only a little bit later, after the winnings have been invested at six percent interest. In the meantime you do the best you can. Now tell me where you live and we'll have it out with those sons-of-bitches and then we'll be ready for the greatest epiphany of all."

"What's an epiphany?" she says.

"It's a feeling invented by James Joyce," says Foster.

EIGHT

She lives in a hotel for women, not a whorehouse as she described it but one of those dim, sweet-smelling, thickly populated residential hotels which Foster has been in only once or twice in his life on staid dates and which even at the remove of a decade or so can fill him with terror and remorse, terror for the immortal soul of any man trapped there after visiting hours, remorse for the infinity of lost opportunities held in the shell of institutions like this. Once, in his mid-twenties, he had, during one of his working periods, dated a girl who lived in a hotel like this and he knows that he will remember for a long time, Winner or Loser both, the true and interesting case of *penis captivus*, which he had suffered in the very lounge of that hotel, one Sunday morning just before curfew when the matron was working out the last remnants of the evening's corruption. The girl had been one of the typists in the clerical department of the large financing agency in which he had worked and something about the way that she found the most terrible things amusing—she somehow still thought that letters of collection were a private joke between the company and the victim which were carried on only to keep the collector happy—to say nothing of the fact that she never wore a brassiere, even under tight sweaters in the subway, had enticed him enormously but all the enticement vanished when he found that he was unable to withdraw his prick from its crucial juxtaposition at a moment when this could not have possibly been less convenient. It had taken him some three hours of mumbling, insistences, promises and pleas to get this far, he had long since passed the question of marriage and had constructed for them an old age full of desert sands, winnings in Las Vegas and fine German Shepherd puppies to protect their estate against the ravages of the grandchildren by the time the prick was fully lodged in its dry decanter, huffing away, not anywhere near an orgasm but a damned sight better situated, or so he wanted to think, than it had been when this all had started. Throughout, the girl, by some witchery of manipulation, had managed to act as if she had no idea of what he was doing, her eyes off in some abstract corner of the drapery, her hands disengaged, loosely toying with one another, only a slight quiver of her nose betraying some relationship to the fact that he was performing upon her a possibly unprecedented act, unprecedented that was to say if he could take her dryness and the poor way she held her limbs as any indication of her history. On the other hand, it might merely be the fact of trying to make it in the hall of the residence hotel; you had to give her that much credit. In any event he had managed to slip it in while sitting apart from her and maintaining an upright position, a feat of gymnastics so unusual that he had never been able to duplicate it or, for that matter even been able to remember, much later, how he had accomplished it; whatever distinction he had achieved had nothing to do with the length of prick or maneuverability of the girl's cunt but had, he decided, better be put down to Youth in the same was that boisterous antics or strange drunks were supposed to be—and left at that. Deeply within her, gesturing with his hands to sculpt out what kind of gravestone he intended to have placed above them in their Final Resting Place he had been astonished and then terrified by the patter of the matron's heavy, sensible feet, the click of her flashlight and had quickly jerked back, expecting an instant release of his prick and an embarrassed but rapid readjustment; instead he felt only a terrific, stunning flare of pain and a sensation of heaving which, beginning with the girl, passed rapidly enough to him and left him absolutely frozen, stricken with the kind of terror he had only read about in Army novels.

In the Army novels it was always some kind of physical test that was terrorizing the protagonist or maybe a siege of bullying of the Sensitive College Graduate by a group of yokels who had no appreciation of English Literature but whatever emotions those protagonists felt could hardly touch his own responses which in their frenzy and uncontrollable assault upon his senses went far beyond anything that he had ever read about; in fact, for Foster at the vulnerable age of twenty-three it was an excursion onto a level of feeling he had never before previously known and of whose existence he had never been aware; much later, even a matter of years, thinking about it he could encourage quivers of terror and relief because the worst thing about the entire incident was that the girl never acknowledged it. It was as if she too could not admit the existence of this simple physical disaster and was able to respond to it only by composing the planes of her face into a bleak Madonna-like composition which would have gone well with a nun's habit and sturdy shoes, assuming such had been available in the residential home.

Foster tried talking to her, giggling, whining, saying, "There seems to be something wrong here," all of this engendering further tugs and winks but the harder he pulled the more firmly he seemed lodged and meanwhile the matron was prowling the vicinity, mumbling to herself, growling absently, flicking her flashlight on and off into various corners to spot intruders or random rapists who might not yet have been flushed from the premises. The flashlight skittered to their right and left and finally came firmly upon them and Foster frantically adjusted his jacket, tossed it over their mutual lap with what he hoped looked like cunning, debonair ease and smiled brilliantly into the glare of the bulb saying, "Ah, well now, we were just saying goodnight," and the matron said, "Curfew's passed; you've got to leave now," and Foster, not having to feign an emotion but only its direction said, "But I *want* to say goodnight, I care for this girl," and the matron said "Well, that's very nice, you so rarely find a man around nowadays who really has any use for a girl but you have to go anyway, it's after one o'clock," and advanced upon them, the beam now glittering and sinking in a sputter of impromptu Morse and Foster said with a tremble in his voice *"Please, please* now," thinking that at the very worst of it he supposed that he could urge the girl into standing, they would stand together, holding one another, then sidle over to the elevator like a four-footed, four-tentacled beast, holding each other with what the matron would take for genuine passion and maybe the act of walking would jar him loose; in any event, he would be able to play for time. What he would do at the elevators if not dislodged he had no idea; he supposed that he could ride up with her on the pretext to the matron that he was insane; shortly troops would be dispatched to remove him by stunning force but there would be a few private moments during which he could work his will. He supposed in the last analysis that he could always cut his prick off; it would be painful and embarrassing and in the bargain would cause him to bleed to death; also it would sentence the girl to an embarrassing life as some kind of cripple unable to consummate a relationship but all of this would be a far better thing than the obvious alternatives. The matron, however, perhaps being reached on a level of sentimentality she had never previously suspected, said suddenly, "Well, a minute for a *proper* goodnight and no longer than that, young fellow," and stunned by his luck and the possibility of salvation, Foster had resumed his grunting efforts almost before the flashlight had been taken from them.

Throughout, the girl's silence continued; only some frenzy in her lower limbs, blocking them even more tightly around his tool betrayed her discomfiture and he mumbled to her "Relax, relax," hoping that the matron would take this for his desire to soothe her at his imminent parting. "It's only a matter of time," and put his hands down to her invisible hole, trying to poke and pry her apart but some virginal stifling caused her to squeeze even more tightly and Foster on the instant made himself a promise, one that he had never subsequently broken (the only promise he had ever kept as a matter of fact) that he would never, under any circumstances and for whatever reason have a date with a girl who had not given him good evidence beforehand that she was not a virgin but was a cunning, knowledgeable fuck. It simply was not worth it; if sexual inexperience always equaled something like this then it was far better to engage in fantasy. Later of course, having gone out to become an expert on the terrible subject, he learned that *penis captivus* was a very rare phenomenon which had more place in folklore than in fact, being restricted only to medieval tales about chaste wives and clumsy husbands but at the time he interpreted it as the kind of phenomenon which was almost inevitable to any young man seeking to perform too much upon a given virgin in her residence hotel. "Oh, come on," he mumbled and gave an enormous yank: the girl shuddered, sighed, squeezed, fluttered her eyes, moved toward him, gasped and some conjunction of angle plus the sturdy shrinking of his prick worked with him, perhaps it all went to prove the existence of a Merciful and Just God after all because he felt himself coming free, literally expelled from the girl with such force that he lost his balance (but oh gratefully, gratefully!) and tumbled off the couch, sinking to his knees, a ludicrous position but, ah God, the *relief* of it! and by the time he had regained his footing the girl had adjusted her skirt and stood, looking at him with a strange, unblinking expression. "Well, Harry, I want to thank you for a lovely evening and do call me sometime," she said in a toneless voice and Foster came to understand that she was doing everything within her power to restore the situation to normality; that was all right with him, he didn't even want to discuss it. "I surely did," he said. "I mean, I will." He put a heavy arm around her, guided her toward the elevator, the matron reappearing to flick her semaphore at them in some approbation of their deep relationship and at the elevators he kissed her once gently and she responded feebly with her tongue mumbling again, "Thank you very much for giving me such a nice evening," and turned, went into the elevators, out of his life forever, he trusted and toward a destiny which he hoped for her sake would be very special and meaningful because no girl capable of carrying off the situation with such aplomb deserved a mediocre outcome. Perhaps she would marry a contortionist or a middle linebacker for a tough professional team.

The matron stopped him on the way out to smile at him, say, "You understand, I don't generally let young men stay after hours but I thought it was so sweet the way the two of you couldn't say goodbye," and he said, "Yes, yes, well, it's one of those serious relationships, a serious thing," and resisted at the last moment an urge to swat her behind in relief and fury and passed out of the door, the flashlight still shining behind him, guiding his way into the snow where, unfortunately, on a deep winter's night, he fell unhappily down three stairs and landed with a slam on his thigh to induce such a pain as to make the other only a memory ... which was probably just as well because due to the aftermath effects of such an experience or maybe it was only an accident of biology and would have turned out that way anyway, he was totally unable to screw for a month after that and for six months after the restoration of his capabilities he found himself undergoing certain strange tremors when on the point of entrance which he was hard-put to explain to his partners, even the most willing ones.

He found out much later however and by a kind of coincidence that he had company; long out of work and deep into his Second Trotters Syndrome (he had discovered a system by which, playing the trotters only to show and parlaying back only a certain proportion of the winnings he was guaranteed to turn a profit each and every night only the system didn't work out so good when he found himself having to bet fifty dollars to show on a horse for a two dollar and fifty cent return and then watching the horse cheerfully, aimlessly break and drag his driver through the infield post) that he had not been the only man involved in that way with a girl; drinking in a Third Avenue bar late at night he had begun to aimlessly bullshit and then earnestly talk with a man about his own age who kept on saying that he should go home and get a night's sleep but he just couldn't face the idea of the welfare department anymore and had to drink himself into unconsciousness. The man began to talk about sex after a while and referred to a certain girl he had gone out with recently who had trapped him mercilessly in his car in her cunt for almost an hour and had had to be literally talked out of her fit through a skilled application of casework techniques that had been learned at the Welfare Training Institute. The girl lived in a residential hotel in the neighborhood and Foster, more than half drunk himself, started to compare notes, found out that they were talking about the same girl and then related his own experience for the first time. The welfare investigator, for reasons which made Foster eternally grateful, did not laugh but listened to him with careful solemnity, only certain vagrant twitches and scratchings of the forehead indicating that he was relating all of this meaningfully to his own experience. "Well, my God," he said when Foster had finished, "my God, that's worse than anything *I* went through, I at least was alone with her and had a chance to talk it out. You got to almost talk yourself out of something like that." He went on to say that he had done his own research on the girl and although the details were not final yet and largely fourth-hand hearsay, it seemed as if the girl, at the age of twenty-four or so, had managed to trap enough men to fill out a medium-size football league and that all over New York, sitting in saloons or lying in marital beds were men who owed at least part of their range of experience and metaphoric insights to this very girl. It seemed she was part of the New York underground; one man who was a writer had even written a carefully disguised story about her which had appeared once in a third-rate men's magazine. "It's remarkable," the welfare investigator assured Foster drunkenly, "absolutely remarkable, but you shouldn't take it personal if you follow what I mean. I mean to say, she'd do it to anyone and it's not her fault; it's some psychological tension or something like that. Maybe she deep down wants a man so bad she'll do anything to keep him," and they had both giggled at that, giggled loud and long until the bartender came over to check on their sobriety and they had been induced to stumble into the outdoors where Foster found himself very anxious to buy the investigator a redemptive drink but the investigator, unfortunately, passed out cold over the hood of his own car while trying to open the door and after manifold consideration Foster had decided to leave him there rather than to push an involvement which could only circle somewhat more deeply into explication than at the present time he really cared to go.

But that was far in the past, far far indeed, he never thought of things like that, having been vaulted to other levels even before the Big Win, and so he only drove calmly to the girl's hotel, smoking one cigarette after the other—they had stopped for a couple of packs shortly after leaving the house and were now cheerfully trying to make up for Lost Ground, letting Dolores set the tone of the drive which seemed to be silence. Somewhere on the Gowanus Expressway however, she sighed and said, "This is ridiculous. I think you're crazy."

"No I'm not. I promise you—"

"We're going to go back to that place and you know Al and Eddie are going to be there. They'll have it staked out. They've got guns, Harry, don't you understand that? They're desperate men and very mad."

"But you don't understand," Foster said with sweet exhausted patience, leaning forward to flip an unfortunate bug off the windshield and into the driveshaft. "That doesn't mean a damned thing. Those men are losers. They can't do nothing right."

"Oh, yes they can."

"No, they can't. They have no timing, no luck. So they have to lose every time."

"You don't understand. Al—"

"Al what? Al is the clever one and Eddie the stupid one but aside from all that stuff which you've seen in the movies, what's the difference?"

"The things they made me do. The things that they do. The things—"

"All right," Foster says, feeling some vagrant titillation; there is, after all, a great deal of perversity in the world and all of it is interesting; someday he will have to quiz Dolores in depth, right down to the last detail, and learn what was invoked upon her breasts, her belly, her cunt, by this pair; what if anything besides money drove her to the telephone yesterday. But the interesting thing at this moment is that he does not care; he is purged, shrunken, has fucked away most of his curiosity and all of the perversity; probably if statesmen were condemned to bed with concubines for twenty-four straight hours once every three days the world would function much better too. "All right, so I'll grant that they like to think they're tough. What have they done?"

"The syndicate—"

"There is no syndicate," Foster says with contented positiveness, fishing in his pocket for thirty-five cents change for the Brooklyn-Battery tunnel, the goddamned thieves. "There is merely an overall set of operations which keeps on speaking terms with the others, that's all. These guys couldn't be eligible to be hit by the syndicate. They got no room for losers in the mob. Don't you think?" Foster says, swerving the car with some enthusiasm and flipping the quarter and dime in his hand, "don't you think for God's sake that if the syndicate had a place for losers, I would have been in it long ago? And every other goddamned bum at the track? Don't you think that that's all they think about, seeing the money being lost, knowing that someone there is making the money, desperately wanting to get a piece of it, seeing the operations network so clear they think that they can touch it. But there's nothing there, just a few success stories and a lot of blood. Believe me," he says and drops thirty-five cents in the attendant's hand. "Believe me, they have no future, they have no past, they got no possibilities, all they have is bad luck and enough of that to keep them going for decades, bad luck can be so subtle and so interesting that sometimes it smells like good luck.

"Like listen," he says, guiding the car into the tunnel, flicking the headlights on, not for illumination so much as for emphasis, "like listen to this; I went out to Aqueduct one June day, maybe six years ago, with a horse to bet in the ninth, Filatonga, the damned horse was and I figured she couldn't lose. She was a distance horse who had been running in sprints against males; they had primed her for this one, they were dumping her into a route race against fillies for the first time and the price was right. I didn't even need information on this one; it was all laid out in the *Telegraph*. Hell, it was so clear what they were going to do with this horse that my mother saw it, sent me out there with twenty bucks of her own to bet on the bitch. Well, I got there in plenty of time; as a matter of fact I had meant to show up only for the ninth race, make my one bet, collect my winnings and go home but I got nervous and anxious like I always did—shit, I thought that they might close up the track and take it away if I didn't get out there by the third or that something would happen to the roads, a traffic crush because every bastard in town was aiming to head out late and bet the ninth on Filatonga. So I got out there for the third race and right away—right away, mind you, I don't even buy a program, I don't even look at the board; all I know is that there are two minutes before post-time and if I hustle I can lay down a bet—right away I run to the window and see that the number one horse is the favorite in the third race so of course I bet the number one. Just to have some action. Just to have some interest there. Because it's like going to a whorehouse to watch television if you don't bet; you follow what I mean?"

"But listen," Dolores says, "listen, I don't really want to hear your horse-racing experiences. I heard enough from Eddie and Al. I hate the horses; I can't stand to listen to it anymore. I'm not even interested in horses, you know that? And besides that, I'm scared."

"But listen," Foster says, bumping the headlights down to *park*, "listen, because this is very important and really ties into the situation and will give you some fascinating metaphorical insights; believe me, everything I tell you is a message because everything that happens to a horse player has a meaning; there are no accidents at the track, can't you understand that? No accidents at all. Anyway, the goddamned favorite who is 4-5, a nice little horse named Anchored who later on went to do some pretty good things but was running his first race that day and was pretty green and goddamned Cardone didn't even know how to sit on a horse in those days, Anchored runs second in close quarters which sounds very good except that I had the chance to get to only one window before getting shut out and the window with the shortest lines was the ten dollar win. So I lost ten dollars on Anchored. There's a protest on him too, an objection and I think maybe that he's going to get moved up but it turns out that he's moved down for interference, put last, no sweat, what's the difference; it hurts less when the horse you bet on finishes last than second. So I'm ten bucks behind and you'd think I'd be cautious, right? I mean, I only come out with fifty that day along with Mom's twenty to bet, now I'm down to forty less expenses, you'd think that I'd hold off, have a couple beers, play it cautious, maybe bet only two dollars for interest on a race, bet it to show just so that I'd be ready for the Filatonga *coup* but do I do that? Do you really think I do it?"

"Harry," Dolores says, and puts her cool palm on his over the wheel, strokes him with a finger, "Harry, you're shouting. Harry, calm down. *Watch that truck, Harry!*"

He hits the brakes with enormous skidding force, coming up on the enormous van before him all too rapidly; where in hell did it come from? And regains control in plenty of time; no sweat, the hell with the truck, the hell, for that matter with the tunnel, coasting to an easy glide which settles him six or seven car lengths behind and says, "Now, I was talking about Filatonga."

"Harry, you've got to calm down. I can't even follow you anymore. I'm scared, Harry," Dolores says and tosses a cigarette butt to the floor of the car, stamps on it, then grabs the pack from the windshield for another. "There's no need—"

"Ah, you silly bitch," Foster says with an enormous and rising sense of power, "you silly, silly bitch, you, *you don't even know what's going on here.*" There had been a time, a long ways back, when he had doubted that he would ever be able to talk harshly to a pretty girl; had, in fact, looked with uncomprehending awe at men in movies who he saw abusing beautiful actresses and once, seeing a tall man make a lovely blonde cry in a cafeteria he had been tempted to go over to the man and punch him until he had arrived at the decision that nastiness was its own reward; the man would lose the girl. But now he understands all of it, there is no limit to what Foster could now see, there was a simple trick to it and the thing was to get them so deeply involved with you, for better or worse, that they simply didn't care; needed the abuse, in fact, as much as the other things in order to assure themselves that they weren't only being used by you for their bodies; that you had emotions for them which went beyond simple lust and could risk the complexities of anger. Marvelous, marvelous; nothing has been the same for him since he got the big score, not that he looks back on those old days of course with any particular regret. Like the light at the end of the tunnel, rushing upon him in its blandness and reward, seeking him out to strike him with the bolt of power and knowledge, so Foster feels that reason, after years and years of eluding him, has been caught at last in the trap of Circumstance and he is about to unhook the squalling creature, watching the blood run in rivulets from its mangled claws, sling it over a triumphant shoulder, take it home and eat it. It is a pity that the only way the trap for Reason can be baited is with dough, lots of cold, clear dough but on the other hand that is the way the game has to be played. He strokes his wallet reassuringly, feeling the thick bulge, and hurls the car from the exit onto the West Side Highway, misses sideswiping a tow truck which is carrying a derelict Cadillac on its last journey and says, "Now, about Filatonga."

"Harry—"

"About Filatonga," he says again firmly, coming down a bit on the *Fil* and the girl quiets down. "So there I am, right before the fourth race, screwed up on Anchored but still eager to play. I spot something in the fourth I like—by this time I have bought a program although not a *Telegraph*, being deep at that time in my Mystic Period during which you made your selections through program and tote when you got out, the only horses I studied were the ones the night before—and I bet the favorite in a turf event for ten dollars and he loses. Oh, what disaster! What pain! What horror! I had lost fifteen bucks, you see. Now my stake for betting this horse was down to about twenty dollars, not including my mother's own twenty. So of course that wasn't enough money to bet, no sir, how could I possibly invest only twenty dollars on this *coup* horse, this sure thing? I needed more money. So I had to build up a stake through safe, careful bets that would restore me to my original forty or fifty so I decide to bet the favorites to show, simple bets. Guess what happens."

"You lost them all and had no money left by the time the horse ran."

"That's right!" Foster says with enormous enthusiasm. "That's right!" Apparently her days with Al and Eddie, of whatever hue, have not left this girl uneducated; there is a distinct possibility, as a matter of fact, that his pedanticism is wasted on a girl capable of such apprehensions. "I lost every single fucking bet and when the ninth race came I had my Mom's twenty—oh, I never went into the old lady's money when she did something like that; it was a point of honor between us—and a subway token to get home on and about fifty cents in change, just enough to buy a beer. So I bought the beer and Filatonga came romping in home while I watched the race from the grandstand and she paid $8.60. The bitch. She got away at less than 7-2; all of the wise money was out for her that day."

"Terrible," she says, in a mollifying voice. "You must have felt terrible."

"Oh, my," Foster says, backpedaling rapidly to reverse his opinion of this girl, only thirty seconds old. "Oh, my, how could you miss the point and after all the trouble I've taken to try to set you up for it. No, no, I didn't feel terrible. I felt wonderful! I loved it! I flourished on my agony! My mother's money, all $86.00 of it burned and burned in my pocket as I took the subway home not even being able to afford the subway special. I felt my agony corkscrewing in me as violently as sex! The remorse, the dismay, the shame, the horror, the grief! I loved every bit of it! Don't you see that? That's what I'm trying to explain to you!"

"I think I know what you mean," Dolores says. "We're near my exit now. Do we really have to go back there? Those guys—"

"I'll protect you," Foster says. "And you don't have a thing to worry about. You see, the point is, the only point of all of this, the reason I told you this story in the first place, the reason I filled you in on all this background was just to make you understand that these guys love to lose. They have to lose! They wouldn't know what to do with themselves if they won."

"Do you, Harry?"

Foster thinks about that for a moment while he pumps the brake, listens to the pistons clatter, hears the dim, sliding thunk of his transmission warning him that the Plymouth is exploring limits which it may not be able to test much further. "Well," he says after a while, "well, I'm thinking about it."

NINE

There appears to be no one hanging around the hotel when they come up to it; the block is deserted except for a few cars parked illegally— Manhattan has recently instituted a total ban on all midtown parking during the days which, Foster has already concluded, is only a plot on the part of the city administration on behalf of the physicians, public officials and mafia statesmen who will now be able to find spaces without delays or inconvenience—and Dolores lets out a low, long whistle of breath, visibly uncoiling on the seat behind him, a look of relief and release suffusing her features as intensely as an orgasm ever would. Foster nods to her to show her that he knew it all the time and then makes gestures that she should leave the car. He has not planned this out completely but the idea will be to go back to her hotel, see her up to her room and if not intercepted by Al and Eddie already, wait down in the lounge until she packs up her possessions and rejoins him. He will then relocate her. Whether or not he will relocate her in a place which he will share is something which he has not discussed with her yet or, for that matter, even figured out himself. The interesting thing however about his sea-change is that he knows whatever he decides to do will be all right. She will have no objections to him shacking up with her; he simply does not know if shacking up is what he has in mind at this moment.

Dolores is relieved that the street is empty and tells him so with her sigh, various hand-squeezes, even an indolent wink or two which seems to recapture, at least for the moment some shadow of the merry mood she had for him at the bar but Foster knows better than this: knows that appearances can be deceiving as the wise saying goes and that the absence of seemingly threatening elements does not mean that they are not there but most likely only hidden, out of sight in order to be prepared to strike the unwary. This is not paranoia but, at least to Foster's mind, what he takes to be cold, hard fact: it stems from an experience he had several years ago which culminated the second and last time he was able to connect with a woman at the track.

The first time was with the college girl and in a way that didn't count, because college girls who had been bumped by their dates were not the kind of thing which you could expect, by common luck, to run into at the track ever again but the second experience was more typical in a way, more intimatory, more universal, because Foster connected with a woman who turned out to be a regular horse player, a housewife who said that it was her "pleasure and obsession" and who, unbeknownst to her husband, was able to get out to the track, she said, three or four afternoons a week while having the groceries and various home duties attended to by certain willing friends whose background and motives she would not explicate further. Her main dread, she said, was that one of these days she was going to get pregnant, the son-of-a-bitch was going to knock her up, and that would be the end of that; she would be confined for at least the last week of her pregnancy and the kid wouldn't be able to go out with her to the track until it was at least a month old. Also, her husband was some kind of a lunatic about breast-feeding, maintaining that anything his mother didn't do for him his wife better do for his child and had told her shortly after they were married that any kid of his was going to get the tit for the first eighteen months or he would personally make someone responsible. This woman did not believe that breast-feeding in the Aqueduct grandstand was possible and feared for her experiences if she did so; there was always the clubhouse of course where things like this and other activities were rumored to go on but who the hell had the money for the clubhouse? And anyway, the people who were there were so dedicated to losing that they made the people in the infield look like winners.

The name of this woman was Margaret and she would not tell him much else about her background or circumstances: she had no compunctions however about filling Foster in on her husband in great detail which she did all the way between races and also a little bit during them by screaming things like "You son-of-a-bitch, you run like Jerry fucks" and "Come on, you little bastard, sneak in through the wire like Jerry sneaks a beer!" and so on and so forth. Foster had picked her up after the third race by the simple expedient of being behind her on the winners' line at the ten-dollar window where, it turned out, they had both bet a little beauty named Absalom Absalom to win, something which already gave them a great deal in common and the basis for a profound relationship. Since Absalom paid $13.60 or the amount of $68.00 for a ten-dollar ticket this did not hurt things either, giving them a mutual fifty-eight dollar start on what Foster immediately took to be their mutual life. Even the fact that the fifty-eight barely pulled him even for the screwing he had taken on the second didn't sour his mood.

It was quite obvious to Foster from the beginning that he was going to be able to screw her; no problems, no doubts, no questions. This kind of thing happened very rarely at the track but if you were a reasonably sane and alert man and kept your wits about you it was easy to take advantage of the few times that it did come along. The trouble was that 90% of the men out there either had no alertness or didn't care anymore; this was what gave the track its well-deserved reputation for being an almost impossible place to make connections and in the bargain Foster knew that he had missed opportunities himself, probably, because so many afternoons he was so sunk, so deep into his own problems and conditions that a pair of bare boobs would have looked like nothing to him so much as a tip to bet the number two in the race upcoming or maybe the number four if you threw in the nipples. But Margaret made things even easier for him than necessary; she took his hand almost at once and suggested that since they were both winners they ought to stick together and noted that Jerry, who was fully employed as the driver of a distribution truck, wasn't due to come home until eight o'clock off the route tonight so there was no reason why they couldn't wrap up the afternoon in the style to which Foster, who had concluded years ago that everyone at the track had an angle and, besides, there was no such thing as free lunch, shrugged and went with it. The important thing was that she not only had firm tits and a kind of nice face in a cheap way, not only knew how to wear a brassiere and the real purposes to which a brassiere should be put which was modification not amplification; the important thing was that she seemed to know more than a little bit about horse playing and the interesting thing is that they did rather well that afternoon; she restored his luck or at least helped him to hold onto it and that was one of the truly good afternoons; he ended up about a hundred and seventy ahead, much thanks to Tropical Flight II who came in in the starter handicap in the ninth race and Plaid Doll who managed to hold on all the way to the wire in the eighth. Thanks to his tips, insistences, squeezes, nudges, and gestures he had persuaded her to go off her original selections and join him on these and the way it ended up was that Margaret was in a most merry mood as she set sail from the track arm-in-arm with him, heading toward his '58 Oldsmobile in the lot, singing gently to herself about side by side and when we win this world together and it was the most natural thing in the world for him to kind of half cup her tit as he opened the door for her in the nearly-deserted parking lot, then kiss her gently on the lips and squeeze a bit as he eased her in. She had excellent breasts, firm and high and altogether remarkable and Foster found himself enjoying the afternoon very much: horse playing had its ups and then it mostly had its downs but there were times like these during which it most assuredly beat not only work but not working and feeling very pleased with himself he drove her to her house in Astoria, singing all the way, joining her in duets, the pressures and nudges of her fingers on his cock giving him no small additional pleasure or intonation as he guided the car into her massive underground parking lot, took a ticket from the attendant and got back a wink in return, a really nice wink, the attendant was a good fellow, no question about it, and if he was too aware of what was going on in general, well you had to blame those high-rise developments in Queens which created all this tension, loneliness and human anonymity, God bless every bit of it if it led to screwing.

Which it did, which it did: once inside her three-room apartment all poses stopped, dropped as rapidly as the clothes they wore and he put his hands, his fingers on her, feeling the even texture of her flesh, the rosy roundness of her thighs, the beat and sigh of her breasts and barely able to contain himself, staggered across the sill into the bedroom and fell heavily on the bed waiting for her while, casting a few glances left and right she followed him, coming with enormous power and force against him and then, with absolutely no preliminaries—what the fuck were preliminaries but rationalizations and delays? when you really were in need of it they didn't mean a goddamned thing—they began to fuck.

She was, possibly, the strongest woman he had ever screwed; her power was not only in the fullness and arch of her breasts, a sleek sheen of hardness under his touch (her breasts were incredibly hard, a quality he had only read about in a few sex novels and which had always struck him as kind of disgusting but it was a different thing entirely when you realized you could suck and fuck and play with this kind of breast and it would *always retain its shape*) but in the enormous power with which she was able to drive him; he was literally able to ride her body as she supported him with ease, and the sheer effortlessness of her carrying him, the power of her thighs, the driving wedge of her cunt which seemed to be fucking *him* rather than he her drove him to almost unbearable excitation; he dropped his load into her so quickly that he was embarrassed, felt that he had to tell her that nothing like this had ever happened to him before, which was not, of course, quite the truth but which was the thing you were supposed to say to them if you came too fast just as the thing that you were supposed to tell them if you couldn't come was that nothing like this had ever happened to you before. In both cases, it was that they were both too beautiful. But Margaret only giggled with the ease of long familiarity with him (he understood a little later that it was familiarity with self which underlay that giggle and should have been warned about something right then) and said, "Well, I suppose not; nobody who's with me has ever had that kind of thing happen before. An old talent," she moaned, "an old talent," and drew him down to her muttering. He licked her ear, licked her neck, squeezed her breasts, slipped down her belly and began to eat her passionately, finding that she was so slippery as to encourage the foolish illusion that he could get his entire mouth, perhaps even his jaw in and he was almost perverse enough to try but then his flaccidity by some fortunate stroke had restored itself below him and he did not have to run the risk of getting choked or drowned; instead he eased his head up, surged up on his legs and knees, scuttled into her gracefully while the trap of her swung shut behind him and then began to fuck her even more enthusiastically, glorying in the variations, the time, the sheer *patience* of it because of course now he was in no rush at all; there was little danger that he would spill out rapidly twice in a row although, of course, in this world there was so little you could be sure of that you better watch yourself; he watched himself through the use of her tits which were just as firm down as up, coming up at him in hard halfspheres, delicate nipples molded into exclamation points to her own groans and comments as she directed him. "Oh, wow," she said. "And wow again," and "You're really a little bit of terrific," and "Skiddoo, buster, twenty-three skidoo," and similar archaisms which puzzled him until he decided that probably she had learned most of her sexuality through an older relative who had come out of that mild and gentle period of history during which people were hep rather than hip and hung out rather than got strung out. He zipped in and out of her with smooth and increasing ease, built to a point of surging, then spilled the bulk of him through the tiny portal of his prick, an enormous, lunging, aching orgasm so painful in its delight that he began to scream in absent sighs and pants and she said, "That's the ticket, keed, give me some skin," and kissed him enthusiastically to stifle all recollection as he worked incredibly into a second orgasm on top of the first, tumbling away from her with great reluctance, panting, only several moments later. She lay with a smile on her face, both enigmatic and prognostic by turns; the kind of thing which women always got after fucking and then raised a finger with a flourish. "Okay, Jerry," she said, "you can come out of the closet now." And Jerry, stark-naked except for underpants in which a huge bulge could be detected, drooping moustaches and sweat, came out of the closet with a pleasant bow, nodding in the friendliest fashion to Foster and stood before them.

Well, what did Foster expect? The scene eventually came down to, much, much later, what did he expect? It wasn't every attractive woman, after all, who would be expected to pick him up at the track and lend him her good company and take him home and screw him for no obligation, not a penny asked or a favor demanded, after all…. He didn't think he was so attractive that an attractive woman would find him irresistible, did he? I mean, he wasn't that bad-looking but Margaret would have to be insane to carry on this way for no reason, right? The point was that there had to be something in it for her as well; there was always something in it for people, just like at the track even the losers won to the degree they lost in different coin and Margaret's problem was that her Jerry, her beloved Jerry, her only husband Jerry had found himself completely impotent after the third month of their marriage and could get it up only by hiding himself in closets and watching his wife fuck other men she had seduced; then, restored to a magnificent Gallic capability—he was a Frenchman, Jerry was, well not by birth but his *mother* had been born there and come over here at an early age and she had passed on to Jerry her hot-blooded romanticism and brooding intellectual continental brilliance—Jerry was able to pounce upon his wife and in the oldest and most meaningful of life's embraces perform upon her those duties and functions which were the only thing in the world which gave her true pleasure, all the other being unselfish sacrifice on her part done only for the purposes of restoring Jerry to full vigor so that he could love her as once he had so romantically and beautifully in the front seat of his Renault which he had had to give up unfortunately for economic reasons after they were married. It was only for love of Jerry that she was doing this and Foster should be pleased, *pleased* at being the unwitting beneficiary of her sacrifice to say nothing of knowing that he was performing a service for a fellow human being who was the dearest, that is to say the *dearest* person she had ever met in her life when understood in his own way, Jerry that was to say. Jerry was seeing a psychiatrist once every other week, that being all they could afford, and had explained the whole problem in detail to the good doctor—also a Frenchman, one of the few French psychiatrists in the city and therefore by definition among the very best—and the doctor had pulled on his similarly Gallic mustaches and had said that the question of voyeurism was very difficult, very profound, very complex, but he recommended that Jerry continue with it, at least until a cure could be implemented, since the important thing in sex according to the works of the good if German Wilhelm Reich was to obtain a true and beautiful orgasm, a purgative flowering, by whatever means. So Jerry was doing what he had been ordered to do by medical advice, his wife only performing her duties out of marital love and in the fullest and deepest sense of the word the vows, the marital *vows* were being implemented so what was Foster complaining about, was he some kind of homosexual creep or like that? Through all of this Jerry stood by the side of the bed, a submissive grin on his finely-chiselled features, the huge lump protruding from his pants and listened to this with small winks and sighs which he communicated to Foster by occasional nudges. Margaret delivered the first half of the lecture prone, the second and more interesting half crouched on her haunches, hard breasts dangling only a little bit and toward the end her spouse found himself so genuinely moved by what she was saying, the true and terrible marital sympathy which she maintained, that he found it necessary to express his love by reaching around and palming her breasts which he did with excellent Gallic flourish and, Foster noted, with no diminution of his own fixed gaze on Foster which, in fact, seemed to sharpen to a kind poignancy. Do you want to join in? Jerry seemed to be asking. I can need all the help I can get. Foster decided not to.

By the end of all this he was not even sure what was going on anymore or why he should be ungrateful but it was not easy for him to leave so easily: it turned out that Margaret had explained only the first and less shameful half of Jerry's difficulties; the second part consisted of the fact that after having intercepted wife and lover in a state of tumescence, he was able to continue his functions to their normal conclusions only if he could do them in front of the lover, have an encouraging, envious witness so to speak and Foster, who had never previously noted a voyeuristic intent, decided that it was all right with him, the hell with it, if they were willing to fuck, he was willing to stay and so, assembling his clothes slowly he was treated to the sight of Jerry Fucking His Wife, an interesting performance to see, even more interesting because Foster had never—although he would not have admitted this—ever seen fucking before, even in stage movies, and it was certainly something to watch even if ineptly done. It was so physical, so vigorous, and he had never been so previously aware of the crucial role which the buttocks muscles seemed to play in fucking; just like the fingers they are, always flexing and unflexing, coiling and uncoiling, why the whole goddamned prick was controlled by the ass when you looked at it that way, it was probably measuring out the very amount of semen. Margaret cooperated enthusiastically with all of this, looking over Jerry's shoulder with an expression which he took to be somewhere midway between pedantic interest and a student's submission; that is to say that she seemed to want his opinion of what she was doing and how Jerry was doing and he obliged as best he could with nods and smiles of encouragement while the grunts increased and the groans resounded and the breast-sucking became a series of snickers and slurps to fill the room and finally, to his vast relief and Margaret's to say nothing of Foster's, Jerry was able to commit the holiest and most ancient of marital responsibilities, delivering himself unto his sweet bride with all the power and skill which Frenchmen had commanded at the Battle of Verdun as well as in so many other famous engagements, a couple of military screams at the climax indicating that, De Gaulle to the contrary, his own Gallic spirit had remained unsuppressed, and collapsed beside her with a whoop, small sprays of semen seeming to lance through the air. Either Jerry, Foster decided, had very occasional orgasms creating a huge backlog of goods or he did this quite often and, inspiration being its own reward, was able to produce in mass quantities what was, for other men, something of an occasion. Or something like that. It was difficult to say. In any event, it became possible for him to take his leave at that point; Jerry, in the aftermath, was even more apologetic and benign than before; he smiled at Foster, winked at him, gave him nods of encouragement, indicated with gestures that Foster was free to take his wife himself again if he so desired in payment and Foster said that that was all right; he felt fine and Margaret indicated with a few grunts and sighs that there was no reason for Foster to feel shy; he had been very nice and cooperative—far more sensible than most of the idiots who had been involved in this—and he was perfectly free to fuck her again if he wanted because he was not only a good guy but a nice fuck. Foster had found this second invitation well-nigh irresistible and, Jerry scuttling to the other side of the room, had settled himself over her with a kind of joyous release, the familiarity of her body—which he always found the second time he fucked a woman—goading him along with a certain exciting taint of corruption, it being after all, a rather unusual situation but as he began to work himself down the well-worn path he felt a gentle touch, no more than a pin-prick—but it turned out to be a tongue-touch—in his bobbing and extended asshole and turning in rage and dismay found that Jerry had taken his secondary sex-responses to a new level of direct connection instead of going to the closet where Foster had logically expected him to go. That was pretty well the end of it; no serious horse player could say that he had moral objections to anything but Foster knew that he would be unable to come in such unusual circumstances and begged off, reaching for and settling rapidly into his clothes. Meanwhile Margaret explained that this too had been explained to the French psychiatrist, Jerry's need for reaming and buggering of the male guests, that is to say, and the psychiatrist had expressed hopefulness, saying that this was a more dramatic evidence of Jerry's disturbance but would probably be the first thing to go as the cure was effected; he was only displacing his desires to perform these acts on Margaret and was using the guest as an intermediary. Foster thanked them very much for that and said he was flattered and got his clothes adjusted and got the hell out of there as quickly as possible, trying not to listen to Margaret's faint, lazy protests and indications that he was acting like a child instead of the mature adult she had taken him so hopefully to be when all of this had started. Jerry, stark-naked, saw him through the hall and down the floor to the elevator— "No one is in this place during the day except wives and salesmen and they're all locked up fucking" he told Foster with a giggle—and there shook his hand and told Foster that he appreciated everything that he had done for him and would be delighted, absolutely delighted, to have Foster back any time at all, he had been one of the nicest, most civilized and most productive guests that he and Margaret had ever had and his house was Foster's house, at least in that one essential detail. It was very difficult finding a man who had shown the consideration and understanding that Foster had demonstrated and Jerry wanted to have Foster know that he appreciated it. "I mean, it's just one of those things, right? You can't help yourself, you've got to go with it," Jerry said and put Foster lovingly on the elevator, stood and waved at Foster until the car dropped; Foster could still see him, peering down the shaft for some diminishing trace perhaps of his asshole as the car sank with a groan the fifteen flights of the housing development and sent him out into a bright, airy, glittering lobby filled with old women and their dogs. He looked at them in confusion; they looked at him with loathing and he got the hell out of there with enormous speed to find that his car had a flat tire and he had to call a garage for help. All in all, he was eight hours getting away from Margaret from the moment he met her on line and a hell of a lot longer than that in getting away from the sense of situation which oddly enough, as time went on, made him giggle somewhat less and tend toward insomniac periods when he would roll over, regarding the white bloat of the ceiling behind closed eyelids, trying to piece out all of this and that together and wondering if there were percentages on human relationships that could be calculated as neatly as the odds on horses; not that the horses always ran right or the humans always ran wrong but even the lowest milk-wagon plug of a plater had something that the highest-bred human didn't: he had some god-damned consistency and he tended to run back to his past performances and it was possible to establish a certain view of the horse which excluded treachery, excluded the explosion of possibilities, put the horse into some kind of reasonable relation to you where you could begin to look at the whole thing in logical rather than emotional terms.

What the incident with Margaret had taught him, of course, was that just because there didn't seem to be anyone in the vicinity didn't mean that someone couldn't be hiding. Jerry, after all, had had to be in the closet in order to make his exit possible. One had to be in need and loss and deprivation in order to have sex. One had to have a horse lose sometime so that he could win another at better odds. Similarly, he supposed that Al and Eddie were somewhere around, waiting.

As a matter of fact, they were in the lobby, slumped into chairs, half-asleep, only the guiding, dull lights of Al's eyes and the clench of fingers in his pocket indicating that they had retained any wakefulness, any hope. Dolores gasped and said, "Harry, Harry," and tried to back them out of there but it was too late, of course, Al stood up sleepily, a slow look of shock coming over his features replaced then by sheer hatred and he came briskly up to Foster and, lobby and all, clerk at the desk and all, hit Dolores once across the face and says "You stupid bitch, we knew we'd see you again."

"I didn't have nothing to do with it," Dolores says. "It was all his idea. To come back here and all. I told him. I told him."

"But we knew he would, didn't we, sweetheart? Because he couldn't stay away from wanting to meet us again. Right, and we couldn't stay away from you either. Come on, Ed." Al whispers in a hoarse, urgent tone and, groaning, Eddie detaches himself from the chair, staggers toward them still asleep, awakening apparently only in the final stages of his journey toward them when his eyes come open slowly and then begin to glisten as he sees Foster. "Well," he says, "well hello. Patience is a virtue."

"Hello," Foster says.

"Hello, hello," says Al. He is no longer Al all-blue; somewhere in the interim he has switched into a rather dapper brown with numerous pockets, fore and aft, the pockets seemingly jammed with merchandise of all kinds but Foster is disappointed to see Al withdraw from one of those pockets nothing more interesting than a pipe which he puts into his mouth with a lurch and then begins to struggle with, lighting and relighting a large cigarette lighter which he has been concealing in his hands. "He drove away with me," Dolores says. "I mean, I couldn't very well stop him."

"Sure, sweetheart," Al says. "You drove away with him. You were his helpless victim."

"Victim," says Eddie and then, apparently understanding the word says again, "Victim" and begins to laugh uncertainly.

"If I try to stop him I wreck the car and then where are we?"

"Dolores," Foster says. "Don't make it any more difficult for yourself than it has to be. Watch what you say; watch your loyalties. I mean, we got a lifetime together."

"Lifetime together?" she says and turns toward him with a strange, spreading anguish, "I don't know what a lifetime is. All I know is moments, don't you understand that? There ain't nothing else."

"Only for losers," says Foster.

"Enough," Al says, patting them both easily. "Now, you know what we are going to do? We are going to work things out nice and easy and utterly reasonable; what we are going to do is to send Dolores up to her room to do a little bit of packing while meanwhile we wait downstairs for her and then all of us are going to take a nice little ride in Harry's excellent car which I am sure he brought."

"Still public transportation, huh?" Foster says. "You're the first damned hoods I ever knew who had to make it on the public service busses."

Eddie grunts at this one and tosses Foster a looping right hand which catches him casually behind the ear, not enough to make him crumple but there are a few solemn moments of reflection during which he can sense Dolores lunging forward to take him by the arm and lead him uncertainly toward one of the couches, moments in which he senses that Al is telling Eddie a few things about maneuvers like this, moments, in fact, in which the clerk somewhere off in the corner seems to give them numerous strained glances without doing too much about it. When the haze has passed, Foster finds that he is sitting facing Al on one of the couches and Dolores and Eddie are gone. He tries to stand but Al shows him the gun in his palm carefully, nods at him and then helps Foster ease down into place. "Don't worry about a thing," he says. "They're both fine. Eddie went to escort Dolores to her room to get a couple of things and I'm just down here keeping you company. Soon we'll all be together again and then we'll go places. Still got your wallet, friend? Check."

"There ain't no men allowed in those rooms," Foster says.

"Well, you know something, that's right," Al agrees, turning one of his pockets inside out and shaking a few scraps of tobacco onto the floor. "That's absolutely right; it's a long-standing rule of the organization. But you know something? Eddie and I had a little talk with that nice girl over there behind the desk and in thirty seconds she changed a policy that has been in effect for all these thousands of years. It just goes to show you that institutions can be responsive."

Foster looks at the clerk who is sitting in a rigid frieze, fingers spread, palm supporting her aged head, a few wisps of blonde hair darting in and out of her ears, a strange, concentrated glare in her eyes which at this distance he takes for hatred. "We had to show her the gun," Al says regretfully, "and then we had to remind her that if she makes any moves to make a phone call while they're up there, I'm still holding it. I think she'll stay put. It really wasn't a very nice thing to do but we didn't fig- ure she'd be reasonable. See her staring at me? I can face her without even turning. I really think she likes me, Foster, you know that?"

"Angles," Foster mumbles. "Angles. You're full of angles and moves."

"Well, of course," Al says. "You don't really think that that mistake yes- terday was the usual thing, did you? We operate very slick, we got a lot of moves; generally we try to know what we're doing and keep a step ahead. Of course that twenty-three grand threw us off a little bit yes- terday, I admit that. It's quite a lot to think about, all in one piece, isn't it, Harry?"

"How do you know I still have it?"

"Oh, come on, Harry," Al says with enormous sincerity and patting the gun, crossing it under his arm, leans forward and looks Foster in the eyes, "Come on, Harry, be sensible, be clear-thinking about this. I know you as well as I know myself; we know each other terribly well, Harry, I recognize you for being what I am and so on and I know if I were you I'd have that money with me right now. There isn't any place to put it, you see. You don't trust anyone in the world well enough to leave it in a house with them and you sure as hell wouldn't give it to Dolores—you got to watch that girl, incidentally, not that you're ever going to have a chance with her but she's an aggrandizing bitch and not as much of an idiot as I once thought she was—and you can't put it into a bank because you've never had a bank account and to walk in and just start one would lead to all kinds of questions. Besides, you don't want to give that money up, Harry, any more than I would if I were in your shoes. It means so much to you; you've struggled for something like this so long. You can hardly believe it. You want it right next to you, warm against your ass, warm and snug in your pocket, drifting and dreaming with you. You wouldn't give it up for a second."

"The hell with you," Foster mumbles. He reminds himself that there is only one way in which this can come out and that Al is a Loser, Al will always be a Loser, there is no way that can change his stripes; still it is a hard thing to accept even abstractly under the present conditions. "The hell with Eddie too."

"Oh, Eddie's all right. I mean he's a little stupid, Harry, not like you and me; we're really bright, talented people, if we ran in luck we'd probably be doing something useful with our lives although not half as interesting and we need someone like Eddie along just to remind us of who we're dealing with. The reason you don't hang around is that you're a horse player and you wouldn't trust anyone. But Eddie's simple, a nice, stupid type; his vicious streak can be controlled, he has the simplest and most sentimental sexual tastes you can imagine and he believes everything he sees in movies. He's fine. He's no problem. Besides, he's probably slipping it into Dolores right this minute; I told them to take their time. He'll make them take their time, be sure of that."

"You son-of-a-bitch."

"Oh Harry, Harry," Al says with gentle regret singing in his tones. "Harry, Harry, we knew this girl long before you were even looking for her; you got into her twenty-four hours ago and you've stopped being sensible but the fact is that we've been travelling with her one way or the other for a long, long time, and don't you think we know what's best? And what she is? And how she's got to be dealt with? If anybody's making the wrong move up there it's probably her, not poor Ed. Ed really believes in virginity. He thinks that when actors and actresses do it in films there's no one around them except one guy with a camera and he keeps his eyes shut. You don't know sentiment even when it reaches out and belts you in the mouth."

That at least, Foster decides, is probably true and there seeming, for the moment, nothing else to be said between them, he lets time drift, for a time. It is almost a pleasure to sit like this with Al because Al is a good silent companion; he has, it seems, no more urge to speak than Foster does. This is all to the good.

Looking at it now, sifting it through, Foster is willing to make certain admissions to himself in the form of questions: questions that he guessed he would not have been able to have asked himself before so maybe this, if nothing else, proves that he is coming along. He is not sure now why he has brought Dolores back to the hotel in the sure knowledge that Eddie and Al would be there and things would turn into this kind of situation.

It had seemed easy of course: the point about having a Big Win was that you could now confront and by the confrontation exorcise all of the demons, only losers lived continually in that network of intimation where all *doppelgangers* clamored for passage; winners were strong and sure and knew that the only way life could be taken was through confrontation. He had come back to Al and Eddie wanting to show the girl— and to show himself—that there was nothing that they could do to them because winners and losers dwelt as apart as poor blacks and landed aristocracy in the Old South. He had forgotten about the plantation riots.

But the thing to do was to come to terms with damages and prove that the price could be met; what Foster is willing to ask himself at this moment however is whether he did not bring the girl back here precisely because he was not seeking to transcend disaster but merely to meet it. Certainly, his motives could be more easily explained that way; the infusion of twenty-three thousand dollars into his life may have risked changing things so unalterably and terribly that he will never be the same ... and will not know how to come to terms. More simply stated, Foster is willing to admit that he may not know what to do with himself as a Winner; having been a Loser for so long he knows one estate without in any way being prepared for the other.

But if he came back only to confront Eddie and Al and to be destroyed by them, that says very poor things about Foster: it suggests that he has lived all of his life not in a truth as he had believed but in a lie, that the racetrack was not a means but an end, and that he, no less than the blasted old men and women who skulked the grounds between races for tips and mutuel tickets, was linked to this horror for all of his life because it was the only thing he knew. He had long been aware that if one of these people were actually handed the proceeds of a large daily double, they would not know what to do with it but would inevitably, as the sea recedes in the tide, have to turn it back over to the machines. He knew it was not folklore that winners almost never quit; that losers want to lose. But he had somehow imagined himself as being in a different category. He came from better stock. He had had better educational opportunities. He had had the advantage of Mom's tips and counsel for these many years. His old man had been one of the least famous ex-jockeys in Bensonhurst and he had learned a few things from him too about waste and dread. He had expected better things from himself. Also, he had never doubted that he would make the Big Win. That was the difference, perhaps, between him and the old people; they laughed and talked about it but knew that they were never going to strike. Foster was sure. It was only a matter of time.

So time had passed and he had quit jobs and gone back to jobs and battled shylocks and moved in and out of the rim of his luck, waiting for the thing to happen; he had wept and grinned, smiled and jeered, won and lost, researched and played by hunch and finally, just as smoothly as if it had been intended all the time and was only a matter of waiting, the Hit had come through. And now that he had it he seemed dedicated to losing more fiercely than he ever had been before. Or was he only trying to prove that winners could not lose and must stop living in the fear of it? It was very difficult, too complex, he could hardly keep up with it anymore. Also he was tired and his limbs ached. He felt himself sliding in the chair, felt pain surge in the place where

Eddie had hit, sat up with a bump and found Al tugging at him.

"Here they are, sweetheart," Al says, motioning to Eddie and a very sullen Dolores who is carrying out her own luggage, two black bags full of it, white things sticking out the sides. "Time to go now. This is going to be the last mile."

Sighing, Foster stands; all things being equal, he'd rather be sweating out a wheel-to-the-favorite in the bottom part of a daily double. But that too, he hastens to remind himself, is not quite the answer.

TEN

Once, only once, and that a fairly long time ago, Foster's sexual adventuring had gotten him on the verge of serious trouble. He had picked up a whore and had found himself in the process of being waylaid by her pimp. It was a very rough process but it worked out all right and from that, he thought, he had learned something.

It was his own damned fault almost all the way: in the first place he had no business looking for whores at his age and in the second he had just had a killing day at the track, was down to his last fifteen bucks and had come off the subway special absolutely numbed, ready for nothing other than one of those long, comatose sleeps which always seemed to restore him from shame. But he went out into the greasy air instead to stop at a bar for a fast beer and at the bar he met the whore. He should have known it was a phony from the start: for one thing she was very young and pretty and in her blondeness and wide-eyed attention to the bullshit he started to rap out to her had the kind of vulnerability and soft edge of fright which is almost unknown among big city whores and in the second place, after they got down to business, she asked him for only seven bucks including the price of the room and that was so cheap as to indicate that something was seriously wrong. Being only twenty-seven at the time, however, which was still relatively young as compared to thirty-three, Foster had put it down to his attractiveness, to the way in which he listened to the whore and brought the full force of his attention on her and to the season and had not investigated it any further.

He had told her that he was an executive in a large international show company whose name he dimly recollected from commercials and spent the better part of fifteen minutes, both before and after the bargain, telling her exactly what the coming styles were going to be and why teakwood sandals, appealing as they did to the deepest yearning of the population, were a can't-miss item. The sound of his own rhetoric had filled him, as it so often did, with a feeling of power and possession so large as to make the girl almost irrelevant and he had strode from the bar almost oblivious of her presence, almost oblivious of those impulses which had started him talking to her in the first place. The fact was that the bullshit was beginning to restore his spirits and ease off the shame and being caught between the two emotions as he was, on that high pendulum of swinging circumstance, Foster could not have conceivably been less in a mood to get laid. Still, a bargain was a bargain.

She took him to the hotel which was wrong news number three because it was a very nice, respectable place just a block from Macy's, the kind of hotel which appealed to the kind of tourists who were all around the lobby when they came in: big, red-faced, shouting men and women presiding over hordes of children, the children seemingly atomizing in various directions over the lobby, waving baseball pennants and calling wholesome midwestern curses to one another over the shrieking of the parents. It was, in short, an excellent hotel well-known for its security and good atmosphere but Foster simply put it down to the fact that this girl was an upper-class whore, definitely a finer type of nymphomaniac who did it for social reasons only and then only for the most attractive of men, the money being merely a gesture she accepted in order to keep the roles straight and probably to titillate her further. Undoubtedly she was an ex-debutante run into perversion and despair, like most of them. He went up in the empty elevator with her; the operator, hunched over, seemed to be having some mild difficulty controlling his breathing—but that again was only his lust—and she took him into her room which was a very nice, quiet cubicle filled not only with the usual furniture but with an array of stuffed animals which peered at them from the window ledges, from the floor, from an alcove, from high shelves which had been installed. There might have been a hundred of them: all of them bears of various varieties, black bears, brown bears, pandas, and so on, sharing only a rather stupidly benign expression and a fine gloss of fur which indicated that her fetishes were as expensive as the rest of her seemed to be. Foster was fascinated. He felt that at long last he was beginning to live the kind of life which he knew everybody really had (and which came out in books written by some of them) but which somehow he had missed out on, mostly due to poor luck. The girl took off her clothes indolently, showing him every part of her body carefully and Foster felt a flash of disappointment because everything was somehow smaller, less elaborate than it had been promised to be inside the clothes, in the bar, but this was an old problem and he put it down to naivety, nothing serious. Who *expected* breasts to be hard and rising after all? He went over and petted her a bit and she curled and moaned in his arms and began to pull at his clothing with such insistence that he had to stop and strip himself down, tossing everything from him in heaps and then he put his arms fully around her, feeling the trembling excitement pass from his limbs against her and almost ready, drove his prick right against the cloven wall of her belly, panting. There was the sound of a key in the lock and the girl's pimp came in. He was a thin nervous man about twenty years old, could not have been much more; in one hand he was carrying a gun and in the other, strangely enough, a pipe. He took nervous puffs from the pipe as he spoke, the gun fluttering in his hand in a most frightening way. "Oh God," the girl said. "Oh God, I thought you'd never come."

"Elevator troubles," the man said. He looked at Foster with some interest. "Okay, buddy," he said. "Just hand over your wallet and your clothes and we'll beat it. That should keep you occupied for a while so I don't even have to hit you over the head if you play it nice. The wires in this damned hotel never work anyway so just forget about calling for help."

"Listen," Foster said, "you don't really want to do this."

"Oh, yes he does," the girl said eagerly with an encouraging nod toward the boy. "He's a desperate man. He really is. Both of us are. We'd as soon kill you as take your money or both."

"Listen to her, mister, and you won't get hurt," the boy said, the gun shaking in increasing arcs. He puffed desperately on the pipe, produced a thin cloud of smoke, seemed to choke on it. "Oh, Jesus," he said weeping and removed the pipe from his mouth, gasped, knocked it against a heel, wiped tears from his eyes. "Oh, *Jesus*. Just give me that money now, will you?"

"But you don't," Foster said. He was not exactly sure why he was making a fight of it but the thing was that he felt such a goddamned fool, such a mark; it compounded his racetrack shame to the point where he knew that any emotions he felt when this was all over would be so insufferable that he might as well be dead. It wasn't possible to get seriously nailed twice in the same day and for the same reasons—simple greed; there had to be some kind of statute of limitations. It had to be worked out. "Now, why don't you put down that gun and be sensible?"

"I'll shoot you. I mean, I'll *really* shoot you. I'm not doing this for kicks. We need the money, mister. For God's sake, we need the money!" the boy said and put the pipe back in his mouth with a flourish, inspecting himself in the side mirror. Meanwhile the girl, very skillfully, was getting into her clothes, her eyes cold and removed. *I have no more to do with any of this* her bearing seemed to say. *I work strictly on guaranteed draw; no commissions.*

"Then don't go to me. I just busted flat out at the races today."

"That's what all of you salesmen say. I'm not listening. Turn it over!" the boy said, puffing and huffing out great clouds of smoke, levelling the gun at Foster. Meanwhile the girl with a farewell wink and nod more directed towards victim than assailant went to the door and out, leaving in such haste as to give a momentary illusion of flight; seeming to skitter above the level of the floor. The door closed and the boy took the pipe out of his mouth, breathed an enormous sigh of relief and set the chain with trembling hands.

"That's the last time I'll ever get sucked into something like *that*," he said to Foster and then went on to explain that the girl had picked him up one night and had made this arrangement with him; she would lure customers into a room and then he would use her pretty little gun to rob them and split the proceeds with her—75 to her, 25 to him for the risk—but none of it had worked out too well and a couple of the recent cases had been really nasty and anyway he suspected that the girl, just to be perverse, was deliberately now picking up weirder and weirder customers to increase his own problems in the arrangement. At no point did the boy explain how he had decided to get into the arrangement in the first place and what was in it for him although he vaguely referred to working his way through a municipal university this way and on a few other jobs. But recently it had all gotten more and more depressing, the girl had gotten harder and harder, the customers stranger and stranger, the take lower and lower and he had just about reached the point of quitting anyway when he was signaled that Foster was on the scene and decided to make another appearance. "So it's just your lucky day, mister," the boy said, "and if you want to show any token of your appreciation; I'll be glad to have it, not that this gun fires anything but blanks I have to explain to you, otherwise I'd be in violation." And Foster explained to him about the horse-racing disaster then until the boy finally stopped nodding and nodding and said that it was a damned shame, he couldn't be sorrier. Foster didn't find it necessary to mention his Mom's winnings of course. So he said goodbye to the boy and even shook his hand and got out of it in good style, excellent spirits, but not a little bit later he began to think over all the angles of this particular swindle, the personalities involved, the way the girl had led him on in the bar, the way she had disrobed with real skill and involvement when no nudity was needed at that point, the way the tiny flowers of her nipples had seemed to curl up in anticipation when she heard the sounds at the door and Foster decided that the logical thing to conclude was that there was a hell of a lot more to this arrangement than one would see on the surface just as there was as hell of a lot more to a 40-1 shot than you might see in the past performances. Life was passion, fury, complication, bitterness, pain and vision and it was a shame, all these things being equal, that they had to come together in something as banal as flesh, as unyielding as the breath, as cold and graven as the heart.

"Now this time," Al said. "This time we do it this way. You open the door for us and you let Ed and I in the back seat first. Then you open the door for Dolores and let her in the front seat. Then you walk around to your own side of the car and get in and close the door behind you. Then we all drive. That sound reasonable to you, Ed?"

"Yeah, that sounds awfully good," Ed says, and pats Foster on the back. "I hope you listened close to that." He takes Dolores's valises from her, tosses them on the back seat and then follows them in like a puppy on the prowl, hands and knees, scuttling to vanishment and then Ed winks, nods again at Foster—he is getting damned sick of this nod and wink but one thing is sure, he will not forget it—and says, "No tricks now, kid. Not that there'll be any tricks of course. Now where we're going to go and what we're going to do will be a nice surprise but I'll give you this clue, it won't be a long day. Not a long day at all. Still got your wallet? Oh, terrific; that just makes the day." He slides in painfully, squeezing for room and closes the door behind him. Dolores stands beside Foster, panting slightly, whether from humiliation or excitement Foster does not know and then looks up at him, a hopelessness in her eyes which manages to affirm and deny everything simultaneously; he understands what Al has been trying to say to him about her depths. But Al, of course, is a damned fool: it is always unfortunate to find this kind of intelligence in a shell. Foster is feeling very good again, suddenly, and quite out of his previous mood; he knows now exactly why he went back to see Al and Eddie and what he has had to learn. In fact, he knows what he *has* learned. The fact is that he is getting a little bit bored now with Al and Eddie; up to a point they are interesting, but past that point they are not. They look at him from the car now, peering up, their faces bright and piercing and more than anything else, they do indeed look like dogs, alert young ones, but not too bright. "All right," Foster says to Dolores with enormous care and precision, modulating his voice evenly because he has got to say now must be low-pitched and yet, crucially, must carry. "All right, now, let's run."

And so they run. If she is nothing else, she is a girl who listens and responds.

They run. They lurch from the pavement, feet scrabbling and, hand in hand, are around the corner while still gathering speed, Foster still dangling his car keys from the free hand, Dolores hissing with fright and exaltation. They are on Lexington Avenue fleeing downtown; only a sprinkling of early morning traffic still available because it is only 8:30 of a Saturday which is no hour for Lexington Avenue in New York City but nevertheless, Foster has to do several remarkable things to his feet in order to avoid two grey poodles, apparently unattached, who look at him gloomily as he hurdles them, guides Dolores around, breaks into a run again. "The subway," he gasps, "the 59th Street subway!" and breaks the handclasp in order that he can pump to run more easily but she seems to want the contact, forces her dry hand into his and so they run. In fact they run and run.

"The car!" she moans at one point. "They can catch us in the car!" Foster dangles the keys at her and she gapes, then begins to laugh, a helplessness tearing at her from inside, tears moving from her face. "And they don't even have cab fare!" she wheezes and that strikes him very funny too but does not slow down his running. A cop looks at them indolently, poised in front of a call box on 63rd Street and Foster tips an imaginary cap to him, smiles, does a little shuffle with his feet and then carries on. He has never, after all, been as genuinely happy to see a cop as this one; further blocking as it will the deadly pursuit of Eddie and Al who, he supposes, are just beginning to stumble out of the car now, looks of woe on their streaked faces. Well, he makes this deal to himself, for all the favors and acts of grace they have performed, if they can start it, Eddie and Al may have the car. He, Foster, is not an ungiving or ungrateful man and certainly the 1961 Plymouth is the least that he can offer in exchange for the various lessons and verifications he has gathered from those two. True he will call the insurance company the very next morning and list it as a stolen car which means that the loss is not so much his as the million other customers of the carrier but that diffuses guilt to the vanishing point, a matter of pennies, that is all, and then too, even if they are able to jump the ignition wires or get a master key—and they are fairly resourceful boys; Eddie and Al probably will—they are going to have a little bit of hell when the transmission falls through the floor which it is bound to almost any day now but that is their problem, not Foster's and it is not every loser who is offered half ownership of a 1961 Plymouth in good condition, the body only slightly rusted. Feeling enormously cheerful, he admires the swing and canter of Dolores's breasts as she jogs slightly in front of him. "The suitcases." she says to him in gasps. "The suitcases, my suitcases are in the car." Foster tickles her elbow with a confident, winner's hand, winks at her, increases the pace of his jog. "Doesn't mean a thing," he says. "Fresh start, all new clothes. Replace everything. Everything." They run, bumping one another now in their fatigue, into the kiosk of the 59th Street station of the Lexington Avenue line and Foster finds himself reeling lightheaded on the steps, far more winded than he would have thought possible but then, on the other hand, he has not been much for physical activity in recent years, having sublimated most of it in the action of racehorses. They stand puffing, looking bemusedly at one another in front of the token booth, Dolores for all her dishevelment looking very good indeed, streaks in her face, spots on her cheeks, gasps in her chest and he reaches out, takes her hands, squeezes them and says "You really were fine, I mean that; you were really great," not even sure why he is saying this except that it seems the proper thing to say after you have run several blocks with a girl, fleeing from very bad company. She comes against him, all yielding, all moisture, sobs deep in her throat, moderating to growls, and heaves against him, sinking her face in his chest. He feels her body shaking and coils his two arms around her, bringing her toward him, feeling the warmth and submission in this girl; feeling it in a way which he never really has with any girl before. It is an interesting experience. A young transit policeman, standing behind the turnstiles, looks at them with bemusement and Foster looks back, then breaks the embrace and says, "Okay now. Okay. Okay."

"They frightened me. You don't know what they're like. The things they did—"

"All right," he says, not wanting to start the biography again, not feeling biographical. "All right, it's all done for. I told you they were losers, didn't I? I told you that they couldn't stand to make luck unless it was bad."

"Oh, I don't know; I just don't know anything anymore. Where are we going to go now? What are we going to do? Are you going to stay with me?"

Foster reaches behind, fondles his wallet, slips a finger inside a crease to feel the cool firmness of the bills, pressing tightly against him; they seem to cling to, encircle his hand with familiarity and affection. "Well," he says. "That's pretty obvious, isn't it?"

"Nothing's obvious anymore. We've got to get out of here. They're following us."

"They have no luck. You'll probably never see them again."

"What do you mean it's obvious?"

"What?"

"You said, where we're going to go is obvious. Oh, Harry, I'm so cold."

"Well, think a bit about it," Foster says, an edge coming into his voice. "Think about it. There's only one place where we could go now. Exorcism, remember? Diabolism. Dybbuks. The confrontation of strange forms, the removal of damaging history."

"I don't understand you. I don't know what you're talking about anymore, I swear to God."

"The purgative aspects," Foster says. "The need to face the demons. Where could we go?"

She looks at him, a wistful nod of understanding firming her lips and they stare at one another in the cool strangeness of the roaring basement for a moment while the transit cop begins to shake his nightstick back and forth, manipulating it like a tool and then with stunning Freudian accuracy whacks it with a flourish against a turnstile and then puts it meditatively against his teeth, chewing on it.

"The track?" she says.

"Of course," says Foster. "The track. Where else? What did you think?"

ELEVEN

Foster's first lay had been very educational, very symbolic, and he was grateful that he had had it in that fashion although it lacked a good deal of being the kind of thing you would have preferred to read about in books. He had gathered over the years that the first sex experiences of almost all the men he knew were horrible: distinguished by their shame or uncertainty or sheer, bleak sense of obligation; it was only one man in a thousand who got inaugurated into sex in a decent fashion and that man, odds on, would turn out to be a screaming pervert in later life because he felt his differentiation from the norm so enormously and thus felt separated from the magic mainstream of American life. There was probably, at least in the ideal sense, a better way to do things like this: at some ritual age, like fourteen, the young man could be escorted to the local whorehouse accompanied by older male relatives bearing gifts and song; he would be turned over to one of the youngest and lushest of the harlots, one trained for precisely such affairs as this and there in wine and roses, bed and song he would consummate not only the act of sex but one of entrance into a new world of possibility while underneath his relatives chanted hymns to him and made their own busy preparations with more cynical whores. In certain primitive societies he had read about, they did things something like this. But in America it was catch-as-catch-can; the whole point of the society, it seemed, was to make the first act of sex as seemingly peripheral to the content of experience as possible and maybe this was the reason why almost every American man struck Foster as being insane, at least in one particular fashion. On the other hand, if sex was only a symptom and not a cure as the modern psychiatrists liked to theorize, then there was no point in looking for sex to change until a lot of other things did and in the meantime you did your best to struggle along.

In any event, his own experience, in the relative perspective of things had not been too bad at all although it did have certain side effects which in the long run looked as if they might be permanent. He got laid on a date in a motel in Westbury, Long Island after having been with the girl at Roosevelt Raceway; she was a nice enough girl although too simple in certain basic respects and the evening was suffused with a rosier hue than most because it had been his first time out at the trotters and at the age of twenty, he had won over a hundred dollars, even including the ten dollars that he gave the girl to bet which she lost playing long-shots to show, an old habit it seemed of almost everyone he knew. The girl who was named Carol was all in all not too bad at all; she was a secretary in another one of that succession of small firms in which Foster seemed to have spent most of his time during his early twenties—a long, bleak period broken only by long, refreshing gaps of unemployment insurance and confrontations with his superiors before those gaps when his superiors told him off and fired him. It seemed to irritate them primarily that when they asked Foster if he didn't want to work there—this was always the question they asked when they were getting ready to fire you—Foster said he didn't particularly care; there was very little in the whole prospect of the firm that enticed him, not that it was anything personal having to do with all jobs but he would rather be dead than be in the eventual position of the man sitting opposite him. For some reason this always infuriated the superior at issue to the point where even the gentler ones seemed on the verge of making threatening gestures. But this time out at Roosevelt was before the Obligatory Firing Scene at the job; he had only been there for three weeks and the salary was not too bad and besides, he was enticed by Carol who had a hairdo and facial expression very similar to that of Brigitte Bardot and indeed was called "Brigitte" by some of the people in the office, something which seemed to send her beyond pleasure into ecstasy as with little winks and nods she confided to Foster later that, yes, Brigitte Bardot was her idol, not only a wonderful actress but a very fine person as well and she hoped that she could only turn out as well as Brigitte had in her love life and career, not that she knew she wasn't missing out on something by not being French.

Carol was beautiful to look at or at least seemed beautiful to Foster at that time and even at that early age having demonstrated his ability not to worry about girls—he had always been mystified by the kind of man who found getting sex difficult; it was really an inevitable kind of thing, it only took a certain frame of mind and consciousness—he had no trouble starting a relationship with her which passed through a couple of drives, a restaurant date and finally the Roosevelt Raceway affair which was both the consummation and closure of their relationship. Up until then he had only done the usual with her; a little necking and fondling in the car, a couple of hushed, groaning pleas at her door one night when she made the mistake of conceding that her parents were off somewhere for the weekend, but nothing in particular, certainly nothing memorable. She told him that he was a remarkable person and there was something about him which thrilled her deep down but all things being equal she wanted to save it, whatever it was, for the man she was really sure about and nothing personal she wasn't yet sure about Foster. But might be, these things took time. No, there was no way of saying how much time; sometimes it took her a week, sometimes a month, sometimes longer than that to make up her mind and she really had no control over her emotions because a woman felt in very strange and appealing ways. She was clever. She was really not stupid at all. She knew her business.

She had, in fact, only one really annoying habit; she constantly sang popular songs with the same nervous carelessness and intensity with which Foster, even then, was smoking down three packs a day; she not only knew the latest hits but the period pieces as well, fragments of nostalgia from a borrowed past, movie music, folk songs, folkways, folklore, and she mumbled them constantly almost all the time, except when they were necking when they slipped away with a 78 rpm clatter and clash, and she applied herself to her work most diligently. Otherwise she hummed and moaned, muttered and sang, played the radio in the car almost all the time; even carried along a small transistor in her handbag which she begged Foster to let her play when they went places because it relaxed her and she would keep it low. Foster could understand where in due time a habit like this might easily drive a man crazy but he was not operating in terms of the long run. Just as in his job, he had mild hopes, mild inventions: he intended to put in the requisite time and earn the Unemployment Insurance of her cunt and then he would see what he would see.

The Roosevelt Raceway expedition was a "treat" in honor of Carol's new salary raise—her boss was trying to lay her but Carol said that it wasn't going to work out, the man was married and had children and anyway had no idea of how to come over "softly" to a girl—and Foster's part of the treat was in turning over money to her to bet; she had asked for it so casually, so straightforwardly, with such innocence in her voice that he had passed over the ten dollars to her without even realizing until much later that he had been maneuvered intricately and cleverly into something that was absolutely outside the context of the relationship; he read an "etiquette" book much later which explained that the gentleman "out for a day with his lady at the races" was not obligated beyond paying for her food, admission and amusement and could salve his conscience by reflecting that "the money he bets is being bet for both he and his companion." Foster did not reckon much with books on etiquette but he had learned there a lesson he had never forgotten and from then on, on the rare occasions when he had taken a date to the track (the track had to be a solitary occupation) he had told the girl that what he was doing was being done for her own amusement and she could like it or leave it; she had better like it, however, because Foster's winning would put him in an excellent mood but his losing would be something else again. This in any event was his first time out at the trotters; despite the fact that he had literally grown up in the presence of the flats and had, by the age of ten, known everything necessary to know in order to study the charts intelligently, he had been aware only through various side-remarks of his mother and father that there was, "somewhere" out on Long Island a place where "they run pigs and pigs bet on them." His parents hated the trots with a loathing which Foster, once he got into them, could never understand; granted they had neither the speed nor the possibilities of the flats, still they offered interesting profit-making opportunities and the class of people who attended them—because they were run at night and a lot of these people worked during the days—was a far better type altogether, they even seemed to have a sense of humor. What so infuriated his parents, Foster later decided, was the fact that the trots were not run all-out but contained losing as a very necessary part of the operation; the horse had to run in a set gait with the driver holding him to an even canter and therefore a horse which went all out to win a race was necessarily breaking the rules, was penalized and was dropped to last position. This could be infuriating if you had bet on the horse, had sympathized with its efforts and had at least vicariously exulted when the horse made an effort to win but on the other hand, Foster could have pointed out to his parents, on the other hand losing and control were more important parts of life than effort; almost everything, when you came right down to it, was repression so what the hell? The trotters were closer to the sense of things than the racers. Of course people didn't go to the racetrack to get nearer to the sense of things, that was a point. A more important thing was that it was possible to win money at the trots through cautious parlaying for show. Foster learned that right off. He won a hundred dollars while Carol lost her ten and at the end of the evening, her face deeply flushed with wonder or possibly only envy, she said, "Do you want to go to a motel? I feel in the mood tonight."

Her sudden capitulation, the unabashed way in which she put this made Foster's abused cock begin to straggle to attention within his clothes barely before he could say anything and then he said, "Yes, yes, that's fine," trying not in any way to betray his lust—because that was part of the game—and failing, of course, dismally. All the way out to the Westbury Motor Inn she regaled him with a virtual catalogue of the swinging hits of the 'fifties, the transistor humming Muzak in the background, the car radio blaring forth Dixieland in the foreground, Carol went from "Cry" to "Little White Cloud" to "Delicado" to "Kiss of

Fire" to "Shake Rattle and Roll" to "Rock and Roll Is Here To Stay," all in a high, sweet piercing voice so penetrating and idiotic that Foster could feel his insides twisting; whatever sophistry she might seem to have lacked however came back when they pulled into the motel where she sat ever so demurely, ever so confidently, hands folded in the car while Foster left the motor running and went in to get a double for him and his wife who were just whirling in from St. Paul, Minnesota, boy those roads were hell and you couldn't find a rest stop for miles, thought the kidneys would burst. The clerk who probably had kidney trouble himself said that the thing you had to do was to find a nice big sign and pull the car over near it and then go behind but Foster pointed out that on those modern interstate highways signs were not permitted, there was not even a blade of grass for miles and only a midget would be able to spout inconspicuously behind his parked car. This shut the clerk up thoroughly, some trickle of woe passing over his features as if he had intimated in a flash his own eventual prostrate operation and Foster went back to the car with some aplomb, dangled the keys in victory for Carol to see, drove her into Unit 12 and there, with the air-condition-ing humming his love better than he ever could, the hiddenflush and tinkle of war singing the song of his emotions he laid his first true love who less than ever, disrobed and spread under sheets, looked like Brigitte Bardot.

The thing about it was that he had no sexual fright at all. He knew from all the books he had read and jokes he had heard that first sex was supposed to be kind of terrifying to a man who usually either went limp or came too fast but he had such a cold clarity of purpose, such a fixity of need that the whole question seemed irrelevant and, in the bargain, the girl already owed him ten bucks plus the price of the motel room which more than anything else demanded that he get his price back without complication. Naked, she proved to have thinner breasts than he would have thought; too, they hung a bit more radically than those of the girls in the magazines, but her nipples were hard and warm, her thighs were good and he buried himself in her willingly, feeling her tongue touching all his spaces and she hummed and moaned a lot to him while he worked her over although not, surprisingly, about sex.

"The hundred dollars," was what she was saying. "A hundred dollars, you won a hundred dollars; isn't that wonderful? Isn't that just the neat-est thing you've ever heard of? A whole hundred dollars, just for betting on horses; why I didn't know that there was something like that in the world, why go to work?" and flicked a clever finger at his joint, cupped his balls, urged his semen to pour forth with such insistence that Fos-ter would have thought it came out in spurts shaped like dollar signs. "Oh, it's just wonderful, wonderful," she moaned, handing him a breast, flicking out a nipple, warning him that it was "distended" and "very sensitive" and so he should "watch his teeth please" but rather than watching his teeth—she left him to his own devices on trust—she closed her eyes and sang to herself softly, beginning for the first time during their mutual sex to lapse into song and she began to sing to him a whole catalogue of songs about money. She sang "Side by Side" and "Sitting on Top of the World" and "I Found a Million Dollar Baby at the Five and Ten Cent Store" and "Pennies from Heaven" and "My Heart Belongs to Daddy" until he thought that her affectionate little heart would burst from the combined effort of shoving her cunt back at him and regaling him with the popular literature but far, far before her little heart burst his enormous cock did, thudding into life like Hanover Hanover in the seventh race charging for him on the rail, moving toward the wire, singing and flowering and pouring and he put all of it into her, feeling the hush of applause in the room around him, feeling a sensation as if Flowers were being draped around his sweaty, graceful neck, feeling as if a halter were being slipped gently over him and he was being led to the barn for a well-deserved blowout and a nice pail of oats. Oh, it was one explosion of metaphor, that was all there was to it and he fell away from her feeling much relieved; it had been like nothing in the books, he had neither panicked nor been betrayed by a too-quick tool and he supposed that even though he had actually started off getting laid rather late in life he'd made the right decision by waiting to get it from a nice girl in the proper context rather than going to a whore and getting all fucked up like poor Eugene O'Neill. O'Neill really scared him; that was an example to be shunned because O'Neill had a play in which a man came onstage to meet a girl at the opening and before three minutes had gone by he was standing alone, talking to the audience about this dreadful experience he had had with a whore sixteen years ago and how it had made him impotent for life even though he really loved this particular girl. He raved on and on about his impotence, this man did to such a degree that Foster had been embarrassed not only for him but for the playwright, but when the girl that the man was waiting for finally came onstage Foster began to judge, even from his eighteen-year-old perspective, that if there was any impotence it was more likely due to the personality of this particular girl than any poor, hard-working whore who would have been by the time the play opened at least sixty years old and therefore paying proper penitence. But O'Neill had apparently gotten all screwed up by whores not to say drugs and almost singlehandedly had kept Foster away from them, this being for all Foster knew—he didn't know too much about plays—the most lasting effect which the work of Eugene O'Neill would have on anyone, anywhere, but the hell with that, feeling very prosperous and almost kindly he lit two cigarettes, just like they did in the movies, and passed one to the girl and sat up taking cognizance of her body which was steaming only slightly from the efforts he had put upon her. That was the interesting thing about women which Foster had never quite gotten over; you could do almost anything to them and they would come out of it looking fresh, bland and untouched five minutes later. They only showed the effects of it when they wanted to for their own reasons.

"Actually," Carol said, "actually when you come right down to it, half that money belongs to me, don't you really think so?"

"Why is that?"

"Well, I mean, I was with you and all that. I was giving you moral encouragement. You wouldn't have even been out at the track if I didn't say okay. Remember, you asked me? If I wanted to go? And I said it was all right with me. So because I said it was all right, I won you a hundred dollars. I think I should get fifty."

"Why?" Foster said with a slight twisting sensation in the stomach, doubtless due to the enormous amount of smoke he had just inhaled. "What does that have to do with it? I made all the selections."

"But you checked with me. You said, I'm betting so and so, this Adios, that Adios, this boy, that boy. And asked me what I thought."

"Well, what the hell, Carol, you always said that was fine with you. What were you going to say? What do you know about trotters?"

"But I could have said no; I could have said that I don't like this one, I like that one better. This way you would have lost the money instead of winning all that. I helped you make your selections."

"But for God's sake, you made your own selections. I gave you money to bet any way you wanted. Everything you picked lost. I didn't make you bet the horses that you did, Carol."

"I only did it to please you. I wasn't even thinking or anything like that; I just picked by the names. Women are supposed to do that. But your selections I really studied. Oh, I don't think that I should have *half*. That was just kidding. But I should get *something* out of it, because without me you wouldn't have won, without me being there right next to you. I think forty dollars or twenty-five dollars anyway."

"No, Carol," he said and then The Scene had commenced: it had been a very bad scene, one which he was capable, thirteen years later, of regretting almost as keenly as he did then; it was a Scene full of accusations and recriminations during which, being very young and stupid, he had accused her of being a whore and going down for him just because she wanted money and she had told him that he was the worst fuck she had ever had in her whole life and he had said he bet that she could make that judgement out of her massive experience and she had said that she was going to use the phone and call the clerk to get him arrested and he had said that she was twenty-five if she was a day and he wasn't too worried about it. She had said that she was twenty-three and he said however old she was she looked older than that and was twice as hard-bitten as any whore and then they had begun to throw things at one another and it had gotten very nasty. Eventually, of course, they had had to face up to the facts of the matter which was that they had to get out of the room in some reasonable semblance of order; there were no battles that could be won or lost in such small quarters and far away from the possibility of escape and so they had gotten dressed, leering at one another, her eyes round and spiteful, his taking on the slow confused gaze of the Loser … he had not lost that expression for thirteen years, he supposed; actually for a long time he lived in a reflexive mode of total astonishment … and they went into the car and he drove her home. Somewhere in the middle of the drive she recovered her voice if not spirits and began to mumble torch songs in a low, spiteful voice while she turned the transistor up loud to the news and listened to all the disaster reports, ship dockings and commodity exchange listings. As far as he recollected, they did not say a word to one another when he dropped her off at her home and after he drove away he parked in a deserted area to check over his wallet on an impulse and found that through some magical exertion which he never understood she had managed to rob him of thirty-five dollars. When or where was beyond him. He put that down, along with the experience he had had, to the price of learning how to get along in this society but later on he came to realize that instead he had only learned how to get along at a racetrack which was a different kind of thing and the lesson, hardlearned, would be hard unlearning. It was going to take him twenty-three thousand dollars and a good deal of time to learn to differentiate life from the track but he supposed that he was getting there.

They were going to go out to the track, Foster was definite about this, but before they did, he wanted to check into the big motel near Aqueduct and spend a couple of hours with her. By this time Dolores was numbed, beyond resistances or approvals of almost any kind, and he didn't even have to explain to her why he wanted to do this; she only nodded when he explained that he had always wanted to go to that motel, there was something about the ambiance of a place near a track which had fascinated him and said yes, but she had to pick up some clothes, she had no clothes. Sitting next to her in the empty IND local, racketing and rocketing their way toward Ozone Park, Foster had shown her his wallet once again, opened it up and demonstrated the bills to her, their width, breadth, density, the feel of them and any mood of denial which had been within her shifted to a weary, snug kind of approbation and she took his arm and held it tightly. Now, however, at the motel Foster wonders if this was really such a good idea after all; it has been a long, weary walk from the subway station to the highway and furthermore, in their bedraggled condition, they are getting some very strange glances from the clerk who is looking up from his *Morning Telegraph* to relight a cigar while shifting his gaze between them and the clock on the wall. "Yes," he says finally, "anything we can do."

"Well, I want a room," Foster says. "For me and my wife here."

"Your wife, huh? Well, I don't know; I think we're kind of booked up."

"Listen," Foster says, "it's eleven in the morning; that's check-out time. You couldn't possibly be all booked up at this hour."

"You couldn't possibly be looking for a room either," the clerk says rather nastily and takes a card from the desk, pushes it across. "Fill it all out and I'll see what we can do. Your wife, eh? License plate and auto registration number and the driver's license too, if you will. No charges or check. Cash."

"Well, that's it," Foster says. "You see, I don't have a car."

The clerk raises his eyebrows into the bald sheen of his forehead and taps the pencil on the *Telegraph*. "Don't have a car?"

"Well, no."

"Then how the hell did you get here?"

"We walked."

"You walked. You walked all the hell the way over to the highway because you wanted to stay in a motel. Of course. That makes sense. Happens every day of the week. Listen, friend," the clerk says rather kindly and withdraws the card. "I don't think we're for you or you're for us. It's nothing personal—"

Foster takes out his wallet, gives the clerk a good look, removes a hundred-dollar bill and places it on the counter. Behind him, Dolores sighs, the sight of the wallet possibly having brought her to lust again or maybe it is only her enormous weariness. "I'll pay cash," Foster says. "No problems."

"My God," the clerk says and riffles the pages of the paper. "Uh, yes. All right. If you want to. I mean, I just couldn't understand why someone would come in here without a car. It doesn't figure."

"Nothing figures," Foster says, taking the card from the affectionate clasp of the clerk and circumspectly putting down a false name and address and listing Dolores with a different last name. "You've just got to go along with the tide."

"Sure. I can understand that."

"Depends."

"Listen," the clerk says and with an uncontrollable eagerness, loses the last of his Clerkly Mask and leans forward over the counter, his hands trembling, "It's none of my business or anything like that but did you have a big score out here? I mean, you know …"

"Yeah," Foster says. "I had People Trap."

"You had People Trap?"

"Yeah, quite a bit."

"Well I'll be damned," the clerk says. "I wanted to bet that horse myself. Yesterday at this time I was sitting here right in this room in the same position with the same goddamned copy of the *Telegraph* looking at me in the face only the date and horses were different and I was saying to myself that People Trap, you better watch that cat, those people are going to put him over one of these days real soon. I liked his figures."

"So did I."

"I didn't think that the horse could lose. Matter of fact, I was going to lay twenty on him, just for the hell of it but then I got stuck here, I couldn't get relief and the boss would have given me hell if I had taken off. Twenty bucks I would have had, maybe fifty. You win a lot?"

"I did fair."

"I bet you did. I would have done too. You look like the kind of man who always bets to win and to win only. Bet you did."

"I did all right."

"Friend," the clerk says, taking back the completed card and looking at it, "I mean, Mr. Agamemnon, I mean, not to impose on you or anything like that, but what do you see today? You got anything you like? You come out here with your … uh … wife to play something special?"

"I haven't even had a chance to check over the entries. I don't know who's running."

"Well, take this," the clerk says and thrusts the *Telegraph* at him, open to the fifth race, a turf event. "I'm sorry, miss, I mean ma'am," he says to Dolores. "I mean, I just wanted to talk to your husband for a minute; I hope you don't mind."

"I don't mind," Dolores says. She is sitting on the bench, her eyes closed, her arms folded, head leaning back against the wall. She seems to be wrapped into the beginnings of a deep, dreaming sleep and Foster wishes for her sake that it could continue but there is still much to do today; it will never work out.

"This one," the clerk is saying, pointing to Williamette's Creek, the third post position. "What do you think of the chances of this one? I have a friend who says today's the day but I don't know."

Foster looks at the chart briefly and says, "I know it from way back. It couldn't run on dirt, it couldn't make the hurdles and the fact that it ran a little in the slop only shows that it has sore feet. I don't think I'd play it if I were you. Of course it all depends; it could win. They all can win."

"Well yes sir," the clerk says, "yes sir, I don't have to ask you anymore;

I'm delighted to have had your opinion. No, I had the same fears about the horses; I don't really think I would have played it, friend or not. You have anything that you ... uh ... like better? In this race or in one of the others?"

Foster tosses him the hundred-dollar bill, stares the clerk down calculatedly while change is fished out and put in front of him; the clerk is apparently charging them only ten dollars without even asking how long they intend to stay, takes the ninety dollars and stuffs it into his pocket and says, "I told you, I didn't even take a look at the entries this morning. Didn't I tell you that?"

"Well of course, but general knowledge, background, the possibilities, the feeling of horses—"

"Forget it," Foster says. "I have nothing. No news, no information, no tips. I'm just a loser reformed. A bust-out in luck. A wrongheaded tip that got the rest of the field stiffed. You wouldn't want to hear from me even if I had something." He goes over to Dolores, takes her by the elbow and coaxes her out of the office, nodding at the clerk. "I mean, I'm you, just twenty-four hours later; it could be you, have hope keep on with it," he says to the clerk and takes her down to cabin 12. She trots at his side obediently, gently, you can do anything with women once you work them into such a state of emotional exhaustion that they can barely function. He wishes that he had learned this years ago. There was nothing special about them; it was all a question of manipulation.

TWELVE

Inside the room, Foster busies himself with the usual motel preparations, locks the door, flushes the toilet, runs the water, flushes the toilet again, checks the cabinet for toothpaste or scumbags, sets the air conditioner on humming, closes the shades, checks out the wall for hidden speakers, throws a couple of towels around to loosen up, then looks over at Dolores who is curled up on the bed, yawning. "Oh Harry," she says, "Harry, I could just sleep for hours, I really could."

"Dolores, baby," Foster says and puts into his voice now all the conviction and sincerity he can muster; the next couple of hours have to go just right or everything will be blown, all of it, totality, all for naught and he will be back where he started from, there is simply no room left for any false moves. Losers don't worry about things like that but Winners cannot make mistakes, "Dolores, I promise you that very soon now you'll be able to get all the rest you want; we'll stay in a beautiful room with a view of the park and ducks and swans and children and sleep and sleep but for just a little while now we have to keep on going; it isn't much longer now, just for me."

"Oh, I'm so tired, Harry," she says. "I'm so tired of pushing and running and putting up with things, so tired of having to look good and act sexy and be attractive and optimistic; all I want to do is to sit down somewhere and have a little peace, peace, Harry, it's been too much." And he says, "Yes, yes, I know how you feel, I feel the same way but we've got to clear out the last demons, Dolores, get rid of them, this isn't for me, it's for you, both of us, the thing we have and want to be," and he begins to remove his clothes then very deftly while she stares at him with shock and exhaustion chasing one another through her eyes and says, "Oh, Harry, Harry, I can't do it now. I just can't do it for you; I'd like to, baby, but I just don't think I have it—"

"Don't worry about it," he says. "I'll do all the work, there's nothing you have to do there except to take your clothes off and lie pretty. I promise you. I promise you that but Dolores you must do this one thing for me, you must now get up from the bed and stand for a few minutes; I have to do something." He slips off his last garments, feels the strange coolness of the air conditioner moving into pockets of sweat of him, goes over and flicks it off. "Please," he says but has misjudged her, she has already stood up and shaking her head is stripping down. Her body looks even better than he remembers it but there is no time for that kind of thing now.

"You see, Dolores," he says, going to his pants, removing his wallet, double-checking the door to make sure that it is locked and then, opening the billfold, "you see, what we're going to do now Dolores is something very special and very important. We're going to fuck on money."

"What?"

"I said, we're going to fuck on the money, Dolores, that's what I said."

"Fuck the money?"

"No, sweetheart, fuck *on* the money, how could you fuck money; you'd have to be perverted." He removes the huge clump of bills from his wallet and begins to put them on the bed.

To her credit she surprises him again and stands wistful, naked, looking down at him as he does what he has to do. Perhaps she is only thinking of how desperately she wants to lie on the bed and the sooner he is through with his insanity the more quickly she will stretch out. Or maybe she is really titillated and bemused. In any event, the hell with her, it makes no difference. Foster knows exactly what he is doing now. It is only the second time today that he has; the first being when he ran from the car. He puts the hundreds down neatly, laying them in careful, even rows on the bed, head to toe, side to side until every part of the bed is covered by a fresh, glistening bill, then, since he has at least half the pack remaining, he doubles up, covering each bill with a gleaming companion, moving his palm across them now and then to keep them in place. It is good thing that he turned off the air conditioner, he decides, because otherwise this would never do, they would flutter like hell.

"What are you *doing*, Harry?"

"I'm making a bed of money," he says. "A bed of money for you and me to fuck in; I want to see if there's any difference screwing this way. I want to screw on money. And you, Dolores, you're even luckier than I am because I'll only have my palms and knees in it but you're going to be back all the way into it, deep inside all the way, that lovely curly crispy money all over your back and ass and legs and neck; oh, you'll love it. There's never been anything like it. That's the way to do it," he says and having completed the job with the hundreds considers adding the few tens and singles and twenties he has, then decides that this would corrupt the whole affair mercilessly. The hell with them. He flings the remnants into a corner and then motions. "Come on, Dolores," he says. "Get down there for me."

"Oh, I don't know, Harry," she says with a strange giggle. "Doesn't it seem, oh well you know, a little bit perverted to you?"

"Why?"

"Well, the money and all."

"Well, don't worry about it. Don't you understand, Dolores, that's the whole point of it. To screw in a bed of money. That's what everybody wants to do and I want to do it too. Think of the opportunities, the possibilities, the memories. How many girls have ever done it before?"

"I feel strange, Harry."

"It's the power of all that money getting to you," he says and puts his hand out, cups her breasts, feels them flap to his clasp, then pushes her gently and she falls away from him down on the bed with a thump, some of the bills scattering like fireflies in the impact. She moans and stretches her arms above her head. "It tickles," she says.

"I bet it does. It's supposed to. That's money, after all."

"It's weird," she says. "It feels something like velvet but it's pointy. Whoops! I think I've got one in my asshole," and reaches underneath her to extract a slightly moistened hundred which she passes over to him with a flourish. "That's a strange thing," she says.

"Oh, yes it is, it is indeed," he mumbles to her, delighted by the idea now, by the affair, by the way it is working out and the best part of it is that she is really getting into the spirit of the thing, really cooperating with him, working deep toward his purposes and not against; she is, when all is said and done, a very nice girl if a bit too much on the treacherous side. "Whoops!" she says again and bounces enormously, clearing enough space underneath her so that in the momentary opening he can reach down and seize a fistful of bills which he raises above his head with a shout, then slowly allows to drop on her. They are caught by some vagrant breeze in the room, drift, momentarily encircle and shroud her face so that she has the aspect of a Madonna in Search of Money and then he reaches down, grasps her breasts, squeezes them urgently from the aureoles outward while she moans ritually and pants. He frees a hand, takes another couple of hundreds, puts them over her breasts and covers as much of their area as can be permitted, then fondles the hundreds, feeling the flesh quiver underneath. Eventually he bends his head and begins to suck at her nipples tasting greenness, seeds, power, other vague things as the nipple comes to a rapid point and seems about to erect through the one hundred, tearing it. He bites down, tasting the crispness of the paper, enjoying the slight sensation of give as it curls around the nipple and she moans, thrusts it deeper into his mouth. "Oh suck it, suck it," she says, whether referring to the bill or tit he has no idea so sucks both, moistening them, slobbering over both, crunching down on the bill and tasting money as he withdraws finally, spits it out and concentrates on the other tit which she has kept covered only by snaking out a hand and holding it down on the bill. He sucks this one too until the paper is filled with saliva and then, moaning, thrashes on top of her, feeling himself already guided with surges of power toward her dim hole. "Oh, my God," she says, "this is fun, why didn't I ever think of doing something like this on my own?" and he smiles at her, runs a gentle, gentle hand over her forehead, wipes off some of the sweat and dew, then takes another hundred and slides it up her thighs, moving it toward her cunt, tenderly touches the outer lips with the point. "Aah!" she screams. "Ah God, give it to me!" and he wraps the hundred tightly around his finger, holds it at the base with his thumb so that it will not be dislodged and begins to finger fuck her with the hundred while she bounces and screams, breasts juggling, bills flying, toilets down the corridor, flushing; he feels her little cunt-muscles squeezing around the one hundred with affection that quickly turns to greed; he can feel her literally sucking at it with her interior and so, regretfully, he sends it on his way, removing his thumb, letting the bill spiral softly away from him and she goes "glug!" in a high shrieking voice and begins to pump with such enthusiasm that the bill after a time passes out of her, falling moistly to the bed. "Ah," Foster says, more excited by this than he would have dreamed, "Ah, look at that little son-of-a-bitch, *you've made it all wet!!*" and full of love for her own love of what he has done for her, takes two more hundreds from underneath him, wraps them tightly around his tool and guides himself into her cunt slowly. She screams when she feels the first touch of the hundreds, thrashes, then relaxes so that he is able to move up slowly, slowly. Friction is enormous of course and it is a difficult passage but so enthusiastic is her cooperation, so fine her commitment that he is able to make the righteous passage without any substantial difficulty; in due time he is all the way in, only the ball of his thumb holding the hundreds to him, keeping them from mindlessly swimming their way up her channel and doubtless to her most secret parts. "Fuck me, fuck me!" she shrieks but he stands in little need of such encouragement; he is, in fact, already fucking her, the hundreds flying left and right now, the bed having the aspect of a hundred moths scurrying their way in the vicinity, the faint swish and *ping!* of hundreds as they hit the floor working in counterpoint to his own efforts. "I love it, I love it," she shrieks. "I'm going to come now!" and seizing her breasts, squeezing them into fullness, abandoning touch of him to touch herself she goes into an enormous, groaning orgasm, eyes closed, nose twitching, face breaking open to show him all of the secret parts of herself and he takes it in, takes in the aspect of this woman completely: he feels at this instant that he has never known any woman as fully or as well as he knows this one and she renders him encouragement toward this suspicion opening her mouth, forcing her mouth against his cheeks, moaning, "Oh God, oh God, you're beautiful, Harry, you're just so beautiful; this is the most beautiful thing that ever happened to me in my whole life" and falls back, far away from him, curling to herself. Tenderly he removes himself from her hole, looking at his red, diminishing organ with some dismay. The two one hundreds seemed to have vanished somewhere inside her.

"Dolores," he says. "Dolores?"

"Oh God. Oh boy. Oh dear. What is it?"

"Two c-notes."

"What about them?"

"The two c-notes I had around my prick when I went inside you. Where are they?"

"They aren't around you?"

"Nah. They must have slipped inside."

"Well," she says, bringing up her arms to squeeze him, embrace him, drag him into her again, "Well, they're inside, then, how about that; they seem to have gone away. They feel wonderful in there, wherever you are. Do you mind?"

"No, I don't think so."

"You don't really want them back, do you? You wouldn't poke and pry at me and tear me all apart just to get two c-notes back."

"No," Foster says. "I couldn't do anything like that to you. I'm no pervert, for God's sake."

"That's good. Then just lie on me. Forget it. Maybe they'll come out of my mouth or something like that later. Oh, you have no idea how it feels. Oh, it's the most incredible thing." She is talking in short gasps now, complete, full sentences apparently beyond her depth. "It was terrific. Oh, Harry. I have an idea. I know what I want you to do now to me."

"What?"

"Eat me. Put your mouth inside me. I want you to taste me."

"I have a better idea," Foster says. He reaches down, takes yet another bill, smooths it carefully—in their flurry it seems that many of the bills have become unfortunately creased—and then wraps it around his mouth, tonguing it to hold it in place, then moves down and puts his mouth against her hole. He tastes her steaming moist cave or maybe it is only the hundred that he is tasting, that cove of possibilities.

"Oh yes," she says. "Oh dear God, yes. That's what I wanted you to do. Oh stick it in there. Stick it all the way in." And snorting he drives through her, inhaling deeply, smelling and tasting the fragrance of the one-hundred-dollar bill and then forces himself into a conjoinment as deep as anything he has ever known, literally trying to immerse himself and the c-note in her cunt, drowning in it, falling into it, his tongue licking frantically and he feels the rough threads of her vulva or maybe it is only the rough threads of the hundred-dollar bill, he tastes the smooth sweet taste of her cunt, the scent of her walls although maybe it is the hundred-dollar bill he is tasting and then, using his tongue, he begins to lap her, driving in and out of her rapidly, hearing moans and gasps above, dipping his hands into the layer on the bed to affix two new bills and then begins to knead her breasts through them, then, for the hell of it, drops a hand once more to toss a few c-notes on her belly and then, buried in lust, attacking his mountain of green, he moves into a long, timeless wanting period during which he feels that he has come closer to the sense of this girl than he has ever done with any woman in his life. As a matter of fact, he knows he will marry her. Eating her is like nothing less than eating all of Aqueduct Racetrack in one sweeping gesture and he had always known that he would never marry until he found a woman who would do this for him and at long last, after all these years of struggle and backtracking he has.

He has, he most definitely has: eating her is like taking hold of all of it; he is tonguing the tote board and Clocker Lawton's Orange Sheet and Jack Powell's Green Leaflet to say nothing of the New York Turf Letter; he is able through her cunt to take hold simultaneously of the infield and of the swans puddling in the polluted lake behind the backstretch; he is clamping the grandstand and the clubhouse and all of the horse players there too, the jockeys and the bugle calls and the high lonely sound that the trumpet makes before the first call to the post; he is eating out the hundred-dollar window and the parking lot and the unshaven little men who always know what is going to win the ninth but never what will take the next race, all of them bursting and skittering and jumping in his mouth and underneath him Aqueduct Racetrack says uh from a long, long distance and *ah!* and *oy* and *eh!* and it is all he can do to keep himself from hurling himself into this pit for love, for love clamoring in between her heavy thighs and perching there a rail-bird forever, moaning for the horses in their flight while the endless trumpet calls. *It is now post time*, Aqueduct Racetrack says over him, *it is now post time and now they're off*, that's lust on the rail taking the lead; love is second, remorse third, that's memory fourth and on the far outside it's prophecy. Far back are indulgence and possibility and trailing the field at this point is hope. Now they're coming into the first turn and that's still lust by three and a half lengths, remorse coming up on the outside now second, memory bird. That's indulgence coming outside to be fourth and from far back, prophecy is now picking up ground. Now as they come into the stretch turn that's lust still on the lead, a length back remorse now coming up head to head, memory is third. That's prophecy now the strong horse on the outside. In mid-stretch that's lust and remorse with prophecy. It's lust and remorse and prophecy. Now it's lust and prophecy, remorse and indulgence, lust and prophecy, lust and prophecy, and as they come over the finish line, that's prophecy by a nose. Lust was second, indulgence third. The complete order of finish has not been posted. Please hold your tickets. This result is not official.

"Oh God," he moans and comes away from her; she has pumped his mouth and her cunt to submission, does not protest, looks at him weakly with the glimmering light of sensuality still in her eyes as he settles above her again, commits himself once more to the ancient posture of generation and then for the last time possibly and then again you never know performs upon her the act of vigorous fucking, one-hundred-dollar bill clenching and unclenching in his distended palm as he moves, bounces, rides, screams, bucks, forces, whines, pleads, incites, insists, coaxes, prays, necessitates and finally vomits onto her a drop of scum so tiny and yet so perilously raised that he thinks he is going to faint when he finally discharges upon and into her and collapses on top, falls into a muddy pool of silence then for a period whose length he cannot judge and only comes to awakeness through the convulsive jerking of her arm as she tries to get it free. "It fell asleep," she smiles and he falls asleep, they both fall asleep, darkness settling upon them in that room, hundred-dollar bills rustling to the right and left of them, the sliding sound of money easing their limbs in the convulsive postures of sleep as together Foster and the girl dream the dreams of the dreamless, waiting for Post Time to come.

THIRTEEN

When he got up it was 1:10 on his watch and Foster felt quick fury giving way to panic; surely they were going to be late. There was no excuse for it, none at all; they had no business sleeping, that was the original mistake. "Dolores," he says. "Dolores, please get up, it's late; we're going to miss the daily double already; we'll barely make the first if you hurry now," and she stretches, moans, opens her eyes, says, "Oh my God, what time is it?" and Foster says, "One ten, can't you see? Come on Dolores, come on," and prods and kneads at her flesh, this flesh which has roused him to such passion but which now only fills him with dread because it is the cause of his lateness. "Oh, Harry," she says. "Oh Harry, for God's sake, let's sleep, what's the point?" And he says, "We've got to get to the track, Dolores; I ask you this one last thing for me, that's all, then it's all over and we can live like what we've always wanted to be but it started at the track, it has to end at the track, don't you see?" and reaches for his clothes, gets into them stumbling, on instinct. Aided by many slaps, pleas and even a few mild threats, Dolores comes groaning to her feet. Foster now begins to chase the hundred-dollar bills so that he can get them back into his wallet: it is a very difficult thing to do because there are hundreds all over the place, on the floor, in the bed, on the sheets, stuck to Dolores's body, stuck to his own skin, on a lampshade, caught in the shade, a few dangling from the ceiling, under the bed, on the chair, under the chair, even a couple in the bathroom. It is like roach infestation only more infuriating because roaches are not valuable. Many of the bills are sticky with dried semen and Foster, cursing, tries to keep these separate from the others; he hopes that all of them will not become contaminated. There is no time to count but when the wad seems large enough, he folds it on itself and sticks it back into his wallet, remembering at the last moment to search the chair for the tens and twenties he has so casually tumbled there. What a mess. It is all too much for him. He must have been out of his mind. "Dolores," he says, "we're going to miss the first post. It's already too late. Hurry."

She is struggling into her sweater and skirt, her mouth a thin, crazed line, probably from fatigue, and she stops suddenly and says, "What is this? Are you crazy? Is this going to go on forever?" and Foster says, "No, Dolores, it's almost through now, I promise. It's almost over, but I told you that it started at the track and it ended there; we have to go there today. I have to. We have to come full-cycle. And then it will be over, I promise you it will be all over and we can get married and live happily ever after with twenty-three thousand dollars in the bank—well, twenty-one, we'll buy some furnishings and have a honeymoon—and I will definitely get a job and become respectable and take good care of you."

"Is that a proposal?"

"Yes, of course it's a proposal, don't you think I know what a proposal is?"

"No one's ever proposed to me before," she says and begins to cry. He comforts her aimlessly, patting her on the full back, squeezing her flesh. "Well, I've never proposed to anyone either, Dolores, so there we are but we can do all of this later. We'll have all the time in the world. We have to hurry now."

"You really want to marry me?"

"Of course I want to marry you, damn it; I didn't ask you for my health, you know; I would have to have a real relationship with the girl I married in order to do it, you know what I mean, come on, Dolores."

"In spite of what I did to you?"

"Forget it," he says. "That's in the past."

"You're not mad. You haven't been taking it out on me? You really care?"

"Of course I do," he says and is embarrassed and infuriated when once again she collapses on him sighing, moaning, sowing like a pig in heat, reaching blindly for his face. It is really all too much; he has learned a thing or two about women during the last day or so. "Oh, come on," he says. "Be reasonable, Dolores; I've got to get to that track. Believe me."

"You really want to go?"

"Yes, I really want to go, damn it."

"Then we'll go," she says and finishes putting her belt together. "Then we'll go. Anything you want to do I'll do for you. Any place you want to go I'll share. Your way is my way. My way is your way. I'll—"

"Oh, for God's sake," Foster says and flips open the door, makes a last hurried check to see that there is nothing of value left in the room other than Dolores, then snatches her by the wrist and pulls her out of there at great speed. Somewhere during the past couple of hours it has started to rain, a fine, dusty sprinkle that sends up clouds of filth and humidity from the sidewalk. He knows that if it keeps up for any length of time he will be soaked and probably catch pneumonia but that is a risk worth taking. He has to get to the track. Anyway, the rain will keep the crowd down; there shouldn't be much more than twenty-seven, twenty-eight thousand on a day like this. He will have, with luck, plenty of time to catch the second anyway.

"If we get a cab we can make it," he says, moving her in the direction of the highway. "They go by here a lot; we should have luck."

"I read that in the Book of Ruth," she says.

"Read what?"

"That business about where you go I will go, what you do I will do, what you want, I will want. I thought that was beautiful. I used to read the Bible a long time ago. It's such a nice book. I wish that all things could be like they were in the Bible."

"Here we go," Foster says and without even checking the interior, dives into a cab which has been idling in some confusion by the roadway. He pulls Dolores behind him, slams the door closed, notices that he has virtually crawled over a tiny man with bright eyes perched in a corner of the cab. "Son-of-a-bitch," the man is saying to the driver. "Son-of-a-bitch."

"What the fuck is this?" says the driver.

"Let's go," Foster says. "Aqueduct. We're going to the track. Don't worry about a thing, I'll make it worth everybody's while."

"Aqueduct," the little man says. "Aqueduct. How the fuck we get to Aqueduct? This son-of-a-bitch lost me. I miss out on the double because this son-of-a-bitch."

"I'm a *Manhattan* driver, mister, I can't know goddamned Queens. I try to stay away from the track."

"It's such a beautiful book," Dolores says.

"All right," says Foster. "A little calm, a little control. Let's all pull in one direction. You got no problems, no one." He leans over, tells the driver where he is, guides him out into traffic again and talks him carefully, devotedly toward Aqueduct. The little man moves over slightly on the seat, begins to look at Dolores with some interest. Dolores reaches a hand forth, strokes Foster's ass lovingly. The cab sputters, comes to the parking lot entrance at Aqueduct. "They refund the dollar," Foster says. "You pay them now to let you up to the grandstand area and then when you go right out you get the dollar back."

"I'm not paying out any dollar, buddy. My wife almost left me because of the horses; I used to play them down at Narragansett. I don't have nothing more to do with this anymore. You walk from here."

"Oh for Christ's sake." Foster says and stabs for his wallet, gets a hundred out, gives it to the astonished attendant who looks at him with a faintly stricken gaze as if he had just been informed of the presence of a titillating but terminal illness. "Give that back to this guy when he comes out," Foster says. He flags the taxi driver into action again. The cab staggers forward, moves into the lot, misses a couple of attendants by not too much, comes into the grandstand area. Foster gives Dolores a nudge; she opens the door and gets out. He shakes the taxi driver's hand, gives the little man another hundred, scurries after her. He is not sure what their expressions are nor does he particularly care. He grabs her by the arm—she seems to be walking in rather a somnolent state— and guides her away from the clubhouse toward the grandstand entrance. "We have to go grandstand," he says. "We're not dressed for the clubhouse. Anyway, the grandstand is better." Impatient, he almost does not wait for his change when he gives the attendant another hundred but forces himself to do so because if there is one thing he does not want to strike people as, it is a lunatic and therefore he must cover his traces. The important thing is to put up a good front, no matter how desperately you want to get to the races. He grabs the change, hoping that the attendant has had the decency to short-change him—it is the least that can be done—and at a full jog pushes Dolores up the ramp and into the infield, narrowly missing people right and left as they get into the huge, foul arena of the under-grandstand. He checks the tote. It is twelve-horse field and it is now 1:29. He has one minute to get his bet down.

"All right," Foster says. "Let's make a bet."

"What?"

"Time for a bet!"

"I thought you were quitting," she says.

"Soon," Foster says. "Soon." He checks the tote carefully, wincing in the glare. In this twelve-horse field, the four horse is 99-1, the eight horse is 80-1 and the twelve horse, which is probably a field entry is 6-1. The odds change as he looks and the eight goes to join the four at 99. Good. Interesting.

"Who do you like?" he says.

"I don't understand this. I thought you said you were off betting. I thought you said that you were never going to bet a horse again."

"You silly bitch," Foster says to her for only the second time. "After everything you've been through and you still don't understand. A dead wipe. Experience erasing itself automatically. You really don't see a thing here, do you, none of the significance at all?"

"Harry!"

"Well, do you?"

She looks at him and he sees fright passing over her features along with other things; well good enough. He seizes her hand, squeezes it roughly. "Well," he says, "who do you like? I asked you something."

She looks at the tote, back to him. "I don't understand horses," she says. "Al and Eddie, that's all they would talk but they never took me there. I don't know a thing about them."

"I didn't ask you for your biography, you idiotic cunt. If I wanted that I would've got it, no? I would've got it in spades. I asked you who you like!"

She is crying. "The five," she says.

"No good. He's 3-1. He's the favorite. Try again. Give me another."

"Harry—"

"Well? The eight or the four. You like the eight or you like the four."

"I don't even know who they are!"

"But that's the whole point!" Foster says with a mad, merry laugh. "That's the whole point! You don't have to know who they are! If you do, that just screws up everything! I like the eight myself because he's got to be the longer shot. He was 99 when the four was 80. So he figures stronger. How about it. Do we bet the eight?"

"Bet the eight?"

"I said, do we bet him?"

"Okay, Harry," she says, "Okay, okay, bet him. I don't care. I didn't say you couldn't bet him."

"Good," he says. "Excellent. That's more like it." He leads her over to the hundred-dollar window, just a few feet down the line. The betting area is full of sound: screams, shouts, bells, whinnies, amplified hooves, groan of announcer but around the hundred-dollar window it is very quiet. He should have been into this a long time ago; it is a whole different way of living, just a couple of yards away from the two-dollar window. He leans over to confront his friend the clerk, a large, red man with a pink scalp, fine intelligent hands, an alert nose. "The eight," he says. "The eight."

"Very good, sir," the clerk says—in the hundred-dollar window they always call you *sir*, and punches out a ticket, waits respectfully while Foster removes his wallet. "That's not enough," Foster says. "I want it again."

"How many times?"

Foster takes out all of the money, puts it on the side of the window nearer the clerk. "Cover it," he says. "Just cover it all the way." It is the most significant, most powerful statement he has ever made, the first order of substance he has ever given. The clerk's eyes flip all the way open and he begins to shake. "Cover?" he says with a slight break in his voice.

"Just start punching, you son-of-a-bitch," Foster says, "don't you see we're going to get shut out?" He clamps his hand down hard on the clerk's and the machine begins to spit tickets. He and the clerk watch it disgorge for quite a while, counting out the sounds. Every time a ticket comes out there is a whirr and belch and the clerk, fooling around with a pencil in his free hand makes a mark. Foster has counted 158 whirrs when Capossela says, "It is now post time."

"Faster," Foster moans. "Oh God, faster, they're going to lock the gates."

But the machine, the damnable machine, can only print and record in its own monolithic way and the movement seems agonizingly slow. Twenty-three more tickets come out. A bell rings. "They're locked," the clerk says, "The machines are locked."

"No, they're not, you son-of-a-bitch," Foster says, tossing all the money at him. "That's just something they tell the losers. I made an investigation of this whole thing, I got friends. We've got thirty more seconds at least until the lock, they don't freeze up until the starting gates open.

"Sir," the clerk is muttering, "sir, my *hand*," but Foster holds him firmly, lovingly in place until, miraculously, the machine makes a 225th *whirr!* and Foster says, "that's enough; that's all I have," and grabs twenty-two thousand, five-hundred dollars of win mutuel tickets on number eight and turns from the window. Dolores is nowhere to be seen. Perhaps she has vanished somewhere in the crowd. Perhaps she has thought better of marrying him. Perhaps she has failed to understand the true sense of the affair. It is too bad, too bad. "And they're off!" Capossela says and Foster runs, runs through the betting area to get to the back of the infield in time to watch at least part of the race. Hurtling past the tote he glances for the final figures, notes that his twenty-two thousand five-hundred has driven the number eight house down to 5-2. At last he has had some real effect upon things in his life; he has converted a 99-1 shot into favoritism. The crowd moans its pleasure at this task. Foster jumps, vaults. He comes into the open air, clustered behind bodies, hundreds of them, grey, black, brown, drab shades and peering, looks over to the stretch turn to try to get a glimpse of the race. On the board showing the order of the race the eight is not one of the first three. Good enough. Make his move later. Make it or not. Son-of-a-bitch. They'll always do it to you.

Foster stretches, jumps, leaps, screams, curses, pleads with his horse to come in. Out of a corner of an eye he notices dimly, somewhere in the distance, that Al and Eddie are standing with Dolores, looking at him with enormous interest as Dolores leans over to touch Al on the arm, whisper something into his ear. Al listens tolerantly, winks at her, reaches inside his jacket pocket. He takes out what seems to be a gun and points it at Foster.

The hell with it, it is only an illusion. Although he had always known that there would be a third time of intervention and that it would be out here. Maybe, as a matter of fact, that is what was driving him here. Foster will never know. He does not care. Fuck the metaphysics of the thing. He is raving, screaming, pleading, cursing, dying to get the eight up at the wire when Al with a casual and final flick, a massive show of proficiency, blows his brains out at twenty yards dead down range so that Foster never sees his horse run last, never sees his body fall like a pulped flower into the loveliness of his blood, never sees Al's gasp or Eddie's grunting embrace; never sees Dolores smile as she reaches to put her arms around them and hold them close, never sees anything at all although there will come a time of reckoning and he will, you bet, he surely will and when he does it will not work out the way that it did the first time. He will know far better, he will know how to come to terms with it, he is through with losing—

Forever.

January 1970: New York, New York

THE END

Afterword: *A Bed of Miscalculation*

"Well, he couldn't enjoy it because the Losing had already done for himself what the sex was supposed to do and it was like jerking off a corpse..."

"Fuck the metaphysics of the thing."

A Bed of Money is a horse-racing novel poorly disguised as pornography; the sex is clinically, often lavishly described but it is a mask for the real passion which is that of win/place/show in the shuddering infields of possibility. I was in the net cast by Maurice Girodias and his new USA version of the Olympia Press, the hardcover *Screen* and *Oracle of the Thousand Hands* had inaugurated in 1969 his second failed attempt at a literary line, pitched at two-handed readers and Girodias, a self-destructive and cynical man had pronounced both of them DOA; "I asked for pornography and you give me literature" he said of the first and "It is a masterpiece like Balzac but it is not your number one best seller" he said of the other, agreeing with a disappointed shrug to publish them both but with doom, his most characteristic, most desired posture in his soul. Of course he was correct. Then, in mid-1969 I settled in, I thought, for a long career of Traveler's Companion green paperback originals, all of them to be ancillary to my Pilgrim's Progress as a science fiction writer. That did not quite work either, not for Girodias, not for me, and half a decade later, his green card personally revoked by Henry Kissinger, he was heading back toward Paris on a slow boat to death. That boat docked in 1990 in a television studio where he had completed an interview for the second volume of his autobiography and as Budrys wrote of H.P. Lovecraft, that heart attack might have been welcomed, it was salutary in speeding him out of the 20th century before that dying century had done its work on him.

A Bed of Money is, however, as passionate a novel as Maurice was cynical; the graphic sex (perhaps the most graphic I had produced to that point and in contention for the eventual career gonfalon) is beyond mechanical, it is in its sly way desperate and the point it was seeking is well embodied in Foster's final statement before the collapsing grandstand, the collapse of all possibility. *Fuck the metaphysics of the thing* was Foster's and the novel's and for that matter Nick Tosches' crowning statement; he quoted it to close a long political essay sometime in the 90s. (I met Tosches only once, in 1999, he brought this very trilogy to the table and had me autograph the novels which, he said, "Have been very important to me." Their importance to this wild, transgressive, outlaw writer, everyone that Hunter S. Thompson wished to be, has become a sustaining factor over the next two decades.

I agreed with him; the three were also wildly important to me, *Underlay* might have been the crowned head and the earnest catalogue of pathology at the three-eighths pole that became *Overlay* was the knighted court jester but *A Bed of Money* in its ferocity, naked metaphor of track for sex, sex for horseplaying, horseplaying for copulation, copulation for the prospectus of Benny the Chart of *Underlay*, the members of this trinity had individual and collective roles in tracing suggestively the pattern of their author's life which he was only to come to truly understand decades later. Of the three novels this is the most naked, the most ferocious, the most—if you will—ill-spirited because it offers no way out. Harry the Flat had the metaphysic which Foster had discarded, Simmons the Horseplayer of *Overlay* could clutch at least to some residuum of belief in a rational, chartable Universe but Foster at the end had nothing but that Bed of Money upon which he pounded and pounded not only the hapless Dolores but himself to oblivion. Joining him in oblivion would be Citation, Native Dancer, Swoon's Son, Swaps, Bold Ruler and a host of what the publicity mill would call "others" and at the end which Foster runs up and down, in and out, ten strokes to the bar, there is nothing but the shimmering yet turgid discard of the exhausted century, the ever more exhausted millennium which presided over Shakespeare and the Spanish Inquisition and the Holocaust and Huey Long and the String Symphonies of Mendelssohn; riot and color, tinkle and tune, fire in the hole, fire in all of the cities and the countryside ... the millennium like those ships packed with refugees and their children staggering from port to port, looking for protection, finding instead Rooseveltian decree and gun boats. Oh, that was some millennium, a Garden of Earthly Delights. Here Foster still reads the charts and pounds Dolores to ash. He has no alternative.

May 2020: New Jersey

Underlay

Barry N. Malzberg

For Joyce, Stephanie Jill
and
Erika Cornell Malzberg
and for
Fred Caposella

"We would of all by now been wearing diamonds; But we ran out of money too soon."

Public Domain

I

MY MISSION AT AQUEDUCT RACETRACK IN OZONE PARK, QUEENS, NEW YORK

My mission is to recover the body of the late but famous Harry the Flat and to present it, only incidentally, to his widow Gertrude, so that he may be given a respectable funeral. It is high time that this honor was paid him. He died four years ago of a cerebral accident and now lies encased in heat and ice, sweat and dust, death and connection, underneath the backstretch of this well-known race track which is one of the top sporting centers, it is widely understood, on absolutely the entire East Coast of the United States. Gertrude is most unhappy about the indignity of Harry's station, to say nothing of his many friends and acquaintances who did not abandon their friendship for Harry the Flat simply because he died and was thus unable to reimburse his debts. In addition to these emotional factors there is a practical difficulty: his continued presence under the backstretch has been lousing up the mob's figure, this being the prime reason for the recovery action.

Unfortunately, and as is usually the case in this fiction called life, there are complications. The NYRA, for one thing, which is short for the New York Racing Association, the governing authority of racing in this state under the aegis of the popular and successful Nelson A. Rockefeller, would not look kindly upon its backstretch at Aqueduct Racetrack, in deepest Queens, being dug up . . . nor does it appreciate the recreational facilities being used as an arena for anything other than the simpler human passions. Accordingly, as the one charged with this important mission, I must move cautiously and with a certain overriding sense of the dignity of my position.

There are several reasons for this sensation of great pressure which afflicts me, the most important of which is that the recovery must be made today, June 9, 1971, and not a moment later. Precisely at midnight tonight, the bomb which the mob has implanted within my thigh as the signature of their seriousness will explode and blow me out of reach of all saving parlays unless I have, sometime during the interim, presented the body of one Harry the Flat as ransom for being defused. The excellent George Needles, who is the mob specialist in occupational and internal therapy, will do the defusing if given the proper word. If anyone else so much as looks at this area in a compromising fashion the bomb will blow up. I am assured of this by Tony Winner, who has never lied to me about a thing in his life.

This would be an irrevocable disaster, the bomb going off inside me, I mean. I am really only forty-one years old recently, even younger than the great John Fitzgerald Kennedy was when he was assassinated and I retain an even greater enthusiasm than did this famous historical figure for, what I like to think of as, life.

II

A DESCRIPTION OF HARRY THE FLAT AS I REMEMBER HIM. OF COURSE, IT HAS BEEN A WHILE

He is a small man, crushed halfway between his hat and the ground, the white tremble of his features alight with occasional grins and nods, the strangely heavy lips pouting in a thin bow when he is verbally assaulted. His frequent talk is in an uneven slang composed of mid-Manhattan and outer Queens. Because he served in the Army, he is also capable of cursing with a fluent Southern bias, usually in anal inferences. When he walks he bounces, and so has cultivated a loser's trudge to conceal imminent fortune. He wears damp, sagging suits which seem to glisten with sweat and purposeful creases. His pockets are filled with papers of every description: tip-sheets, scorecards, computations, mathematical tables, pornographic playing cards and so on. He prefers Lawton's Orange Sheet but has been known to buy a Powell. He distrusts the *New York Turf Letter* but has been known to play its criss-cross double selections. He dislikes touts but will solicit strangers' views on forthcoming races. He appreciates longshots whose odds drop consistently to post and go off at less than eight to one.

He has been married for the seven years up to the point of his death to the lovely Gertrude nee Hawkins who comforts him, prepares his meals, and arranges occasional loans and grants to him. Every night, whether he wants it or not, she offers the precarious advantages of her large white body, endowed under stress, with an almost plastic mobility. He prefers Scotch but will drink beer. He prefers beer but will drink wine. He prefers wine but will drink rum. He will not abstain although he is concerned about his liver. Occasionally, he has gone through periods of abrupt withdrawal from alcohol, composed of gloom and an obsessive determination to urinate less. He believes that Johnny Ruane has never reached his true potential and that Eddie Belmonte is dishonest. He does not believe in wheeling to favorites on the daily doubles, particularly if the favorite in either race is less than eight to five. He sweats, eliminates, excretes, and performs other human tasks but has never been known to have regarded them as much other than horrid necessities. If he goes to the men's room with you it is silently understood that this is only because he is trying to be sociable.

III

WHY I HAVE BEEN SELECTED FOR THIS MISSION

I was the oldest living friend of Harry the Flat when he was with us; now that he is gone he remains my closest dead friend. Furthermore, I am the only one who is sufficiently aware of the metaphysical, not to say philosophical, underlay of so many of his most famous opinions. Thus there is a good deal of sentiment wound into this. It is not an annoyance which I will be removing from the backstretch but a sacrament, meaning that I will take especial care of the decomposing layers of Harry the Flat as I cradle him across the infield lake and out into the parking lot. A less involved person might do work less neat, leaving various evidences for the law.

Also, and aside from all this sentiment, I am in dead hock to the mob, which has their own important reasons for wishing to remove his body. These reasons have nothing to do with salvaging the good will of the widow. The way in which they will aid my recovery is this: they are rigging the eighth race. In this race, Knockover, a one hundred and fifty to one shot, will win by four to five lengths breezing. Thereby, the mob feels, it will cause such astonishment and consternation in the grandstand, infield, clubhouse, and steward's offices that I will be able to stumble into the backstretch undetected and, spade and shovel in hand, do the disinterment, hurl the uncoffined corpse over my strong right shoulder and speed away. There is no possibility that Knockover will not win this race. I have been informed that it has been irrevocably manipulated for him, barring the omnipresent prospect of poor racing luck or blind switches. In which case, of course—well, in which case I will have to remove Harry anyway because the mob has selected today, June 9th, as the target date and there is no tomorrow for the efficient and well-functioning Mob.

(It cannot be done at night. The track is patrolled by thin and solemn guards, busted-out horse-players all, with guns for programs and clubs for Lawton; they will brook neither mystery nor possibility. Also, and I admit this, the Mob is perverse and has an almost literary sense of irony in certain details; they feel it is fitting that the decomposed Harry be removed in this time and in this way. Since the Mob itself need not be up front, this has the aspect of reasonable thinking, to them. I have no choice but to accept this.)

There is no tomorrow for the Mob; there was no tomorrow for the unfortunate and unforgettable Harry the Flat either.

Only the Mob itself can transcend time; coexisting at the poles, moving between eternity and origin like a dark fish in gelatin, the cool, spacious eaves of chronology firming its flesh as it strokes my life tenderly, absently, a dim caress moving me toward such intricate and deadly causation.

IV

A STILL LIFE OF HARRY THE FLAT ON ONE OF THOSE RARE BUT STILL- CELEBRATED OCCASIONS WHEN HE WAS FUCKING HIS WIFE

He hangs over her, mouth open, balancing on the palms, knees at cross-angle to the skylight, looking at the whiteness of the walls, the yellow background, that yawning pit of his wife which seems to smile at him as he guides himself gracelessly into that cavern, feeling it swaddle and surround him while he sucks on her breasts, biting the nipples absently while he computes results, balances, odds-charts—the only way in which he is able to force himself into a state sufficiently abstracted to function.

It is four to five against coming fast. It is seven to two against her coming; even money, however, that if she comes at all she comes first. Make that a round-robin. It is twenty-three to one against simultaneous orgasm, well, make that nineteen to one instead. Nevertheless, even knowing all of this so well he persists; there is really very little alternative after all, the odds are fascinating and in any event there is nothing better to do at the present moment that he has not yet already done to avoid the situation. Caught in that hush, in that slow, clinging languor one can sense his trembling eyes as he looks with slow, cold astonishment toward the ceiling. The first drops of the parlay begin to build within him.

He surges toward her then, the heart of him caught in a trap larger and containing more torment than any… any which he has ever known before… any but for this reiterated snatch.

V

THE LAST SERMON OF HARRY THE FLAT AS DELIVERED TO FRIENDS AND ACQUAINTANCES ON THE EVE OF HIS DEATH, JUNE 18, 1967, AT POP WARNER'S BAR AND GRILL IN FLUSHING, QUEENS, NEW YORK

"My friends, we are about to return, but not to a quality of vision. Rather, we seek a vision of quality. The spirit that I now reflect, moves slowly within us to disgorge its own insight. Pain, like a memory drifting through our skulls, in the words of the good poet Aeschlyus, moves past the body's core and toward its own destination.

"We have busted out flatly, once again… but I tell you this: that there has come upon this planet a newer generation of horseplayer, a horseplayer fired and forged in the testing and drone, droned and tested in the forge of the fire… and this generation will not easily sacrifice its margin, nor permit, for two bits, the denial of a program. It is not a generation which will submit cheaply to the lash of dime breakage, one which will accept the slavery and humiliation of an eighteen percent take out.

"No, I say to you my friends and brothers, no! To all of you, sharers of one destiny, I say that we have come to that time when the reversals will begin, a massive turning of the time, and friends and losers alike, parlaying our nine to one shots across the board, we will get out of the slime hole of history and move toward that greater achievement which once we dreamed was our contract when we got into this game. Why did we get into this game?

"I will answer that question: we came to this game not for a victory of personality but for a personality of victory. And I say to you now, letting the word flow forth, that there will be an end to losing favorites, worthless longshots, missed wheels, terrified and cowardly apprentices ruining our figures. The war is now turning around and in our favor. Daylight through the end of the tunnel. We will clean out the poison from all crevices that exist and then move on to other things.

"And so I say to you… I say that we will go into the streets now and toward our homes tonight, performing the old, cold, graceful motions which we have carried on so many times on the way to wipe out. But I tell you that this time, this night, is different and the motions are not an intimation of loss so much as a loss of intimation. On the other hand, they may be neither intimatory nor lustful but only a grave sensuality, that slow dance of the spirit. We cannot lose. And we will not lose. For we have seen the reign of the good and evil in our time: Marshall, Rainey, Cordero, Rotz, Jacobson, Fitzsimmons, Baeza, Smithwick, Shoemaker, P.J. Bailey, W. Lester, and we have survived. Our survival becomes mute witness to the century's terror.

"We turn toward the night knowing that the night will yet turn toward us. And now I bid you good evening. Good evening, gentlemen, and quiet to your homes: we shall assemble later and there will be a greatness among us."

VI

FURTHER EXPLANATION OF MY MOTIVES

I am enlisted to disentomb the body of the late and famous Harry the Flat because my own position with the Mob is precarious. Simply stated (I might as well come to the point) I owe out fifteen hundred dollars which fifteen hundred dollars I do not have and only because of being carried along by the good graces of Tony Winner for several months now have I avoided a rock in the head at any moment. Now is the time to function; I have been given this excellent chance to redeem myself, recoup my debts, and live a free life. If I can only perform this one service for the Mob, things will be good. I am dedicated to success. I know I will not fail.

I want to make the Mob happy. The alternative, after all, is too hard to contemplate. Not only have I put my life on the line as has been previously annotated, I have this enormous and very far-reaching sentiment for the late Harry the Flat to further my overall sense of dedication.

VII

HOW GERTRUDE NEE HAWKINS FELT ABOUT HARRY THE FLAT

"He's a stiff. What I mean is he don't produce. If he produced, that would be one thing, but half the time he's straight down the drain. The other half he's telling me he's on the way up but I don't see no evidence of the fact. I don't see nothing but that he gets deeper and deeper which I can always tell from his eyes. Call me a pessimist but I have my opinions on this.

"I got to have my head examined or something like that just to string along with a guy like this one let alone be married. But there's something very lovable about him, okay, okay. Anyway, I got to admit that with him every day is a difference. Not that I was getting any younger, either. You never know what's going to happen next with him though except it'll be something bad, but nothing else, so there's all that anticipation which can be really terrific. The other way I know how I would've ended up. This way there are lots of questions. You follow?

"Besides that, Harry arranged for the sterilization right after the accident and everything. So that's out of the picture which is a relief knowing that nothing like that will ever happen again. I wouldn't bring children into this world, anyhow.

"Oh, it's not a bad life, not the worst life, when you look at it from the outside. From the inside is a little different thing, but I read somewhere where one of these guys wrote that everybody's life, from the inside, looks terrible. And there's a kind of security in it, too.

"But who would believe, would you ever believe, that there could be such pain in that place? Would you?"

VIII

THE TEXT OF A TIP SHEET WHICH HARRY THE FLAT SENT OUT TO A LARGE RANDOM MAILING OF PEOPLE ONE WEEK WHEN HE WAS IN DEEP AND UNABLE TO RAISE MONEY FROM THE SHYLOCKS WHO WERE GETTING A SEVERE CASE OF THE HARRY-THE-FLAT SHORTS THAT WINTER

"I must win or I'm out of business! I must win Tuesday, August 10, 1960, or never be heard from again. This is serious business. Do not destroy this notice. Read it carefully!

"Yes, on Tuesday, August 10, 1960, selected associates and I have elected to put over one of the great sporting COUPS of the New York racing season, a COUP in which investors will find a solid horse, well-placed, in clever hands and ready to win. This horse will go off as a SLEEPER at a guaranteed payment of twelve to one or more!

"This COUP has been in the planning for several months. My associates and I have worked carefully toward this day, using our avenues of connection to assure happiness for selected investors. Now at last the time has arrived. And you are invited to get aboard. Your name has been given me by a confidential source who I cannot mention who assures that your confidence may be respected and your sincere interest in horse-racing cannot be doubted.

"We ask you for no money!

"That is correct, we ask you for no money. My associates and I, we stand behind our predictions one hundred percent, without fear and without favor. If you wish to know the name of this horse you may do so at no fee whatsoever. Simply call us at the number given below between the hours of nine a.m. and twelve noon on Monday, August 9th, 1960.

"Your only obligation will be to forward us the proceeds of a five dollar win bet on this COUP *AFTER* the race has been run.

"In order to cover the modest expenses for this mailing and to obtain proof or your own serious interest in this once in a lifetime opportunity, we do request only that you give us a small deposit prior to our release of the name of the COUP horse.

"This deposit may be deducted from the eventual sum you will forward when the horse wins. If you will mail this deposit to the address shown below and sign the name of the person to whom you wish the information released, my associates and I will then accept your call on Monday, August 9th, and release to you the name of this horse.

"The deposit required is only fifteen dollars and since the horse must pay more than fifteen to one, you will see how reasonable this small statement of faith and cooperation is.

"This is serious business. We are not fooling! The horse must surely win because if it does not I am out of business. It is not my intention to play on your faith, time, small deposit, or risk unless I can produce for you. So I say once again, as I did before, that this horse will win at odds of no less than twelve to one or better.

"Send your deposit in immediately. If you have a friend who, you feel, might want to accompany you into the COUP, please pass this letter on to him. We must advise you, however, that we will accept only a limited number of investors, inasmuch as the odds must be kept as high as possible on the horse in order to guarantee a real PLUM to my associates, myself, and to those willing to join us in this fantastic day of fun and games at the track on COUP DAY.

"Remember, the deposit necessary is only fifteen dollars, the best investment of your life.

"Only fifteen dollars."

IX

HOW I GOT HERE

I got here in various and circuitous ways beginning with the difficult and always interesting moments of conception-and-birth but most specifically, which is a question of keeping things in direct context, I followed the turf advice of Harry the Flat.

I followed his turf advice in relation to the system number 34, which system involves playing platers or two year old claiming geldings in a modified-progression situation. I got took to a considerable extent, even though I was able, in the middle of all the troubles, to hit a ninety-six dollar and seventy cent payoff only to see it taken off the board because of a tiny little disqualification. This was frustrating but did not break the basic pattern which was disastrous.

I do not, however, blame Harry the Flat for what has happened to me, inasmuch as he prepared this system a long time ago in the Eisenhower era. So he is unaware of the more current realities of racing in these terrifying times to say nothing of the declining health of claiming stock. Also, he has been dead for quite a while, and I can hardly get directly at him for dialogue.

What must be taken to task, instead, are my own foolishment, gullibility, and vulnerable good nature which should have long passed with that time when I was able to place faith in easy answers. To believe in platers, I am trying to say, is like believing in virgins but only worse because there is no evidence that platers were ever anything else, even in the maiden-specials where most of them start, whereas for virginity at least there are certain precedents. I have seen young girls, public school girls, who I could clearly state were probable virgins.

According to Harry the Flat's special plater-system instructions, I selected a given plater, Silent Sun, a four-year-old $3500 claimer at the beginning of the season in Tropical Park because I liked his name and large ankles. I then played him faithfully all year. The principle is that he would finally win and in the process would enable me to recoup all of my losses with much excess since I would be doubling up my bets consistently. Meanwhile, the Mob who controls all the horse races, (I believed this at that time) would be working nicely with the horse's owners to make sure that when the animal won he would produce a fine price.

The heart of the system is that every plater must win once during a given year if he stays sound. That is because owners and trainers must bail out on what is essentially a losing proposition, since it costs so very much to keep a horse these days and bad horses act just the same as good ones in the eating and shoeing departments. Everyone's turn must therefore come in order to keep the wheel going. ("Racing is a wheel," Harry liked to say, "but this doesn't necessarily mean that it cannot come full circle.") It is important to say, however, that the given horse must stay sound in order for the system to prevail and one of the reasons platers are platers is because they are not celebrated for their good health, either.

Silent Sun, unfortunately, was beaten in eight straight races and then forced to retire for permanent repairs, due to a broken left tendon his front knee got, and which caused the trainer to have him shot most sympathetically in front of the stands at Aqueduct one fast but sloppy afternoon in July. Resultantly, I was never able to recover my losses since one of the eligibility requirements for a cheap plater race is that the horse at issue be alive at the time that his name is dropped into the entry box.

Silent Sun had several stablemates, of course, as is common with this kind of public training operation responsible for most of the platers, and one of them, I discovered, to my bewilderment, won and paid fifty-three eighty the very next afternoon. However, this did me no good, since, in tribute to the late Silent Sun I had spent all of that day mourning the deceased animal in the premises of Ferdie Lender, where I was trying to redeem a very shaky financial situation from the ruins.

"Consider," I said to Ferdie Lender, "it is true that the animal is dead but in March he won a race and would've paid over ninety-six dollars, except for the disqualification which knocked him back to fifth. Not only did I lose my money then, I suffered. Certainly I am entitled to some kind of support for this; the system works, it is only a matter of timing." Ferdie, however, was not particularly sympathetic, claiming various family troubles and missed round-robins which had temporarily sewn his funds up tight. At the root of it, I believe that Ferdie has some connection with the Mob, himself, but this is an accusation which I could not possibly prove. Raising it without proof would only tend to hurt his feelings; beyond that constant aspect of pain which he wears like a sheath even now. "I cannot help you," he said, "even in memory of Harry the Flat and his system, I cannot give you the kind of backing you need. Of course, if you wanted me to book a few of your bets when you run the system again, that's something else. But, although I can be a sportsman, I can no longer be a financier; things have changed in the last few years and racing is no longer the same." He then offered me, for my diversion, a modestly-commissioned shot at his runner, Dorothy Wheels, if I wanted to forget about business. This I had to decline. Long losing streaks tend to make me impotent, which is one of the reasons why my sexual life is somewhat sporadic, even with people for whom I feel affection.

Therefore, I was in the hole for the tune of some one thousand, eight hundred and three dollars after this unhappy event occurred. Since I did not have this money but had, as a matter of fact, been forced to borrow most of it from the Mob at steadily increasing rates I was in very dire circumstances since the Mob had advised me that my credit was being cut off after the final loan and some means of repayment was now expected. The thought that Silent Sun would run into footing difficulties had never occurred to me.

After a few routing attempts, then, at minor evasion, I had to come to terms with the Mob in the person of Tony Winner. Tony Winner, I am led to understand, is only a minor functionary in the overall scheme but is important and respected enough to be permitted to handle matters such as this. The Mob, sad to say, fails to take emotional losses into account when attempting to settle its books and it also, contrary to popular legend, chases smaller amounts even harder than big ones since they are more visible. Tony Winner was acquainted with my pain but unwilling to take it as repayment.

I do say this, however: I do not blame Harry the Flat for any of these grievous problems which have overwhelmed me. By being in person, dead himself, he can be counted upon to have paid off all his dues. Also, I am simply thrilled to have the opportunity to do this one little favor for my old and trusted friend.

X

A GLIMPSE OF AQUEDUCT IN JUNE. THE NATURE OF THE TOTE, THE WELTER OF THE GRANDSTAND

It is a grim, bleak, blank track, this; it seems to have been slammed in colors out of concrete, only those hues—pasteboards, the drab color of tickets—relieve it at all but in their aspect of chewed and ruined candy, somehow only increase the depression, nail to the senses the poison that is in this still, rising air. It looks like a child's toy of a track, imagined to enormous size, lacking the context of maturity and it is instantly apperceptible in this obstacle of a shell that nothing can go on here that will have any tragic dimension whatsoever. No laughter, none of this, none of anything, only small, grim debacles and shame enacted over and again in some frozen graveyard of the spirit, a trick which seems to simultaneously propound and deny responsibility. A dream, a conception this thing, even an escape: call it a mental institution in which the inmates wander around in a kind of perpetual occupational therapy listening to the magnified drone of the Counselor telling them over six hundred speakers that everything will be all right, eventually, somehow, next race, could be. No changes. The tote glimmers and blinks, dazzles out its own messages to the crowd which have nothing to do with horses and in the bowels of the grandstand, in the swelter underneath the plane in which they sit, bodies are packed like fish in their density: mouths opening, gasping querulously, a flicker of newspaper, jot of sweat, a howl of rage the nearest one can come in the apprehension to those emotions which took one here in the first place to deposit him in this house of pulp.

Murder. Murder. Ah, Harry, there is murder here yet.

XI

THE POLITICAL THEORY OF HARRY THE FLAT

Harry the Flat was at Aqueduct racetrack on the well-recollected 22nd of November, 1963 on which date John F. Kennedy, the beloved President of the entire United States was assassinated. The announcement of the President's severe medical problem was made by Fred Caposella over the public address system at one twenty-five p.m., just before the third race and the popular Fred M. Caposella added that the condition was still uncertain and all racing fans should pray for the health of the young President, to say nothing of his future, while standing by for bulletins. In the third race number six was two pounds over.

"Ha, ha! it ain't got nothing at all to do with the form charts," said Harry the Flat. "They're going to put this one over under the record, can't you see it?" and went to the window to make his bet. The horse on which he bet a hunch, New Times, was fourth in a tightly-bunched field, being unfairly crowded on both turns. "Fuck this shit," said Harry the Flat, "I need a winner, I got to get out of this, got to move along, otherwise it all ends up in the Dallas way," and went back to bet on Bob Lynn Sue in the fourth race. The information on this horse had been passed onto him by a tall Greek in the grandstand who said that he knew the owner personally and that the filly must win today, otherwise they were out of business. This information thrilled the Flat, not only because it let him onto a possible score, but because a tall Greek in the grandstand would think enough of him, a local stranger, to pass this word on. Just as he placed his bet he was informed, along with others, that John F. Kennedy, once the President of the United States, had died in Dallas just about twenty minutes ago because of certain peculiar, mortal wounds. Scurrying out to the infield to be part of all this excitement, sticking his cigar between his teeth, Harry the Flat joined the majority of the infield crowd in vigorous applause. Bouncing up and down with the exertion, his small features winding their way with intricacy to some point of conjoinment on his round face, Harry radiated much of the excitement which America must have felt at that moment. "Teach him, the son of a bitch," he said, "but then you can't win them all now, can you, really?" and went back to the window on a hunch to throw another twenty on Bob Lynn Sue to win since she had the same first name as some relative the President had . . . but this proved to be his truest and most unfortunate undoing since Bob Lynn Sue Placed but did not Win.

Harry blew the twenty he would have made on the original win-and-place bet by the extra stab. The missed tip, the maddening, elusive Greek who he wanted to straddle in rags and pulp, the high, clinging scent of ozone in the air, the blare of the megaphone, the glare of the sun, the news that they were going to cancel the program after the seventh, came together in Harry for his one, great political insight and he said, "The trouble is that something always gets between you; between you and it, and I'm not talking about fucking now, because the fucking you get simply ain't worth the fucking you take."

Several horseplayers looked at him with interest but there were no real comments.

XII

HOW HARRY DID IT TO HIMSELF

I think this is the way it happened: Harry the Flat committed suicide on June 19th, 1967 at Aqueduct racetrack, a fine, warm, late spring day in Ozone Park when the temperature was eighty-five degrees, the humidity thirty-one percent. This is how it must have been: the suicide occurred immediately after the fourth race when Rock Diver, let go at five to two, finished fifth in a seven horse field, unaided by blinkers and the enthusiastic and sexual pumpings of his jockey. "Son of a bitch," Harry must have said to the large crowd of friends and onlookers, including Tony Winner in the upper grandstand, "son of a bitch, I can't stand it anymore, I can't stand it! The system stinks, I see that now. Why did I ever get taken into this pursuit?" and without waiting for an answer removed a small point, twenty-two caliber pistol from the inner pocket of his plaid sports jacket, put it firmly against his sweating temple and pulled the trigger.

"Gee," I think he added, "that was stupid of me," just before the rictus of death, a curiously soundless explosion, overcame his now-smiling features and he plunged inert to the ground, a copy of Lawton protruding cheerlessly from his breast pocket. His death was curiously bloodless and artistic the way I think I remember it; a fact which more than any other permitted the Winner and other acquaintances to say as they considered his corpse that it was certainly a shame Harry had to go this way but on the other hand he could at least be granted a last wish often expressed to have Aqueduct as his final resting place.

"Bury him here right now," someone said and picking up the form, his friends conveyed him to a vacant Harry M. Stevens free-flow pushcart which had been abandoned by its vendor after the daily double; the pushcart and its horrid contents were then conveyed down the escalator, onto the lawn and in a few nimble but clamorous twitches across the rail. Then to the backstretch itself, I can see it now, so clear and distinct that it could have been in no other way, past a few indolent swans on the infield lake who looked at the excursion without interest but terrific knowledge.

Excavations were rapidly and successfully accomplished; Harry was joined to the turf which he had so judiciously calculated for most of his adult life and then his friends went off singing, if not drunken, into the bright remnants of the afternoon. "The least we could do for him" and "this should hold up the early speed a bit more" were among some of the comments passed, comments which seem rather indistinct in my mind, however.

As a matter of fact, it all seems indistinct: what happened is the only possible explanation for Harry's burial and I know that it must have been in this way but the Winner, among other abilities, has the talent of clouding men's minds and perhaps my memories of this are not all that they should be. Perhaps what we did was to wait with Harry until nightfall before burial. Or then again, I have a vague feeling that Harry might have dug his own grave out there and shot himself in solitude, maintaining only enough sentience in his ebbing life forces to cover himself up for ascending. One does not know. I cannot pursue explanations further. I have immediate, pressing business, and the present is all. It has been four years now, after all, and so much has happened since then.

The early speed did tend to hold up a bit during the next couple of days' racing, but by the end of the week, things had settled down to their usual dismal level and the Harry the Flat system, along with so many of the others, was also discarded. Harry would have been proud of the ability of his friends and acquaintances to discount his presence on the back-stretch once it proved unavailing. "Flexibility," he would caution us in his days on earth, "flexibility. Never stay with an angle if you can disentangle."

XIII

MY RELATIONSHIP WITH GERTRUDE NEE HAWKINS IS HEREIN EXPLAINED FOR THE VERY FIRST TIME

I have been in love with the remarkable Gertrude nee Hawkins for several years, ever since, in fact, the first time I met her in the company of Harry the Flat on their wedding day.

Harry and Gertrude were wed in the Hollis Avenue Sacred Shrine Union Church of the Sacramental and Beloved Divine reception room on a fine autumn afternoon, and as one of his oldest and closest I was invited to the wedding. This made me participate in the Bringing of Gifts, though I had not previously even glimpsed the bride who had always been kept concealed from the Flat's companions during the period of his courtship. Probably he wanted to lay off his bets and not let her know what kind of acquaintances he was having or not having luck with. Gertrude was then and is now a lovely female with matron-like breasts, full and wide, white and thick in the suddenness of repose and exposure. I dreamed often of the Flat's adventures in paradise until I was informed by her, during our second adulterous tryst, that he had not gone to bed with her more than fifteen times in the course of their marriage. Harry settled for fucking only when he had lost huge bets or felt himself, via an important tip, on the verge of the enormous rim of chance. And all of these events, to make them even less convenient, seemed to occur during the early morning hours, that time being the only period of day when Harry could find an erection.

"You see, you see, he just ain't geared that way," she reminded me, laving my guilt with the flow of desire below and thrust her complacent flesh skillfully into my clamorous mouth. Oh God, I could have died that way: the softness of her flesh entwined with memory; images of the madonna circling thickly into lust, her rising nipple plunging my throat like a dancer, all meaning, all sensation darkened to that high, bright flame of purpose as I probed and probed her again, muttering my Love, Harry's foolishment, the anguish of the machinery into whose pistons we had fallen, cut to ribbons, bright blood moving swiftly, circles of spreading dark, streaming to the floor.

XIV

FINALLY REVEALING HOW LAWTON IS ABLE TO GIVE WINNERS AND MAINTAIN THE ILLUSION OF SUCCESS WHEN ACTUALLY IF YOU PLAYED HIM FAITHFULLY FOR A FULL YEAR YOU WOULD LOSE EVERYTHING THAT YOU COULD OWE

Lawton gives two horses in each of the nine races. They are almost always the strong morning line favorites in their races and if they aren't favorites they will rapidly become so because of the pari-mutuel system and the wide distribution which all of Lawton's picks receive. Of these eighteen picks, then, four or five will win on a normal day since better than one third of favorites do win and favorites and second choices combined will win half the races. This means that Lawton can thusly claim twenty or thirty winners a week but the prices are short and he does not remind you that it is as well to lose two win bets on longshots blowing four dollars as to win on one out of two races-four bets-on favorites and collect three eighty. Lawton is thus another illustration of the principle of disequity in the universe. This principle has much to do with my current adventures at Aqueduct racetrack in Queens, New York.

Also, I have had it out for him for a long, long time and think that this is a good opportunity to get that one thing off my chest.

XV

A FEW WORDS FOR THE WIDOW

Harry the Flat signed a telegram which the crowd at Bailey's Bar & Grill in Brooklyn sent Jacqueline Kennedy, the international beauty, on the eve of her first husband's funeral. He was hanging around getting drunk, when the thing came up. When the collection was made, he felt that he could not stay out of it easily without generating certain unpleasant hostilities in a bar whose tab he needed badly to sustain. He was able, however, to short fifty cents on the split by claiming that he had no loose change.

WE ARE TRULY SORRY FOR WHAT HAS HAPPENED AND WISH YOU AND THE KIDS THE VERY BEST IN THESE TIMES AHEAD STOP KNOWING THAT YOUR STRENGTH AND SPIRIT WILL COMFORT YOU AND ALL AMERICANS ARE WITH YOU TO-

GETHER AT THIS HOUR OF TRAGEDY AND PAIN STOP FOR THE UNITED STATES, the telegram said and the very next day the Flat read about himself in the paper in a story which noted the flood of sympathetic telegrams pouring into the White House including not only messages from simple Americans but from dignitaries of politics and the arts. That almost made the whole thing worth the expense and he certainly *was* sympathetic, even though the goddamned funeral bombed out the whole Monday card . . . including several very interesting choices which Harry had been teaching himself to watch for several months.

XVI

CERTAIN FINANCIAL CONSIDERATIONS

The Ultimate Tip on Knockover, the horse, will pay three hundred dollars or more or Tony Winner is no longer a winner. I intend to place one hundred of my own sequestered dollars on this horse, the better to exacerbate the pleasure of the mission. It will be impossible for me to cash my tickets immediately after the race, unfortunately, since I shall be otherwise occupied with the details of disinterment. I will be able to cash them at the previous days' windows on the next day or the day after that and when I receive this money, I am not able to talk of what will become of me other than that my life will radically change and very possibly for the better.

Fifteen thousand dollars.

Fifteen thousand dollars back for my hundred—small reparation for where I have been and what I must do. The sum I need, to consummate my existence then and, for all I know, to begin a newer and more complicated way of life with the lovely Gertrude, *for* the lovely Gertrude.

For her and for myself. We have been running in this season of chances too long; too long, now the entries must be changed.

XVII

A CHAT WITH TONY WINNER

"But why do you want him dug up? He's been buried there quietly all those years; what's the difference? He could stay there until the year ten thousand; how would they ever know it? No one, no one at all could tell."

"No he couldn't. He got to get out of there, that stiff. He always loused us up; now even when he's dead you got no peace."

"Why?"

"You're not supposed to know why."

"But I'm entitled. Think of the risks I got to take here."

"That ain't no matter; you're just the messenger. The hard detail man we call it. If you were supposed to know, I'd tell you. They'd give me the orders because that's the system. I read all about it in this book about the Mob. It was very interesting. I never knew they worked that way."

"I'm entitled to something for the risks."

"So what? It's your problem; I'm not taking them so what the hell?"

"I ought to know."

"I told you, we got our orders. It's the higher ark. I'm not even sure that I know the reasons for it."

"Oh come on, Tony, be reasonable. I'd take it as a personal favor."

"Maybe I don't know."

"Sure you know."

"That was just a joke, okay. I'm an inside man; I know everything. I wouldn't kid you that way, it isn't fair. Of course I know, they tell me everything. They know who the Winner is."

"Tell me then."

"You really want to know?"

"What do you think?"

"Well, if I gotta say it then, he's lousing up the figures, that's what the stupid son of a bitch is doing."

"Huh? Who?"

"Who? That stinking bum, lying under the sod there. He's done something to the dirt, it don't come down even. He's screwing up all the figures, the past performances, he's making figuring impossible. They run over that backstretch and they gain two seconds, lose four seconds, start crossing over in front of the field. They can't tolerate the error no more. Probably he's been doing something to the turf when he started to decompose."

"The burial did this?"

"The burial, fuck the burial, I mean that stiff is lying in there and lousing up everything. For a while they could compensate: Billy Chart was able to figure out speed and windage and variables so we could take the stiff into consideration but since they done so much racing over the track with the dual meets and Belmont being out of action until so late and the December racing and everything, something's happened. The arrangements don't stick. It's getting unpredictable, goddamn it, and we got to get that loser out of here before he louses up everything. I'm telling you, we're having plenty trouble making any kind of results with that kind of stuff going on in there. And then where would we be? We ain't making no money off the conventional operations, they're all taxed and it's mostly public relations. The only area you get yourself a little edge is in the arrangements and now we can't be sure of nothing."

"That's really something."

"It sure is. You tell anyone you're wise, bum, or that I put you up there, I will blow your head off with a shotgun or more likely use some kind of good and efficient hammer which is more reliable if somewhat less cleaner."

"Then if that's so, I got one single question to ask you."

"You got one. Exactly one and no more. I hate to sound like a tough guy or anything but they really make things hell if you don't stand up to it. It's a whole policy."

"If the figures are loused up, how can you be sure you can put over this Knocker?"

"Knockover, dummy. The name of the horse is Knockover. What you got on your mind?"

"I meant Knockover. Couldn't the figures get loused up on that one too?"

"Sure," Tony Winner says, "that's a sure thing, of course it could. But if they do then you get good and loused up too, meaning that you ought to be very concerned and involved with what you're really there to do and the hell with the tip. Forget about the horse. Because everything is chance, life is a chance, and I am sitting in this chair right here this minute only because one bit of sperm won out over a couple billion others and the four guys who sat in this chair years previous had to resign owing to these tiny little accidents with their circulation."

XVIII

HARRY THE FLAT ON THE SUBWAY SPECIAL ON THE MORNING OF THE DAY HE CANCELLED OUT OF IT

He will meet his friends at the track; he insists upon travelling there alone, because in no other way can he find the time to himself, to think. Now, the *Telegraph* folded on his lap—it is hopeless, he can find no spots, he has for the moment given up—he sits alone on a double seat, drawn in gracefully upon himself, a small man, not to say delicate in appearances. The seat could with ease have been occupied also by a very large woman, for some reason, however, that very person who entered the car at the Hoyt Street station and seemed about to sit next to him changed her mind at a critical instant and, instead, sits across from him in a tiny single seat, glaring uncomfortably, muttering, but unwilling to join Harry. She holds her glasses between the thumb and forefinger of her left hand, twirls them, looks at Harry with energetic hatred and he finds himself wondering vaguely if there is something wrong with him, something which makes strangers in public places seek other accommodations or pass him by sniffling quizzically. He thinks for an instant of leaning over and asking the woman why she hates him so but decides that he cannot, she might take him for insane, and this is something with which he cannot deal. Instead he thinks of Gertrude who not three hours ago permitted her smooth, bland warmth to lie quietly beside him, deep in sleep, small nestles of her hair turning gently with his breath. Surely, he thinks, if such a woman would lie next to him there can be nothing wrong with his public aspect; the large woman is obviously unstable and he, the Flat, has nothing to fear. He tries to fixate on Gertrude, to get down in his mind exactly what she looks like and how he feels about her, but it is too difficult, too painful for reasons too obscure to identify. So he returns to the *Telegraph* opening it to the entries for the fourth race, and for the seventh time that day spots the figures on Rock Diver, a four-year-old gelding. He has been in and out of spots with this horse for a year, now it is time for all losses to recoup and he is positive that even as the favorite today it will win. "It's got to win, I know it will win," he mumbles and involuntarily clasps his hand, the woman stares at him, the train lurches, a whiff of subway filth comes through a window and into his nostrils, panels away and he clutches for a handhold as the *Telegraph*, unheeded for the moment, slides to the floor and turns gently in the wind. *Rock Diver, Rock Diver*, Harry thinks and the lights in the car wink out at a momentary circuit-break; he stabs in the darkness at what looks like stars, the lights go on again, the train stumbles into daylight. Unhappily the Flat does not take these events as an omen which is one of the keys to his problem; for all his faith in mysticism, he has been selective about his anguries.

XIX

A BRIEF DIFFICULT MOMENT AT THE ENTRANCE TO THE GRANDSTAND

I have driven out on the Long Island Expressway in a Mob Ford leased to me by Tony Winner, inasmuch as it has been agreed that the conveyance of spade and shovel on the subway special would be more conspicuous than truly desirable. Since the subway special is my usual habitat and accustomed means of travelling to Aqueduct it has been an uncomfortable drive, although the power steering and brakes on the

Ford are considerably easier to manipulate than a subway strap. Tony Winner has thoughtfully provided a stereo tape collection of bugle calls and announcements of interesting races to hold my attention during the trip. Because of the nature of the mission, I have been compelled to put the car into the grandstand parking section and hike my way into the grandstand itself, the spade and shovel packed neatly into an excellent leatherette cello case which was given me by my sister a long time ago as an inducement to a musical education. Everything goes relatively well up to the time of paying admission, although several of the customers, walking in with me through the parking lot, want to know whether I am playing a cello concert on the grounds during the day and what selections on the cello would be the most appropriate for a very cheap card. Although I appreciate the humor of these remarks, and in different circumstances might have made some myself, I find that the best response to them at the present time is complete silence and disapproval. Music, although it has never been one of my great interests, is not to be sneered at and to be a concert cello player would be a fine and remarkable thing, although not strictly applicable to the picking of winners. At the window, however, when I extract my wallet to pay two dollars admission, a terrible thing happens: somehow, the zipper on the cello case becomes undone, or perhaps it was undone all the time. And from the opened case spill the two implements which, in gentler circumstances, have been referred to as gardening tools. They fall in the area of my feet with a dreadful clatter, managing to somehow stub the toe of a large blonde in attendance with a short, serious horseplayer type. "What the hell do you think you're doing, friend?" the short horseplayer type asks of me while the admissions clerk and ten or fifteen people on line eye the scene with interest. I cannot say that I blame them.

"Oh," I say, having never been particularly graceful at social banter, "Oh, I'm sorry. I don't know how that happened." I bend and snatch the two dreadful implements, trying to stuff them back into the cello case but in the heat of the moment and because of certain cross-angles I do not have entire success. The line begins to mutter and the admissions clerk seems to curse me, a most embarrassing interlude since whatever moderate success I've had in my forty-one years on this planet has come from making myself inconspicuous in most situations. "My toe, my toe," the blonde says and begins to poke and flex the member. "I think you really hurt it."

"You hurt her toe," the short horseplayer says and removes a cigar from his inner coat pocket which he places into his mouth with some concentration. "Did he hurt you bad?"

"He bruised it, can't you see?" she says, showing him something pink, not the only pink protrusion of female companion flesh since she is wearing a halter which shows off what she has to some slight advantage, "I mean, what kind of people are there in this place anyway, honey? Here I was thinking he was so sensitive and fine and all that. How many times do you see a cello player coming into Aqueduct and he turns out to be a bum who makes an attack upon my toe with his shovels? What do you think of that?"

"Yeah, what *do* you think of that, friend?" the horseplayer asks. What was an implicit inconvenience seems to be rupturing into a major confrontation and fear rushes through all of my stick-like limbs, to say nothing of my white cheeks and intelligent eyes. It is not physical fear of these circumstances so much as what I know will happen if Tony Winner gets wind of the way in which I have made my entrance to Aqueduct racetrack. For reasons which I have long felt to be obvious, Tony is a big fan of quiet entrances and exits. "I'm sorry about your toe, lady, I really am," I say, the tools at last snugly back into the cello case and the case neatly zipped. "I really didn't mean anything personal by it." Carrying the case tightly now, I could be a symphony instrumentalist, making my entrance into Carnegie Hall but somehow it does not carry as it should. People are giggling and the ticket seller has opened his window to look at me, with a distinctly unhappy expression. "My toe," she says again, "you really hurt my toe."

"What right you have calling my wife 'lady'?" the horseplayer says. "You think that you got to show some respect, do you?"

"I don't understand," I say, "I don't follow what you're saying."

"Pain," he says, "lots of pain can happen to men who make remarks like that. What are you staring like this for? Get a move on before I bend your guitar case over your pointed head."

Thankfully, I reach into my pocket to produce the two dollars which one way or the other will buy me out of the scene but I cannot escape one final disaster, the handle of the case slips from my hand and hits me a stinging blow on my own big toe, that very toe which I use to poise myself on at the finish during happier days, to cheer home a winner or at least a Place horse. The pain is astounding and I crumple with it, meanwhile becoming momentarily oblivious of my surroundings which turn out to contain not only the usual cast but two large, grim Pinkertons who eye me with suspicion and dread as I massage the appendage with the hand still containing the two crushed dollar bills. "I'm sorry," I find myself mumbling, "I'm really very sorry."

"Has he been a nuisance to you?" I hear the Pinkertons asking the blonde and at that instant I want to hear no more; counting upon the demeanor of the Pinkertons to say nothing of the distractions of the track I thrust my two dollars at the attendant. In astonishment he presses the catch that releases the gate and I whiz through, followed by the cello case. With much rapidity I make my way into the track proper, past the program stands, past the tipsheet stand, past the *Telegraph* stand, past even the famous and dedicated Sister Annie who sits by an entryway in full costume rattling her plate for the Sacred Sisters of Mercy in the Heart of Benevolence in the Chapel of the Little Holy Sisters of Triumph and Saint Anthony.

It is an excellent indication of my mental state that I have forgotten, on this of all days, to give Sister Annie a contribution. She stares after me as I scamper through the alleyway. I do not need sensory organs any more delicate than those in my back to partake of her look: composed of revulsion and dismay it fairly convulses her saintly little features as her eyes darken and glint in the sun. Sun in her eyes, sun over the parapet, a hint of sun over the toteboard as I take the stairs two at a time and find myself in the main level grandstand of Aqueduct racetrack and still a long, long way to go to the elevators.

It has been graceless but at least I am here and I induce myself to feel, true or not, that somehow Tony the Winner and his supporters would cheer. I decide that before I go one step further I deserve a drink, a single little drink, to carry me on my way and on my tragic mission.

XX

HARRY THE FLAT ON THE NEW MORALITY

Prior to his marriage to Gertrude in the fall of 1960, Harry the Flat would occasionally frequent bars in the vicinity of Ozone Park and points east on winning weekday evenings. These neighborhood bars were apt, at any given time after nine p.m., to contain a large scattering of single girls, some escorted and some not, some seeking companionship and some not. The Flat was often the subject of amused and affectionate kidding from his friends because he steadfastly refused to become involved with any of these girls, even to the point of noticing their presence in the bar, much less buying them a drink. Since his reputation had spread along with his single-minded dedication to horseracing in the years of the 1950s, this was not as easy it looked, inasmuch as the Flat from time to time, rumored large scores which would be of particular interest to some of these unescorted girls. When confronted by one of them, which might happen once or twice every six months, the Flat would upset his drink and scamper rapidly to the men's room in which cool spaces he might stay for minutes or hours until he felt the more immediate pressure-points had eased and he could safely make his exit. "What's wrong with you, why are you afraid of girls?" one of his acquaintances once asked him, being careful to add in the confidence of a rye-and-water that, of course, he did not suspect the Flat, even in the least of faggotry. Once this inference had been raised for kicks by the drunken Marvin Beers during the running of the third race at the old Belmont. The Flat, not otherwise known for physical accomplishments, had stopped witnessing the race long enough to destroy the helpless Beers, who had vomited most of his day's intake, to say nothing of his hopes darkly in the aisle, while their mutual selection ran fourth in a six-horse field. "I mean, they don't mean no harm, these here and they got their purposes."

"You do not understand," the Flat said, indicating with a shrug and a wink that he took no offense and that the question was safe, at least for the course of one evening, "I am saving myself for the time when I get married, which hopefully may be soon—just as soon as I can establish enough of a score to give my wife some security. The marriage is a holy and sacramental act in which sex can be beautiful to both of the participants but in addition to that, I think that these girls are very cheap and are just looking for superficial things, which I cannot give them, my attention being wrapped up elsewhere. I have too much respect for what women should be to pay any attention to the goings-on in Pop Warner's,"

"But they're easy, it's just a simple score," his friend pointed out, "and anyway it isn't as if Queens is the East Side, the price is right. You don't have to promote and they're simple enough to take it for what it's like. Not meaning any offense of course."

"It breaks your concentration," the Flat said, "the whole thing just shakes up the rhythm and this rhythm is very important to establish and to stay on with. They just use themselves and sex to distract you but if you let yourself get distracted then you can't accomplish nothing no more. Once you start getting involved it's just like chasing longshots, you get in deeper and deeper and you always think the next time is the last, but the fact is that you never get out. They won't leave you alone. Not having anything against women of course. I told you, I hope to get married just as soon as I can make some of the breakage."

"Well, that's your decision."

"It isn't a question of a decision, just noticing the way things have changed. Have you noticed how things have changed? These girls are a different type altogether from the way they used to be. I used to get involved you know. Before I got serious and really found out what I wanted to do in life, I chased around a lot. But these girls are different. They're more aggressive. They won't leave you alone. They're always hustling you for something, have you noticed?"

"I try not to pay too much attention to them myself," the friend said. "My feeling being that one takes one's drinking and one's sex at different times and places and in most bars the best thing for one to do is to drink."

"Well then you see my point. I don't know exactly what's happening but I see them all over now and they all seem to be the same. A lot of them come into the track with their boyfriends and the first thing they want is money to bet with and the second thing is that they have ideas exactly how to bet the double. It ain't no good. It's no good at all. I tell you, the whole thing has changed, it used to be that you could count on women being in one place and you being in another when you wanted to keep it separate but no more, no more. Someday, I tell you the truth, someday I can see it happening, we're even going to have girl jockeys. They'll be doing that too and once they get into the racetrack that way you know that we're all finished. But at least it will be a long, long time and I have the comfort of knowing that I shall be dead when this horrendous event comes to pass."

The friend and acquaintance was about to continue on the discussion raised by this horrifying possibility, when we were interrupted by the sudden entrance into the bar of two girls. They came trailing all the way down the length of the counter, stopped before the Flat, and said they had heard confidentially that he was the toughest rock on Queens Boulevard, and since they happened to be slightly drunk they would test this out for themselves. The larger of the two then attempted to kiss the Flat, precipitating a series of events which I will not discuss other than to say that in their intensity and polish they added up to some of the greatest moments the Flat had ever had. The consequences, although minor, seemed at the time to be totally past any kind of reasonable control for a long, long time.

"I can't stand it, I just can't stand it," the Flat said when at last the floor was cleared, "can't you see that I'm just trying to save my seed?"

XXI

A GLIMPSE AT MY BACKGROUND, SOME APPREHENSION OF THE KIND OF PERSON WHO MIGHT COME THIS WAY. INFERENTIAL TECHNIQUE BUT SO ARE SELECTIONS

Like most of my friends and acquaintances to say nothing of the celebrated Flat himself I did not come to my present occupation on a straight-line course like the way that a doctor or lawyer or architect tends to utilize the Pipeline Technique. Instead, like most horseplayers, I wandered my way back and forth, in and out, and finally kind of fell into it backwards and with a stunning and discovered sense of involvement. In this way and only in this way, I am led to understand, can horseplayers be compared to writers and some other people in the Creative Arts. In all other ways, they command a far more useful occupation and a more meaningful future.

"You've become totally irresponsible," the girl who was my wife stated. "I don't know what's happened to you but I don't like it. You're not the same and you do not even pretend to be. If this keeps on, I will have to get a divorce."

"I cannot be frightened by the prospect of divorces," I said to her, rearing up from the pillow and snatching a copy of the *Telegraph* from the adjoining night table. Whenever these discussions reached a certain peak, the girl who was my wife had a specific habit of attempting to destroy the *Telegraph*, which not only was a fifty cent investment shot but contained all of my figures for the following day. Hence, I had become protective. "Divorces are only a state of legality, it's a question of relationships which count. I told you, the fact that I have become interested in horses has nothing to do with my feelings to you, which remain the same. You must trust me."

"You have a good future. You've got to think of that future and children. We've got to have children and you're responsible to them. Don't think you'll find answers in that disgusting paper of yours."

"Now you have me being responsible to things that don't even exist," I pointed out to her, tucking the newspaper into a safe and unreachable place under the bed, "I have enough trouble being responsible to what is. You can't scare me with that kind of talk because it doesn't even matter anymore. Don't you see that the angle will work?"

"I don't even know what you're talking about!" she said and yanked the sheet from both of us, exposing her nude expanse which I note, parenthetically and in retrospect, was most enticing, but which had absolutely no momentary interest for me. "You keep on mumbling about systems and angles and charts and possibilities, but all I can see is that you're losing all of our hard-earned money. Don't give me any song and dance about how I don't know the figures, I see what's going on here. We're living on my salary now, yours is going down the drain every week."

"It just takes a little time to break in," I observed. "You can't come into a game cold and beat the hell out of it anymore than you can start off in politics as President. It takes time. Believe me, everything will shape up. The system is infallible and I'm starting to get it."

"You're totally irresponsible," she said, flinging the covers at me and rising to her full, lithe height of five feet six inches. She then leaped off the bed like a swan and beginning to stride around the room, the very vigorousness of her exercise not concealing from me the fact that she had no idea what she was doing. "Totally irresponsible, and the thing is that you have potential, you could make something of yourself."

"Now you listen to me," I said, similarly striding to full height and capturing her somewhere in the vicinity of the mirror. From that aspect I pinned her arms and forced her to look at the two of us in the streaked glass, forms wavering whitely in the fluorescence, "You listen to me because just this once I am going to say it and short and sweetly and I will not repeat myself. I do not want to hear about responsibility and potential. I do not want to hear about either one of these two important qualities because it is responsible people with potential who have gotten us exactly in the condition we are in now. It is responsible people who have been elected to the government, responsible people who are running the corporations, people with potential who have their hands on America, and you can see where all of this has gotten us. We have been put exactly where we are by sane, responsible men who meet their obligations in an approved way and I do not, speaking personally, want any part of it. It is time for a little irresponsibility, a little reality, if you will, and that is what I am after now. If you want to go along with me you will find that in the long run things will work out better and more sensibly this way. But if you don't want to go along with me, I should point out that I lived in the theoretically divorced state for almost twenty-two years before I made your acquaintance, and that can be returned to without any great sense of loss on my part. Now it is your decision but I no longer want to hear easy phrases, because I do not think you know what you are talking about."

"Oh," she said, "Oh you," and only then did I realize that during the latter part of this dialogue she had been moving against me, pushing her buttocks against my steadily erecting genitals which responded to my rhetoric in their own fashion. She was grinding her little ass against me as if the prick was the flame and she the moth and unresistingly I slid my hands to her breasts and began to touch them, press them, indent them. "Oh you're impossible," she said, "you're impossible, I can't take it any more," but the body was talking its own dialogue, the body was making its own adjustments, its own connection in the sudden and stinging dark. Lunging into one another we made slow transverse toward the bed and on the bed we fell into one another the way that two horses, one lugging in, can connect near the rail in a tight race. Try as I could to suppress images of horses from my mind they rose with the other heat, blended with the other necessity and that is the way I took her for the next-to-last time, lunging again and again toward the toteboard of her body, watching the crazy-lights flicker as I plunged endlessly into and around her hole. Finally, the lights went out altogether as I drove past the finish wire thinking of the responsible men, the generations of responsible men who had taken us here, all of them tight-faced and stunned against the dark as the final sense of it began to come slowly home toward them. "Crazy, you're crazy," the girl who became my ex-wife said, and in the aftermath of orgasm, drained and stricken myself, I could say nothing but "I had to, I had to," until I began to believe it myself. The sheets were sliding like snakes under us, the dazzle of summer insects in the air somehow in their fluorescent, encompassing buzz making artifacts of the two of us as I made what accommodation I could in the descending and sensuous night.

XXII

A DRINK FOR OLD TIME'S SAKE BEFORE THE FIRST. ETERNAL RE-ENACTMENT IN THE GLOW OF THE INNER TOTE. A BARTENDER WHO ONLY WANTS TO HELP. A TIP THAT MUST BE GIVEN.

At the bar I order a Whiskey Sour straight up and check the odds on the inner tote while the bartender gets the drink. It is one eleven, only nineteen minutes until the first race and the number three horse, eight to five, appears to be the favorite but my sense of time, to say nothing of selection, has been suspended by the astonishing events of a few moments past and I conclude that I am highly entitled to the drink that I am about to get. The fact that this may be a rationalization means as little to me as the knowledge that in some three and a half hours, a mere two hundred minutes from now, I will be deep into the profound act of disinterment. All of it is too abstract. The bar is surprisingly empty for the time of day at Aqueduct and I am treated to an unobstructed view of my bartender's neck and shoulders as, busily, he suits himself to obtain my pleasure.

He is my bartender because in the six or seven months since he has joined the Harry M. Stevens Institute and administered to me behind the grandstand bar, which has been my own special enclave for some years, he has given me a daily double selection each and every day. This bartender, whose name is Alexander, spots one double pick every day as a means, he says, of supplementing his wages from the cheapest corporation in the modern western world. Although in all this time not a single one of these selections has hit or even come close, he still passes them on to me with an intimate and dreadful kind of confidence along with the first beer. "You'll see, you'll see," he says, "they come in and pay a mint and I'll be all straightened out nicely. You want to hear from me what happened in Latonia?" and he goes on to tell me, the same story repeatedly. It's about when he was a singles man at Latonia Downs, not too many years ago, his 9-6 double came in to the tune of three thousand and eighty six dollars, this sum being sufficient to finance him in the opening of his own bar & grill outside Thistledown Park. The bar & grill failed after a time, along with most of the Thistledown chalk, but Alexander the bartender, now back in the concession business, still is way ahead of the game and is willing, the higher virtue, to share his knowledge with me. Now as he puts the beer before me in a glass gently steaming with curls of ice and Harry M. Stevens refrigeration he says, "I got a good one for you today, the real thing, the real article. What's with that guitar case? You play with the band?"

"No," I say, "my sister takes cello lessons at the Juilliard Institute but was forced to go to a social event uptown today to which she could not bring her cello. Her lesson is at seven this evening and I will meet her outside of the Lincoln Center with this very excellent cello which she will then proceed to play and play. Speaking for myself, however, the musical gift in the family is specific rather than general and I can't make a sound with it."

"Well, that's very interesting," he says. "Personally, however, I am a great lover of music when the Seuffert band comes to play for us on spring Saturdays. So take no offense."

"There are no cellos in a band," I say, knocking off the beer with a dazed sense of completion and pushing across to him the mandatory fifty cents which is my greeting tip, "a cello is an orchestral instrument like with the one hundred and one strings or the Hollywood Bowl."

"Nevertheless," he says, pocketing the tip and rattling the coins in his apron until a slow, stupid grin of satisfaction spreads over his oval face; I hate to say it but Alexander, the Stevens' bartender, is not the brightest of persons, being, as too many limited people are, more addicted to the feel of money than its symbolic purposes, "nevertheless, I have something for you. I got it from a very 'in' source. It's the best information I've heard in weeks."

"I'm laying off the double today," I say, which is completely the truth, since I have not bet any of Alexander's picks since the first disastrous weeks. "Actually, I'm just kind of here for some fresh air; there's nothing really good on the card."

"Sure there is," he says, "nine winners, and besides that, I got this information from a very privileged source and you must not let it get around. This is no double. This has nothing to do with the doubles, it's in the eighth race."

"The eighth?"

"Exactly, the eighth. Now listen to me and remember who it came from because personally I am going to bet the horse ten and ten, ten to win and ten to place and this would be one of the largest bets I have ever made on a horse in my life, excepting that one time in Latonia. Do you want another beer?"

"All right," I say, feeling the horrid pressure of the cello case now digging me meanly in the hip as I shift my weight; meanwhile fighting off the dismal feeling that once again the case is attracting somewhat of an excess of comment. "If you want."

"Sure," he says and gets me one from behind the counter, pours it into the cup two-handed, staring at it with enormous concentration, slight wrinkles and twitches appearing over his forehead. "Warm in here," he says, "no pleasant environment."

"I am still waiting to hear about this tip," I say, passing Alexander a dollar and waving away the change.

"Oh sure, sure," he says, putting the bill into his apron—I suspect that he is working this one off the register— "I just wanted to know that you were really interested. The horse came from the most inside of sources— who, I cannot reveal. It is a horse named Knockover."

"Knockover," I say and regret to add that a slight dislocating tremor causes me to tilt the cup and pour a small but upsetting quantity of beer over my right pants leg. "Knockerover?"

"No," Alexander says tolerantly, producing a bar cloth and tenderly wiping the counter, "no, just Knockover, that's all. Surprised a little bit at this, are you?"

"Oh no, no, how could I be? I never really think I noticed the horse."

"Well, you might be surprised; you'd have a right to be. He figures to be at least eighty to one, even after the inside action. The horse hasn't won in two years, not since a maiden race at the Fairgrounds and he didn't even win that one. He was third and there was a double disqualification. His figures are terrible. But I got word."

"It don't figure," I say, trying to retain my cool and some quantity of Harry M. Stevens beer which seems to be moving around my insides rather unevenly; the fact of the matter seems to be a minimal but definite nausea. "It simply don't figure."

"Well," Alexander says and shrugs, "of course it don't figure but neither did the burning of Belmont. As I say, I got it from a very strong source. If I didn't trust you I wouldn't even spread it. Don't let it get around."

"Oh no," I say, "no, I won't. I'll sit on it tight," and at that moment three or four horseplayers, it is hard to make out numbers, approach the bar talking in Spanish about some of the jockeys, looking at my cello case with uneven, lascivious glances and I decide that it is time for me to make my exit. I seize the case, clamp it tightly under a shoulder, feeling it prod like a piece of deadly armament against me and putting another dollar bill on the counter for the sake of Alexander, I make my way away from the bar, into the open area and finally toward the escalator. Through all of this I move through another forest of glances toward my equipment but I now pay them no heed; my mind is far away, my mind in fact is on other matters entirely. My mind, to tell the truth, is occupied with a hundred different issues or at least one of them and I see nothing whatsoever as swaddled within myself I ride in stately fashion up the escalator toward the roof of the grandstand.

I am not sure exactly why I have left the extra dollar bill for Alexander but I suspect and have reason to trust my instincts, that it has to do with a decision I will shortly make, never to see him again. Whether this applies to Alexander specifically or the establishment in which he works, generally, is something I am not prepared to tackle directly at this time but I know that that too will come, will come, will as all things, percolate slowly, and then flower like a bullet within me.

It is all strange and with one hand I fumble in the inner coat pocket for a program to check whether Knockover's morning line odds remain at the cheerful fifty to one printed in the morning paper. Too late I remember that I have not yet bought a program and am thus caught in frieze on that escalator, one eye cocked toward my chest, the other blinking away sudden water, gracelessly poised in the act of diving into myself only to come up, like so many horses and jockeys I have seen, empty.

XXIII

SNAPSHOT: HARRY THE FLAT WATCHES A LONG ONE COME IN, A PARLAY COLLAPSES, THE NIGHT QUICKENS

Stretched on the rail now, hunched into a dwarf's posture, the heat of the crowd knifing him against himself, the Flat's concentration seems to have dwindled into a small pinpoint, a gleaming tunnel of light squeezed on all sides pressure from within and without. His horse, the six horse, is still on the lead as they stagger toward him around the stretch turn, the six beginning to stumble in the mud, heave for breath but nevertheless retaining three lengths over the rest of the claimers. The horse's eyes, Harry thinks, are somehow bright with anguish and cunning as it struggles thickly to do what is asked of it. It is only a furlong to the wire, maybe a little less, three lengths to hold onto and if the horse can hold, it will pay seventy two or seventy three dollars, seven hundred and twenty or thirty to the twenty the Flat has on him. In addition it will nail down the second third of a modified parlay which the Flat was up until three o'clock this morning doping out as he lay twitching in bed in a posture of consideration past the dawn. *Son of a bitch, son of a bitch*, the Flat murmurs, seeing the horse weave toward the rail and then shy in dismay, *they ain't got no fucking right to do this to me*, understanding, not for the first time at all that it has been madness, madness. He has turned over his life and any sense of its control to beasts which are utterly mad, utterly beyond influence and as he thinks this, something tickles at the base of his scalp, wants badly to be thought. He chases vaguely after the thought which (he realizes) will be very important to him but too late, too late for any of that thinking nonsense, the horses are coming by him now and the six is in deep trouble. A horse on the outside has hooked it on the rail and the six is stumbling, spitting, showing all the signs of a horse which has been whipped. "Oh for God's sake!" the Flat murmurs, "please, a little more, just a little more," and perhaps the horse hears him and perhaps it does not. It gears up for one final effort and breaks its right foreleg, the cannon bone, right above the knee, and falls flopping, fish-like to the ground. The other horses go by. The Flat and the six horse confront one another in a seemingly infinite expanse of acreage, the jockey thrashing on the ground in pain, his own cannon bone seemingly destroyed and numbers begin to go up on the board as the six horse, shaking its head, stumbles to its feet and swaying, attempts to finish the race on three legs.

"Crazy, crazy," the Flat mutters because watching this the thought which he had pushed away assaults him full force and although he cannot verbalize it at all he understands almost everything or feels he does. "It just doesn't make much sense," he adds with a near-boyish confusion as the jockey, twitching, his face grey, stumbles to his feet and starts to hop away. The horse whinnies, the crowd cheers, the hackers' truck comes with the rifleman, and the announcer, God bless him for his omnipresence, says that in the sixth race there are no changes and posttime for the sixth race is four oh two.

"Shoot him dead," says Harry the Flat, "the whole fucking parlay is right out the window."

XXIV

SOME SIMULACRUM OF HISTORY. SOME SENSE OF REITERATION

Hovering over Gertrude, easing myself into her with slow, burning thrusts that seem to move her above as well as below, watching her face change in the receding light I find myself thinking of the girl who was my wife. It is the first time I think of her in several months or years but some aspect of illumination, some hint of tension around Gertrude's eyes remind me of her. I realize then that one of the factors which has always rendered Gertrude so appealing to me is this resemblance. In certain postures, at certain times she could indeed be my wife and perhaps it is this and not longing more direct which has sent me to her. I do not know. There is no way to be sure. Pounding in those crevices in which the Flat has dwelt once or twice in his lifetime, I find myself thinking of him too and my orgasm, seizing me like a noose, is bitter, bitter, winding and full. I pour into her, groaning all of the lamps of my love, and then hover there for a while as she comes back at me. Her orgasm, as always, is reciprocal to my own, known only as an aftertaste and response and it is hard, hard to maintain myself within her but I know that I must. "You, you," she says, just as my wife used to call my name in her own heat and I reach down, touch her nipples like a penitent, waft my hands over all the surfaces of her body and finally tumble, tumble, fall to her left side, crouching on the bed, reaching as always for the cigarette that will mean finality. As if she were unaware of my leaving her she moves on the bed in concentration, squeezing her thighs, her eyes closed and I feel that I should, as I did with my wife, put a finger into her to finish her off but again cannot do it; cannot accept deceptions on any level and so instead only work on the cigarette, tonguing it slowly like a nipple, watching the sun come fully into Gertrude's room. Strange and distant, distant and complete to understand that Gertrude embraces some forgotten necessity for my wife and I try to embrace the thought, accommodate myself to it but her hand is on my genitals, clamping away. After a time I turn back and do what I must, thinking small, gloomy retracted thoughts of maidens and platers and odds-scheme, two demented flies battering one another in the lamp somehow fixating all of my consciousness, if not desire.

"Horseplayers," Gertrude says after a long time, "horseplayers. Is it true that you're thinking of it all the time? Can't you get your mind off that stuff for one second? I mean I understand how involved you can get and how interesting the whole sport can be but don't you think you could pay a *little* attention? There are lots of things that I could think about too you know but I try to show some decency."

Snorting clouds of smoke, adjusting my thighs more loosely on the bed, I begin to understand that my relationship with Gertrude may be edging into a sea-change and that something critical may have to be done if I wish to maintain it. The thought titillates me, although hardly in the more conventional sense and I chase it down an alley or two briefly. But the alley turns into the straightway at Shenandoah Downs and on that flat the horses scamper joyously, free at last. I close my eyes, the cigarette turned to ash, and dream and dream that afternoon of a week ago away.

XXV

THE GENERATION GAP AS ARTICULATED IN THE TIPSHEET BUSINESS. PATERFAMILIAS DEPLORED. YOUTH AS IT ENABLES RISK

Rumor has it that two of the top turf-sheet experts have not only their skill with the horses in common but are father and son: specifically the rumor is that the George Lawton who writes the selections for the New York Turf Letter is the one and only son of the well-respected Clocker Lawton who is the author of Lawton's Orange Sheet. If so, and there is no reason to disbelieve this rumor since it is the very excellent Billy Chart himself who is responsible for its forgatherance and credibility, it leads to many interesting reflections and possibilities because the two Lawtons disagree all the time and also have an entirely different way of regarding the races.

In the first place, Lawton's Orange Sheet is sold for seventy-five cents while the New York Turf Letter goes for one dollar and five, tax included. Also, the Orange Sheet is merely a slip of paper with the horses on one side and a picture of Lawton on the other telling his record for the year previous, which is always very good. Whereas the Turf Letter is red, white and blue and comes sealed into its very own envelope which contains no writings of any sort. The front of the Turf Letter contains the selections and a few tips on how to bet them while the back is entirely blank. The younger Lawton perhaps believes that his selections are their own reward and that no public relations are necessary.

But this is not the half of it as any regular patron of the two important tip sheets will swear to. It was Harry the Flat who pointed out almost ten years ago that it looked like the father was giving the chalk while the son was giving the longshots and he suggested that it came from a desire of the two relatives to cover all possibilities in several ways. Certainly, the New York Turf Letter, particularly in the cheaper races on the card, would almost always spot longshots at or near the top while most of the Lawton horses seemed to be always closing at eight to five. But this in itself was not precisely the point; the point was that every now and then the two letters would give the same horses in approximately the same order. It was these instances, never more than one a day but less than three a week, which led me slowly toward the Insight and that Insight was that the father and son, who loved each other basically very much, were having a big quarrel but would take time out from the quarrel every now and then, just to indicate that their feelings were in the same place. It was as if the younger Lawton, with all the impetuosity and bravery of youth was showing up the old man in his willingness to take flyers. The old man showed the stolid lessons of a lifetime but both of them had a weakness for unraced shippers and both believed firmly in the principle of the Single Gelding in the All-Colt Race. It was an argument, of course, that the Flat and Billy Chart suspected would never be settled but there were enough signs of accommodation, now and then, to indicate that father and son, in the long run, might be able to get out of it together and alive.

But in the meantime, the quarrel, like so many other quarrels, still seems without solution. In one sense it is settled because Lawton the Clocker picks more winners and sells four times as many copies of his Orange Sheets as the New York Turf but then the New York Turf sells for thirty cents more and has a very devoted if limited audience of its own. Also, enough of its longshots will come in to give it only a very modest proportionate loss over a season and sustain Lawton the George's argument that a modified progression will always get a player out.

Only one last problem remains. It is contained in an issue raised by George Needles, who in his capacity as resident medicologist for most of the people with whom I am associated, is both insensitive and stupid about the horse-races. As a matter of fact, George Needles has not, to my knowledge, made a single bet on a horse-race since his time of flunking out from medical school, over forty years ago, and compulsively refuses to read the *Telegraph* inasmuch as the figures give him a headache and his wife objects to the decor. His arguments, therefore, can be assumed to come out of the arrogance of misunderstanding. Yet it was Needles himself who suggested that the father-son question was merely a cover story for the Lawtons and that actually it was just one of them, one Lawton that is to say, who was talking out of the two sides of his mouth on every question, creating two personalities with two distinct points of view, so that no matter what happened on a given day, sales of tipsheets overall could not go down. If longshots won Lawton was covered through the George and if the chalk came in the Clocker himself would register a small but gratifying increase in the next day's sale. The use of two personalities in one tipster, George Needles' theory went, meant that almost any eventuality, including dead heats, was well-covered. "As a matter of fact," he added at the time he propounded this to us in the pleasant but unremunerative circumstances of a Blarney Rose at midnight, "if you want me to tell you something, just making a guess you don't understand, I'm not even sure that the guy's name is Lawton. It could be Smith or Beal or Goldstein or something like that. But Lawton has a nice ring, it sounds like authority and truth and the police, a ton of law, you get me? and anyway it means that he won't get no calls at midnight telling him how he screwed up on somebody's rent or obstetrical money. I wouldn't be surprised if that were the case. Why should you trust any of these guys at the track? I did it just once and as a result of this I am not a top-flight surgeon in the East working with neurology schemes but instead a very different kind of circumstance entirely, which is not to say you understand that I am knocking it or that neurology is so particularly fascinating."

But this we could not take. The doppelganger theory, the simultaneous inhabiting of two persona by one mad but cautious individual engaged in self-protection was bad enough but barely within the scheme of possibility. Worse things than this have been known to happen even in top and honestly-meant stakes races. But the inference that Lawton was not named Lawton, that there was not behind the orange, the red, the white and the blue some clear identity which could, in the last analysis be dealt with if everything collapsed, some living individual who functioned for all of us now and then as an imaginary court of appeal, this was too much. It was too much if Lawton were not really named Lawton because if he lied about something like that, then he could lie about everything.

So we took out George Needles from the Blarney Rose and gave him a little education and sent him home a chastened man. But as to what good it did and whether it affected George in the long run, I cannot possibly say, being too dependent upon him, ironically at this moment, to perform certain delicate adjustments which will be necessary within eleven hours if I ever want to dream of Lawton again.

XXVI

THE FIRST RACE. A FORETASTE OF ECSTASY AND DOOM

At length I find myself in the upper reaches of the upper grandstand which will be my place of assembly during the entire day, up to the point of my assault upon the turf. It is not at Tony Winner's suggestion that I have selected this spot, he having rather left the question open, except to suggest that it would be worth my while to be at the track from the very opening of the card so that there would be no possibility of getting impeded sometime before the moment of connection. Winner is actually rather flexible. One could not, I have come to understand, have achieved his rather high and mysterious state unless one is willing to make adjustments—and he even left the question of the concealment of the implements to me. But just as the cello case seemed to make consummate sense when I borrowed it from my sister, so, similarly, the upper grandstand seems to make sense now. Not my usual post along the rail (which I have occupied for over four years as a tribute to the late Harry the Flat) because the possibilities of concealment would seem to be better with height and distance and also the tools are very cumbersome. They feel, more and more, as if they were going to spring out of the case in a series of deadly cleaving gestures which, for all I know, might emasculate people or effeminate them, depending upon one's point of view. It is in the upper grandstand therefore, that I now sit, suspended at some high angle, only the corner of the tote visible in this westernmost seat poised over the stretch turn. It is one twenty-nine, one minute before post, and the horses, whose numbers if not appearance I know very well, are being fed into the starting gate.

Through the excellent pair of binoculars, which I purchased with my first winnings some years ago, I scan the goings-on at the gate. It is a six-furlong race and I can spot the place where Harry is buried just a hundred yards or so up front from the gate; framed in the binoculars it can be seen as a slight discoloration of the dirt, hardly noticeable except to those already attuned Flatward but in that pinpoint of connection, that small slice of light coming through the glass it is obvious that it is a definite discoloration indeed, or possibly even a luminescence. Unquestionably something of this distracting nature could affect the break of the horses, to say nothing of their eventual performance. As I look at this it occurs to me, perhaps for the very first time, that Tony Winner and his cohorts are serious. They mean business. I am genuinely expected to remove the Flat from this space and bring him to another resting place. Before this moment, I now see, I had approached these activities in the same spirit in which I used to approach the racetrack; the question of losses or involvements was not serious because surely if the losses were noteworthy, my money would be refunded upon appeal. It seemed impossible to me that a fine and legitimate state like New York, presided over by an excellent and responsible Republican administration, could possibly be party to an experience which would tap out a man seriously and ruin his life. At the heart of it I was sure that a reasonable letter, spelling out all the difficulties and background, would certainly turn the trick. Sooner or later I came to realize that this was not so and that New York State no less than Nelson Rockefeller thought of me as an essential abstraction. It was this attitude which took me through my first two thousand of losses and by that time I had achieved a cynicism which made me feel that I could work it through on my own . . . that New York State might someday write *me* letters inquiring as to my interest in refunding winnings so that the mental hospital program could continue. The evolution of the horseplayer is an interesting study, not to be touched in these plain and simple facts which

I am setting down in the form of a memory book, but someone of more skill than me should someday do the job. It is a fraud and a pity that not one single journalist writing about the splendid sport of horse-racing appears to be very literate.

Looking at the mound and now away I understand that Winner is serious, it is not a joke: the Flat is out there and they want him back. Surely, I, less than almost anybody at Aqueduct racetrack, should doubt the convictions of the people who have sent me there and the presence of the Flat: still, somehow, it becomes apparent to me that I have. Even hustling the Flat's body through the darkness, scent of grass and the urine of horses coursing through my nostrils four years ago, I was not truly believing. I thought that it was only a device or an imagining and that the Flat, like so many of his tips, would have no substance or meaning after his perishment. Still, there he is and quite a bit of trouble in the bargain. At the clang of the gate the horses come out poised in a stiff file, noses strained alertly toward the breeze, a panorama of attention and commitment rarely seen anywhere else. Then as they hit the Flatship a few strides out, the line begins to break, wander, and two of the horses caught in the middle of the pack seem to be in nothing less than severe trouble as, knocked off stride, they fold to the rear of the pack and inspect clouds through the slots in their blinkers.

It has not been my intention to make this a betting day, not up until the eighth anyway, but some hard core of purpose within me, some sportsmanlike facility, demands that I have something on every single race ever run on the track in front of me on the off-chance that I might have picked a winner. There is nothing like the frustration of having the horse you would have bet come in first. It adds an element of the truly diabolical to the sport or as Billy Chart once put it, in a rather high-class fashion, it "increases the projective elements." Nothing gives me more dread than the fear of my elements becoming too projective and so I make my bets in all circumstances, circumstances which often are so confusing and maddening that the sum of a night's work on the race has assured me that nothing can possibly win it. But projective elements might do something very bad to me, it not only has a medical (as George Needles pointed out) connotation but somehow a vaguely sexual one and so the bets go in. In the present case, the first race at Aqueduct on Tuesday, June 9, 1971, I have bet five dollars on the number eleven horse, Royal Return, to place and ten dollars on the field horses numbers twelve, thirteen, fourteen and fifteen to win. The number eleven is a very strong horse, eight to five in the morning line and he should at least definitely place. As far as the field, I am getting four horses for the price of one, four horses going off at the splendid odds of seventeen to one and in a large field composed of poor horses—the race is for maiden fillies three years old and up—any one of a number of things can happen, rendering a four-way longshot an excellent bet. At least this has been my philosophy. I have not this one time, and for understandable reasons, studied the card particularly intently on the previous night and thus my ego is less bound with the results of the race than usual. Also, Tony Winner has kindly provided me with twenty-five dollars betting money, which money is to be considered the car expense account but which can be used in any way which seems fitting. My plan is to win out or lose the twenty five as soon as possible and in any case to then bring my own rather substantial financial resources into the picture by no later than the fifth race or time enough to get warmed up before the central eighth. I have taken three hundred and forty-eight dollars, my total assets, painfully secreted and kept away from any question of the Mob and it is these resources which are critical. What the Mob has given me is merely excess which must be treated with contempt, this being my theory, but what happens to me is the thing that happens to me during every race I have ever watched. All of this speculation and detachment to the contrary, in other words, I become almost frantically involved and by the time the horses hit the head of the stretch I believe, once again, that I am possessed of a very special destiny, known only to me and working through all levels of connection and that this race, like all the other races, addresses this destiny. This is neither sane nor profitable thinking and is certainly no way to make a serious dent on the sport of kings but nevertheless it is my approach. The cello case, to say nothing of its possessions huddled embryonically within, is forgotten. Only a slight bulging pressure against my calf, which I maintain, links me to the grandstand at all as the horses spread across the track and begin their final run for the four thousand two hundred dollar purse which is now the minimum in New York, thanks to the horsemen's strike of some years ago on behalf of their livestock which they felt to be unfairly abused.

I follow them with the binoculars, feeling myself twisted into some agonized posture of attention. The eleven horse is clearly beaten, some five or six lengths in back of the first flight and stopping, having lost his early speed which is exactly opposite to my calculations and expectations. Nevertheless there is a good deal to hope for because the thirteen and fourteen horses are coming on the outside with a good deal of purpose and the twelve horse itself is fighting for the lead with the number two. One hundred and seventy dollars for ten if things can hold up in this fashion, nothing exceptional but a fine tribute to my ability as well as the first winning bet which I will have cashed in nine or ten races. "Come on, come on," I find myself shouting, losing once again all sense of removal and propriety in the scent of money. I think of the Flat, who at certain tense moments would scream obscenities and sing jingles, lapses which at least I have never maintained and the twelve horse quits suddenly, throwing its head up like a virgin being felt underneath her skirts for the first time and repeating, losing its action, cantering gracelessly sidewise toward the rail and one would hope oblivion. The two is left on its own whipping and driving but the thirteen and fourteen are still with the pace, their jockeys too frightened or stupid to know that the two has put it away. Everything now funnels down into a telescope, the events as deadly and contained as if they were artifacts on a distant planet. In that removal I see the thirteen take cognizance of its number and bolt slightly toward the outer rail, just enough to throw the race (but the jockey must have lost control; horses never throw races as clumsily as that, not at Aqueduct racetrack). Now it is solely a matter of the fourteen which strains and strains, moves within half a lap of the two, moves within a neck's distance, moves to a nose and then a head advantage but the last two are past the wire, the margin at the wire, that is to say, being a neck which means that the two horse has unofficially won the race and officially as well since ninety-eight of every one hundred winners in New York stay up on the board. The jockey on the fourteen, a sixteen year old apprentice, shakes his head and grabs the reins as they go around the turn, muttering to himself. Through the binoculars we exchange a single, hopeless look of loathing which I know I will be making more of than he and then I put the binoculars down, gasping, white with sweat, open to the heat and sit on the hard wood, the cello case falling limply across my lap like a woman. I fold my hand around the place where the breasts would be. No comfort. No comfort.

The two, another longshot, pays thirty-eight forty, twenty-six sixty and seven eighty across the board. The place horse, one of the field, pays fourteen sixty and six eighty to show. I have, however, bet straight win only as instructed by all the instructors of handicapping this important and fascinating sport. Therefore I can only comfort myself with the knowledge that the place and show payoffs are disproportionate to the win. While the win bettor battles only a seventeen percent takeout, the place and show are often fighting margins approaching fifty. This is instructive and helpful since the fact that a ten dollar place bet on the field would have paid me a profit of some sixty dollars would be otherwise disturbing, disturbing if I did not know that I had been shrewd and careful and had as always played with the odds on my side.

The first race is over and has thus cost me fifteen dollars, slightly more than my average per race but close enough to the norm to once again drive home to me the fact that the disastrous losing streak is not yet over, that it might never be over, that I need all the help, not to say alterations in personal circumstance that I can get. It is probably best that something dramatic will occur today to yank me permanently, one would hope, from this grim and terrible course. It is only in the moments immediately after a losing race that I can face what I push off at any other given time and that is twofold: that I am extremely mortal and that I am a lousy horseplayer. In some careful way these two seem to be connected but not so that I can make much sense of it. I do not think, for instance, that I would necessarily be a better horseplayer if I were immortal, only perhaps somewhat of a more patient one.

I put down my binoculars and turn around stiffly to look at the people surrounding me in the grandstand, once again aware of circumstances and the pressure of the cello case which I dare not take off my right kneecap. There are not too many people in this section of the grandstand and most of the standees have already departed on their errands. Of those that are left scattered around me most look unhappy and one or two look happy. Some are winners and most are losers. A few can face the day with an edge and the majority are into the sack and must start behind. I am aware from my marginal contact with what we like to call the "outside world" that this is not an unusual situation in life but it does not make the losing any sweeter or get the fourteen horse up to show some kind of bravery in the deep stretch.

XXVII
STILL-LIFE: HARRY THE FLAT LOSING ON A DISQUALIFICATION

The horse's number has come up on the board, ten clearly to win and the Flat, patting the moist tickets in his shirt pockets has succumbed, once again, to the illusion that he is omnipotent, that he is on top of the game, that he has within his own hands the means to shape his destiny. But then the *inquiry* light came up, only thirty seconds later or so and now the track announcer has stated that the jockey on the horse which finished fourth has claimed foul against the winner and the stewards will examine the films of the race, do not discard any tickets. A deep thick grunt of rage has come from the crowd at this announcement. The ten horse has been the solid favorite, going off at seven to five or a little bit less and in the bargain this is the second race, the bottom half of the daily double and thousands of students are locked into the favorite for the second race. Thus it is rage, rage and astonishment which seem to filter from the crowd in uneven waves, a haze of emotion so thick that could it be converted to weather on the spot, the track might sink beneath its own purposes and vanish into the surrounding mud. Poised over the rail, his accustomed spot, the Flat has had a few moments of great difficulty in simply assimilating the problem. To contain the single emotion of the accomplishment or loss after a race is difficult enough for him nowadays, now when he must sustain two, balancing them off into something between hope and revulsion. It seems as if the very scatterings and joints of his mind are buckling, the Flat wipes moisture off his forehead with a limp hand, caresses the pages of the program, bends the program over the rail, reaches for and then discards as pointless a cigarette which would only make him inhale upon the foul foretaste of decay, disassembly, death. "Goddamn it," he murmurs which is the best he can do under the circumstances. He has bet fifty win and place on the ten horse and since the objection has come from the horse finishing fourth it means that he cannot even hope for backup money if the horse is disqualified. It will be bumped all the way down to fourth itself while the others scuttle in precedence. He takes out the tickets, looks at them, feels a stab of utter dismay overtake him as he sees that the twenty-five dollars he thought he had bet to place had instead been for show; he must have called the wrong slot to the seller or maybe he is really losing his mind. Not only his mind but his guts, he simply has no stomach for this any more, no sense of control whatsoever, a feeling of large, dim events somehow overtaking him and imploding his life from within. The Flat finds himself wonder if he made a wrong decision many years ago, maybe his father had been right, maybe he should have looked for a trade, something steady that he could do with his hands, no large possibilities in it but no disqualifications either and a union card for the times that it all got too hot. He might have been working in a lumber yard right now or perhaps a metals shop, Harry the Handler, bent over his tools, his face shining with perspiration, intent with involvement, happy in himself and his work because he could see the goddamned results right in front of him and something to come home to at the end of the day too, something that made sense, a wife and a couple of kids and a television set and a few cans of beer too, what the hell, it wasn't much but it beat this. Anything except that goddamned Gertrude who would never shut up and was so full of ideas that if they were turned into parlays little streamers of loss could be ignited over Bensonhurst. Gertrude who was satisfied with absolutely nothing that he did, ever (but then why the hell did she marry him?) and in the bargain was full of small resentments and twitches of her own. Odd long evenings she would spend in the kitchen, drinking coffee and mourning her lost piano lessons, long afternoons on Sunday when he was only trying to squeeze a little percentage out of the *Telegraph* entries and she would ask him, to start a serious discussion, whether he really felt that Bensonhurst was the whole world. There was just no future in it, nothing at all, he had married her for his own reasons and they made sense at the time, they might even make sense now if she would leave him the hell alone but of course that was precisely the one thing that she would never do, leave him alone. If she was able to leave him alone maybe she wouldn't have needed to marry him in the first place, could have done all those things that she said she was about to do but instead it was only a question of Gertrude in the kitchen, Gertrude in the living room, Gertrude every damn place you went and absolutely the same thing in all of them. She would never change her expression or tone of voice, even when she was fucking. She had a good body but what the hell. On balance it simply didn't add up, it didn't figure any more but the kind of backgrounds that they both came from divorce was out of the question, so what was there? What the hell was there? Well, about the only major thing there was was the hope that he could win himself out so big that he could pay her up to and beyond what she thought she deserved, pay her off and the hell with her and then be able to get into the game with some kind of edge. But that was harder and harder all the time, his luck had never been so good in the first place and although he had been able to beat the game in small ways right through the time they had gotten married, everything seemed to have fallen apart since then. His selections weren't working, his timing had fallen apart, he had become superstitious and he had lost his courage as well. Everything was going to pieces, no question about it. The blinking number ten comes off the board at that moment, the crowd muttering and screaming and praying and gets knocked down to fourth position. The announcer says that after their consideration of the films the stewards have found that number ten was guilty of interference on the stretch turn and the objection has been sustained and the revised order of finish is now official. Harry takes out his tickets for the last time, symbolically kisses them, which he has always felt is a pretty gesture, and tears them into colorless shreds, casts them twinkling over the rail. They land in a few puddles of yesterday's slop. Now he feels collapse, a sensation of buildings falling to the right and left of him as he stands on a vacant street somewhere holding out against the wreckers who nevertheless, needle and ball, have moved in to take his life apart. Dwarfish laughter in the skies, terrific power in the rolling concrete, flickering and incision of light behind him as he turns to run but there is nowhere to run, they are demolishing the whole fucking city it now turns out and so Harry the Flat stands as best he can against all these difficulties, man holding out against his destiny, reading the one remaining copy of the *Morning Telegraph* which they have kindly lent him to provide illustrations for his prescience. At length someone in the sky says that in the third race the number three, Royal Red, is four pounds over and he hastens to make the alteration on his program, knocking out the three who is going from nowhere, strictly from nowhere, underneath all that weight.

XXVIII
AN EXEGESIS OF BILLY CHART

There has been dispute for some time as to the true nature and function of Billy Chart: whether he merely figures out the races for the top connections and gives them an experienced opinion supplemented by research, computation, intuition and the kind of academic knowhow which can only be provided by a college degree in mathematics . . . or whether, as some have proposed, he is not predicting the races but actually manipulating them, giving over to the top connections every evening his planned program of intent for the next day. If the latter is true then the Chart is absolutely diabolical. He is able to muddle in his head not only the records and potential of several hundred horses but is able to decide exactly in which fashion their histories should be recorded, the timing of wins, losses, run-ins, disqualifications, and so on. It is because this second task seems to me to be utterly out of range of man or demon that I have opted for the point of view that the Chart is merely a brilliant handicapper but every now and then, when particularly insane things happen at this track of my choice, I am not so sure. In either case, the likelihood of definite word is quite slight; the Chart will talk business to no one and after an evening's effort will go only to Tony Winner in whose backroom premises he is often known to be locked up for several hours, discussing, no doubt, the nature of the weather at Aqueduct and his reminiscences of his college days and so on.

The Chart is visible at most times if one knows where to look; he does most of his work at Pop Warner's and now and then, on weekends, at the Little Invalid. His appearance is so characteristic, not to say distinctive, that it is impossible to mistake him for anyone else. He is also, as the saying goes, a reasonably accessible man in that he is willing to put down his charts and memoirs at almost any given time to talk with someone he knows. The only problem is that he will discuss absolutely anything except the horses. On the horses he has absolutely no comment and those who have attempted to break this policy with strong drink or threats have found that the Chart, under pressures of this sort, is apt to become ugly and full of false information . . . and that the Winner, the next day, is apt to become even uglier. It simply does not pay then to become too closely involved with the Chart although he is a fascinating man and in other circumstances, say at a college of higher learning, might be well-received and highly-respected for his articulate nature and his rather liberal points of view on contemporary subjects of particular interest. "This country is absolutely post-technologized but what the social scientists do not understand is that the post-technological era began way back, began in 1900 as a matter of fact and that what we took to be the beginning of the industrial revolution was in sociological terms really its end. The whole life-style which we thought of as technologized really is a reaction to it," is a characteristic statement of the well-spoken Chart and although there is no one in or around the vicinity of Pop Warner's capable of discussing the point with him at his serious level there is no question but that the Chart makes a good argument for himself and that almost anything he says is likely to be of great interest.

It is of great interest from the scientific point of view at any rate, although the woods and prisons are filled with men who tried to piece together from the Chart's conversation hints on the next day's selections and horses to watch and so on and so forth. These unfortunate horseplayers, perhaps being more adapted than I to the theory that the world is essentially a benign and meaningful territory to occupy, theorized that the Chart was under Tony Winner's thumb but carried around at all times the desire to do fellow workers of the turf well, and tried to do this in various oblique ways for which all of his academic discussions were merely a cover. Thus when the Chart would say, "we're in an age of declining consumption I would think; per capita consumption has actually gone down within the last twenty years because there's simply an insufficiency of goods which you can convince the urbanized they really desire. As far as the disadvantaged, there are simply more and more of them fighting for the same amount which is disproportionate not to say reduced," some unfortunate punter might get the idea that what the Chart was actually pointing out was that Per Capita, the roan filly in tomorrow's fifth, looked like a spot at the odds or that Insufficiency, the bay plater in the starter handicap might be a very good bet. Many serious horseplayers came to grief because of their speculations on the philosophy of Billy Chart but since it was well known in and out of the trade that Billy Chart's health and well being was under the paternal aegis of Tony Winner, it was felt injudicious for any of the losers to point out to him the difficulties involved by being a serious student of the Chart's metaphysics.

I could have pointed out to any of them (but of course did not, having my own troubles, not to say complexities of the inner life) that it was almost hopeless to deduce tips from the Chart because he was sincerely and passionately dedicated to his intellectual theories when not on the figures and obtained genuine pleasure from the use of his mind as entirely apart from the company it produced. Beyond that and more importantly, the nature of modern racing and breeders' naming is such that on any given card there were apt to be at least three or four horses whose names had been bounded into the Chart's lectures and these horses could be assumed to be connected to the Chart inasmuch as he had studied their background and had, perhaps, subconsciously, incorporated them into his essays of the higher life. It is, in any event, a point of fact that Utica and Troy, New York are filled with plumbers, bricklayers and mortician's assistants who at one time in their earlier years felt that the path to revelation lay straight through Billy Chart's philosophical studies and spent many weeks or months at his feet trying to gather the word from him.

Because Billy Chart is known for his linguistics, his computations and his overall quietude about the matter of his employment, his intercepting me on my way from the Winner's studio after my dialogue last night was particularly surprising and what transpired after that is complex enough to lend something of an overage to the tasks which I must perform today. Chart took me by the elbow as I was midway poised between the bar and door and the street and escorted me quietly to an upper level of the bar to the rear, his glasses glinting in his characteristic scholarly fashion. His intelligent face had a certain pallor, reminding me once again, if I ever needed reminding, that the Chart is a serious man and that serious consequences await anyone who does not see him in that light. "It is important that I talk to you," he said, passing his drink over the bar to me, "the Winner is very, very upset about certain things and I must advise you of the urgency. Finish my drink, I don't want it. I was only drinking to pass the time away until you emerged. Actually, despite the fact that half my life seems to be spent in saloons, I am really not a serious drinker."

I tasted the drink which appeared to be one of those deadly sugared concoctions which, when I was younger, had caused me so much difficulty and said, "I'm not quite sure what the problem is." Caution was the watchword of the time, the Chart, as I hope I have suggested is, perhaps, not to be trifled with and in the bargain I was shaken by my conversation with the Winner who I did not need to be told was extremely serious. "Would you care to tell me?"

"You're doing the job, aren't you? I mean, that's what he arranged with you, right? I mean, I couldn't stand it if after he promised and promised he wasn't doing it."

"All right," I said, finishing off the drink in a single horrid gulp, feeling it recede within me, as my fond memories for Harry the Flat had somehow passed away before my eyes, when I became involved with his widow, "there is no reason to be concerned. I have been detailed to do an excavation."

"Ah," the Chart said, keeling over the bar with a groan of relief and then raising one of his thin and deft hands to curl hair away from his forehead as if he were handling a pencil, "ah, that is very good to hear. You must do this. It must be done quickly."

"I am doing it tomorrow."

"You don't understand," the Chart said, "no one understands except me and I don't know if I made it clear to them back there at all. The whole thing is falling to pieces. I can't make the computations anymore. It's all screwed up due to that stiff. Nothing works."

"So I have been advised."

"It's out of control. The whole thing is that it's out of control and I can't get my hands on it anymore. Listen, there was a time up until very recently when the sprints were being affected but I always knew that I would be able to work out a mile or a mile and an eighth race because in the routes, class tends to stand up and they can come back from being knocked off stride and do what they have to. So you could lay off the sprints and still make the figure but the point is it's gotten so bad that nothing works. Not even the mile and a half stuff which they run occasionally over the main course. The conditions are so bad that they don't ever seem to come back. It don't affect the turf races of course, the turf races are still all right on the inner grass courses but how many turf races are there a day? and anyway the factors don't stand up too well there for other reasons. I don't know. I just don't know what to say. The whole thing could drive you crazy; they got to get hold of it."

This was the first time that I had ever found Billy Chart in the actual act of discussing horse-racing and it was this more than anything else that made me tremble. Not the cast of his face or the movement of his hands but the fact that the Chart would actually get into the subject of horses filled me with a distinct and unpleasant ominousness which made all the difficulties with the Winner pass away as if in an inner breeze. I ordered a martini, which is a very unusual gesture for me, and then ordered one for the Chart—whose rate of respiration and internal movement seemed to be on the increase. "Be calm," I said to him, passing down an excellent wooden dish of nuts, "be calm, everything will be taken care of in the long run." This advice sounded strange coming from me but on the other hand the whole conversation was very strange. When the drink was put in front of the Chart he knocked it off in one swallow as if it were beer and then, wiping his lips, turned to me and jolted the nuts onto the floor. "Leave them," the bartender said from down a distance, "just leave them. Let them scramble for it; they'll think it's selections."

"I used to be an alcoholic," the Chart said, "in fact, I had a very promising career as an alcoholic until I got sidetracked into a mathematics degree by virtue of the GI Bill of Rights, which is an actual swindle. You see, the thing is that I think I'm losing control. It was nice for a while, you could move them in and out, up and down in class, work out things the way they appealed to you. There were limits, of course, and actually you were kind of tightly controlled, like being sure to make the favorites win one out of every three races and be in the money two out of every three times. They are very strict about that and there are also tight percentages for second favorites and longshots and like that. Actually, you'd be surprised how little freedom you have in the job. But every year you could do one or two things really interesting and creative; you could take a liking to a thirty-five hundred dollar gelding, for instance, just on his name or looks and you'd work him into a couple of races and move him right up in class and maybe by the end of the year he'd be running for twenty five thousand or even in allowances. That would always keep things interesting and the prices were good too. Or you could work it the other way; there would be a stakes gelding, for instance, who you didn't care for and maybe you had something against the trainer and they got to listen to you so you'd start to drop him down and down and by September *he'd* be running for thirty five hundred. You know what I always liked to do the most? You know what the most fun was? You would take one of these and drop him down and down and finally he'd end up in a thirty five hundred dollar race which you knew they couldn't stand. What I liked was to have him win galloping and then he'd get claimed away from them and start moving up in class. Oh, I loved that! But it's all gone to hell the past year; I can't stand it anymore. Could I have another drink?"

I passed him over my martini, feeling very sober and in possession of my faculties for possibly the first time that day and extracted a cigarette, trying to light it calmly and preserve the tenor of the discussion. "Look," I said, "look, do I gather right? Is it the truth? You're the one who arranges all the races and makes the results come out. You mean you're setting the whole thing up?"

"They won't let me bet," the Chart said, working on the second martini as if it were the solution to the first. "They won't let me bet, they're very strict about that kind of thing, the betting has to be tightly controlled and if they ever discovered me doing any betting, even through a cover-up, it would be very bad. They pay me two hundred dollars a week and my expenses. Two hundred dollars isn't all the money in the world but you'd be surprised—" and he stopped dead at exactly that moment because Tony Winner, looking very determined, emerged from his office, turned toward the bar, saw us there and came toward the Chart meaningfully, his hands gripping and ungripping. Behind him, two of his associates, who I had but rarely glimpsed before, looked at us with unusual intentness, then went to the door and leaned their shoulders against it convincingly. In all the books and papers I have read about the Mob, this kind of action indicates that serious trouble is brewing but as it so turned out I was so numbed by the Chart's series of inferences, to say nothing of the martini atop the Winner's instructions, that it all failed to connect. "You people having a companionable drink together?" the Winner said, stepping between us. I should have pointed out somewhere along the way that the Winner is a very small and strongly built man, five foot six or so but well over one hundred and fifty pounds and exceedingly menacing in appearance with a face and head that seemed to have been transplanted from a man much taller. Also he had massive shoulders and all in all, even without the question of the associates, one would not want to get into a serious difference of opinion with the Winner. "I thought that you were told to go home."

"No," I said, "you didn't say that. Not that I ain't. Not that I wasn't going to head home this minute. It was just the Chart. The Chart invited me to share a drink and I felt it sheerly propitious—"

"Don't look at me," the Chart said in a high whine, raising his hands and backing away from the bar, "it had nothing to do with me, he just wanted to share a drink. Anyway I was just heading back home. Look, I am not even married, I have no wife and children, I can not even claim pre-marital associations. You are not dealing with a man who has very much. I can't even handle liquor too well. Show some sympathy, some understanding."

"You have a loose head," the Winner said. "An extremely loose and disjointed head and there appears to be no dealing with you."

"But you don't understand, we were merely talking about social dislocation and cultural dysfunction in the post-technological, secular society, chief. That's all and then he started to get argumentative—"

"I think we will give you an escort," the Winner said. "That is to say, I think that we will help you get home, inasmuch as you seem to be having some difficulties on your own making that journey."

"Well, all right," the Chart said rather trepidatiously and ran a hand over the bar, "if you insist, that is all right, but I do not think—"

"It is highly necessary," Tony Winner said, "and I will, with one of my companions, perform that duty. The other companion will take you home," he said to me, "since you seem to be having concurrent difficulties."

"I'll do it," I said rather pointlessly. "Believe me, I'll do it. This mission to me is not only a job but an act of a sacrifice, a penance for an old dear friend. Nothing in the world would give me more true pleasure than to perform this act well and to—"

"Of course you'll perform it," the Winner said, "you will perform everything because you are one of these people made to follow orders but I do not discard the possibility of a little education after the fact." He motioned his companions over; dropping their shoulders, looking with some loathing at the Chart, they joined us. "William and I," the Winner said, "are going to afford the Chart a drive home. David, you will take this gentleman here to his destination. Is that clearly understood?"

"That's all right," the one called David said. Close up, from a view I had never inspected before, he seemed to be a somewhat enlarged and fuzzier version of the Winner but in a dim light this would be no help. "I would be pleased to escort this man home." He put his hand on my shoulder, creating a definite and unpleasant pressure to which I submitted, having learned at a different period of my life (but one no less important) that submission at certain times is the best of all possible worlds or at least not the worst.

"Just home, David," the Winner said. "I appreciate your enthusiasm and dedication to our point and purpose but there is no need to take further action at that time. The man is to be taken home pleasantly, swiftly and courteously."

"Oh, that's all right," David said, "I wouldn't think of doing nothing else any wise. I'm not one of those sadists."

"Cultural inferences," the Chart said, "and the slow dislocation of time. We will continue our discussion at some later interval and I will be able to fill you in on the quantum theory."

"Quantum Theory," the Winner murmured and with the help of his associate took the Chart out of the bar. David and I followed at a respectable distance, his arm almost lovingly around my shoulders. "I have an excellent air-conditioned 1971 Impala," he said, "which premises I am sure you will enjoy. There is no need not to relax with me, everything, as you know, will be all right."

"Fine," I said, making no effort to escape the grasp, "that's fine."

"You're the guy who is supposed to be doing the job tomorrow, is that right?"

"I'm the man."

"How does the bomb feel?"

"I don't feel anything," I said. "It's just kind of a pressure in the thigh. It went in very quick and they closed it right up. You'd hardly know it except if you bump yourself which I do not intend to do in any way whatsoever."

"It isn't, uh, sexual or anything like that, is it?"

"Huh?"

"The bomb. In your thigh. I mean, it don't give you sexual feelings."

"It's nowhere near there," I assured him, "nowhere near that part at all," and we continued in silence to his car; in the car he put the air-conditioning and stereo on and loosened up quite considerably, even to the point of advising me how badly the Chart had been suffering in these recent weeks, how badly all of them had been suffering under the surprising and unfortunate circumstances and how grateful he, speaking personally, was that the condition was being rectified. Imbued with too much information already that evening I kept a respectful silence all the way home, not even taking the bait from him when he began to curse Billy Chart who, he said, he believed to be somehow involved in the problems himself and might have lost his touch or his connections and was only blaming the stiff to take a little of the heat off his own directions. "I don't know," I said, "it's all too complicated for me, I never went to college," and we went home and he escorted me out in a lover's embrace, into the vestibule of my two-family in Bensonhurst. A long, firm, careful gaze followed me up the stairs away from him as if I were a woman he was trying to promote, but only in the most inferential way.

I listened for his car to drive away which it did not, expectedly, for a very long time, but finally it did and then I tried to make myself as comfortable as possible in the circumstances of the time bomb and the anticipation, trying to lie on the other side, trying not to think of George Needles' handiwork. But as I tried to sleep and then to dream, all that I could see were pictures of the Chart: the Chart was in the infield lake at Aqueduct, huddled with the swans and he was drowning, drowning naked in the pond. "Help, help!" the Chart screamed but could not attract sufficient attention to his plight because a race was in progress and the crowd otherwise occupied, the noise volume high, the attention fixated elsewhere. "Help, help!" the Chart screamed again and went belly-up in the pond, swans coming then to pick at his tiny genitalia as the horses stumbled by toward the wire, the fluttering of swan's wings concealing from the preoccupied crowd the picture of this deeper and more significant swindle.

XXIX

HOW HARRY THE FLAT'S TIP-SHEET SCHEME IN AUGUST OF 1960 FINALLY WORKED OUT

To his random mailing of one hundred appeals, the Flat received fourteen answers, one from an account executive in metals and one from a promising young starlet who even he had heard of. The replies all came into his post office box within two days of one another and when it became apparent that it would come to no more, the Flat sat down in his apartment, surrounded by his single friend and associate and fanning them out on a table said, "now you have to look for an angle. Two hundred and ten is hardly worth the trouble of going into it unless you find an angle."

"Two hundred and ten dollars provides the expenses and makes it worth your while," the associate pointed out and the Flat said, "that is quite true but now I am in the awful position of having to give out a winner and I am not quite sure what would be the best way of doing this. In the meantime, I must do some thinking," and took the proceeds down to Winner stating that this was a good faith payment and indicated that the Flat was trying to meet his responsibilities and would, and thus only needed a little more time. The Winner said that he would think about this and the Flat returned, the whole visit having taken only three minutes, since at that time, due to certain extrinsic influences, he had rented rooms right above the Winner's then habitat. "I know what I'll do," he said as if the conversation had never been interrupted, "I'll scatter fourteen longshots through the nine races and give each of them out to one. I ought to hit at least two or three of them and the five dollar win bets will give me enough finance to go into this in a bigger way. In addition to that, those who win will love and trust and depend upon me and I will find it much easier to raise their ante in the future." The Flat then took out the entries for the following day's races and hastily made some notes. "The calls will all be coming in at the same time," he noted, "I will have to arrange with Sally so that she doesn't object to the booth being tied up for a while."

The Flat then proceeded to pick fourteen horses in the nine races, all of whose odds were upwards of twenty to one in the morning line while his friend and associate comported himself with drinks, confidences and that other regalia of friendship which had been his due with the Flat for some time. It was not so much that the friend and associate was in awe of the Flat as that he felt the perverse desire to protect, which sometimes came over him also when he looked at apprentice jockeys. The Flat, oblivious of all those significances did his work and went to sleep with a justified smile on his benevolent (in that aspect) face.

Unfortunately, the scheme did not work out so good. In the first place, the Flat by this system was able to locate no less than five winners on this day of longshots, handed out to the various people, and in the second place not one of them found it fit or necessary to pay the proceeds of a five dollar win bet. The prices on the five winners were $59.20, $86.40, $32.70, $114.50 and $49.10 and a ten dollar win bet on even the smallest of them would have been worth eighty dollars to the Flat, leaving out of the question the nearly three hundred that would have been returned on the largest and leaving entirely to one side the issue of parlays which the Flat might have considered.

"People," the Flat said a week later when it became apparent that his correspondents had vanished into the same place where yesterday's Top Turf letters do, "fucking people. They got no honesty. They got no respect. They are nothing but a bunch of dishonest charlatans and that will be my final evaluation after all these years of living."

Much later, in somewhat different circumstances, the Flat tried the approach again but it drew no responses and as it turned out the horse that he genuinely intended to tip on was scratched out and shipped permanently to Dover Downs. More direct means, from then on in, appealed to him.

XXX

BEFORE THE SECOND, A SURPRISING INTERVENTION: A SCENT LIKE GAS MEANWHILE DRIFTS FROM THE INFIELD TOTE

Fifteen dollars, therefore in the hole. Locked into that curious insulation which takes over any serious horseplayer before a race, I am examining the *Telegraph* carefully, deciding what would be the most propitious horse on which to lose money in the second, when I am startled by a tap on the shoulder. My first thought is that it is one of the Winner's assistants come to check on my presence and the second, even more difficult to assimilate, is that it might be George Needles's time bomb which, due to certain mechanical defects, is making its presence known some ten hours too early but when I turn I find myself confronted instead by a small, dignified, grey man adorned by a goatee and a set of random jewels which infest various parts of the jacket he wears. The jacket is also grey (I should mention that so are the pants) and the jewels, being of many different colors, lend a certain cheerful relief to his appearance although not, unfortunately, enough to entirely relieve me. "Pardon me," he says, noting the cello case and my program with one judicious sweep of his eyes, "you are the man I believe I was meant to see. Won't you come along with me, please?"

"I don't believe I understand you," I say, my normal racetrack surliness being compounded by all kinds of circumstances, "I'm not seeing anyone."

"Oh come on, my friend, don't be ridiculous. We don't have the time. I was advised to locate a man in the upper grandstand with a cello case and a certain expression around the eyes and you have both. Will you come with me? There are certain matters that must be discussed."

I put the *Telegraph* down in as circumspect a way as possible and say, "if there's anything to discuss it can be settled right up here. I'm rather busy and I don't have any winners."

"Oh yes you do," he says rather vaguely and tips his head, regarding the tote. "You know something?" he says in rather confidential fashion, "I really hate the races. I don't understand them and I don't know what's going on. How people can get involved in something like this, throw their money away is beyond me. The whole thing sickens me."

The circumstances of being locked deep into some kind of defensive discussion with a grey little man in goatee and jewels thrusts me, perhaps, deeper into surliness than I have been for a while and I say, "listen, friend, I told you, I'm very busy. I got a lot of things to do up here. Why don't you just leave me alone? You want a contribution for something, I have a few cents."

"Oh come off that," he says in a harsher tone. "Stop that nonsense, we have no time for it. I told you, a discussion is in order."

"So discuss it up here. You have anything to say? I'm listening."

"You don't understand. It's not me, I am merely a messenger. I have been detailed to contact you and bring you to the appropriate place. On my own, I have nothing to discuss. I don't even understand the races. How could anyone?"

"That's it, buddy," I say and stand to my full height which although only five feet ten is relatively somewhat impressive at the racetrack which is generally filled with shorter men. "I want to hear no more of this starting right now."

"Don't be an ass," he whispers to me with an unusual and flowing sibilance, bending his little lips back so that his teeth, grey and pearly, fairly glisten in the clouds, "do you think you're really going to get out of this alive? You're the only definite witness they got to the whole thing, the only one who can spill the business and you got a time bomb in you set for midnight which will conveniently remove you from the picture. You think they're really going to take that thing out? Like hell they are; I bet you six to five that they don't even have a removal device *on* that thing, it just goes off."

"You said you didn't know nothing about odds," I say rather weakly but it is merely a weak complaint, not attuned to the general situation whatsoever and I find myself staggering, the very air seeming to dissolve and stagnate around me, impression of birds fluttering in the heat and I sit down abruptly, feeling a dangerous pressure around my inner thigh which instantly reminds me not to be abrupt. Somehow it seems difficult to pull myself into momentary accord with the situation. "How'd you know?" I find myself saying, "how'd you know anyway? The whole thing was supposed to be being kept under wraps. I had it promised—"

"Come now," he says, taking me tenderly by an upper elbow and helping me to my feet again with far more vigor than might be expected from such a delicately-chiseled man, "come now, don't be ridiculous about this again. Did you really think that something like this could be kept under cover? Everybody knows, believe me. We only want to help, to discuss this whole thing reasonably. There are things you ought to know, we feel you're entitled. Or I should say *they* feel; I'm not really involved in this being a messenger of sorts. There now, isn't that better? Come along," and so I do come along, reaching my free hand to take the cello case which I balance uneasily and permit myself to be led down the steps and up the ramp and through the door and then to the escalator. Having accomplished his mission, the little man seems to have detached himself completely, only the hand retaining connection, otherwise he shakes his head, mutters something, checks his watch against the tote and escorts me tenderly.

It is a strange sensation being conducted through the maze of Aqueduct by a small, neatly-constructed little man while carrying a cello case; I feel as if I were a musician being led to an important date by the conductor or perhaps a cello repairman being taken by the cellist to the home of his condition, all of this detachment and fantasy heightened by the density of the escalators, the noise of horseplayers, the blaring of the announcer. I had never realized until this time how noisy the racetrack was, having been so much more involved in my own self-excursions, but now I see that it is, perhaps, the noisiest place available in all western society outside of a construction site and I try to visualize in compensation an orchestra playing quietly, the *Swan Lake* possibly, or maybe one of the Boccherini cello concertos, anything to detach me from Aqueduct. Obviously, it is too late to entertain ambitions of this sort and in addition, my thigh, aided by the bump, is beginning to itch dreadfully. I want to put my fingers into the spot and dig and scratch, but obviously think better of this kind of impulse. At length we come to the first floor of the grandstand and my escort leads me toward the rear, the cashier's window section and finally to a Harry M. Stevens cigarettes & candy concession station, station number 161 as a matter of fact, where a large blonde woman behind the counter sights me and smiles and then takes me from the grasp of the grey man as tenderly as any woman has ever touched me. "Hello there," she says, "I'm so glad you came. You got him then with no trouble?"

"No trouble at all. I had to shock him a little bit I'm afraid, but that's all."

"Well I can see you shocked him a little bit, you look just terrible honey. Why don't you sit down?", she says and pulls a stool from the side, pushes me gently down into it, removes the cello case from my limp fingers and puts it to one side. "That's fine, Gerry," she says, "that's just great. You can go ahead and take care of your business now."

"Do you want me to hang around?"

"It's up to you."

"I really hate the racetrack, Julie. If it's all the same to you, I'd really rather get out."

"Well that's fine, hon, you just go ahead and do anything you want to do because now we've got the man of the hour here," she says and allows her fingers to dribble across my forehead, coolness against the damp, a scent of gas wafting in from the inner tote and causes my body to contract and then yelp with sweat. "Everything's great," she says and the grey man nods, pokes me gently in the unimplanted thigh and leaves. "He's all right," she says. "He doesn't understand the horses but he's efficient and he has a very gentle streak."

"I didn't even bet the second," I say, "listen, I'd better go and bet the second—"

"Oh sweetheart," she says tenderly and produces another stool, seats herself next to me, puts up a sign on the counter saying OUT OF OR-DER so that two customers tapping the counter shrug and prepare to look for their outlets elsewhere, "oh, sweetheart, it's too late for any of this now. Please don't be coy; it isn't fair to anyone and it doesn't become you. Let's talk very directly."

"But who are you?" I say. "I mean, I've never patronized this stand before. Usually I buy my cigarettes and other stuff before I get here; the charges are just too much so I don't know anyone."

"Lots of guys feel that way," she says, "this is just such a cheap company that they squeeze every nickel, they don't understand that they'd do ten times the business if they gave the consumer a break but you see the way they figure it is that the turnover at the racetrack is so quick all the time that they might as well get them while they're here because next time they won't be. This is my theory anyway."

"That's very interesting."

"I try to think a lot about these things when I have the time," the woman called Julie says, "but we really don't have the time; I have to make this very fast. You know why you came down here, didn't you? I mean, I don't have to start from the top, do I? he told you everything."

"He didn't tell me nothing," I say as two more customers, released like birds from the coop of the crowd come over fluttering to look for cigarettes, see the intensity of our conversation and mumbling walk away, holding one another's arms. "I don't know nothing at all but it looks like business—" and at that point the cello case which I have been supporting on my lap falls to the floor with a horrid clunk, rolls painfully on my instep and settles, quiescent. I look, fascinated, to see if the implements will once again follow but they do not and the remainder of my attention is diverted by a hand on my knee: clamping, viselike, but with a distant warmth that might under different circumstances even excite me, as horrid a thought as this must be. "Oh Lord," she says, "I thought you had been filled in; I mean I figured that they had had the decency to at least tell you what you were doing out here. But then again why should they? that's the way they operate, in absolute contempt for people. I see then I'm going to have to take it from the top. I have to do this quick you understand because we just don't have the time but if you listen to me for just a minute or so I can fill you in and then you'll understand. You a bright guy? You see, the thing is that you have to grasp all of this fast."

"I don't know," I say, "I wasn't figured for bright, which is maybe why I ended up here."

"That's true of all of them," she says, "but it ain't brains missing, it's just organization. Listen to me now. Listen intent and listen quick and I will give you the total smarts on the situation here and make you understand what has been done to you."

"I wish I could lay something down on the second," I say wishfully, deterred by the grasp on my knee from any more definite reaction. "It's just an old policy, I never missed a bet."

"Forget it," she says, leaning forward and fixing me with her cool, storming gaze which like her grasp, locks in and hints at depths far beyond the rather simpleminded nature of her occupation and Harry M. Stevens concession hat, "forget it, I can always tell by looking at the way the Adam's apple in the neck moves. Although there's nothing personal in this, you understand, and you got to look at it only as a scientific explanation, the fact is that you're a loser. A loser, my friend. A loser now and in the future and you got to begin to deal in accordance with that fact.

"Now hear me out."

XXXI

WHAT JULIE TOLD ME

Now the first thing you got to understand is that this Mob of yours, which like all the simpleminded people you associate with, you take to be the end and center of all existence, is only part of the question. There is a Mob, of course, and that's not to be denied, but they control only half of the situation. The other half is controlled by an organization which is set up in about the same way but for exactly the opposite purposes, antithetical to it in every way, to use the kind of word I rarely do and hate to but find it fits the present circumstances. We might as well call this other organization 'the Counters' just to give you a convenient tag to call it because I know that you don't make it very well with abstractions. Gerry and I happen to be members of this organization, not very high of course, make it in the middle-levels, roughly where the Winner is with the Mob.

Now the thing is with your Mob that they've moved up in the world, they've been around for a long time and for most of it were a kind of small-time organization without luck or skill, just hanging around on the fringes. Post-technology, which came along in 1900, pretty well knocked them out of the box even though they had been around for a hundred years before that because they just weren't able to deal with the post-technological devices too good, they weren't set up for it. So they just kind of moved along on the underside for a long, long time, picking up the fringe energy and hustling off the margins. It's pretty safe to say that the whole arrangement was being run by the Counters who were a newer, smaller, more adventurous organization back in the nineteen hundreds and were able to see the way the drift was going and were able to make adjustments. But the Mob fell into a kind of luck after its long wasteland and period in the desert. In about 1963, late 1963, they were able to get hold of the situation and from then right up until a few months ago they were pretty well running things themselves. It was quite a reversal as you can expect and the fact that the whole world seems to have turned around in these eight years is because of the change of direction, but I really can't get too technical about this because it would take too much time and you wouldn't be able to grasp it. Even I'm not able to grasp it: it takes a lifetime of study and preparation at the highest levels to grasp the reasons and there's no time for them at the bottom.

But as best as we can figure out it was at the time Kennedy was assassinated, whether or not they were actually responsible for it or whether they simply saw an edge, a way to move into a difficult situation and fake it out we aren't quite clear yet. Certainly, this can be admitted: the Counters had been running things for a long, long time and the organization had gotten kind of frozen; back in 1963 there was a lot of dead wood at top levels which maybe was on the way to being eased out and maybe not but it was ripe for some kind of takeover. Most of the theories do hold that the Mob was able to maneuver the assassination and then slip in right quickly to take advantage but that's only discussion and it doesn't matter. In any event, it's been their ballgame for seven years now and I admit that they've given the Counters a run for their money. On the other hand, there was a big shakeup in the Counter organization right after the assassination when new blood moved up and a lot of realistic people took over the situation. Certainly if those people had been around at the time this never would have happened. But by then it was too late.

So the thing is that they got hold of the situation, opportunism or luck and they've been calling the shots now for a while. They've been running the races and the other stuff pretty much as they wanted to but you see what happened, when your friend the Flat had that accident back in 1967, even though they didn't know it, that was the beginning of the end for them. It took a long time for the excavation to begin to penetrate to the actual soil of the backstretch but as close as we can figure it they lost the ability to get hold of the races a couple of months ago. Their figures have been knocked all to pieces and they just can't control the races anymore. And if they can't control the races, you see, they can't run the world. It all runs in a straight line from the races right through everything else but the races come first. If they lose the ability to maneuver those, then that's it.

Now I understand that this is kind of a hard thing to grasp, how being able to control the races would mean that you'd be able to get hold of every single other thing in the world and if that's an explanation you want, I'm afraid that I won't be able to help you very much. I studied very little of it myself. Everybody in the Counters gets a full survey course in which you learn the history and background and elements. I picked up a few things but it was only a couple weeks course many years ago and even then I wasn't sure what they were talking about. The fact that the Counters, at least, try to teach the people working for them why the system is that way and how they work means that they're a better organization right off the top than your Mob, which can only move through fear—but I just throw that in as a selling point. The fact is that I'm not one of the theoreticians, I'm just more of a lookout, an observer you might say, used in this Harry M. Stevens concession location so that I can keep a lookout on the races which are central to almost everything else. More or less I'm a reporter and investigator although now and again as you see I'm licensed to do contact work.

Now the fact is that we know exactly what's going on with the Mob, we know exactly what they're up to and it came to our awareness just as soon as it did to theirs, that the only way they could regain control of the races was to get your friend's body out of that backstretch. Then it was a matter of simplicity to find out when and how they were going to do it and who was involved and so on and their methods. So we've had our eye on this all along and that's why I'm able to speak to you now.

So you see, the whole thing is very simple when you come right down to it. If you dig your friend out of the backstretch like they hired you to do, then the backstretch will be all right again and the figures will work and they'll be able to handle the races again because we just took over and frankly we're not very strong and we've had the upper hand for so little time really that we just couldn't resist their strength once they got back into control again. And then things would pick up just the way they have been since the Mob took over: the atrocities and the riots and the rigged races and the wrong speed ratings and the suffering and dislocation and so on. Just if you take care of the backstretch job.

On the other hand, if we can persuade you not to do it, then the figures will still be loused up, they won't be able to make the charts stand up, the races will continue to get away from them and we'll be able to reassert our control. We'll be able in a year or even less, just granted a little head start to run the thing all over again just like we did before. And tell me, wouldn't that be better?

Wouldn't you rather have peace and justice and good prices and formful ratings than what you been putting up with the last seven years? Wouldn't it be nice if things went back to the way they used to be and life made sense again? The Counters have always operated by trying to make sense of the world; the Mob is so bizarre and greedy that they don't care. Don't you remember how things used to be? Don't you remember how it was when you could live your life as if it mattered and could make a difference and wasn't being fought over by fifteen hundred bastards? When you could work out speed ratings and consistency charts and they mattered? They could be that way again. Nothing's changed in the world; it's still the same spot that it was a long time ago. Only the management changed but now we got a chance, for the first time since the Kennedy business, to change the management. Wouldn't that be better? Wouldn't you rather have it that way?

So it's up to you. Only you can make the decision. If you follow through on what the Winner instructed you to do we'll go right back to where we were before and things may not change for fifty years . . . and the way your Mob is running things, in fifty years they'll have finished off the whole thing because they're so damned incompetent. On the other hand, if you have the bravery and strength to resist and to stand up against the Mob and tell them that you won't rescue the Flat, then the Mob can't save the races, they'll lose control of things and things will pass to us. Things will get better, finally. The planet will have a second chance and wouldn't that be nice?

So I don't want to overemphasize the urgency or sound melodramatic or anything like that at all because the Counters try to believe in justice and decency and temperance but we might as well lay it straight on the line because it's called for, and say that the whole fate of the world is up to you. It's on your shoulders and only you can make that decision. It's kind of a big thing to ask of a man but if you think of what's best for the whole of mankind rather than for yourself or the Mob you'll see that there's only one thing to do and I know you'll leave him there. You'll leave the ashes in heat and ice, leave him filtering slowly to silt in the darkness so that once again a little bit of beauty and reason can return to this tortured world. I get all carried away when I think about it.

No sir this booth is closed, I'm not selling any cigarettes until at least the fourth. You can pick them up the next booth down by the escalator or you can ride the escalator to the third level and meet this very nice lady named Margaret who will take care of any of your needs.

XXXII

THE QUESTION OF CONSCRIPTION. A SURPRISE IN THE SECOND

"It's all too much," I say, when I have absorbed this as well as I think I am ever going to be able to absorb the matter. "It's too much for me. I don't think I understand any of it. Counters. Mob. The Flat. Besides, the whole thing's improbable. It's insane. You must think I'm stupid."

"I had to give it to you fast, sweetheart," she says. I should point out that through all of this her clamp upon my knee has not relaxed and the knee now feels absolutely bloodless. Slowly I move it away from her cupped palm, and perhaps trusting me to be immobile now she relaxes the grasp and pats her hair into place. She looks exactly like a Stevens concession lady; flighty, tired, a crinkle of malice around the eyes. It is hard to accept that she is not your everyday Stevens lady. Perhaps she *is* your everyday Stevens lady. The kind of job she holds could make any-one unstable. On the other hand, there is nothing particularly sane about the condition of Harry the Flat or Billy Chart's suggestion of the evening previous. "I don't know," I say. "I just don't know."

"I can't explain it again."

"Listen lady," I say, finally allowing a little bit of my personality ooze forth and it is a pleasure, after the constant oppression of the last days or months (it is hard to distinguish which) to finally assert myself, to suspect that there is something inside still worth asserting, "listen lady, I'm not entirely stupid, even though this cello case and the time bomb might give you the wrong ideas. Accepting everything you say, which I don't, because I think that the Mob is only one organization, not two, accepting all of that, why are you talking to me? Why are you appeal-ing? An organization like the one you describe—"

"The Counters," she says.

"Well, yeah, the Counters, whatever you call yourselves, an organization that you say ruled the world and wants to rule it again, well why are you talking to me. Why don't you simply make sure that I'm not around at the beginning of the eighth to do the job and that would solve the whole problem? It just doesn't make sense."

"It wouldn't, you poor chicken," she says and hands me a pack of Philip Morris filter king cigarettes, courtesy of the house apparently, helps me unwrap the cellophane tenderly and then puts one into my lips and lights it almost lovingly, "it wouldn't because you don't understand the way the Counters work or what kind of organization they are. All your life you've been deep into your Mob where the only means of doing things are violence and coercion and you can understand nothing else. You're so used to being beaten by them that they've made it all you understand. We don't work that way you see. We can't. The Counters aren't that kind of organization and never were."

"I don't get it," I say, puffing on the filter king which seems to have a rather ratty taste; a hint of filly dung in it or possibly the sweat of a maiden gelding. I do not smoke often enough to make informed criticism so keep quiet about this. "I just don't understand."

"Well, then you won't. The thing is," she says, now sounding like Billy Chart, "that your Mob is Dionysian while we are Apollonian. The Mob believes in passion, cruelty, violence, destruction, indulgence, polarization, confrontation and pain as the means and methods of human affairs. We do not. We never have. Didn't you notice the change in things? We believe in reason, order, control, temperance, patience, the pastoral virtues. Discussion and engagement. The moderation and modification of the baser passions. If we tried to deal in the way that your Mob dealt we would lose all of our powers. We wouldn't be the Counters any more, we'd merely be another division of the Mob and that means that we couldn't possibly beat them. Then it would have to be the Mob that was ruling the world. We have to do it our way."

A female horseplayer comes over in slacks and a halter—I had not realized what a popular and loyal clientele Julie has acquired—and asks for a stick of Wrigley's chewing gum, very soft. "I'm sorry, she says, "this stand is closed."

"How can it be closed? It's never closed during the races."

"I'm off duty. I'm having a discussion."

"Yeah, you're making time, you bitch, making time with a cello player. Don't tell me; I know everything that's going on here, you people aren't happy rigging the races, you got to screw around too," the lady horseplayer says and goes away again or at least she disappears, leaving Julie shaking her head with a rather bemused expression. "That's exactly what I mean," she says, "this kind of generalized hostility and hatred. The crowds have never been more violent and pained. You can thank your Mob for that."

"Listen," I say, "stop calling it my Mob, it isn't nothing of the sort. A man in my occupation picks up certain obligations and responsibilities and has to deal with them through the means he has. The Mob was the only thing that there was, so I got involved. It wasn't nothing personal and I have nothing to do with the Mob one way or the other; it just worked out that way. Granted your argument that they're such evil."

"Oh, that's the pity of it," she says, sounding less and less like a Stevens lady or even a disturbed Stevens lady, "that's the pity of it: the evil, the malice, the way they work, they make couriers of you all and none of you ever feel culpable. It's diabolical. Diabolical! Surely, you should appreciate the opportunity you've been given. An outfit like this has to purely be put out of business."

"Leaving that to one side for the minute," I say, "there's another question. Suppose I listen to you and I refuse to do it. I don't dig up the Flat which incidentally means that at midnight this evening or slightly before I am blown to sky-high ribbons or smithereens as they call it in Pop Warner's. So what? So what about it? All that they'll do is tomorrow to get someone else and the whole thing will happen again, don't you see? If it isn't me it will be some other guy so I don't understand what the point even is of taking this time with me. If I say no it will only be someone else."

"Ah," she says, "but that's the point too if you'll only think about it. That's precisely the point, don't you understand? You can only function for yourself. You can only make your decisions for yourself and go on from there. If you refuse to do it, then it means that the next one may refuse too. If enough refuse, it will eventually be too late and it doesn't matter whether he gets out or not. You live your life to yourself, no one else has the responsibility. You must do this one thing for yourself, that's all. Why worry about the others? That's Mob thinking. Think of the integrity of self."

"It's too much," I say and stand, reach for my cello case. "I'm a simple man. I went to Utica College a division of Syracuse University for a single semester back in 1957 but it never took and I decided that I'd probably be better off in the Army instead. I am not highly-educated. My opportunities are limited. I just don't know how much of this I can take." This is a perfect lie, of course. It is a true fact that, my educational disadvantages to the contrary, I have always considered myself a highly intelligent man who in different circumstances would have made lights go up in the intellectual world. Nevertheless, it seems time to terminate the discussion and if what Julie has said is to be interpreted truly, the

Dionysian Apollonians or Apollonian Dionysians believe too much in temperance and moderation to stop me. "Thanks a lot," I say, "I'll think about it."

"I see I'll have to convince you," she says, "you won't listen to reason unsupported by myth and prophecy; it's an old habit but maybe in terms of your background it's a good one. Listen to the call of the second race. It will be won by number eight, Tinker Bell who will pay three dollars and forty cents to win, two sixty to place and two twenty to show. It should be on right now. Would that convince you?"

Standing, I feel somewhat better to say nothing of more control of the situation and I say, "I'll listen to anything."

"It's too late to bet if you're thinking of that kind of thing."

"Who bets even-money?" I say and at that moment, prophetically or otherwise, the amplifiers come on for the call of the second race and Caposella says that Tinker Bell in the middle of the track, takes the lead. The under-grandstand is almost empty, only a few senile old men and women wandering around with shopping bags looking for droppings and even fewer crazed optimists who pile onto the cashier's windows to collect their bets early in case they win. Julie yawns and leans back on her seat, feigning, as the word goes, an elaborate casualness and I follow Caposella's call with interest. As always it is characterized by its individuality and distinctiveness; Caposella's diction is the surest indication that nasality, contrary to medical superstition, does not lead to lower articulation or a reduced degree of intelligence. Tinker Bell, Caposella gives us to believe, leads by three lengths coming into the stretch turn and then begins to pull away. By herself, says Caposella, and I am willing on the merits of the case to believe this. The mumbles and grumbles refracted inside vanish and Caposella advises that the result of the race is not yet official and all pari-mutuel tickets must, please, be held and the amplifiers go off with a loud tick. I wish Caposella well and wonder whether he ever makes selections of his own or whether the public relations statements are correct and he is a dedicated non-bettor. Julie looks at me with a slow glow of triumph illuminating the corners of her face and taking some sort of the edge off the crinkles and says, "you'll find that the prices stand up. Does that convince you that we know what we're doing?"

I shrug, and hoist the case. I am about to try something difficult and totally out of context but on the other hand it has been a terrible set of times so far and every indication is that things will become even more difficult before the day is over. I am entitled to this. I am entitled to one gesture and as I start it I know instinctively that I will be able to carry this one thing off and that Harry the Flat himself would be truly proud of me.

"So," I say, looking at her and preparing for a magnificent striding exit, "so listen to me, what kind of organization have you got there that would go to three to five shots in a cheap race like this? What kind of minds operate there; don't you have any sense of humor? And besides that," I say, pointing at her with a distinct flourish, "besides all that, tell me how much real smarts it takes to call the winning and prices on a three to five shot? Answer me that, my smart lady, and by the time you do maybe I'll be able to give you the results of my decision on my poor, stinking friend the Flat who only deserves after all these times a decent burial and who was closely related to his widow by marriage for several years before his problems became insuperable."

And leave her standing that way, striding to the escalator, holding the case nimbly, like a violinist, even daring to wink at her when the steps begin to move. The escalator carries me skyward; vaulting above the crowd and Julie like this I feel for an instant as Tinker Bell herself must have felt only a minute or so before, throwing herself from her field for daylight, vaulting above them for her own brilliance, superseding the claimers behind her, as for once in my life, I have also superseded something, I suspect well, there will be no payoffs made on me.

It is all true, all too true, and by the time I have reached my seat again I have returned to a proper solemnity not to say trepidation as I begin to understand that the real thinking of the difficult afternoon now lies ahead of me to say nothing of the horseplaying too.

XXXIII

SAMPLE SYSTEMS OF HARRY THE FLAT

1) Play only maiden-specials, allowance races and lower grade handicaps. Claiming races and stakes must be discarded because there are less variables. Play the three horses in each race which go off at the longest odds on the board for five dollars to win and place. Double the amount bet after every loss but do not exceed three doublings, that is, bets of forty dollars, but after three losses return to the amount of original investment. If a hit is made in one of the first three races bet, take the money and immediately go home. Leave. Do not remain for any of the races. Do not even think of remaining for the following races. Do not parlay winnings. Only losings are to be parlayed.

2) Restrict play to bottom claiming races for fillies and mares, age three years and up. These should be races in which the claiming price of the most expensive horse in the race does not exceed five thousand dollars. Bet all horses in the race listed at odds of between eight to one

and twenty to one to win and double the bet after every loss up to a maximum of forty dollars. A lower percentage of favorites win these than any other kind of races on the New York circuit, meaning that this system has a chance to win. Be reasonable however and if two or three eight to five shots come home in a row in these bottom filly races, then try to think of another system.

3) Play only cheap claiming races for mares, fillies, colts, geldings or ridgelings. Look for a horse which finished last in its previous race, next to last in the race before that and third from last in the race before that. This indicates that a trainer is maneuvering for a bottom performance from his horse in order to catch a big price. Bet such a horse to win and place and double the bet after every loss. This system gets enormous prices. Only three or four plays in a season will emerge but they will be on horses at prices ranging from seventy to one and up and should not be ignored.

4) Look for a horse which won its last race in a driving finish, that is by a margin of a length or less. Driving finishes tend to knock even better horses off form but the crowd doesn't know it; three times out of four, such a horse will be a favorite in its next race. Ignore that horse as long as its odds are less than three to one. Instead, dutch the book among the other logical contenders so that you will cash a bet no matter which one of them wins. Try this angle for repeaters.

5) Jockey system: play one of the ten leading jockeys on the circuit to win on every one of his mounts *after* he has lost ten races in a row. Top jockeys fall into losing streaks but these streaks rarely exceed six or seven in a row and when you find a leading jockey who has lost as many as ten you know that he is determined to win. Since the average losing streak for a jockey is 3.2 you know that you have an excellent bet through this system. Double the bet after every loss and play straight progression here.

6) Play a horse that won its last race to win again if it is not moving up in class, won its last race by three lengths or more, is ridden by a top jockey, has a history of at least two back-to-back wins within the previous year, is not carrying more weight than it did in its previous victory, is running within five days of its previous victory and is listed on the board at odds of more than ten to one. Very few plays emerge through this system but those that do are worthwhile and should be awaited.

7) Hundred-dollar betting window system: shortly before post-time for the race, go to the one hundred dollar window and stand diffidently to one side, close enough to the window to hear the big bettors announce the numbers of the horses they are playing to the mutuels clerk. Most of the smart money comes in at the hundred dollar window and the most

popular hundred dollar window is the grandstand; too many wise guys try this system in the clubhouse and tend to pick up only false information. The grandstand is the play therefore. It is important to remain nonchalant and at ease in front of the Pinkerton guard who stands by the hundred dollar window. He is there for precisely the purpose of protecting the hundred dollar bettors and if he feels that you are too obviously seeking information, he will ask you to move along. If he does this to you, comply without argument and discard the system for that week. Pinkerton guards change on rotation every week and therefore the system can be put into operation the following Monday. Be discreet. If you do pick up information, bet the horse you hear to straight win as big bettors are only interested in playing it on the nose. Parlay after losses. If three or more horses are heard played at the hundred dollar window skip the race; if only two, play them both to win. Try to be at the window as close to post-time as possible. It is wise to bring a cup of beer or coffee along with you to give the impression that you are merely having a bit of a snack and are not actually in pursuit of information.

8) Paddock system: stand by the paddock as the horses take the track before the race and listen to the paddock guard at the gate who often engages in friendly conversation with passers-by and some of the grooms who walk through the gate to make their own bets. Try to deduce, if he does not actually say, what his choice is for the forthcoming race and bet it. An alternative system is to try to cultivate the friendship of the Pinkerton guard by being in the same spot at the same time for several weeks, etc., until he takes you into his confidence. However rotations, illnesses and conflicting information from the grooms can make this system unsuccessful if played too singlemindedly.

9) Men's room system: attend the rest room between races, at that time when it is most crowded and ask the man at the next urinal who he is betting. Leave the rest room and return five minutes later when there will have been almost total turnover and again ask the question. If the same answer is obtained twice, the horse is the bet. A correction-system calling for three straight selections of the same horse will cut down losses but reduce the prices.

10) Clocker Lawton system: Play Lawton's choice to win in every race on the nose. No progression, no doubling, no reduction. The same amount must be bet every time. If Lawton has a bad day, try the New York Turf Letter or Powell's Green Sheet.

XXXIV

SNAPSHOTS OF A MARRIAGE

Lying on my wife, working myself heavily into her, I feel myself edging into some kind of connection, some movement and blending that I have never known before and it is not the orgasm I feel overtaking me so much as a complex of emotions so moving that I know it will take me a long long time to sort it out. She moans against me, opens herself top and bottom, the panels of her skin slide roughly through me and I work myself through the last necessary inches, thinking of her, thinking of what we could have. But at the last moment, once again, the damned vision comes of jockeys and silks and colors and toteboards and flickering in the grandstand. Odds seem to sift in my ruined brain, to say nothing of program entries, and I feel myself moving away from her, moving further, weakening within her limbs and it is all shrinking, shrinking. Desperately, to avoid failure once again, I close my eyes and jounce upon her frantically, holding her limbs like reins, snorting in her ear and think of nothing but the need to finish, the necessity not to disgrace myself. Slowly, slowly, I feel myself rising, slowly the aged flowers below open up and almost without sensation, in a kind of catalepsy I pour my seeds into her, my eyes opening at the moment of immersion to stare at the blank, ruined surfaces of the wall. "I can't stand it anymore, I can't stand it," she says, but whether she is referring to what has just happened or all that went before, I did not know. I reapply myself the more gloomily to my tasks, finishing her as best I can in the only way I can finish her, hearing a flap like the pages of the *Telegraph* in the background signalling my separation from my more meaningful destiny.

Finding her in the act of dressing, her head cocked to an odd angle, confronting herself with a kind of astonishment in the mirror, I feel an emotion toward her I have not known for a long time, something midway between lust and protectiveness. I go over to her quickly, put my hand on her shoulder, feel the skin move up against me and then begin to circle downward, reach around, and cup her breast. It is then that the nipple retracts, seems to flare inward with a kind of eloquence she has never otherwise possessed, and she says, "get away from me, just get out of here; I'm dressing, can't you see that I don't want to be bothered?" "I want you," I say, which is strange because it is so rarely the case, but it is the case now. I can feel necessity lumpish in my trousers and say, "come here," and she says, "you've been at that whorehouse all day and now you want me? How can you say you want me?" and I say, "It isn't a whorehouse; it's a business, it's like everything else, it's a question of being systematic, that's all. It's a business. It's life. Surely it is, you've got to give me some credit." She wheels around, her breasts flopping on her chest, the slow dangling movement pressing me into further attention and she says, "How much did you lose today?" "I won," I say, "I won seventy-three dollars, a day's pay. I caught the seventh and I caught the eighth. Now come here," and reach toward her again and she gets up, backs from me, her palm against her mouth and says, "you bastard, do you really think that it makes any difference whether you won or lost? You can't seduce me with that crap, it's the whole system that I can't stand, what do you think I am? Something you pick up there, that's what you think." "There's no pickup, there's no sex," I try to say to her, but it is hopeless, it goes far beyond reason, there is no question of dialogue anymore because spreading over all her features as she backs into the wall is something with which I cannot contend, something which causes the heaviness within to flop uselessly with gravity, something which causes the very stomach to churn and I feel that I must leave the room. She is looking at me with the heightened, darkening terror I have seen in so many of the faces around the walking ring before the last race and I cannot take it anymore. I cannot take it. The seventy-three dollars is pointless if this is what it is doing to me. I feel that I must change my life but by the next morning everything is entirely different and several stops have opened up in the sixth through ninth races. It is only in the evenings when she can move me still and then only through a kind of memory.

I have read the note on the table twice and it says the same thing, it says that she is leaving because she no longer sees any hope for anything which can happen in the house. Numbed, I turn toward the refrigerator, perhaps a beer will help. . . but as I close the door, beer can in hand, I see her at the entrance to the kitchen holding her bags and she says, reaching toward me, "I couldn't do it, you bastard. I wanted to do it so much but I just couldn't, I can't leave you," and comes toward me. We press against one another, the damned can falling with a clatter, and I can feel her hands on me as they have not been in months, seizing, groping, scratching, that birdlike whisk of hands which will always be my most characteristic memory of her and right there in the kitchen, somehow, I do not know how, we manage to do it. It is good, it is better than it has been for a long, long time, and aching, gasping, we fall to the floor still clutching one another. "I can't leave you, I can't leave you," she cries, "you're impossible but you just need me so much," and I promise her then that things will be different, that they will not remain in this impasse forever, that I will, as a matter of fact, try to take an entirely different tack just as soon as possible, because only she is important, and that is the way we huddle for quite a time. The night is good too but in the morning I have to leave for the track and two days later she does leave me after all, no note this time just a scribble in lipstick on her vanity mirror THE HELL WITH THIS and maybe papers come and maybe they do not and maybe lawyers write and maybe they do not, but the track, like all central things, goes on and on and on, and only past the time of its necessity can I think of anything else. She was a gentle girl with luminous eyes; freckles all over her, even on her breasts and when she opened against me for the first time she made a sound like crickets and sighing took me into that deepest part of her, so filled with light and tumbling, that one could forget it was darkness.

XXXV

DEEP CONTEMPLATIONS BEFORE THE THIRD: WHAT WOULD THE FLAT HAVE DONE?

My seat in the grandstand is still unoccupied, despite the fact that in the haste of exiting I neglected to fold down a page of the *Telegraph* as a signal of my presence. This is not really unexpected; by the second race on weekdays, a certain kind of companionship has already established itself in this sparsely-settled section of the grandstand, and names, faces and identities tend to be established to say nothing of seating arrangements. Scattered around me seems to be roughly the same cast as previous although there are slight alterations. A pretty young girl and a rather nervous escort have taken the place of an old couple two rows behind and a strange woman slicing oranges and eating the peels is three seats down to my right, supplanting a musically-oriented gentleman who had whistled all the way through the first. All this is normal, however, there is turnover at the races just as there is in life and the basic circumstances remain the same. Only I have changed. I am, to tell the truth, distinctly unsettled.

The thing that I wish to do more passionately than anything else is to take some few moments off to myself and think the situation through, but this is not easy for several reasons. In the first place, the Needles bomb is now beginning to itch like crazy; I had had the best assurance of all the attending surgeons that I would not even notice it was there until and unless it blew up, but it is now a massive, heavy load sitting darkly in my thigh and sending out waves of tickling through the lower and upper limbs. It is the kind of tickling which might be entertaining if one were lying on a bed on a Sunday afternoon with nothing else truly to do but under these circumstances pretty unsettling. In truth the bomb is giving off sensations which I can only interpret as malfunction or imminent explosion and this does not lead to the kind of quiet reflection which has been recommended by Julie, the Dionysian Apollonian. In the second place, the third race, what with one thing and another thing, is almost upon me now and it is the third which was the object of some moderate interest last night; there is a horse in it named Social Scout who I have been following on and off for a year now and whose record is just bad enough and recently unsuccessful to make possible the question of maneuvering. I want to put ten dollars on Social Scout to win and thus have even more money to put on the ultimate tip of the eighth but there are other horses in the race too that I had noticed: No Monicker and Fast Cloud and Arabian Spy and Inch by Inch in particular. All of them have proven capable of winning in this company and all of them need that kind of careful investigation and separation in which I modestly specialize. All these distractions work against the lecture and instruction which I have received below just a few moments before.

Nevertheless, one must try to return order to one's existence even in the most difficult circumstances and therefore I work out a program. First, I extract the Mob's last ten dollars from the special Mob compartment of my wallet and while I finger it, look over the entries quickly. I decide that Social Scout might stand up in this company precisely because his record looks so awful, and hobble to the window to make my bet. It is then my intention to return to the seat, and in the four or five minutes before the third, give the whole question some very serious thought. But instead there are problems, my mind scuttles around in my head like a rat in a cage and instead of taking the breeze and working out factors in my seat I find myself doing some very serious thinking on the line to the ten dollar window, which is not the place to do serious thinking of any sort except selection . . . which selection is not truly serious thinking as any experienced horse player can tell you.

Jammed between a couple of thin types who have separated themselves and are exchanging confidences over my shoulder, I began to consider the question of the Counters versus the Mob. It is all very confusing because this business of the world being divided into two opposed types of people who battle over it, I have always felt to be associated with the youthful thinking of my retarded years and have instead tried to cultivate that mature weary sophistication which tells you that everybody is really part of two groups or perhaps three, depending upon whether or not he is also, in addition to all this, religious. Certainly nothing in my experience would make Julie's theory or truth stand up very well and yet there is a kind of horrifying realism to it. It is the kind of thing which just might work out if you looked at circumstances in a certain way. I am not the only person I know who feels that the world has gotten much worse since late 1963, but on the other hand this is more the personal than the political operating because it was in 1963 that I began to play the horses truly seriously. It is quite possible that 1963 was the year that a number of people decided to or were forced to stop playing them seriously, in which case the years since then would have seemed better rather than worse.

In short, everything is relative, a good perspective and one I have always tried to cultivate through thin circumstances and thick. I return to the figures on Social Scout, indulging in my usual window habit of trying to pick up some last bit of information or possibility which might spring the whole speculative nature of a bet into a good solid investment. But my concentration is broken by the question of Counters and Mob and also the two horseplayers spread out over me are having a furious argument of their own over the merits of the race to come, an argument of which I become slowly more and more aware, like sniffing gas odors during sleep or becoming cognizant of the fact that one is missing a limb. "Arabian Spy," the one in front says, "the figures on Arabian Spy confirm. He had a thirty-two windage."

"That's absolutely true," the one behind me says, gesturing in such a fashion that he taps my shoulder blade painfully, "but the windage factor is not an absolute in terms like this, considering the level of weight carried and the outage of the track, the banking interval alone ought to cut down the windage fifty-five percent. You can't credit him with more than a twenty-three windage and that's at the outside. Fast Cloud has to get the plus marks on bankage so where are you?"

"Where are you, where are you, who the hell knows?" the one in front says, jamming his finger at the *Telegraph* and slamming me uneasily in the ribs as the line moves forward a notch, "there ain't no easy answers but the horse broke in the last time and the bolting consideration has got to be invoked. There is an eighty-two percent possibility of going wide on the turn by any figures you use."

"But the horse goes to the outside to accelerate, you can check the leverage," the one behind says and knees me rather violently in the rear of a joint, causing me to stumble, virtually toppling over the cello case. It is really too much, all too much for me, "for God's sake, gentlemen," I find myself saying, as I pull the case to rigidity and advance another couple of paces, "you've got to cut this out; there's a man in the middle here. You want to get together, drop behind me but show a little courtesy."

"He wants us to show some courtesy," one says and the other says, "this man believes in courtesy," and they turn on me then with curiously blunt faces, blunt and intense, the eyes piercing behind the flesh. For all the world they look to me like a thousand men I have seen in the back rooms of Tony Winner and I can feel myself virtually bracing, shuddering in some sudden breeze which seems to come in through the flapping doors. "Make your bet," I say, indicating that the line has indeed broken for us and the man in front is now at the window. "Make your bet and forget the whole thing, will you?"

"A cellist," the man says, "this guy's a fucking cellist and he's telling us how to play the horses." He leans over to the clerk, whispers something, regards me with distinct loathing as he takes a ticket and stuffs it into his pocket. "You better keep your mouth to yourself, cellist," he says.

I go to the window, put down the ten on Social Scout and turn away, prepared to go back to my seat but find that my way is blocked by the two of them who have intercepted my way and hands on hips are looking at me with decided grimness. "We don't need lectures on manners, cellist," one says but maybe it is the other: like so many of the people who come in to discuss matters with the Winner they are relatively interchangeable and it is hard to see whether I am dealing with the one who pushed me or who I warned. In any event, I have a rising disinterest in finding out. Something turns off dully in me and virtually all the way and I can feel a kind of sinking cowardice I have not known for a long, long time. It is not so much that I have gone through recent years without fear as that the more distinctly physical elements of it have been rubbed off by subtler horrors. "Cut it out," I say, "cut it out," but they do not seem disposed to cut it out at all. This is impossible: who among other people, would run into danger of physical assault in the grandstand at Aqueduct and on this of all the crucial days? One of them reaches out a fondling, investigative hand toward my thigh and touches randomly and urgently in the area roughly above the locale of the time bomb and it is at this moment that something within me breaks, I blow more than a smithereen or two of my unnatural composure and backing away I shriek at them in what seems to be a dismaying falsetto although I try not to pay too much attention; "cut it out, will you? Lay off me, huh? If you want a tip I'll give you a tip, just leave me the hell alone and I'll give you something worthwhile."

"He wants to give us a tip, Bertram," one of them says and they look at one another with grins, then wheel back to stare at me. "A tip. You really look like a tipster cellist."

"But I am, I am," I say, wondering how many years ago this scene occurred; surely it must have been twenty or so, it could not be happening now, "Listen to me and it'll be worth your while. Knockover in the eighth. Bet Knockover. He's going to be a hundred to one, two hundred to one off the board and believe me, he's worth it."

"Knockover," one of them says. He turns to his companion and smiles, smiles ever so gently and then the other begins to laugh, setting off the first and then they are laughing very hysterically indeed but perfectly within control, if you know what I am saying. "Knockover, he's giving us Knockover, my God, where'd you pick that one up, cellist? It's all over the lot; you must have heard it in the men's room or maybe I am thinking of that crazy bartender down on the first level or maybe it would be clubhouse Annie. Knockover, Knockover, the *cellist* is giving us Knockover now, is it a sign?" and they laugh and laugh, it is desperate and humiliating but leaves one particular note of optimism which I am quick to take advantage of, their laughter distracts them. Or maybe it is only that they too are willing to get out of this gracefully, and in either event, I scuttle away rapidly, head down, moving rapidly toward the open air. They let me go and I stagger back to my seat hoping that they will take no heed of angles or numbers and it is only as I get to the seat again that I understand what they have told me and what the consequences of this might be.

But there is no time to think of that. This is not my day, it would seem or at any rate, it is a day founded completely upon distraction. Waiting for me at my seat is David, my companion from last evening, and he has a very determined look upon his face, a look of determination that seems to turn to purpose as I approach and before I can even take possession of my seat again his arms are upon me, although somewhat more gently. "There you are," he says, "I been waiting for you. Where were you? gone to make a bet."

"Yeah," I say, "I thought I'd watch the race," referring to the fact that the starting gate is now half-full of horses who are about to break. "If I could."

"Well you can't," he says, "I'm sorry but you got to come with me right now. The boss wants to talk to you this minute; he got reports and he wants to see you and I'm supposed to take you, so make things easy and come along."

"But I can't!" I say, "the Winner is in the clubhouse and I never been in the clubhouse in my whole life!" Perhaps this is not the most rational way to put it, but my reasons are explicit if not my language. "Listen, everything's all right."

David reaches within his pockets, extracts a soiled grey tie and hands it to me. "That takes care of the clubhouse part," he says, "and for the rest of it, I got my orders and you better come right along now or you will be extremely regretful. I hate to be this way but you got to understand that's the way the operation goes, I got to follow my instructions and that's all there is to it. Come on, come on, I'll take the cello case," and as nimbly as Toscanini ever could, he snatches it from my hands, grabs me by a wrist and leads me through the rows of the grandstand, toward the exit and easterly, toward the domain of Tony Winner.

I follow. It is purely a question of geophysics.

XXXVI

GERTRUDE NEE HAWKINS SUBMITTING TO HARRY THE FLAT: THE QUESTION OF CONFLICTING LIFESTYLES

Underneath him, feeling the poised frenzy of his body, his skin slipping smoothly away from her as fast as she can grasp it, she feels that she may have reached some kind of accommodation, that it may, after all, have worked out all right. Harry has her, now and then, to enact his passions upon, such as they are, and as far as she goes, she has the ceiling. The ceiling is dense and white, scarred and faintly pitted, it looks like Harry's flesh although far more distant and resilient and she feels that if she can concentrate upon it profoundly enough, everything more immediate will go away. In addition she will have absorbed from this precarious balance the kind of lesson which will alter the entire context of her life: she will become a different person. "Oh God," the Flat murmurs, running a finger through her hair, twisted off into some intricate alley of his own pursuit, and absently she pushes back. Gertrude dangles a reciprocal hand at the back of his scalp, feels the faint warmth emanating from the back of his neck, feels the timing of his grunts as they come from the deepest, most bound part of him. How hard he is working upon her, and for such fragile outcome! But Gertrude does what she can, listens to the surge of his blood, coaxes him past rising, thinking that if she can only get past the next few moments then it is all downhill from here on. But looking at the ceiling again she finds that it is receding, tracking in some kind of elliptical orbit around her and then she understands that she has been flung upon her belly again. The bastard will not leave her alone when he gets in a certain mood, must have things in his own fashion. She closes her eyes, feels the graze of blankets, the whisk of sheets as they slide past her cheeks and tries now to cleanse herself of all thought. However the tickling pressure begins between her legs and his high, whining moans: this is the worst part of it. It happens only now and again but when it does it is enough to back her off any sense of it. She finds herself wondering with some detached portion of the mind exactly what she is doing here and what she could have had in mind when she decided to marry him.

Was this all she wanted? But his tongue, if no other part of him, knows its purposes, cleaves in and out. Sighing, she squeezes her thighs, shakes her head, takes a deep breath . . . and feels him mount her, sobbing. Now, at last, it is almost over, it is only a question of getting through the next minute or so and then it will all be over. She feels his hands moving underneath her breasts, tearing, rising, gripping and bites her lip not in pain but for the sheer embarrassment of it. What could anyone think of her if they saw her now? He begins to move upon her unrhythmically, broken motion, talking to himself; she clamps her thighs to trap him and feels him slide halfway up. Enough, enough. Now he is talking once again; it happens every so often and that too is predictable and must be gotten through. He is talking about colts and geldings, fillies and mares in a husky, trapped voice, murmuring something about odds and angles and track circumference, and at the moment when his lecture reaches its quickest and most insistent point—but not before, oh no, never before, there is just no way around this—he spills into her grunting, dry, hard, bitter trickles. She sobs in sheer gratitude for this completion and he rolls off her, his eyes closed, breathing unevenly, looking up at the ceiling—*her* ceiling—and for the sheer anguish of it she curls against him and puts her head on his chest and he holds her neck in a gentle thumb clasp. That is the only way the two of them go to sleep. Another day at the races over for Harry the Flat, and a rare one too— for rarely can he afford such special connection.

He is not much, but at least he is there, and for whatever reason, he is all that she now has. She tries to comfort herself with this but it is not easy and when her thoughts, as they have been doing more and more, lately, move toward sleep in a welter of horses, whinnies, calculations and slide-o-meters she knows that something definite will have to happen soon, because she, too, is approaching her limits. But time enough for that tomorrow, sleep at last and seven hours or a little more until she has got to get out of bed and she will take it, she has to take it, she guesses that she will take it as long as necessary.

This is my interpretation of certain scenes in the marriage between Gertrude nee Hawkins and Harry the Flat. It is not necessarily the absolute truth but it is sufficient for me and it is as far as I care to take it now, or for that matter, ever.

XXXVII

A DISCUSSION IN THE CLUBHOUSE: THE ISSUE IS PUT CLEAR, THE FOURTH PROVIDES ANOTHER SURPRISE

Up until what might as well be called the imminent moment, it is a fact that I have never been in the clubhouse, at Aqueduct or anywhere else, in my entire life. The only difference between the clubhouse and the grandstand, as far as I can see reputed, is that the clubhouse costs five dollars to enter and the grandstand two. This difference, of its own, imposes some kind of automatic segregation, not to be otherwise understood, except in terms of the neckties men are supposed to wear. Horseplayers who think nothing of betting an extra three or thirty dollars at the last moment apparently think greatly of an additional expenditure at the outset. Therefore, what you get in the clubhouse, or in any event, what I think you get is a different class of people, more sparse than those in the grandstand and, in my opinion, of a different order altogether. I tend to think of them as not being serious types in relation to horseracing and lacking the kind of application which you will find throughout the grandstand. On the other hand, as far as I know, there are fewer crazy ladies in the clubhouse and the men on fine days are less apt to denude themselves to the legal limit to take advantage of the beneficial rays of the inner tote board, striking fire into their flesh.

All of this may be prejudice, there is no way for me to be sure of anything as psychologically explosive and profound as the reasons why I have feared throughout my life to enter a clubhouse. Once, while performing a minor service for Tony Winner at Saratoga some years ago, I almost found it necessary to go into the clubhouse to get a large bet down at an uncrowded window, but the sight of three or four young girls in necklaces, sleeveless dresses and a fine, cold look around the eyes, as they stared at my imminent entrance, was enough to send me straight around and back to the grandstand where I was able, in the final analysis, to get the bet down after all. (The horse ran out, which made the Winner distinctly uncomfortable, but I had the tickets and the papers had the proof and there was really nothing that he could do to me.) Since then I have never been even in that vicinity again.

I am aware, as would be any horseplayer of my means, experiences and backgrounds, that there is not a single class of horseplayer but in fact two, and that this other class, which has nothing to do with me, is as important and central and necessary to the game as my part. I also realize that this other class believes itself to be at least as serious as I, but somehow I am unable to pay them the true and fine cognizance of wanting to mingle with them. This second class, which is composed of people who come to the races to spend money rather than to win it, is responsible for most of the horses and most of the races and most of the spectator aspects of racing but, as I say, I try to have as little to do with it as possible. I stay in more meaningful niche, and if I never went to a clubhouse in a hundred years, I believe I would be duly satisfied. Particularly, it had never been my expectation that I would find myself visiting a clubhouse in precisely this way: supporting a cello case, limping with a bomb sewn in my thigh, led by a short, tough man with square shoulders and a determined stride whose eyes were never deserted by a certain merry light which could well be madness. Two or three times, on the long walk through the infield, the thought has occurred to me to take evasive action. It would not be difficult to slip his gaze, dodge a handhold and amalgamate myself into the hordes of horseplayers who are studying their possibilities at all angles before the windows, but a certain aspect of David's gaze assures me that this would not be wise. Then too, evasive action would not be very bright since good relations with the Winner remain as essential as always. Only through the Winner's graces, after all, will the faithful George Needles find himself induced to remove the timing device.

On the other hand again, one must have three hands to be any kind of a decent horseplayer, but if the question of the Counters is one to be taken seriously, then perhaps the Winner's graces or Needles' faith are not to be taken into account as confidently as previous. In any event, one way or the other, I stay with David the Assistant who winds me here and winds me there and eventually takes me to the junction between grandstand and clubhouse where, under the gaze of some exceeding grim guards, one is permitted to pay three dollars for the transfer and move over directly to the Holy Land. The fact that these guards exist always as a periphery, seeing the two different classes of horseplayers rushing by them on either side and unable to make any judgment as to their own status (although they stand on the clubhouse side to be assured), makes them particularly surly and there is one very bad moment when I try to push my way through in David's wake. He has shown his invisible-ink handstamp to the guard and gone through. I take it for granted that my way has been planned as well, but the guard stops me with a terrific thrust to the cello and says, "Where do you think you're going, friend? Giving a guitar concert?"

"It's a cello," I say, insisting upon this nicety once again. I cannot stand to hear musical instruments miscalled and people who call orchestras "bands" or vice-versa irritate me more than practically any other kind because there is no excuse for lacking this kind of precision.

"I don't care what it is, where the hell do you think you're going?"

"You have to pay," David says, looking at me from the other side. "He means that you have to pay the three dollar differential."

"I thought that it was taken care of," I say and then understand that in a certain sense it is indeed taken care of and in any event Poughkeepsie, New York is also filled with barflies and welfare recipients who trusted to Tony Winner's instincts and humane nature. I extract three dollars of the Mob's money from my wallet and put it in the guard's hand, take another look of absolute hatred from him and step through. "Listen," the guard says, "there ain't supposed to be none of that stuff playing in the clubhouse. You ain't going to give concerts and beg pennies, are you?"

"No," I say, "I don't really play the cello, it's just something I am converting over to my sister's use after the ninth race."

"People could get very disturbed hearing string music during races. People could get very upset because this is not what they came to the races to hear and they might find it something of a distraction. I would advise you—"

"I think he understands, pal," David says and this for some reason quiets the guard instantly and completely. I drag the case through and we proceed toward a self-service clubhouse elevator. "I always been afraid of these things," David says, pointing to the invisible-ink on the back of his right hand, which of course I cannot see, "I always was afraid that they could give you skin cancer or maybe even bone cancer: how the hell do we know? How do we know what's really going on with this stuff? They got to use x-rays to look at it too, I think the whole thing is very dangerous. There are a whole lot of things they're starting to mess around with that we don't understand at all, not that anybody listens to my theories." We enter the elevator which is manned by a tiny operator wedged against a corner to such seeming invisibility that it could almost be self-service. "All the way up," he says, "the Winner's box," and the dwarf emits a high peep, closes the doors and slowly, groaning, we begin our ascent. The car shakes, David's teeth seem to chatter a bit in the machinery. "You never been up this way before, have you?" he says, "It's a new thing."

"That's right."

"The Winner is high, real high, he's even above Caposella's booth. You ever met Caposella?"

"No," I say, "I never had any curiosity."

"A lot of guys seem to say that," David says, "it's kind of interesting how many decide that Caposella is a voice and just leave it like that. Actually he's a very nice guy, although he don't understand nothing, but absolutely nothing, about the science of horse-racing." The dwarf peeps again and the doors slowly separate themselves, I find that we are looking into an alley so dense and grey that it seems to have absolutely nothing to do with the track and David urges me forward gently, speeding me out of the car. "The Winner is real high up," he says, "take my word of advice and don't look down," which I do, of course, immediately and regret it at once because the Winner appears to be not only on the roof of the clubhouse but several stories above it. We are apparently in a large tower enclosed by glass which looks down upon the clubhouse from a long distance. Beneath that is the paddock and then the track itself and it is miniaturized, at a great remove. It is a Track Under Glass, so to speak, with all the fixings, and I feel vertigo and nausea overtaking me by turns, and desperately clutch onto the neck of the cello which is also swaying. "He's high up," David says cheerfully and takes me through a door and into a small open-air section. In the middle of this box sits the Winner, surrounded by sheets of paper containing calculations and computations. He is dangling field glasses from his neck and wearing a very sharp blue blazer indeed which brings out all his famous and latent viciousness. "Here he is, Boss," David says, "it wasn't too much trouble at all getting him," and before the Winner has even sufficiently raised his head, deserts the box with a clatter, pulling some glass into place behind him. I shake my head and try to keep it down, fixating on the low bench on which the Winner sits mumbling and jotting figures on cards. He does not seem discomfited at all and only this gives me some hope as he finally looks at me saying, "Oh yeah, I see. Sit down, will you? You might as well." I sit on the bench next to him, it creaks and reels slightly under the impact and there is a single terrifying instant when I feel that I might have unbalanced everything by my presence and all of it: cello case, box, bench, supports. The Winner and I might go to the paddock in the quickest way but the Winner's ease is so bland, his absorption so complete that of itself it is almost something to hang on to. Finally, he turns and looks at me up and down and taking the sheets, begins to stack them two-handed. "All right," he says, "we got to do a little talking, that's the reason I brought you here. It won't take too long. Do you like my environs?"

I say without thinking that I like his environs very much. Indeed, it is easy to see under the circumstances of unusual strain or not, that the Winner takes great pride in his surroundings which, whatever their advantages or disadvantages, have the overwhelming power of exclusivity. It is the clubhouse with a vengeance, no question about it and in these circumstances even the Winner seems to have changed physically: he looks taller, broader, more concrete in the organic sense and seems to fit into the furniture of the box in a way that he never quite fitted into the back room of Pop Warner's, having a certain ease and contentment to the crossing of the legs. This is always the sign, in women too, of feeling that they have found themselves a spot from which they can play from strength. The Winner's confidence however seems to be a little thin around the edges, his eyes are a trifle duller than I remember them being and also his voice is hoarse, much unlike the smooth persuasive voice of the Winner who has taken me down so many alleys and byways in my time. "Listen here," he says, "the word around is that you're getting cold feet. Now you'd better not blow this one, character, or you'll be in trouble."

"How'd that get around?" I say, trying to maintain a certain calm, I know how important this is and even the physical surroundings must not counteract it. "I'm just doing my job."

"Time to level, time to level," grunts the Winner and reaches a hand in one of his pockets, crumples paper within and then removes it, shaking the hand from the wrist so that it appears curiously limp and detached. "Time to level, you been sitting down having a long confidential talk with that Juliet bitch who works out of Stevens and she's filled you full of a lot of lies and crap. You better not listen to that lady, she's crazy as hell and Stevens would pension her off if it weren't for the union. But they figure that she adds some color."

"I don't know nothing," I say, "I just came here on time and been playing the races. I spoke to her but I couldn't very well not speak to her, could I? Consider my position. I don't even remember too good what she was saying."

"It's all crap," the Winner says and raises a hand to his forehead to shield his eyes from the sun as he looks down at the twinkling paddock, the stick figures of horses now feeding into it, "it's all a lot of crap, there's no two organizations, there ain't nothing like that at all. Even the Mob is overrated. We don't control nothing, we're just trying to make a few bucks from predictions and with the help of the Chart, that's all. She can't fill you full of that garbage because it don't mean nothing. She mention the business about the Counters?"

"Something like that," I say. Tony Winner is definitely discomfited: I would put his twitchings and palpitations upon the seat down to indigestion or diarrhea, if I did not know his constitution so well, to say nothing of his habit of eating very little until the end of a working day, and then with great caution, under Needles's direction. "I don't remember any of it too good."

"Well," the Winner says, in the midst of the twitches, "it's all a lot of crap, that's what it is; you shouldn't even think none about that. There ain't no two organizations and there ain't no struggle between them and we don't run nothing. I know that's what she said to you because she's a crazy lady and that's the kind of stuff she spreads around to everyone who'll listen. She used to work in the clubhouse a long time ago but finally the patrons got fed up with the craziness so they put her in the grandstand where it wouldn't make no difference, that's all."

"She said," I say, "she said that I wasn't going to be saved in any event. She said, I mean, that whether or not I did the job, the time bomb was going to stay in the leg, in either case, because that was the way that you operated."

"Nonsense," the Winner says with a jerk, convulsing his shoulders, "that's nonsense; of course we'll take it out. It's only a little commission, a little job. An assurance, say. We always have to do it, it's a matter of policy, but just as soon as it's accomplished you'll come right back and Needles will have it out in two minutes and thirty seconds. Look at that bastard three," the Winner shrieks, breaking off the train of his monologue and leaping to his feet, "look at that son of a bitch, he's acting up in the paddock. Goddamn it to hell, he's so twitchy he'll never make it!" The booth sways frighteningly and I cling on for a handhold; the Winner, however, leans precariously and uses his field glasses to stare down at the paddock. "Can't stand it," he says, "I can't stand it anymore. How can he be acting up like that? It's all out of control."

"Was it the thing that he is supposed to win the race?" I ask which is possibly a dangerous question, "is he the one you want to win?"

The Winner's face clots and he sits abruptly, causing the booth to shake a little more, looks at me with a distinctly dangerous expression. "Shut up," he says, "just shut up and stop speculating; it is time that you came to terms with the fact that you are nothing but a messenger assigned to do one kind of job and that you had better do that job and keep your nose to yourself. You'd better get some consideration and some sense of proportion, you, look at that son of a bitch down there. He's gonna kick the groom to shreds. Halter him, will you!" the Winner screams and lunges precipitately toward the rail, almost losing his balance in the act of concentration. It is only simple justice or maybe I mean simple humanity that makes me rise to my feet against my own terror and drag him back to safety or at least to the bench upon which the two of us sit. Shaking his head he drops the glasses to his lap and looks at me with a kind of disgust; spaces in the disgust, however, show a different emotion which I have not really come to associate with the Winner. "The hell with it," he says, breathing hard, "it's just a little spot play, just a spot play, that's all. Listen you, you getting cold feet or anything?"

"I don't understand," I say, "I just don't get it; they took me down under pressure and made me have this little talk with that woman but why the concern you have—"

"It is all nonsense," the Winner says, "all complete nonsense, there is no such organization as the Counters. Why, those people couldn't get themselves arrested, let alone run things. How you could take that seriously is beyond me. Hey you, listen to me, when that eighth race comes along you'd just better do your job and forget about thinking—"

"I don't get it," I say, "in the first place I was only listening, not talking and in the second, why do I have to do it? I mean, what's the difference; there must be a hundred guys the Mob could have hired to do a job like this and I don't understand why it's so important to you that I do it." This kind of discussion with the Winner is perhaps dangerous; I am well aware of the fact that Syracuse, New York to say nothing of Oswego County are populated with a large number of obscure tramps and brain-damaged oldsters who have at one time ventured to discuss metaphysics with the Winner. Still, there is something in his voice and manner to indicate that he is possibly not as much in control of the situation as it would seem, and there is another factor which, as they say, extrudes. That factor is, that I am getting damned sick and tired of the Winner: sick and tired of the Mob and the Counters and threats and timebombs and George Needles and even Harry the Flat (may his soul still rest in peace, my feelings for him beyond this temporary irritation continue to run very strong). Although this would hardly be the time or place to let those feelings come to the fore, it is also a vivid truth that unless I do it now I am likely not to do it. There seems to be very little future in protest, on the other hand there is very little without it. "I mean, I know I'm in trouble," I say, "and that really you're doing me a favor in letting me bail out and all that, but I just don't understand why you got to put the screws on like this. Don't you trust me? Don't you think that I'll go through with it? Or do you think that somebody else might try to stop me?"

"That is enough," the Winner says, peering over the rail once again toward the paddock where the horses are beginning to string out toward the track, "that is distinctly enough of that line of reasoning."

"Because you're all wrong if you think that they'd try to stop me that way; this woman made it very clear that they don't function in that fashion. She said that she could only put forth the argument and leave it up to me to make the decision as to whether or not I would cooperate with them. She said that they used absolutely no force, that this was not their method at all being Apollonian Dionysians, or of that order."

"Apollonian," the Winner says. "Call it right. Apollonian."

"What's that?"

"Forget it. Oh, Jesus Christ, he's starting to run off now," the Winner says, totally abandoning the thread of our discussion as the number three horse breaks from the pack and begins to sprint toward the stretch turn with some speed and dedication. The jockey, a tiny stick figure crouched over it, is trying desperately to hold the reins in place as the horse goes out a further notch. Outriders catch up to the animal and begin to ease it back into place, the rest of the field circles it at some great distance. The Winner runs a hand through his lush hair and looks at me with such open despair in his eyes, such a remarkable expression for this familiar face, that I find it almost impossible not to say, "having some trouble with your selection, is that right Tony? You just can't control him too good anymore can you?" but in fact I do not say this, retaining not only some fragments of elemental caution, but also a real fear of the Winner's left hook. "They'll get him under control," I assure him instead, "these outriders here are certainly literally the best in the country and if the horse has any chance to win they will reserve his resources."

"Yeah," the Winner says, "yeah sure, that is very comforting to know but the fact is that I am all of a sudden and completely becoming bored with your presence here in my box and I do not want to continue this discussion anymore. Oh Jesus, now he's starting to rear. Don't throw the jockey, Jesus, please. I have finished imparting to you that information which now is necessary and I think that you should leave as quickly as possible and return to your place in the grandstand to prepare yourself against action."

"But why?" I say, "why that? I mean, wouldn't it be safer and better for you to keep me right here, under your eye, until the eighth if you don't trust me? I just don't follow." This too is dangerous material but I am in an inquisitive mood and the adventures of the number three horse have done Tony's assurance and stolidity no real good. In fact, although this is not a phrase I would use loosely, he seems to be something of a broken man, or at least considerably reduced from what I would like to think of as the Winner's Vigor. "I thought I'd just ask that anyway, I mean you don't have to tell me."

"I will not answer that because it is self-evident. This box is half a mile above the ground and at least a full mile from the area where you will conduct your activities . . . there would not be sufficient time for efficiency. Then too—" and Tony seems about on the point of imparting some even more important information, perhaps a moral code or a summation of my responsibilities and obligations. But as to the nature of this and my true relationship to him and what appeal he might make to me from the heart, I will never know because the three horse rears all the way into the air, skitters sidewise, tosses his jockey and then rolls heavily on the ground itself, having totally lost balance, just missing the jockey in the act of scrambling away. Kicking and struggling on the ground, the horse looks like a windup toy that has come loose, and as the outriders abandon the rest of the field to have a look, it strikes me and probably the Winner that the horse has had an injury. It cannot get up. "Oh my God," the Winner says, "my God, nothing's right. Nothing works. Nothing works anymore at all. There goes the whole spot."

"I think that horse has broken its back," I say.

"I don't give a shit if it's broken its head, will you look at that, I never seen nothing like that in my whole life. I'll kill the Chart. I'll kill him for this. He can't do it to me. Where is that son of a bitch?" And the Winner stands, flexes his wrists, runs a hand over the back of his head and then moves toward the exit door. "I have things to do," he says, "which demand my full attention for a little while but remember I will be back here long before the eighth and I will expect to see justice done. I will expect to see you function. I am leaving you now but I would not, in short, try any funny business. I'll kill that Chart right where he lays, the son of a bitch," the Winner says and makes an exit somewhat more graceless than his best, but even the bad ones, as happens to be the case with most of the influential people I know, are pretty effective.

I sit uneasily in the Winner's box for a few moments—the view is dizzying but I doubt very much that I will be back and it is an extremely favorable location—to watch the events taking place on the track, which from this viewpoint seem as consequential as an artifact or a child's game. A hacker's truck comes, shielding the horse from view and two men with rifles come out of it. From this vantage point there is no pain in it, it seems only puzzling that men should shoot horses. There is no sound whatsoever and if there are any crowd noises or discussions surrounding the shot they cannot be heard. Something in a sheet is passed into the trunk by ten struggling man and the truck drives off. Now, from this enormous height, all seems quiet, pastoral, removed, only the colors of the horses on the opposite side of the track, moving into the gate, breaking the gentle greens and greys and blues of the nature scene below. At this height one feels both removed from and impelled toward the action; suspended from it at such a remove that it is totally in control, involved enough with it to see it for the series of tiny and pointless manipulations that I always felt God would take horse-racing to be. To the extent that I ever got God involved with the question of horse-racing at all.

It is a very privileged site, a very privileged location that the Winner has in his box and I wonder if this is something that comes with the other privileges or whether it is the box that makes things possible. The whole thing is too deep for me and I find suddenly I do not want to consider any of it, I do not want to think anymore, I only want to get out of this box and back to the grandstand with which, at least, I can deal: can embrace a set of factors and understand them. I am not a person for the clubhouse, particularly not for this section of the clubhouse.

So I do something then which I have never done in my whole life. Just as the horses are about to break from the gate for the fourth, the whole race spread out in front of me, I spring to my feet, turn my back upon the upcoming horse-race, put the horse-race out of my mind completely with the turning and I leave. I do not care what happens. I want only to get back to my place in the grandstand and try to make decisions.

I do not care what is happening down there. If this was a response I had inaugurated about ten years ago, I would have led an entirely different life, but then too I would not have been able to appreciate what a truly remarkable step this has been.

David is not there to escort me, and the elevator, minus the Winner's presence, has lost its dwarf. It is completely self-service but it is waiting for me and drops me half a mile from the sky at terrific speed, into the waiting jaws of the clubhouse Exacta window line where I cannot leave soon enough. The guard offers me a free invisible-ink tattoo so that I can return to the clubhouse any further time that day, at will, but I tell him although I appreciate this, I think I will pass it up. Gesturing emphatically I almost drop the cello case once again on his toe but recover in time. Before the possibility of further dialogue, I make a hell of a hasty exit, indeed, into the pocket of my beloved grandstand.

XXXVIII

CATHOLICISM AS A COMFORT TO GERTRUDE NEE HAWKINS

Although the Flat was a lapsed Catholic and made no bones about it, Gertrude found particularly in the last years of her marriage, that her religion was an enormous comfort to her and sustained her through periods that otherwise she would not have been able to bear. "Oh Jesus, Mary and Joseph," she would say in front of the crucifix-and-offertory which she had had installed, at some expense, in her own bedroom, "Jesus, Mary and Joseph, I simply can't take any more of this, I pray to all the saints to show me the way; I can't stand it. There must be something other than this to life. The man is completely insane and I'm too young to end up this way," she says and the crucifix wafts slowly in the breeze of her breath, giving her the distinct feeling that her appeal was being heard. Even if very little could be done to rectify her situation it was good to know that at least someone was listening to it and proving sympathetic. "Oh God, it's sinful, it's iniquitous, there must be another way," she would say on long summer afternoons when they were running at Saratoga and the Flat was forced to commute all-the-hell-the-way to Atlantic City, "please do something to him so that he will understand what has become of us and make him change. Or strike vengeance into his heart, either way, either way." Although Gertrude had, like most Catholics, had some formal instruction in ritual and formal Latin when she was a child, most of this had gone by the boards after her confirmation and now she was forced to rely upon simple Latin phrases, the one or two she knew, and basic appeals and complaints given in her own language. "Kyrie Eleison, there's got to be a way out of this," she would say or "Dominus Vobiscum, break down every single one of his parlays," or "Pater Noster, may every horse he bets on run last." Sometimes her prayers were answered but then again sometimes they were not; the Flat was relatively close-mouthed about the details of his routine performances. In any event, Gertrude knew that she would be in there now until the finish, she was praying seriously and thinking in the long term.

The Flat of course would tend to mock her religiosity and would, on those rare occasions when she was stupid in her timing and he happened to interrupt her in prayer, become out-rightly insulting. Once he tore the crucifix from the wall and flung it at her, narrowly missing the bridge of her nose, saying, "for God's sake, will you put your faith in something meaningful and try to give me some help instead of this nonsense!" Then he would proceed to curse her so variously and awfully that Gertrude understood that he was offended as only a deeply religious man could be, and actually envied her her ability to get down on her knees and pray for assistance. "I tell you, I won't have any more of this, ever," he would say on those occasions when he would have sex with her. It was always, at her insistence, in her bedroom and under the very glint of the crucifix whose aspect the Flat could not avoid, close his eyes and hunch his shoulders as he might. "It just gives you the willies," he pointed out to her, pleading for her to at least cover it with a cloth or go into his bedroom but she was determined. If the Flat would not respond to her prayers in any other fashion, he would at least see their results. Of course it is possible that she did not phrase this quite so eloquently.

Sometimes, he would come home having hit a small double or successfully chased a ten dollar win parlay through a couple of races. Then he would grin at her, flick coins and bills in the air, and narrow his face to that penetrating squint which the Flat always took on when he felt he had the game at least temporarily licked. When he did this she would absolutely despair, would feel in some dim recess that she was making a fool of herself and that her problems, to say nothing of Harry's were out of reach of the simple saints she could reach. But then there would be nights when he would stagger in past midnight, his face cold and empty, eyes winking death and would go straight to his bedroom muttering and she would know that something was being done; that in whatever fashion, her interests were being considered in that vault where, one way or the other, everyone, sooner or later, came under the glass.

That was all right with her. She was not frivolous. She was not indulging herself or using religion as a cheap release, as Harry had unfairly accused her of doing. Her purposes were serious. Her dedication was steadfast. She was, as a matter of fact, in this thing all the way and was not quitting until she saw some real results.

It was like investing. You put something in and stayed with it and sooner or later you hoped that it would come back, everything you had put in and a little interest too. If she could parlay trouble for the Flat, with a little interest for herself as well, that was all the better, but she didn't want to get greedy about the matter; she would take things in her stride. Take them as they came. Play with the booking percentages.

XXXIX

BACK TO QUARTERS FOR THE FINAL TIME: THE GRANDSTAND LIKE THE VAULT OF HEAVENS OVER MY HEAD

Cello case in hand, I return to my seat. The fourth race has involved an objection-and-disqualification and horseplayers are wandering around in the vicinity of the cashiers' window shrieking and tearing at their hair or as the case might be, scalps: a distinctly unpleasant and odorous scene but so much hope in the air that you could cut it. Not only the people with tickets on the winning horse line up in front of the windows but the people with tickets on the horse which finished second; there is no question but that they have a chance to win as well and if so they will get an edge in. Thus there are two sets of winners warming up in front of the windows rather than the normal one but this is not purely a happy occasion because the winners hate one another and know that the existence of one will disprove the possibility of the other. It is, as I know from my own experiences in such circumstances, a very unpleasant and tense scene and it is no help to be part of it declaring that you cannot lose because you have tickets on both horses; every so often this will get one physically injured or at least close to that point. The only good thing about this scene, in fact, is that at least I am able to make my progress unnoticed: If Toscanini himself were to stride across the grandstand floor followed by the members of the NBC famous symphony orchestra, it would excite no comment at all even though Toscanini, that great conductor as we all know, has been dead for some fifteen years and most of the members of the NBC symphony are busy playing backgrounds for our best modern motion pictures. There is only one difficult moment, as a matter of fact, which occurs as I pass Julie's stand; I do not even realize for the instant that it is her stand and then recognize her. She is selling candy bars to a line of cursing horseplayers and as I pass her she gives me a long and calculating wink. "I haven't decided yet, I just want to think the whole thing over," I mouth to her hoping that she can lip-read and she winks at me, nods, says very loudly, "it's your decision, you do exactly what you feel is the best thing for you to do," causing the horseplayers to wheel and look at me with interest. I proceed toward the escalator, wondering if I am beginning to have some kind of a problem with relationships. It is discomfiting in the extreme to mouth something to someone who screams at you in return, leading you to the feeling that you are deaf or they aggressive. Also, the itching in the leg which I forgot about during my interview with the Winner has returned with what can be called a vengeance, and the very flesh of the thigh seems to be swelling, expanding underneath my touch. It is a very bad condition, in short, which seats me back in place in the grandstand and the sullen mood surrounding is no help either. The winner has been knocked down to fourth place and the second place horse to third. The third horse has won it, a rare double-disqualification, in short, and most of the horseplayers around me are not particularly pleased because the three was a forty to one shot. "The judges had a piece of that one, it was all maneuvered," horseplayers say to one another and express similar thoughts. I hunch myself over the cello case and try, at least momentarily, to remove myself from the situation and obtain a proper moment of rest, but as is usual at the racetrack, there is no rest at all. Three rows down from me a man goes berserk from the June heat or maybe only the double disqualification and stands, ripping off his shirt, clenching his fists, his face reddening in the sun as he screams, "come on, you sons of bitches, who wants to come with me! Who wants to tear that toteboard down!" He is a very vigorous, powerful man with good gestures and a fine voice but attracts only marginal interest. "You aren't going to stand for that are you?" he says, "how much of this are you supposed to take; do you want them to steal you out of everything?" and seizing a beer can which he must have smuggled in underneath his shirt, hurls it in the direction of the tote. The intent must have been wonderful, a scatter and a smash, but the wind catches it and it only sails lightly, daintily to the ground, wafting in the breeze. This problem or act of fate seems to set the man off completely. He mounts his seat and begins to jump up and down saying that the track announcer should drop dead and the races are all rigged, the horses being inhabited by men wearing horse-clothing who manipulate the races at their pleasure, none of it real, not even the odds. The whole thing is a dream put up by frauds, but at this accusation the powers that be at the racetrack seem to lose patience, finally. They have been tolerant up until now, and a number of Pinkertons appear from no point of origin and surround the man to take him away. He leaps sprawling on their shoulders and skillfully they render him unequal to dispute through certain physical maneuvers, then he is dragged out upside down, his hands flopping wearily, his eyes closed. The Pinkertons, I should point out, are a very reputable private detective agency who have been in the business of policing and protecting the New York tracks for several decades and all of them carry guns, meaning that it is somewhat unwise to make comments upon a Pinkerton's complexion or appearance. In his vanishing, the customer still seems to be heard, muttering about the devil that lives in the toteboard, but there is very little attention to be paid to this kind of thing once the immediate diversion is past, and along with the others, I sink back into my own stupor and contemplations. There is really very little to say about such incidents which happen by the score at Aqueduct Racetrack almost every day of the week and can be considered as part of the ritual. I do not mean to minimize the importance of the incidents or to sound unsympathetic but if one responded emotionally to every crazy person or incident which occurred at Aqueduct Racetrack during a given day, one would have no time to apply oneself to the horses which are, after all, the main business of this activity.

As I open the paper to gaze at the entries for the fifth, however, another thought hits me and it is one which makes me drop the paper and gaze out into space, once again abstracted and taken with complex thoughts. I do not care who wins the fifth in any event, sometime between the second race and my interview with the Winner a certain zeal seems to have been purged out of me. I have lost interest in the races or at least in my potential ability to deal with them and this leaves my mind free to deal with the single amazing thought which instantly takes over not the back but the forelobe of the brain and deserves a good deal of speculation. This thought is that even if Julie is telling the truth about the Counters and even if it is so that the Mob has been running things for several years, it was not that good before 1963 or years previous anyway. It simply was not that good.

It was not that good at anytime at all, when you come right down to it, it was downright bad. Racing in the days previous was even more corrupt than it is now, the film patrol and medical authorities having become more and more influential in recent years and also the rigging and manipulation of the races at the old Jamaica racetrack, particularly in the fall, had to be lost on to be believed. Also, there were the usual number of wars, deaths, pain and murder. There were just as many people suffering the pangs of what can be called social injustice, the only difference was that one was somewhat less conscious of it because one did not have the wonderful opportunities for sharing experiences that are available today.

These are deep thoughts, particularly deep for a one such as I who has never shown particular interest or ability for current events and who, along with most of my friends and acquaintances, has tried to avoid them. But the experiencing of them is quite strange; it is as if in some profound way I have never been truly thinking before this moment and if this is thought, I want no part of it. No less than the Chart or Harry the Flat I want easy answers or at least to believe in easy answers and the question of looking at the races from the sociological and political point of view is all a little bit too much for me. There is a limit to the kind of sensations and thoughts which one human being can take and certainly I have gone around that limit; nevertheless, the thoughts will not stop. Peculiar things are happening down on the track with one of the spraying trucks getting grounded near the toteboard and whole teams of men and trucks coming out to get it before it interrupts the proceedings for the fifth race, but this is only marginally interesting to me. It occurs to me that looking at the whole thing objectively, it might even be possible to say that things before 1963 were somewhat worse rather than better because one was not so close to the action and could take it seriously. It was in about 1963 that I overcame my naiveté toward the races, and came to understand what might possibly be going on there. This knowledge, at least, was something of a shield. If you knew they were out to get you, then you could at least handle yourself in prepared fashion, whereas, if you thought it was a clean honest sport, with equal chances for all horses, under the kind supervision of some expert stewards and commission people, you were in trouble from the start.

Too much, too much, particularly since the heat and the noise level in the grandstand seem to have risen from the times previous and it is very hard to hold thoughts in the head in such instances. People are shouting at one another and poking at the *Telegraph* with increasing ferocity, paying more attention to the stalled spraying truck at which they jeer and throw a few objects until finally a couple of Pinkertons circle out from the lower area and surround the machine. It is not easy to remain detached and composed within the area of the grandstand which is probably the reason why most systems, sooner or later, break down; the atmosphere of a fifth race is entirely different from that of a first.

Nevertheless, I am still trying to think, still struggling with the small compass of my thoughts when I am suddenly and perhaps permanently distracted. Leaning with chin on hand, watching them drag the machine away I am trying to remember my exact sensations during the time of change of governments, when there is a tap on my shoulder, an insistent, clammy tap which makes me turn around quickly and ready to strike anyone who would touch me in such a fashion. And then, looking at this person, see that I cannot strike them because this is the only person who might touch me that way.

Leaning over me, a crazy, twisted grin on her face, pain in her eyes, tension in the cords of her neck, is the lovely Gertrude nee Hawkins her hands still on my neck, the pages of a program flapping in one of them. She is wearing a very nice brown dress and looks very well-contained, indeed, except for her face. "Hello," she says, "I hoped I'd catch you here. I wanted to come. Aren't you glad to see me?"

Gertrude nee Hawkins until this moment has surely never been at a racetrack in her life. I sense that this is something of a manipulated job and behind that I sense something else, too, but this is the woman I love, this is the woman I care for, I rise and touch her, and guide her into the seat next to mine and only when her body sinks against me into the slats do I understand what kind of pain she has and now she must be suffering if her fine, rigid body collapses through my hands like the ooze of beer from a torn Stevens container.

XL

THE REACTION OF MY WIFE TO THE ASSASSINATION OF JOHN F. KENNEDY

"Never the same; it will never be the same again. It's one of those public events which happen once or twice in a lifetime which remind you that it's only a temporary universe and that the bottom can drop out of it at any time at all: don't you think that things are disintegrating? Can't you feel it somehow? It's just the most terrible thing that ever happened, will you take your eyes away from those goddamned entry sheets for one minute and listen to me?

"You can't run away from it all your life you know, sooner or later you have to come to terms with it and you'd better do it now. If this won't make you become responsible, what will, let me ask you? Our lives must change. We must understand that what has happened changes everything. What seemed possible before, isn't anymore. Can't you listen to me? Don't you want to hear any of this? Do you really think that there's any answer in the racing form?

"Yes, I guess you think there's an answer in the racing form. If you didn't think there was an answer you wouldn't be acting like this. People end up doing exactly what they want to do and I believe it, I believe you, I believe that you're doing exactly what you're meant to do. But I don't have to take it any more. There are going to be a whole lot of changes here whether you participate in them or not and that's all there is.

"I mean it's a terrible thing, almost a personal thing and if you ignore it you're missing the whole point of it. Public events *can* make a difference in our lives, in anyone's lives, look at the war. Look at the concentration camps. Do you think that just because something happens to people you don't know it has no effect upon you? You're wrong. You're entirely wrong.

"I see you won't listen to me so that's all right. I'm going to go out by myself, I have a lot of things to do. Maybe I'll be home tonight and maybe I won't. Maybe I'll see you and maybe I won't. Maybe we'll get together and maybe we won't. Everything must change. It cannot be the same.

"If I thought you thought that it would really make any difference in studying the racing form, I'd go along with you, but it really doesn't and you're smart enough to know that. You're not a stupid person. Most of the people who you're going to the track with, or who you meet out there, are very stupid, but you aren't. You ought to have more confidence in your intelligence. Just because you don't have all the education you thought you needed, is that a reason to destroy yourself?

"Why won't you listen to me? Why doesn't anything I say make any difference? It wasn't this way once; you listened to me for hours. We listened to each other. Don't you care? Don't you want to care? Is this exactly what you plan to do with the rest of your life?

"He's dead, dead, dead and nothing can change it but unless we become different because of this then it's all too pointless. Things must become different. Oh God, I can't stand to look at you any more."

XLI

THE POST THEORY OF HARRY THE FLAT

"The assistant starters, that's what you really got to watch. That's where most of the really crooked stuff goes on, right at the starting gate.

"These assistant starters, they really know their business. They can do anything to a horse in there and no one would ever notice, twist a tail to make it quit, give them a kick in the knee so that they stiffen up or go sore, do something to their backs that makes them lose their action. I'm not saying that the jockeys aren't crooked as hell too but the jockeys wouldn't even know what's going on there, it all happens so fast. And after all of that, all they have to do is hold them back for a tenth of a second, make sure that the horse's door at the gate doesn't open for a split-second after the others do. A tenth of a second is half a length you know. You can knock an odds-on favorite out of a race before it's even started and who would know? Who could tell a tenth of a second, even on films? The stewards don't care, they get plenty of kickbacks for that nonsense.

"It's all rigged. The whole thing. You haven't got a chance and the funny thing is that all of this goes on right in front of the public and they couldn't even know the difference. They couldn't even tell. The thing to do is to make your bets after the start but that is not applicable in the state of New York, you must make your bets before the race. This is the way that they get you.

"There's no future. The whole thing is too rotten. It's all fixed and they can get you in a hundred different ways. But there's one advantage you got over them, they can't make you bet a horse. You pick the horse you want to bet and you bet him; they can't control that stuff. And that's why I say that it can still be beaten, although how you can beat it is beyond me.

"Let us look over these entries for the third. You will see that it is a maiden filly claimer which right away is impossible. You cannot beat these kind of races. Nobody can beat these kind of races. But I think I see a spot in this one if you will just move a little bit closer and maybe I can help you on some of the angles, if in turn, you can help me."

XLII

PUTTING IT TO GERTRUDE NEE HAWKINS

"I came here to talk to you," she says when she is somewhat calmer and her breathing has returned to normal. "I wanted to see you so badly but I got lost coming off the train and went all the way to the other end of the grandstand and then climbed up and down three flights of stairs. I have to talk to you," she says and commences to pull herself two-handedly back in focus, tugging at her clothing, her hair, and so on. She is wearing a sleeveless brown dress and as she comes back into condition, begins once again, to remind me of the youthful and attractive woman who I have loved for such a long time. But there is also a distinctly ominous overcast which spoils the whole thing for me and also I do not like the fact that she has once again put on falsies to see me. This habit, which she cannot be broken of, indicates that she takes me for being consistently naïve or maybe only counting on the triumph of gullibility over memory. She has very nice and ample breasts and her attempts to move them up in class almost always result in disaster. "I want to talk to you," she says. "I came all the way here to talk."

"You told me that," I say, "and I know that you came here to talk because you simply did not come here to bet, that is one thing. Who sent you here? Did the Winner?"

"Where did you get that cello case?" she says, running a hand over it. "I never knew you played the cello, you never told me. Now my sister—"

"I do not play the cello," I say. "Tell me if the Winner sent you here."

"It's a wonderful instrument. Whenever I hear Picasso play it just knocks me straight out. I wish you did play."

"The man's name is Castles, Pablo Castles, not Picasso. Did the Winner send you here, Gertrude? What do you want?" This is, perhaps, not a very soothing way to talk to the woman you love but the point of this strange afternoon is, that I am not sure that I love her, as I have come to suspect the use of the word and also I do not like the Winner meddling in my private life, having seen the damage that he has already done with the Public. "What does the Winner want?"

"What a strange place," Gertrude says, looking from side to side, peering down at the stretch, looking up toward the eave of the grandstand, "it isn't at all like I thought it would be. It doesn't look anything like what you'd see in the movies. And it's all full of crazy people."

"Gertrude," I say and take her hand, not out of any sexual tendencies whatsoever but merely for emphasis; her hand is like iron in mine and the question of sexuality is impossible anyway, "Gertrude, I want you to talk to me directly because a number of things have happened to me this afternoon and I am somewhat reduced on time and patience. Also Gertrude, I am afraid that I am going to have to make an important decision soon which I am not really capable of making. You must come straight with me, Gertrude, I ask you this one favor and if you don't—"

"Oh," she says, withdrawing her hand and letting it fall to her lap, twitching her lap slightly, then leaning back so that I can get an excellent view of the false front which, like an odds-on choice, has no meaning at all to me, "oh you have no consideration at all, where's your sensitivity? I come all the way out to see you and I get lost and I run up and down three flights and finally find you—"

"How did you find me? How did you know where I was, Gertrude?"

And at this line satisfactory results emerge; she crumples as if a rein had been yanked cruelly into her mouth and folds in upon herself on the seat shaking her head, putting her fists against her eyes, "oh God," she says, "oh God, all right, have it your way, just have it your way. Please do it, that's all I want to say, please do it."

"Do what?"

"He hurt me, I can't take this anymore, he came out to my house and he said I had to get down and make you do it. And I said I didn't have any contact with you that way and never even saw you at the races and didn't see how I could make you do anything. Then he told me what they had done to you and then he hit me and said that he would do the same thing to me. Oh for God's sake, do what he wants, will you? It's the only way out and I can't take it anymore."

"Ah," I say, "ah," leaning back into my seat with a real sense of revelation; it is not pleasant news to hear that my paramour or ex-paramour has been assaulted by Tony Winner but on the other hand, it reconstitutes my shrinking faith in an orderly, motivated universe and this is all to the good. "And he sent you out here," I say, "sent you out to persuade me. So how are you supposed to persuade me, Gertrude?"

"Oh I don't care," she says, flinging her face back from her fists and staring straight out toward the tote, "I don't care anymore, I think that all of you are crazy and I can't stand it. When the Flat died I should have left the state. Why the hell I had to stick around and get involved with a friend of his I don't know. Maybe it was guilt, because I thought that somehow I was to blame and if I couldn't make it for the poor Flat I could do something for a friend of his. But I was wrong, all wrong. He's a terrible man and he's going to hurt you very badly unless you do this. I don't know how to persuade you, he said that I would find a way. All of you people are crazy! Don't you think about anything except attacking one another? Where are your hearts?"

"It works two ways, Gertrude," I say, thinking of certain tendencies which she herself has been known to show time and again. Her revelation has given me the most wonderful sense of detachment, and suddenly (this has never happened before), I feel on top of the situation, "it works two ways but he really shouldn't have made you come, there really wasn't any point or purpose in that kind of thing. The Winner should know better."

"So what do you care?" she shrieks, "what do you care that I think enough about you to come out and try to beg you to do something for your own sake. For God's sake, if you have to do it, just go ahead and do it. I don't care what he wants, do you want to be killed or not?"

"Do you know what I'm supposed to do, Gertrude?"

"Well no," she says, "no, he didn't exactly tell me that. I know that it has something to do with Harry but I don't really care. That wasn't important to him, telling me I mean, all that he wanted to get over to me was that I was supposed to make sure you followed through. So I'm trying! I'm trying! I don't even *like* you anymore!"

"That's not the point, Gertrude," I say and take her hand gently, wondering how I can best put this so that we will remain on the best of terms and yet avoid further emotional complications, "the point is that he really should have told you, although, I grant you that up until now it was supposed to be a surprise. Do you know what I am supposed to do? Listen Gertrude, I better tell you, it's only fair. The Flat is under the backstretch there, he's been there for almost four years. Contrary to the information you were given, he did not fling himself off a bridge into undiscovered waters but instead shot himself on the spot and was carried to a resting place later by his friends and acquaintances. His presence on the backstretch, however, has been lousing up the Mob's figures something terrible, and it has now been decided that the time has come to get him out. The Flat, therefore, was to be removed by me after the eighth race this afternoon—what remains of him that is, so that the backstretch could be smoothed and the figures would stand up. It was the intention of those interests with whom I was dealing to present you with the Flat's remains, very tastefully of course, in a covered box, so that you would have something sentimental to remember him by, but things have now run into complications having nothing to do with the Flat. But the real thing is that the Winner should have told you this. It would have been the decent thing to do, since you are so well-acquainted with the deceased, even to this date."

To her credit, she takes all of this very well, her eyes turning progressively blank as she listens, but otherwise her responses very good, within the normal range as we say, although toward the end she gags slightly. When I am finished I poise myself for any kind of response but she says nothing for an instant and so I say, "did you hear me? Is it all right?"

"Crazy," she says with that fine Catholic finality which has to me always been one of the least attractive sectors of Gertrude nee Hawkins. "Crazy. All of you people are insane. I knew I should never have gotten involved with any of you. But I was trying to hold onto options. You're all totally insane."

"You haven't heard nothing of it yet," I say. Our discussion has, incidentally, attracted some down on the track. The horses break from the looks of intensity I am receiving, it occurs to me that possibly I have been talking too loudly. "Forget it," I say, "everything will be all right," hoping that the listeners will take it as a lover's quarrel. "Meanwhile," I say, "let us watch the fifth, which is just beginning," and so it is right down on the track. The horses break from the gate and run from the six furlong mark through the homestretch and onto the finish wire while around us people scream and curse and pray and throw things. Seated in the middle of this activity, observing the penitential form of Gertrude Hawkins, holding one of her cold hands calmly I feel quite detached from all of it. It is strange that people would generate such emotions toward horses. It is strange that they would carry on so over something so repetitious and dull. It is madness to think that this can be taken seriously. It is impossible to believe that it makes any difference.

XLIII

PREMONITIONS OF THE DEMISE OF HARRY THE FLAT

Harry the Flat's regrettable suicide was not entirely unforeshadowed although it was, for this reason, none the less tragic, of course. Often in the depths of a losing streak the Flat would say things like "I ought to blow my brains out if this keeps up" or "what the hell's the use if this is all it comes to?" and so on, but most of his complaints were taken for the routine lament of the horseplayer. When the Flat would enter a winning streak or an even period they would disappear so completely that friends and acquaintances felt justified in their belief that the Flat was only posturing. Besides, they had their own problems.

Still, it would have been possible to have noted through a careful observation of the Flat that his remonstrances and predictions might have been taken more seriously than otherwise posted. In periods of repose, a slack kind of terror would creep into the corners of his face, moving from the mouth through the cheeks and then to the eyes, the eyes stunned in the center of these panels winking for light, a tremor of the forehead for concentration taking on the aspect of a tic. At times a heavy sigh would overtake the Flat, this sigh being seemingly unrelated to extrinsic events and wrenching his body throughout; causing him to tremble as if ill.

"Someday I'm gonna get a gun and plug someone," the Flat would say, "plug them straight through the head for doing all this that they done to me, I'll get them for this, I'll get them," and who of us was to know, who of us would have suspected, who of us would have possibly apprehended that the person the Flat would get was himself? so neatly and finally in the grandstand, the tissue of his brains in the explosion floating like a halo around his beaten, honest head, the astonishment of the moment seen only in his mouth which pursing toward an *O* dropped toward extinction as gun in hand he dropped to our feet, kneeward, praying.

XLIV

HOW IT ALL WENT AWAY

Looking at Gertrude nee Hawkins then, the fifth race over and in the bag and who the hell knows or cares what has happened? Looking at her I see what she is, as if for the first time: she is a thirty-five year old woman, maybe thirty-six, beginning to crumble slightly around the edges, held in toward the center by bone and conviction, but now in the extremity of the moment, some of this seems to have given out, and coming from the sides of her I can see something weak, soft and horrifying. I can see what she will look like in ten years or maybe less when the interest goes away, and seeing her in that fashion I understand that I am in love with her no longer. It is a regretful insight since I am, basically, a loving person looking only for things I can trust and cherish. But it is better sooner than never, or so I think, and in any event there is something about the way she holds her body that frightens me. There is an edge to the arch that tells me of many things and all of them are losers. "Oh do it," she is saying, "oh just do it anyway, what do I care, just listen to them, what else can you do? They're crazy, they're crazy. But don't you bring that thing to me, I'll kill you if you bring me anything like that."

"I doubt that there is anything left," I say, "he would only be ashes and decomposition by now. I do not think that there would even be any question of a smell to annoy you."

"*Oh*," she says and springs against the seat, then stands, shuttling the program under her arm, "oh, I just can't talk to you, I just can't stand to listen to this anymore. I've got to get out of here, just do it, listen to me, if that's what they want, do it. Do it." She is, I manage to surmise then, very much afraid of the Winner and who, in her circumstances, would not be? "I don't want to see you anymore," she says, "I think you're crazy."

"It's a crazy business," I say and stand. A strange courtliness seems to take me over; what I want to do is usher Gertrude out of the grandstand with style. If there is no feeling left, then certainly style must make up the difference, and it is suddenly very important that the matter be accomplished gracefully. "I'm sorry," I say, "I mean I'm sorry that you had to get involved with this. Did he take you over?"

"This horrible *man* came and took me over. And now I'm leaving. I don't think I want to see you anymore."

"I understand that," I say, "I mean I know that you could get around to having this point of view. But it's nothing personal."

"I don't know how you people *think*. I don't even know what you have in mind, how your mind works." She sways against me, I support her, I lead her toward the door. Some horseplayers are looking at us with interest but most are not. It is something that happens all the time; many marriages, let alone affairs, have broken up in the grandstand. "I just don't even understand," she says girlishly, never so much confusion in the voice of Gertrude Hawkins and I hold onto her, she leans against me, I escort her to the mouth of the exit and say, "well, I guess I'll see you around. Later, or something like that."

"See me around? You mean you're going to just send me away like this? You're not even going to take me out of this foul place?"

"Let us be logical, Gertrude," I say, "if I escort you home or even part of the way then I will never be back here in time to accomplish my appointed tasks and it is exactly those tasks which you were delegated to send me out to persuade what with to do."

"You're not talking straight. I don't follow you."

"You cannot both ways it have done, Gertrude," I say, finding this manner of talking suddenly very refreshing and kiss her gently right on the steps, horseplayers scuttling to the sides of us, then push her gently on her way. "Be reasonable," I say, being prepared for anything, "be reasonable," and she leaves me without another word, holding her shoulders straight, moving into the mob. From the rear she looks like any lady horseplayer. I watch my lost love depart, sunken in the surprising knowledge that I feel absolutely nothing for her and then, in the midst of all this temporary triumph and satisfaction I remember that I have left the goddamned cello case back at the seat.

I rush back and it is still there, although slightly dishevelled. One corner peeks open and I can see the outlines of the implements. A horseplayer, perhaps, wished to comfort himself with some music after a loss but finding to his dissatisfaction that not music but excavation lay within, abandoned it all to go on his own way, perhaps interpreting the presence of the cello as a musical tip, perhaps, on the basis of its elements, deciding against music forever. It is hard to say, either way it will work out in the same fashion. I sit down and open the *Telegraph* looking at the sixth race entries—how quickly and interestingly this afternoon has gone—but being overcome soon enough by boredom, put it away. Scuttling in the rear of my mind like a small animal is the impetus of an idea; I think that I know finally what I am going to do and the sensation of verging upon epiphany is enormous, I can contend with it only by clutching my fists, squeezing my eyes closed and trying to think of neutral things. Horseplayers burble, cogitate, moan to one another; after a while I get up and taking the cello with me I leave my seat yet once again and head toward the nearest men's room. It seems a good enough place to think and I have had the majority of my most original thoughts in circumstances like these.

XLV

THE FLAT DEMOLISHED

Rolling on the ground, the gun falling from his fingers, his head draining, his eyes open one last time and catch mine, I bend over him, looking into his face and it is surprising, for all the damage inflicted, how calm and knowledgeable those eyes are. Now that pain and implosion having taken his life away, it is as if the interior of the Flat can return to a central peace. The eyes flicker, then fixate, he seems to be at rest and in a kind of control which he has not managed for a long time. "Come here," he mutters, crooking a finger and I kneel beside him, a rare honor, the last of the Flat's associates to talk to him ever, "You understand," he mutters, licking his lips, "you understand that there was a whole different way of doing things which I never wanted to take. You don't think that any of this was easy, do you? It had to be this way, bury me on the backstretch so that at least I can feel them running over me when I'm in heaven," and expires with a Calvinist shudder, his hands opening. The death-speech of the Flat, the sincerity of his conviction that after all is done he will yet go to heaven, the brutal shock of the entire instance most disconcerts me and it is difficult to keep the tears from my eyes as I look upward. "He died happy," I inform those surrounding, "he died happy and it is his last wish to be buried where the horses run." Snuffles come from above, and Tony Winner who is not the Winner then but merely a small, hounded guy named Tony Nickels who has dedicated himself to learning everything that the Flat can teach him, nods slowly and says, "if that's what the Flat wants, that's what he gets. It would be an honor to do this thing for my great friend the Flat," and then turns to the others saying, "anybody going to stop me? Anybody say that the Flat can't get his last will and testament?" and because Tony Nickels then and now is a very forceful guy (although then he had somewhat less substance of course) nobody says a word of protest, there are only assenting nods. "I will do this thing for the Flat," Nickels says, "because he is a truly great man, and a little bit of bad luck at the very end does not mean that he is any less great. I will meet his needs because he is entitled to that." I stand, somewhat shakily, and Nickels put an arm around me. "This man and I will be responsible for seeing that the Flat's news and views never die," he says, "but remain and go on and on, isn't that right? Isn't that right?" I assure him that it is. Tony Nickels soon enough catches on to the right connections and begins to move upward and onward very rapidly; takes advantage of certain political events in the Mob to improve his career and unfortunately forgets most of what he vowed but underneath he remains the same strong, simple person, I tell myself, and can be counted on in a pinch. Only later and in unpleasant circumstances do I learn that this is not so but by then the Flat, in the Winner's calculations, is already half dug-up and Gertrude sent on the heartstring detail to keep me in the service of the Plan.

XLVI

THE FLAT'S BASIC DICTA ON HORSEPLAYING

1. Never bet fillies against mares or female horses of any kind against colts or geldings. Never bet a horse moving up more than one thousand dollars in class from his race unless he won that last race easily or lost it in an effort which did not tax him. Never bet a horse dropping down in class unless he ran badly in his last race in which case bet him if he is the only such animal in the field and has a claiming value of at least three thousand dollars less than the highest price at which he has ever run.

2. Never bet a horse of more than eight to one on the board unless there are at least six such horses in a race, in which case, bet each of them to win and place and parlay after every loss. Never bet a horse who goes off at less than eight to five unless you are playing full progression in which case bet him to show only and triple the ordinary bet. These are the basic mathematical systems embraced by the System of Rules Conservation, although advanced horseplayers may find one which is even more satisfactory to them.

3. Never bet a horse ridden by an apprentice jockey unless the apprentice is: a) one of the leading apprentices at the meeting and b) has ridden the horse before and c) is getting the horse a weight advantage of three pounds minimum over the rest of the field and d) has not ridden the horse before and e) is one of the less well-known apprentice jockeys at the plant indicating that the trainer and owner are trying to put something over by getting a price and f) has not had any disqualifications, objections or suspensions within the last thirty days.

4. In two year old maiden sprints always bet the horse which has the best previous time at the distance unless there is in the race a first-time starter who has worked out to within one second of this horse's time. In which case bet the first-time starter unless he comes from a minor

stable or is out of a routing sire or is ridden by a jockey who has not won at least ten percent of his races at the meeting or trained by a trainer who has won ten percent. In which case, the bet on the previously-raced horse should be increased times the amount of fifths of seconds under which his best previous time is underneath the average track record for the distance on that day allowing a three times credit if the jockey is a national or local leader or if the trainer has in the past produced a series of betting coups. Make no allowance for mudders, routers, or horses which seem to run best on a firm but holding track.

5. Rainy day system: give two points to every horse in the race which has previously run in the slop and three points to every horse who has not, unless the ones who have not have shown some inclination to run at minor tracks whose track variants are fifteen percent lower than major track variants. In which case they should be given four points credit and calculated on the problematical percentage play. Of those horses which have the lowest point total, allow the geldings extra credit and bet them to win and place. Of those horses who have the higher point total give fillies extra credit and bet them to place and show as a long-shot system. If this requires that every horse in the race be bet, eliminate one and bet the others unless the one eliminated has a low point credit; in which case, double the bet on this one and remain at the single unit with the other.

6. Try to leave after the sixth race, the subways become very unpleasant after the feature race and it is bad enough to ride home a loser without having to do it without a seat. Think of dignity, live in dignity, and try to cultivate some sense of self-respect.

XLVII

IN THE MEN'S ROOM: AN ASSAULT OF COLOR

Into the men's room on the third level of the Aqueduct grandstand. Aqueduct is short on atmosphere, a place of difficulty for many other reasons, but one thing it has never lacked is men's rooms, running three or four apiece to the grandstand and clubhouse, large and roomy places which may be the safest and most efficient public rest rooms in North America, a place to which you could send your son with pride and security. Moving there, the cello case now under my arm in a professional fit, I pass Julie's stand, mean to pass her a comforting meaningless wink to keep her content during my Moment of Decision but the stand is closed, boarded on all sides, a sign hanging off-kilter from the wall which says CLOSED FOR THE SEASONAL, WE THANKS YOU FOR YOUR

PATRONAGE. Three or four chewing gum wrappers and cigarette packs crumpled in the vicinity are the only testimony that this was, until so recently, a successful, prospering division of the Harry M. Stevens concession belt. Nostalgia would be an insane emotion to entertain under these circumstances and yet, looking at the abandoned stand I feel nothing else: this was where I was told about the Counters, this was where Julie and I established a special and permanent relationship and relationships of whatever sort are not to be discounted in the brutal and interesting world of Aqueduct Racetrack. The fact that the sign seems to be rather poorly phrased also bothers me a trifle: one would wonder what to make of an organization which wants to rule the world, yet has members that are not particularly strong on the language. Despite the fact that I lack extensive education and do not associate with a class of people who worship the spoken word, I have always tried to cultivate a certain elegance of speech myself as being one of those things which truly separate the men from the beasts. I would not like to think of a world run by people who now and then close things up for the season. Still, this is extraneous thinking, not really applicable to the situation and I decide that I will discard it out of hand. I come into the men's room, walk past the urinals and join a shifting, pale line of men waiting for cubicles in front of a white-coated attendant. Most of the men look uncomfortable in the extreme but it is not diarrhea which seems to afflict them so much as constipation; a look of dark blockage, a suggestion in their faces that they know they are committed to try their bowels as their luck, but in both cases, very little will happen. The attendant, who I have known off and on for several years although never in a non-professional capacity winks at me and shouts down the line, "a booth. One booth coming up for the cellist!" and the others look at me with some anger while I shift the case to the other arm and try to look as normal as possible. The policy is for the attendants to call up and down the line, setting up vacancies for the customers and keeping matters regularized but there is something about the presence of a cello case on line which convinces some of the customers that they are once again being manipulated and there are some mumbles and mutters. "No problem," I say, taking out a handkerchief, and wiping off my face with a bit of residue from the grandstand. "No problem at all, everything's fine," and they look away grunting, having concluded perhaps, that I am somewhat mentally unstable. This is a judgment to which they would be entitled. In their places I would feel the same way.

It is hot in this bathroom, terribly hot, even worse here than in the undergrandstand itself because of the compression and bodily acts which are being performed but it seems to bother few of the horseplayers. Not one of whom seems to be even on the verge of fainting. At the urinals men stand holding themselves with one hand and their newspapers with the other. Selections seem to mingle with urine and there is an absence of the harsh whistling and clatter which seems to be the understanding of most public rest rooms and locker rooms. Now and then someone will get an insight in the act of elimination which insight will cause him to forget to close his clothing after finishing. But the attendants are kind about this and never miss the opportunity to remind. Due to the diligence of horseplayers and the conscientious work of these attendants there has not been a single case of indecent exposure at Aqueduct in its entire eleven year history, a record which is duplicated as far as I know by no other public facility.

Some time has passed while I indulge myself with these homey, men's rooms reflections and I am now the first on line, the attendant leans over and asks me if I have anything good for the day and how I have done so far. I give him fifty cents, the normal cubicle tip, and say that the day has not been too interesting and that as far as I know I have nothing for the rest of the day; I may, in fact, even leave early.

"Don't do that," he says, "you'll feel much better after you've taken care of yourself here. Listen, I got something for you. It's been coming in all afternoon and I'm glad to let you have it. I been hearing it so much I'm going to bet that bugger myself in the eighth race."

"The eighth?"

"Sure thing. Knockover. That dog is gonna be thirty, forty to one on the board and there's a lot of inside money working on the horse. Maybe bet down to ten to one with all the tips floating around but any price is a good price if you win and that horse is set up. I'm going to bet him ten and ten and I ain't even a serious bettor. I'd get on him if I were you."

"I've heard a few things about him," I say, "I guess there's some word out."

"Word out, why man, I been hearing that one all day. They've been talking up Knockover since I came on shift at eleven this morning, which you must agree is a hell of a long time to stand in a men's room shuttling folks around, seven hours without a break and my feet hurt. One for the cellist?"

"One for the cellist!" the man way down calls cheerfully and I insert a hand in a pocket, find another fifty-cents, pass it on to my friend and still trundling the case walk down the long line of closed cubicles feeling vaguely as if I were making entrance before the assembled orchestra at Carnegie Hall. "Hey, I'll hold that," the other attendant says as I make my way into a fine, small booth, "no need to go in with that thing," but I wave him off, hearing him mumble something obscene and close the door on him, bolt it and then cleverly use a second hidden bolt at the top to protect my safety. The presence of the second bolt is known only to Harry M. Stevens concession rest room employees but one picks up certain pieces of information after having been at the track for a long time, this is part of the acculturation process or in any event has to do with the process of socialization. With the door inevitably bolted on me now, with no possibility whatsoever of being intercepted in my difficult meditations I do something complex and yet at the same time quite simple, I fold my hands, lean my forehead on them and try to think things out calmly, coolly, rationally, paying as little heed as possible to the disparate goings on beyond the booth.

It is strange, strange to reduce all of the difficult and surprising events of this day to a series of reflections which I can work through in an orderly fashion in a men's room but I have no choice, I need to think now and the men's room is as good an enclosure as the track offers, the clubhouse restaurant to the contrary, the important thing is to return to the elements, so to speak, from whence one came and so sitting that way, fully clothed, upon Harry M. Stevens toilet bowl I work things through my mind as best I can while turning off the murmur outside. From the groans and sighs to the right and left of me one would think that horseplayers were seeking winners in the bathroom as assiduously as release, every now and then a sigh is broken by a small *ah!* of discovery and it is impossible to tell whether it is the bowels or the entry forms which have opened up. Certainly, if all the knowledge which seems to be in the process of revelation in this bathroom were converted into actual results, things would be entirely changed. Or then again, things might come out entirely the same. The question of picking winners, it has been noted, is a highly individualized process.

All of it works its way through what passes tentatively for my mind: Gertrude, the Winner, reminiscences of the Flat, Julie, Needles, the Chart, my own reasons for being here, my own background and history and now as I give myself over to it fully I find that it is literally too much; too much experience for my ability to absorb and shaking my head I retreat, back off it and try to take things item by item, picking them up and inspecting each separately before going on to the next. It is difficult to order all of these factors: to explain a world which can contain both the Chart and the Flat for instance, or Gertrude and myself, but I try, I do, as always, the best I can and I hear small groans and murmurs escaping me no less than my unclothed seatmates, it is difficult, it is so difficult, but I push further into the center of it persuaded that if I think sufficiently all of it will come clear.

And then there occurs to me one of those remarkable moments known only to characters in books and unlike anything which has ever happened to me before, something going contrary to everything I believe I have come to learn about the way the human mind and human affairs work, something so interesting and enormous that I know it will change my whole life thereafter. For what comes over me in the Harry M. Stevens men's room in the middle of all my struggling efforts to think is nothing less than a sudden and complete insight, a whole total insight which explains everything and orders it completely and although this is something which I myself can hardly believe, having grown accustomed to photo-finishes, the eighteen percent takeout and the process of disqualification, I seize onto it, choosing to believe that if it happens one must go no further. I grab onto the insight grunting, poise it between my hands, shift it so to speak from one hand to the other, bounce it in the air, my eyes widening with wonder and still it holds, the more I toss it, the longer it stays and it holds together, it holds together. It is, as the expression goes, nothing less than an entire epiphany, a word that I picked up in the course of my travels but which I have never previously had sufficient cause to use. This is the occasion. An epiphany. I have had an epiphany.

It ties everything together: the Winner, the Mob, the Counters, the Chart, lesser functionaries like Gertrude or myself, it even begins to verge upon a true and final explanation of the races and the way in which they are run. If pushed to even the slightest degree this theory might well tell, for all I know, how to pick winners, but my aims are far beyond greed and I do not explore it in that direction. Instead, I only stay in the center, looking at the lovely and more immediate applications.

"Oh God," I find myself murmuring, "oh God, it's too much, too much," and the attendant, always concerned or at least alert, pounds on the door to ask me if I am feeling all right. I tell him that I am and try to settle lower on the seat. "Too much, too much," I murmur and then, as I pass through it and to the other side the final part of it hits me and I see not only the explanation but the action. I see exactly what I must do. I see how everything can be followed upon to produce a resolution as clear and sparkling as the water on the infield lake must have been a long time ago before Aqueduct Racetrack in the borough of Queens came to grow up around it.

Naturally I cannot reveal the insight. This would not be fair and would also be a violation of the principle of etiquette at the racetrack which holds that if the other man paid seventy-five cents for his Lawton and you have no Lawton because you did not care to invest that money, you do not, in crowded quarters, seize the sheet from the man's hand and make his selections your own through greed and irresponsibility. There is a certain tacit understanding at the track and this is perhaps the only part of its grace, this tacit understanding being that you get exactly what you pay for, you work things through precisely on your own and what the other man has purchased in knowledge you do not seize from him because you must get it only in your own way and through as hard or easy a process as this turns out to be. Only the results are to be shared and communicated, but they come far after the fact.

After the fact. After the fact. Everything is after the fact. Groaning, I hoist myself from the seat, grunting, I seize my cello case and then, loosening the bolts slowly, I edge my way out into the larger circumstance of the men's room and therefrom to perform my final and summary mission.

XLVIII

THE SUMMATION OF HARRY THE FLAT

"It comes to nothing, absolutely nothing. You cannot beat it. The only ones who beat it are the big-edge guys, those who are behind the whole operation and rig the results, but the guy going out there day by day simply has no chance. This guy going out to play them off the newspapers and his best judgment has got to lose because it's all rigged against him. The only way to understand the races is through information and there just is no information for those who are outside because that would kill the whole game. It's an insider's pastime and they're making millions off of us by using us to be there and put the money into the wrong selections.

"There is just no way that you can beat it because it really makes no sense. It just makes enough sense, a tiny little bit on the edges, to give you the feeling once in a while, that you're stupid and if you could only see things the way they were supposed to be seen you would have a chance but they put that in just for the figures. That's the only reason. Mainly it makes no sense at all and the fact that favorites win one-third of the time year after year, track after track, is only part of the whole arrangement that they make so that it turns out looking systematic.

"I have dedicated my whole like to understanding them and now I see that I was a fool, that they made a fool out of me, that there is nothing, nothing, and no way could I have ever beaten it unless I wanted to start at the bottom of whatever organization it is and pick up a little piece of information here and there as I moved along. That was the only way but I didn't do it; I thought that you could study and prepare yourself at the races just like you could for any other thing and that you could make an education of it but I was wrong.

"I was wrong about everything, I was played for a fool and now I can't stand it anymore. It just doesn't seem to be worth it to you if something you spent your whole life learning blows up in your face and it turns out that you should have been trying something else entirely with your time. At least if I was a failure going into business I would be making some money, less than I should be but there would be something in it for me. But this is ridiculous. This part of it is ridiculous. I'm losing money all the time; I'm a guy who goes into the office at twelve every day and doesn't come home until ten at night and stays up all night working and I'm losing money. It cost me money to work. I can't stand it no more.

"No more, no more, I can't stand it: I thought that I saw a system but I was all wrong. But the only thing, the thing that I can't understand, the thing that I got to live with somehow if I want to live, the thing that I never took into account is how beautiful the whole thing was. How beautiful.

"Why did it have to be that way? Why did it have to be so beautiful? That was what made all of the trouble, after that I never had a chance."

XLIX

THE HORSES ARE ON THE TRACK. IT IS NOW POST-TIME

The sixth race. Or perhaps the seventh. it might even be the eighth coming up after all, it is impossible to know exactly how long I was in the men's room. Nor do I care. Pushing through the clumps of men staggering in in small groups I conclude that a race must have just finished; they are talking to one another in high desperate tones, already tearing at their clothing to expose themselves and void fully of the happenings. I give the attendant at the far end fifty cents thanking him for the services of his clean concession and then move into the undergrandstand for the last time. I know it is the last time because nothing I now see bothers me. One can take everything if it is the last time.

None of it bothers me at all; not the heat, the congestion, the sense of the entrapment, the rush of the crowds, the high bleat which seems to have no source but congeals from all of the voices, the ashen flicker of the tote, the clink of glasses from Harry M. Stevens bars, the sound of coffee burbling from the Harry M. Stevens grandstand refreshment counters. None of it has any effect upon me at all because there has been an added starter in this race and the added starter is that I know for me this is the last time. There will be nothing beyond this, all things coming to an end sooner or later in the run of things. Now, looking at it from the vantage point of one spending his last moments there all of it seems to have retreated from its ghastly high proportions, reduced, contained, it has the look of a series of artifacts strewn over the spaces of this vanished racetrack and I spring toward the light and exit of the doors, case bouncing on my back. Some elements of my fine coherency seem to have been lost, but on the other hand I seem to be feeling better, considerably better, at an entirely different vantage point. At the doors I pause only briefly, surrounded by *Telegraph*-reading men right and left, balance myself on the heels, undo the cello case in a series of rapid snaps and zippers and pull from it the spade and shovel, fine, dense, black instruments, not terribly differentiated but still distinct in my mind, there is a *spade* and there is a *shovel* and both of them are for the glory of the Flat. Horseplayers look at me blinking. "I've got business to do," I say, "excuse me please," and hurl the case down the lawn, it bounces off someone's head and then lands in a small, grey, open space, rolls once and is still. Very similar to the graceful dying motions of the Flat. "Important business, important business," I say, lifting the implements above my head and people give me headway, people definitely form an alley for me—how simple all of this is once you cultivate just a little bit of perspective—and I walk down the alley singing, waving my implements, fixating my gaze on the backstretch which is being tilled by one of the wary but loyal NYRA racing trucks, putting the strip into shape again for yet another race, courtesy of the track maintenance department to say nothing of the Government of the State of New York which allows all of this to be run and run again, six afternoons in all the seasons, at only the most minimal percentage of the take. It is good of the State of New York to allow this thing to be done; it shows that as always the Empire State is thinking of its citizens. Down the infield lawn I go singing and waving my instruments, conducting what I feel to be an imaginary fugue as I cut down the alley of horseplayers and approach the gate which separates grandstand from paddock and then paddock from track, the gate manned by a young Pinkerton who looks at me without surprise or interest as I close, for his sake, a hell of a lot of ground. "Coming through, coming through," I chant madly and they let me through, the instruments trailing after me, their glances awed and respectful because of all the people at the track at this moment only I, or have I got this wrong, seem to be doing something meaningful. "Coming through, coming through," thinking how proud the Flat would be of me at this moment, I having accepted the Flat's fourth and fifth lower dictums of the racetrack which state that precipitate action is the best to take when in doubt. Lights flicker on the tote, another odds drop, the four horse appears to be the money what with going down from two to one to eight to five. More maneuvering. More manipulation out of the paddock and the clubhouse for the racing fans to think about. The hell with them. I approach the gate, fling a hand within, use a delicate cellist's grasp to spring the latch and move into the paddock. I have never been in the paddock before and it is something of a thrill to be in this place where only horses, employees and the gentry walk. The air seems less congealed, thinner, higher, truer, one could spend a whole lifetime or at least a good part of it calculating the beneficial aspects of paddock air which is why a long time ago I thought that I wanted to own a horse. But there is neither time nor need for appreciation. "Excuse me," I say to the Pinkerton and walk with monstrous, perfect casualness through the gate, "I have something to do on the backstretch." The Pinkerton, who appears to be about twenty-four years of age with what Gertrude would call cuttingly (this is one of her many deficiencies as a woman, her cruelty) a "social problem" gives me one look of astonishment, a twitch which rolls his eyes back into his head and makes a tentative motion to stop me. "You can't do that," he says, "you can't go out on the track," and I confront him full by the eyes, take him figuratively by the scruff of the neck and say, "listen, let me alone. Let me go. You don't like this anymore than I do, do you?" and let him think about that for a moment while I stroll onto the track, the dirt shifting a little bit under my shoes. The guard is indeed thinking about this, one can see him thinking, the calculations twitching through his head, perhaps he is thinking about all the missed tips that have floated by him in this area, perhaps of all the owner's wives and daughters who in their sleeveless summer dresses have wafted past him as if he did not exist which in any sense they understand is correct. Maybe he is thinking of curses which come down on him from all the heights of the grandstand when something happens that they think they do not like and maybe when all is said and done, maybe he is thinking of nothing at all except how little he cares about the situation and how much he doubts his effect upon it, a common racetrack problem, because for whatever reason he lets me through. He does not follow me. He gives me a gesture which although vaguely obscene obviously signifies respect and dismissal and is awkward only because of his own lack of social grace.

Now, on the track I feel the place where the horses run: it is nothing like I imagined it at all, neither firm nor corporeal but a strange, shifting blend of sand and mud which seems to wobble underneath my shoes as I trudge toward the rail and then, along the rail, toward the backstretch. Saving ground all the way. It is possible that I am attracting attention, certainly there appears to be a sequence of noises behind me, cheers and mumbles, groans and threats, interesting that they would respond to such an ordinary act in such a way. A man going to do a routine gardening job. A man bringing the mechanical tools of disinterment to a simple task. Holding the rail through the clubhouse turn, I continue on my way, looking at the ground for the most part, staring now and again at the sky which shows more horizon from this perspective than one generally finds in New York City. Two astonished swans regard me from a distance and then paddle in the opposite direction. I salute them, these silent witnesses of more struggle than any of us have ever known and continue on my way. The spade and shovel clatter against one another. The crowd moves into the background. There is a strange bucolic peace to all of this, conducted under a hot sun and on turf that feels like loam. Strangeness, strangeness. I pass the starting gate which for the next race has been pulled all the way into the chute, two furlongs behind the necessary six-furlong marker. Man and horses are around the gate but they are at a far distance and make no move toward me; small figures, a quarter of a mile into abstraction they take my salute as I pass and similarly make no move towards me. I believe that I am going to get away with it. At the present moment, everything seems to be surprisingly in control, even my own respiration and heartbeat which continue at a moderate level. Only small spouts of beer curling within me near the belt-line remind me that I have a digestive system at all. I take the turn slowly, slowly, reminding myself that it is around this very turn that some of the greatest and worst horses in history have campaigned: the mighty Kelso used to ease up here after his winning races; here too Branch and Filatonga, two of my all-time favorites used to begin that series of quitting gestures which had such magnificent causes in the backstretch; here Buckpasser would make his positioning movements and Brush Baron begin to bear out, here Priceless Gem would nail down a firm three-length lead and here Coachlight Square would begin to show nothing in mile and an eighth starter handicaps. Too much, too much for the likes of me and I begin to feel like a monument myself as I trudge toward the six-furlong pole. This part, at least, is all mapped out for me. I do not need to do research. I can see the place where Harry lies quite clearly; it glitters faintly in the sun and small insects seem to squirm into the turf as I approach.

Looking at the grandstand from this vast distance I can see what jockeys are talking about, can begin to understand why, even when everything is known about it, one might still want to race and race; move the horses out of this isolation into that distant bulk which sits and glints half a mile away. Now it is very quiet, only the shift of color denoting humanity, the glaze of prisms suggesting pain. It is very beautiful. There are a few forms running at me across the infield but they are a great distance away and at least in this perspective, appear to be in no hurry. I begin to dig.

Simple, simple, spade into the ground, lurch, grunt, shove, dirt flying, shovel discarded to one side since only the one implement was needed, the overly-protective Winner wrongfully insisting upon two. The shovel splits the ground neatly, halving it like the center of an apple, excavation, wriggling in the sun, those of them that are motile, and then going on their way. The sense of isolation, peace, elevation is magnificent, and overcome with intentness, I bend further to the task, peering now for the remains of the Flat. They should, as I recall, be emerging quite shortly; the circumstances of the burial were quite disordered and we were not able to do a proper job.

Birds wheel, dart in the air, I work further. The forms however are much closer, a sidelong glance in the act of digging showing me that they are closing ground rapidly and the stick-figures seem to be waving implements of their own, high in the air. Brown and dense they come toward me and now for the first time I can hear their voices. They are shouting. Here they come across the meadow of the infield, the shouts like singing and I dig harder and harder, trying to at least finish the job before the moment of dialogue begins. A bell clangs in the distance, they seem to be readying the starting gate. Dimly I can hear the sound of megaphones, the track announcer seems to be saying something. Since the megaphones are fronted in the opposite direction, I cannot tell what it is but of whatever nature, I am sure that it is most interesting.

Here they come. Ferociously, I continue the digging, meanwhile beginning to talk in a high singing voice, barely able to distinguish the words, listening to myself with the skill and detachment of an auditor. "Oh please," my voice seems to be saying "oh please, oh please," and the Pinkertons, closing the last piece of ground in a rush, vault the rail with splendid precision, ten of them, twenty of them, oh a most significant lot and now I can feel hands, hands on my suit, hands on the pockets, hands tearing the spade from my grasp. "No," I say, fighting them, "no, no, don't stop me," and lean heavily on the shovel, covering it with my body, staggering into a small eave and feeling something horrid under my feet. The spade is torn from my grasp. I hurl myself toward the spade, stumble, fall instead into the depression and collapse with a groan into some object below, feeling bones clatter underneath, feeling something horrid rasp beneath the skin. A Pinkerton leans over to grasp me, loses balance himself and falls atop me and so we lie on the Earth: Harry, myself, the Pinkerton and I am a most uneasy sandwich filler, indeed, kicking and flailing as a new thought occurs to me, something not embraced by my previous calculations. A thought which should have been taken into account but was, of course, not.

"You crazy son of a bitch," someone screams toward me, "you crazy son of a bitch, what the hell do you think you're trying to do? What the hell is on your mind? What the hell are you after?"

I lift my head, then, holding up the Pinkerton with a massive effort, feeling his pressure on me, slipping and sliding beneath as the weaker Harry disintegrates further under our weight. The question is very im portant and it deserves an answer; I try to phrase things as judiciously as possible so that there will be no chance of being misinterpreted. I could hardly bear, at this late point, to be misunderstood. Clarity of communication is essential; clear linkage in the void. I look at the questioner and lock his eyes and then I speak from the entire heart of me with such force that only the whole world should listen.

"I'm trying to get out," I say.

THE END

Afterword: My Mission in South Ozone Park

Fifty one years ago, still trying to find a voice and purpose, I wrote a short story "The Ultimate Tip" set at Aqueduct Race Track in South Ozone Park in the Borough of Queens, New York. My hapless protagonist (all of my protagonists then and now are hapless), a horseplayer on a terminal losing streak, is visited by the Devil who offers him the Ultimate Tip, the sure winner in the next day's ninth. The morning line is 50-1, the horse's form is hopeless. A four year old maiden filly named Liz Piet has never finished better than seventh in fifteen races and now, unreasonably, is being stepped up in class. The Devil's bargain is the usual. "High of course but that is the standard deal." My protagonist points out that he has no significant money to wager. "No problem," the Devil says. "I'll lend you a thousand and you can refund that immediately from your winnings." My neo-Faust, sunk in debt and self-destruction, sees no alternative. He takes the deal and leaving his miserable furnished room at dawn, arrives at Aqueduct in early morning, the thousand dollars palpating in his pocket like a tumor. Four hours to post time for the crucial second race.

I will elide agonized synopsis. The Devil is—well, the Devil. His Ultimate Tip has been shared it would seem by everyone at Aqueduct this day. Harry—we might as well call him Harry although he is never to be The Flat—finds himself surrounded, finds himself choked and pressed by the largest crowd he has ever seen at this sprawling, noisome establishment. People surge, chatter, whisper, run. Harry hears them murmur, "Liz Liz Liz Liz." The sibilant steams his consciousness, penetrates him like knives. Suddenly everyone is running to the windows. He finds himself carried as if by a tornado. Six minutes to post time, now five, then four. The lines at the mutual windows are enormous. It is clear that he will be shut out. Thousands are going to be shut out. This is the largest crowd in the history of racing. "Liz," they cry. "Piet Piet Piet." Pitter-pitter-patter. Harry gets a glimpse of the tote board in odd, splintered flashes of light. Liz, the four horse, is 1-5. No, she is 1-9. The board can cast no lower odds. If Harry gets to the window, if he makes his bet, he will win one hundred dollars. And lose his immortal soul. The devil has been busy all night, walking up and down the Earth and to and fro upon it. Caught in the endless, teeming, stunned masses, Harry has an epiphany. It is an old one, of course.

The story was rejected by the *Magazine of Fantasy & Science Fiction.* I am not sure that it was ever sent elsewhere. I had other concerns in the Summer of 1963, not all of them disconnected from the writing of fiction, but I knew that this story was no good. Stark, somewhat clumsy, and the pari-mutuel system made a poor villain, even for readers of fantasy and science fiction. I put it away. I got married. I procured a Shubert Playwriting Fellowship at Syracuse University, embarked upon a convoluted and difficult journey. (It is all in "Tripping With The Alchemist," a long essay in the 6/03 issue of that very *Magazine of Fantasy & Science Fiction*.) Many events, eventual publication, a daughter, Stephanie. Science Fiction. A larger West Side apartment malevolently limned in *Herovit's World*. But the short story stayed with me.

It haunted me: the wretched Liz Piet, the treacherous Devil, the surging, shouting, desperate crowds carrying Harry helplessly toward a destiny suddenly not obscure. Glow of the tote, screams of the trainers, rushing in the paddock, the anguished aspirant straining of the cheap claiming horses, most of them able to race only through illegal pain killers. The glint of fading Winter sun in the shabby light of the tote. And the terror, the madness in the grandstand as tens of thousands came alive slowly to full realization of their betrayal.

I wrote a novel, *Overlay*, in a few weeks in February of 1970 and sold it to Lancer Books. It was fair but Harry was missing as was the Devil and the screams of the betrayed horses. Now it was July and my wife was seven months pregnant and "The Ultimate Tip" was still there, hammering, hammering. *Overlay* had not purged that damned story. I wanted to try again. This time I wanted to write the World Novel which like the World Snake would consume itself: a novel which would sweep from Runyon to Nabokov, to Westlake, from Evan Connell to Mailer to Marcel fucking Proust. I wanted the grandstand and the Devil and Liz, I wanted the surge and the broken, splintered life, I wanted the light and darkness. I wanted the world as gigantic tote, I wanted Harry as Harry the Flat as God himself. I wanted a prose high and low and up and down. I got *Underlay*. I started it in August 1970. It went at a pace even crazier than that of *Overlay*. On page 230 or thereabouts, my father called. My mother was in the hospital, her gall bladder was being removed as we spoke. "Terrible," I agreed. "I hope everything turns out all right." I went back to the novel. Writers can be monsters. Writers, as Janet Malcolm observed, are always selling someone out (usually themselves, she did not add). *Underlay* was done a week before Erika Cornell arrived. I mailed it to George Ernsberger and got drunk (I did that daily in those days, had nothing to do with Erika and only a little to do with Erika.) Erika made her debut on 9/16 and the next day, under some pressure, the delivery check arrived. (The other half of $2500 to keep the record clear.)

George Ernsberger knew as did I that the novel was good but we had little company. Esther Yntema at the Atlantic Monthly Press, that big tease, wrote "the novel should be either longer or shorter." Avon, in the wake of Ernsberger's departure in early 1971, held the novel for the fully allowable four years by contract, publishing it only with the greatest reluctance and in a throwaway paperback original package guaranteeing its obscurity. The only review it received in its first 40 years was from Roger Sale in a *Hudson Review* "fiction roundup" in 1975. Not too bad, Sale wrote. Literary sophistication and technical facility had now so penetrated the culture of would-be or actual writers that even Malzberg, "an ordinary paperback hack," showed some real literary sophistication. The novel had at least one fan who persuaded a small press to attempt a second edition in 1986. It then entered upon an even longer period of obscurity, emerging for an audio edition last year and now, through the grace of Greg Shepard, this new edition.

I still, no less than Harry the Flat and his progenitor, believe in exterior force, divine possibility. I believe in this novel. "I am the medium through which Sacre passed," Stravinsky said of his *Rite of Spring,* and so when I engage in this praise it is not self-praise, I did not write this novel, I merely facilitated its birth the way that Doctors Blumenthal and Bitterman facilitated the debut of Erika Cornell. I believe in the damned book, I believe that in that dour summer of 1970 the Fat Kid in the back room got it together as he never had and never would again. Like the hapless author of *They Shoot Horses, Don't They*, like the wretched Horace McCoy himself I believe that this novel will carry me forward into eternity but only if I accept Harry's deal...I have to be dead to win. No account. Like Liz Piet, my race is run.

Here it is: my dearest, my battered child. I have two daughters. *Underlay* is my son. I sent him once again onto the seas in this frail raft. Be kind to me as the world was not kind to Harry. November will fall in slanted light and America's broken son hears yet again the cries of Dealey Plaza.

January 2015: New Jersey

Afterword To An Afterword

As the essay above, written as a postlude to the 2015 Stark House edition would pretty well indicate, I was satisfied with this novel, written in a blur of intention and hoped for closure in August 1970 and felt that it pretty well finished (if did not properly interpret) what I have come only recently to think of as the "Horse Racing Trilogy"; there are aspects to the novel (then 45 years in the past) which I still did not understand but sufficient unto the day thereof and I posited a reasonable grip on the essential material. The track was a metaphor, the tote board the implacable, inflexible and ultimately crushing machine of circumstance; Harry the Flat was mythic in his sacrifice to the machine, Gertrude was the common man and woman helpless witness to the destruction and Harry's cohorts, a disreputable bunch more or less out of Damon Runyon but a hell of a lot less charming than the trio who had the horse right here were the engines and spectators of the night. Behind them, sullen, beaten and in sprawl through the cheap seats and the clubhouse were the rest of humanity, unhappy background to the massive or trivial struggles centering on Harry's grave. Harry's grave signaled the death of hope, the surrender to chaos and that made his disinterment desperate necessity. In his presence the figures had gone outside of predictability and the Mob's neat control of destiny had been sundered. Shovel time. The novel ended with the unnamed narrator digging furiously and with futility on site. "I'm trying to get out," he mumbles to the constabulary circling him. That is where he, Harry's corpse, the Mob and the world are left, in a state of indeterminacy *sine die*. It seemed a proper ending. Kent State had happened three months earlier, Kissinger circled the globe in a gnat's singular procession seeking "peace in our time" and Agnew had more than a word or two for the nattering nabobs of negativity. My younger daughter, Erika Cornell, was within a fortnight of joining the grandstand. This was the world of *The Tempest* and oh such people within it.

The novel, held by Avon for the maximum period allowed by contract before the rights would automatically revert, crawled into release in August of 1974. Its science fiction editor was long gone to Berkley Books and there wasn't much of a science fiction program left and, anyway, *Underlay* was not science fiction. "Any fool could see that," J. Brahms would have said. Like Jonah's Gourd, it grew in a night and died in a night and only suffered one review, that from a *Hudson Review* freelancer and Professor of English at the University of Washington. The reviewer found it slow at the start, livelier in the middle "where it finally found its plot" and ultimately a *quad ad demonstratum* of the argument that sophisticated literary technique had so permeated even the lower classes that "a good paperback hack like Malzberg" was able to put it to relatively sophisticated use. In Teaneck by that time, three and a half years removed from *Herovit's World*, an ordinary paperback hack all too much like Malzberg fulminated but what recourse was available? A letter to the editor? The editor of *The Hudson Review*, Frederick Morgan, had been one of the approximately fifty attendees of the first World Science Fiction Convention in Manhattan in 1939, but that surprising information (which came to my attention half a century later) would not have given any additional credibility to a letter which, the magazine having no letter column, would have been tossed anyway. (Frederick Morgan, 15 in 1939, had later inherited enough money to found, publish and edit *The Hudson Review* and was as careful about his more secret history as any Nazi making his way into the USA Civil Service.)

So, a secretive course for this paperback original, the domestic equivalent in those years of Samizdat. A few horseplayers over the decades might have found it, one of them knew a small press publisher who revived the novel in 1986 to no real moment. A would-be screenwriter somehow found that edition and then its author and asked permission to write and market a screenplay, no money but he really loved the work and could not understand why it had not already been filmed. (He came to understand.) Then a continuation of the Long Result until the sainted present publisher of this took it on in 2015 and now another surge in the Cheyne-Stokes if anyone is monitoring the hospital bed. If the hospital is still extant.

This remains my favorite novel of my own composition, pressed but not seriously menaced by two or three courageous platers dropped long ago to the claimers. My one recent insight, forcing a reopening of a book which I felt had been placed on a high shelf beyond present reach is that Harry the Flat is G-d (permit that evocation of the original Hebrew), that G-d had become unwillingly implicated in human destiny and then had had his heart broken by the assassination of JFK. That assassination had exposed the dreadful and irreversible constant of human existence ... it was irremediable, it was doomed. In the specter of His assumed humanity, G-d/Harry had finally accepted that truth and had taken Nietzsche's advice. Naturally his implantation had screwed up the figures.

Screwed them up pretty good as a quick look at the news today (oh boy) would certainly validate. This good paperback hack speaking for his legion, throws himself on the mercy of the court. Here I stand. I cannot be moved.

April 2020, New Jersey

Barry N. Malzberg Bibliography

FICTION (as either Barry or Barry N. Malzberg)

Oracle of the Thousand Hands (1968)
Screen (1968)
Confessions of Westchester County (1970)
The Spread (1971)
In My Parents' Bedroom (1971)
The Falling Astronauts (1971)
The Masochist (1972, reprinted as Everything Happened
   to Susan, 1975)
Horizontal Woman (1972; reprinted as The Social Worker, 1973)
Overlay (1972)
Revelations (1972)
Herovit's World (1973)
In the Enclosure (1973)
The Men Inside (1973)
Phase IV (1973; novelization based on a story
   & screenplay by Mayo Simon)
The Day of the Burning (1974)
The Tactics of Conquest (1974)
Underlay (1974)
Beyond Apollo (1974)
The Destruction of the Temple (1974)
Guernica Night (1974)
On a Planet Alien (1974)
Out from Ganymede (1974; stories)
The Sodom and Gomorrah Business (1974)
The Best of Barry N. Malzberg (1975; stories)
The Many Worlds of Barry Malzberg (1975; stories)
Galaxies (1975)
The Gamesman (1975)
Down Here in the Dream Quarter (1976; stories)
Scop (1976)
The Last Transaction (1977)
Chorale (1978)
Malzberg at Large (1979; stories)
The Man Who Loved the Midnight Lady (1980; stories)
The Cross of Fire (1982)
The Remaking of Sigmund Freud (1985)
In the Stone House (2000; stories)

Shiva and Other Stories (2001; stories)
The Passage of the Light: The Recursive Science Fiction of Barry N.
   Malzberg (2004; ed. by Tony Lewis & Mike Resnick; stories)
The Very Best of Barry N. Malzberg (2013; stories)

With Bill Pronzini

The Running of the Beasts (1976)
Acts of Mercy (1977)
Prose Bowl (1980)
Night Screams (1981)
Problems Solved (2003; stories)
On Account of Darkness and Other SF Stories (2004; stories)

As Mike Barry

Lone Wolf series:
Night Raider (1973)
Bay Prowler (1973)
Boston Avenger (1973)
Desert Stalker (1974)
Havana Hit (1974)
Chicago Slaughter (1974)
Peruvian Nightmare (1974)
Los Angeles Holocaust (1974)
Miami Marauder (1974)
Harlem Showdown (1975)
Detroit Massacre (1975)
Phoenix Inferno (1975)
The Killing Run (1975)
Philadelphia Blow-Up (1975)

As Francine di Natale

The Circle (1969)

As Claudine Dumas

The Confessions of a Parisian Chambermaid (1969)

As Mel Johnson/M. L. Johnson

Love Doll (1967; with The Sex Pros by Orrie Hitt)
I, Lesbian (1968)
Just Ask (1968; with Playgirl by Lou Craig)
Instant Sex (1968)
Chained (1968; with Master of Women by March Hastings
   & Love Captive by Dallas Mayo)
Kiss and Run (1968)
Nympho Nurse (1969; with Young and Eager by Jim Conroy &
   Quickie by Gene Evans)
The Sadist (1969)
The Box (1969)
Do It To Me (1969)
Born to Give (1969; with Swap Club by Greg Hamilton & Wild in Bed
   by Dirk Malloy)
Campus Doll (1969; with High School Stud by Robert Hadley)
A Way With All Maidens (1969)

As Howard Lee

Kung Fu #1: The Way of the Tiger, the Sign of the Dragon

As Lee W. Mason

Lady of a Thousand Sorrows (1977)

As K. M. O'Donnell

Empty People (1969)
The Final War and Other Fantasies (1969; stories)
Dwellers of the Deep (1970)
Gather at the Hall of the Planets (1971)
In the Pocket and Other S-F Stories (1971; stories)
Universe Day (1971; stories)

As Elliot B. Reston

The Womanizer (1972)

As Gerrold Watkins

Southern Comfort (1969)
A Bed of Money (1970)
A Satyr's Romance (1970)
Giving It Away (1970)
Art of the Fugue (1970)

NON-FICTION/ESSAYS

The Engines of the Night: Science Fiction in the Eighties
   (1982; essays)
Breakfast in the Ruins (2007; essays: expansion of Engines of the
   Night)
The Business of Science Fiction: Two Insiders Discuss Writing and
   Publishing (2010; with Mike Resnick)
The Bend at the End of the Road (2018; essays)

EDITED ANTHOLOGIES

Final Stage (1974; with Edward L. Ferman)
Arena (1976; with Edward L. Ferman)
Graven Images (1977; with Edward L. Ferman)
Dark Sins, Dark Dreams (1978; with Bill Pronzini)
The End of Summer: SF in the Fifties (1979; with Bill Pronzini)
Shared Tomorrows: Science Fiction in Collaboration (1979; with Bill
   Pronzini)
Neglected Visions (1979; with Martin H. Greenberg & Joseph D.
   Olander)
Bug-Eyed Monsters (1980; with Bill Pronzini)
The Science Fiction of Mark Clifton (1980; with Martin H.
   Greenberg)
The Arbor House Treasury of Horror & the Supernatural (1981; with
   Bill Pronzini & Martin H. Greenberg)
The Science Fiction of Kris Neville (1984; with Martin H. Greenberg)
Uncollected Stars (1986; with Piers Anthony, Martin H. Greenberg &
   Charles G. Waugh)
The Best Time Travel Stories of All Time (2003)

OVERLAY

"In the year 1978 (433 Galactic) the attention of the Bureau
fell to the planet Earth which, Headquarters decided, had
reached a point where it furnished a clear and present dang
to the cause of Galactic Unity. With some regret, tempered l
a long and hard-bought sense of bureaucratic anomie, a pla
was put into operation to rid the sector of the menace by
sowing the seeds of disunity within." And so our narrator, a
galactic agent on a singular mission, recruits four members
from the world of Aqueduct horse-racing to fight the Good
Fight against entropy and chaos. Of course, these four
gamblers are dangerous and insane, but one must work wit
what one has at hand.

A BED OF MONEY

Foster the Loser becomes Foster the Winner when he bets o
People Trap in the sixth at odds of 341-1… and wins $23,00
And that's only the beginning. Because George Foster has
always been the Loser. It takes a little getting used to
becoming the Winner. Celebrating with a drink, he meets
Dolores, who is only too happy to accompany him back to a
hotel room. She loves hearing him tell the story of his Big
Win. She is so excited, she calls up Al and Eddie to share in
George's good fortune—and to relieve him of it. But winners
don't give up that easy, and he takes off with Dolores in tow.
And so begins George's best day at the track… with Dolores
and the $23,000, and Al and Eddie in hot pursuit.

UNDERLAY

Harry the Flat is dead and buried in the backstretch of
Aqueduct Raceway. This is causing the Mob no end of troubl
on the betting side, so Harry's oldest and dearest friend—no
carrying on with Harry's widow in Harry's absence, and in
debt to the Mob for $1500—is persuaded to dig him up after
the eighth race. The Mob boss is very specific on this point,
and to that end has had a time bomb surgically implanted ir
our hero's thigh to impress upon him the urgency of this
matter. So with a cello case stuffed with a pick and shovel, of
he goes to the track to dig up the dubious remains of Harry
the Flat.

www.ingramcontent.com/pod-product-compliance
Lightning Source LLC
Chambersburg PA
CBHW070745190726
48292CB00002B/422